Don't Say It!

600個你一定會錯的英文

一網打盡各種
英文常犯錯誤！

apartment
flat
哪個是美式英語？
哪個是英式英語？
參加比賽是
join the contest，
還是 enter the contest？
為什麼不能說
6 a.m. o'clock？
dessert
desert
如何輕鬆區別？
21

EASY WAYS
TO AVOID ERRORS
IN ENGLISH

Dennis Le Boeuf／景黎明 著

前言

本書讀者

英文學了那麼久，您是否總是似懂非懂，老是在文法部分卡關？對英文用法一知半解？本書顛覆您對文法的刻板印象，幫助您解決英語文法、慣用法及易混淆辭彙的難題，辨別英美在文法、拼寫及辭彙方面的區別，以及辨別正式和非正式用語的差異，直擊您最容易犯的文法錯誤，避免一錯再錯！

本書列舉了作者三十多年來在美國、臺灣和中國大陸寫作、校對、教學中常見的英語錯誤，幫您解決文法及慣用法的問題，幫助您準備各類考試（國考、TOEFL 等）或教學參考。

本書風格

本書為您提供了清楚易讀的辨析，讓您知道如何避免錯誤的用法，並提供相關的趣味例句，使您更容易理解辭彙的意思、慣用法以及複雜的文法規則。

本書不僅是一本易讀好用的文法參考書，而且更是一本趣味性強的閱讀材料。書中一些文法解說幽默詼諧，例句內容包羅萬象，充滿了生活味和文學味，而且例句還韻味十足，更重要的是，完全符合道地的英語表達習慣。

本書使用

本書既是一本文法書，也是一本字典。它提供了簡單易懂的文法要點解釋和例句、英美文法和用詞之間的區別、如何辨別一些容易混淆的辭彙，並按字母的順序排列，讓您能輕而易舉地找到所需要的字詞和文法要點。例如，如果您不清楚「Eight hours of sleep is/are enough for Dwight.」應該用單數動詞還是複數動詞，可以直接參見 subject-verb agreement（主詞和動詞的數要一致）。如果您不清楚 bring 和 take 之間的區別，可直接查找 B 字母的條目，或從目錄找出 bring 或 take。

此外，這本書也提供了交叉參考。當您在查詢某單字時，常常會看到其他相關條目的提示。

使用這本書就像使用一本字典。當然，本書的內容比字典還多，因為字典不會告訴您常犯的錯誤，也不會告訴您易混淆的辭彙。

本書內容

您對掌握英語這門龐雜語言的欲望究竟有多強烈呢？您想知道下面這些問題的答案嗎？例如：

1 您應該 see me off at the airport，還是 send me off at the airport ？

2 您應該 smell those fish，還是 smell those fishes ？

3 您應該 continue on，還是 continue ？

4 您應該說 over thirty percent，還是 over thirty percentage ？

5 您應該說 is considering moving to Japan，還是 is considering to move to Japan ？

6 您應該用 escape from school 來表示「曠課」嗎？

7 Brook, I am sorry that I lost/missed your cookbook.
表示「丟失」，應該用 lost，還是 missed ？

8 What/Which color are Lulu's new shoes?
這句應該用 What，還是用 Which?

9 Lulu did not doubt whether/that the story was true.
這句 doubt 後面應該接 whether，還是接 that ？

10 Paul cleaned the third floor except for/except the meeting hall.
在什麼情況下 except 後面接 for，在什麼情況下不用 for ？

11 Ms. Bloom bought a cottage from an old man with no bathroom.
介系詞片語 with no bathroom 的位置放對了嗎？它的先行詞究竟是哪一個？是 an old man，還是 a cottage ？

12 Give a picture of the sun to whomever/whoever asks for one.
這句介系詞 to 後面接一個受詞子句，子句的主詞應該是 whomever，還是 whoever ？這可是一個許多人爭論不休的文法要點啊！

13 Three miles is a long way to jog in the fog.
主詞是複數 Three miles，為什麼動詞要用單數 is ？

14 One and a half cups of coffee is enough for me.
這句主詞（One and a half cups）看起來是複數，為什麼動詞要用單數 is ？

本書列舉的常見錯誤，其中一些就文法來說也許是對的，但語意卻含糊不清，甚至成為笑料；有些似乎遵守了文法規則，但不是道地英語；有些在英式英語裡是恰當的用語，而在美式英語裡卻成了有關「性」的用語。

英語真是一門奇妙、充滿了魅力的語言！然而，因為有如此多的文法規則，又有如此多「不遵守規則」的慣用語，對英語學習者來說，英語的魅力就轉變成了一種「痛苦」。如何擺脫這種痛苦呢？不要發愁，不管您的難題是什麼，本書都能幫您解決，並且保證不用大量的文法術語使您頭痛。

也許您會說：「學語言就是為了交流，只要人們能聽懂我的話就行了。」從某種程度上，您也許說對了。實際上，在隨意的聊天中，很多錯誤也會被母語是英語的人所忽略。然而，當您需要參加國際商務會議，需要進行商務談判，需要寫專業文章、商業信函和商業電子信件時，這類錯誤就會給讀者或聽者留下不好的印象。

也許您會說：「沒關係，電腦能幫我檢查英語拼寫和基本文法的錯誤。」可是，您的電腦不會在乎您寫 is seeing the blue sky，還是 is looking at the blue sky；不在乎您寫 like to play balls 或 like to play ball。電腦的「拼寫及文法檢查」只能保證您的句子中沒有拼寫錯誤。

本書內容範例說明

Type 1 錯誤 ⊗／正確 ✓

這是書中最常見的一種比較類型，將常見的錯誤與正確用法作比較。其中又分為三種：

1 文法錯誤

496 subject-verb agreement
主詞和動詞的數要一致

E)（作為一個整體的）複合主詞 + 單數動詞

1

⊗ Bacon and eggs are a great brunch or lunch.
被看成是一個**整體單位**（一頓餐；一份菜），動詞要用**單數**

✓ Bacon and eggs is a great brunch or lunch.
培根蛋是一頓豐富的早午餐或一頓豐富的午餐。

2 用詞錯誤

189 enter/join 參與／加入

1

⊗ Ann West joined last week's reading contest.
加入政黨、團體、俱樂部才用 join

✓ Ann West entered last week's reading contest.
參與競賽（a contest、a competition）要用 enter（= take part in）

= Ann West took part in last week's reading contest.
安・韋斯特參加了上週的閱讀比賽。

3 辭彙混淆

408 peace/piece 和平／一（個／張／片／塊）

1

⊗ Do those geese want to have some pea soup and then live in piece? ——意思是「一片；一塊；一張」等

✓ Do those geese want to have some pea soup and then live in peace?——意思是「和平；平靜」
那些鵝想喝點豌豆湯，然後和睦相處嗎？

Type 2 美式英語／英式英語

第 2 種類型的辨析句子，告訴您美式英語與英式英語的區別。也分為幾種：

1 文法不同

272 hospital 醫院

1 美式 Fay was admitted into the hospital yesterday.

英式 Fay was admitted into hospital yesterday.

菲昨天住院了。

2 詞彙用法不同

111 cinema/theater/theatre 電影院／劇場

1 美式 I'm in a line outside the theater for the new movie *Love Crime*.

英式拼法 theatre

英式 I'm in a queue outside the cinema for the new film *Love Crime*.

我在電影院外面排隊買《愛情罪》電影票。

3 拼寫不同

107 check/cheque 支票

1 美式 Kitty Beck wrote a million-dollar check for that charity.

發音相同

英式 Kitty Beck wrote a million-dollar cheque for that charity.

姬蒂・貝科給那個慈善機構開了一張百萬美金的支票。

4 發音不同

001 a/an 一個（不定冠詞）

4 美式 She used an herb to make the tea.

[ɝb]，h 不發音

英式 She used a herb to make the tea.

[hɝb]，h 發音

她用一個草藥泡茶。

Type 3 非正式／正式

第 3 種類型比較正式和非正式用語。非正式其中有兩種：(1) 口語中常用或在非正式的書面語中常見，不是錯誤。(2) 非正式場合使用，但不是標準英語，一直受到許多嚴謹的文法家、作家及編輯反對。這類非正式，在一些非英語國家的英語考試中，可能算是正確的，但在英美國家考試中算是錯誤的。

在正式文體中，比如，在考試中、在商務會談和商務信函中，應該用正式用語， 尤其要避免用上述第二種類型的非正式用語。（遇見這類非正式，本書都有提示 。）

030 a.m./p.m. 上午／下午

✗	Evan told Clem, "My bookstore is always open until seven p.m."
非正式	Evan told Clem, "My bookstore is always open until 7:00 p.m."
正式	Evan told Clem, "My bookstore is always open until 7 p.m."
正式	Evan told Clem, "My bookstore is always open until 7:00."
正式	Evan told Clem, "My bookstore is always open until seven."
	（伊文告訴克勒姆：「我的書店總是營業到（晚上）7 點。」）

264 his/her 他的／她的

② 在無法改變句型的情況下，寧願用 his or her 或者 his/her 的結構，也不要用 their。上面及下面的非正式例句，在考試中務必要避免。

非正式	Nobody really understands humankind or even their own mind.
正式	Nobody really understands humankind or even his or her own mind.
	（沒有人真正瞭解人類，甚至不瞭解自己的心靈。）

Type 4 口語／正式

第 4 種類型的辨析，比較口語和正式用語。口語不算錯誤，但在考試、寫商務信函或學術論文、開研討會時，要用正式用語。

064 bad/badly 壞的／壞地

2 美式 口語 Pam and Millie did bad on the math exam.

美式口語可當副詞，與特定動詞連用

正式 Pam and Millie did badly on the math exam.

正式用語要用副詞 badly

這次數學考試潘姆和米莉考得很差。

573 who/whom 誰

1 口語 Who will Harry Bloom marry?

正式 Whom will Harry Bloom marry?

哈利・布盧姆要娶誰？

Type 5 不自然／自然

第 5 種類型的辨析，比較不自然的句子和自然的句子。不自然的句子雖然文法上沒有大錯，但卻不是好文風。在正式文體的書寫時、在考試中、在商務會談的商務信函中，應該用自然的句子 。

288 infinitive 分離不定詞

1

不自然 Lily has learned how to wisely spend money.

不定詞一般來說不分開

自然 Lily has learned how to spend money wisely.

莉莉已經學會了如何明智地花錢。

138 dangling constructions/ misplaced modifiers

垂懸結構／修飾語錯位

4

不自然用法 Ann told, with a smile, her story to the Tibetan man.

修飾語離主詞 Ann 太遠，不自然

不自然用法 Ann told her story, with a smile, to the Tibetan man.

修飾語 with a smile 應該放在句首，靠近主詞 Ann

自然用法 With a smile, Ann told her story to the Tibetan man.

主詞靠近前面的修飾語

安微笑著把她的故事告訴了那位西藏男子。

Type 6 語意不清／語意清楚

第 6 種類型的辨析，比較語意不清的句子和語意簡明、清晰的句子。在口語和書寫中，一定要使您的句子簡明、清楚，才能到達預期的交流效果 。

138 dangling constructions/ misplaced modifiers

垂懸結構／修飾語錯位

1

語意不清　You will appreciate the advice Sue gives you years from now.

副詞片語靠近 the advice Sue gives you，造成雙重含意

語意清楚　Years from now you will appreciate the advice Sue gives you.

數年後，你會感激蘇給你的建議。

2

語意不清　Lee ran up to Lily breathing heavily.

分詞片語靠近先行詞 Lily，包含兩種意思，語意不清楚

語意清楚　Breathing heavily, Lee ran up to Lily.

分詞片語置於句首，片語主詞與句子主詞 Lee 一致，符合邏輯，文法也正確

李上氣不接下氣地朝莉莉跑去。

語意清楚　Lee ran up to Lily who was breathing heavily.

改用形容詞子句，可明確表達是 Lily 上氣不接下氣

李朝著上氣不接下氣的莉莉跑去。

397 parallel structure/parallelism

平行結構

2

語意不清　Brad never gets angry and criticizes anyone who gets mad.

重複副詞 never 意思表達更清楚

語意清楚　Brad never gets angry and never criticizes anyone who gets mad.

把連接詞 and 改成 or ，才不會產生歧義。並列否定要用連接詞 or 表示「也不」

語意清楚　Brad never gets angry or criticizes anyone who gets mad.

布萊德從來不生氣，也從來不批評任何一個發脾氣的人。

本書使用說明

英語的引號用法注意事項

本書的標點符號是以美式英語為標準。

美式英語 逗號、句號任何時候都位於引號內。

英式英語 逗號位於引號外。句號根據不同的情況有不同的位置；如果句號與整個句子有關，句號放在引號外；如果句號只與引語有關，句號放在引號內。

美式英語和英式英語共有的原則：屬於整個句子（不屬於引語）的問號、感嘆號位於引號之外；只屬於引語的問號、感嘆號位於引號之內。

1. The price tag on that old laptop was marked "Sold." 美式
   → 美式：句號任何時候都位於引號內。

   The price tag on that old laptop was marked "Sold". 英式
   → 英式：句號與整個句子有關，句號放在引號外。

2. Paul said to Clark, "Let's go to the park and play ball." 美式／英式
   → 美式：句號任何時候都位於引號內。
   → 英式：句號與引語有關，句號放在引號內。

3. "Dainty," "funny," and "saintly" are some of the adjectives that can be applied to Olive's personality. 美式
   → 美式：逗號任何時候都位於引號內；通常在 and 前面要用逗號。

   "Dainty", "funny" and "saintly" are some of the adjectives that can be applied to Olive's personality. 英式
   → 英式：逗號放在引號外面；通常在 and 前面不用逗號。

4. Ann asked, "How long did you live in Japan?"
   Annette shouted at the mouse, "Get out of my house!" 美式／英式
   → 無論是美式英語還是英式英語，問號或感嘆號屬於引語，位於引號之內。

5 Did Sue say, "I will go with you"?
Bing, please stop saying, "He is a nice king"! 美式／英式
→ 無論是美式英語還是英式英語，如果問號或感嘆號不屬於引語而是屬於整個句子，就放在引號之外。

本書翻譯英語人名的原則

1. 要和英語人名發音儘量接近

本書中出現了許多人名，而為了幫助您正確地讀出這些人名，大部分人名都與句中的某個字押韻。正因為這個原因，人名的中文翻譯就得儘量接近英文的發音。比如 Larry，一些譯名手冊翻譯成「雷裡」，但 Larry 的發音非常接近「賴瑞」。當然，有部分人名翻譯雖然和英文發音差別較大，但因為多年來人們已經習慣了這樣的翻譯，我們也就沒有修改，而沿用傳統的譯法，比如 Mary 譯為「瑪麗」。不過，要真正做到發音準確，還需要您大量收聽英語節目，比如聽錄音、看英文電影。

2. 中文人名翻譯要顯示出性別

人名是台灣學生的一個薄弱環節，不少學生分不清某個人名究竟是女性名，還是男性名，如果中文翻譯體現不出性別，勢必會給學生造成很大的困擾。

現出版的許多譯名手冊，都沒有注意這方面的問題。比如：一些譯名手冊把 Brook 和 Brooke 都翻譯成「布魯克」。Brooke 是女性名，而 Brook 既可以是女性名也可以是男性名。如果男女都翻譯成「布魯克」，而句中又沒有代詞 he 或 she，那麼就比較難區分男女。

在本書裡，男性 Brook 翻譯成「布魯克」，而女性 Brooke/Brook 翻譯成「布露可」。女性名中使用了「琳」、「黛」、「梅」、「麗」、「莉」、「妮」、「姬」、「露」等，可以讓人聯想起女性。

結語

這是一本類似字典的簡易、趣味文法書，兼顧知識性和趣味性。本書不僅可以幫助您準備各類考試（或用作教學參考），還可以激起您的閱讀興趣，因為本書也是一本趣味閱讀書，裡面有大量栩栩如生的例句，以及琅琅上口的韻腳供您欣賞。我們希望您在解決英語無止境的難題過程中，發現本書對您不僅有用，而且趣味無窮。語言學習者應注意，很多文法規則都有例外，不能一味地用規則去硬套，得遵守慣用法，而掌握文法規則及慣用法的最佳途徑就是大量閱讀，這一點需要牢記。英語教學領域的國際著名專家，美國加州大學 Stephen Krashen 博士研究得出的結論是：趣味閱讀能有效地擴大辭彙量，提高拼寫能力、閱讀理解能力、寫作能力，有助於更有效地運用文法，擴大知識面。

本書就是基於「大量趣味閱讀」的理論寫成的。在這本書裡，您可以找到您需要的許多重要文法規則，辨別英美英語的區別及正式和非正式的區別，還可以讀到許多押韻、道地、真實的趣味例句，並學到許多人名。我們希望您通過閱讀這本厚厚的趣味文法兼字典書，擴大辭彙量，改進拼寫，提高文法理解和閱讀理解能力以及寫作技巧。

Dennis Le Boeuf & Liming Jing

丹尼斯 ‧ 勒貝夫 & 景黎明

Contents

B

C

F

Q

R

U

V

W

A

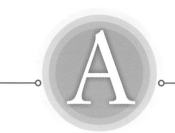

001 a/an 一個（不定冠詞）

1

❌ She has a earache.

✅ She has an earache.

她的耳朵痛。　　母音 [ɪ]，用 an

earache 是以母音 [ɪ] 發音開始的字。在以**母音**發音開始的字前面需用 **an**。以**子音**發音開始的字前面要用 **a**。注意，這裡指**發音**，不是指字母。

2

❌ Bring a umbrella when you come to London. It might rain.

✅ Bring an umbrella when you come to London. It might rain.　　母音 [ʌ]，用 an

你來倫敦時帶一把雨傘。也許會下雨。

umbrella 是以短音 u [ʌ]（母音）開始的。所以要用 **an**。

3

❌ Do you have an university degree?

✅ Do you have a university degree?

你有大學學位嗎？　　母音字母，**子音發音** [ju] 開始，用 a

university 的第一個音節是子音 [ju]，所以應該用 **a**。

（母音 [ʌ]）（子音 [ju]）

- Take **an** umbrella, because **a** Ukrainian dog lives near there and it is not friendly.（帶一把雨傘，因為那附近有一條兇惡的烏克蘭狗。）

4

美式 She used an herb to make the tea.

[ɝb]，h 不發音

英式 She used a herb to make the tea.

[hɝb]，h 發音

她用一個草藥泡茶。

(1) herb（草藥）發音：美式 [ɝb]　英式 [hɝb]

(2) 常見的 **h 不發音**字（前面不定冠詞需用 **an**）：

heir [ɛr]	heirloom [ˋɛr͵lum]	honest [ˋɑnɪst]	honor [ˋɑnɚ]
hour [aʊr]	honorable [ˋɑnərəbl̩]	honesty [ˋɑnɪstɪ]	hourly [ˋaʊrlɪ]

5

✗ Why is Pete driving the wrong way on an one-way street?

母音字母，**子音發音**開始 [wʌn]，用 **a**

✓ Why is Pete driving the wrong way on a one-way street?

為什麼彼特在一條單行道的大街上反方向地開著車呢？

one 雖然是以母音字母 o 開始，但 one [wʌn] 是以**子音發音** [w] 開始，因此，應該與不定冠詞 **a** 連用。比如：

- a one-day trip（一次一天的行程）
- a one-dish meal（一道菜的一餐）
- a once-in-a-lifetime event（一個千載難逢的事件）

6

✗ A FBI agent is talking to Ann and Jan.

✓ An FBI agent is talking to Ann and Jan.

子音字母，**母音發音**開始 [ɛf]，用 **an**

子音發音開始 [ˋfɛdərəl]，用 **a**

= A **Federal** Bureau of Investigation agent is talking to Ann and Jan.

一名聯邦調查局特工在跟安和珍談話。

(1) 縮寫詞 FBI 是以子音字母 F 開始，但字母 F 是以**母音** [ɛ] 發音開始，因此要與不定冠詞 **an** 連用。

(2) 縮寫詞以字母 F、H、L、M、N、R、S、X 開始的，要用 **an**，因為這八個子音字母是以**母音發音開始**。比如：

- an MBA degree [ɛm]（一個企業管理碩士）
- an X-ray machine [ɛks]（一台 X 光機器）
- an RN [ɑr]（一名註冊護士）

7

❌ A "2," a "8," and a "11" are in 2811.

✅ A "2," an "8," and an "11" are in 2811.

母音發音開始的數字 [et]、[ɪˋlɛvn̩]，用 **an**

2811 裡面包含有數字 2、8、11。

如果**數字是以母音發音**開始的，要用 **an**。比如：

- an 8-hour bus trip（一次 8 小時的公車行程）
  [et]
- an 18-year-old soccer player（一名 18 歲的足球運動員）
  [ˋeˋtin]
- an 80 mph wind（一陣時速 80 英里的風）
  [ˋetɪ]
- an 11 p.m. meeting（一場晚上 11 點的會議）
  [ɪˋlɛvn̩]

文法加油站

A 用 a 還是用 an，關鍵在於母音發音或子音發音，而不是母音字母或子音字母

- Pam's a European, and Sam's an Egyptian.
  [ju]　[ɪ]
  （潘姆是歐洲人，山姆是埃及人。）

• Is that an elf with an umbrella riding on a unicorn?
[ɛ] [ʌ] [ju]
（在一隻獨角獸上面是一個拿著一把雨傘的小精靈嗎？）

• Is that an orange sports car on a one-way street?
[ɔ] [w]
（在一條單行道上有一輛橙黃色的跑車嗎？）

B 注意下列的縮寫詞和非縮寫詞的冠詞用法

• Is Amanda happy as an **FBI** agent?
= Is Amanda happy as a **Federal Bureau of Investigation** agent?
（當一名聯邦調查局特工，艾曼達感到滿意嗎？）

• Does she have an **MBA** degree?
= Does she have a **Master of Business Administration** degree?
（她有企業管理碩士學位嗎？）

• She owns an **NFL** team!
= She owns a **National Football League** team!
（她擁有一支全國橄欖球聯盟隊！）

• She wants to become an **RN**.
= She wants to become a **Registered Nurse**.
（她想當一名註冊護士。）

• Does she live in an **RV**?
= Does she live in a **recreational vehicle**?
（她居住在一輛活動房屋旅遊車裡嗎？）

002 a/an 不需冠詞 a/an

1

✗ What a fresh air!
✓ What fresh air! — 不可數名詞前面不能用 a 或 an
— 不需冠詞 a 或 an

空氣真新鮮啊！

air（空氣）：是**不可數名詞**，不可數名詞前面不能用不定冠詞 a 或 an。

2

❌ That's a bad news about Brad!

不可數名詞，前面不能加 a 或 an

✔ That's bad news about Brad!

news 不可數，不需冠詞 a 或 an

✔ That's a piece of **bad** news about Brad!

不可數名詞 news 可用 **a piece of** 修飾

那是一條有關布萊德的壞消息！

news（新聞、消息）：前面不能用不定冠詞 a 或 an。雖然 news 看起來像一個複數名詞，實際上它是一個**不可數名詞**。

003 a/an 需要冠詞 a/an

1

❌ "Dentist fixed my tooth," stated little Ruth.

✔ "A dentist fixed my tooth," stated little Ruth.

✔ "That/The/My dentist fixed my tooth," stated little Ruth.

單數可數名詞前必加 a/an 或其他限定詞

小露絲說：「一名（那名／我的）牙醫治好了我的牙齒。」

dentist（牙醫）是可數名詞。可數名詞用作單數時，需有**限定詞修飾**（如 a/an、the、my、his、that 等）。

2

英式 Sue West went to hospital for a blood test.

泛指「去了醫院」

美式 英式 Sue West went to a hospital for a blood test.

去了（非特定的）一家醫院。**不常用**

美式 英式 Sue West went to the hospital for a blood test.

美式：特定／非特定的一家醫院。**常用**

英式：特定的一家醫院

蘇・韋斯特去醫院驗血。

(1) 第一句裡的片語 **go/went to hospital** 只用於英式英語，泛指「去了醫院」。美式英語認為這種沒有冠詞的用法是錯誤的。

(2) 第二句中的 a hospital 是泛指任何一家醫院，可以翻譯成「去了一家醫院」。片語 go/went to a hospital 無論是英式還是美式都不常用。

(3) 在英式英語中，第三句中的 the hospital 是特定的一家醫院，說話者和聽話的人都明白是哪一家醫院。而在美式英語中，無論是泛指還是特指，都常用帶定冠詞的片語 go/went to the hospital。

3

✗ "It's only about ten-minute walk," announced Lily.

✓ "It's only about a ten-minute walk," announced Lily.

莉莉宣稱：「只有大約十分鐘的路程。」

作可數名詞時，要與 a 連用

walk 作可數名詞用時，指「散步、步行距離、路程」，要與不定冠詞 a 連用。

- take/have/go for a walk （散步）
- a twenty-minute walk （二十分鐘的路程）
- take somebody/something for a walk（帶某人／某物去散步）

文法加油站

由「數字 + 名詞」構成的複合字，名詞要用單數形式

- an exam lasting three hours = a three-hour exam（三小時的考試）
- a journey of fifty miles = a fifty-mile journey（五十英里的旅程）

004 a(an)/one 一個

1

✗ Gus said, "Only a passenger was injured when that truck hit the bus."

✓ Gus said, "Only one passenger was injured when that truck hit the bus."

強調數量，用 one

加斯說：「當那輛卡車撞到那輛公車時，只有一名乘客受了傷。」

2 ✗ Would you like one cup of coffee or tea?

✓ Would you like a cup of coffee or tea?

數量不重要，用 a/an

你想要一杯咖啡還是茶？

- only one passenger：強調數量（不是兩個，不是三個，只有一個）
- a cup of coffee：強調某一類物品中任意一個

005 a lot of/a great deal of 大量的

1 ✗ Brooke's sister has read a great deal of English books.

「大量的」，修飾**不可數名詞**

✓ Brooke's sister has read a lot of English books.

「大量的」，修飾**可數複數名詞／不可數名詞**

布露可的姐姐讀了很多英語書籍。

⑴ a great deal of 意為「大量的」，修飾不可數名詞。

- Our high quality honey makes us **a great deal of money**.
  （我們高品質的蜂蜜為我們賺進了很多錢。）

  「大量的」，修飾不可數名詞

⑵ 請參見 a lot of/many/much。

006 a lot of/many/much 許多

1 ✗ Ms. Potter didn't drink many water.

只能用在**複數可數名詞**前面，不能修飾不可數名詞 water

✓ Ms. Potter didn't drink much water.

只能用在**不可數名詞**前面

✓ Ms. Potter didn't drink a lot of water.

可以用在**不可數名詞／複數可數名詞**前面

波特女士沒有喝多少水。

2

❌ Dad boiled much eggs for Brad and Chad.

much 只能用在**不可數名詞**前面

✅ Dad boiled many eggs for Brad and Chad.

many 只能用在**複數可數名詞**前面

✅ Dad boiled a lot of eggs for Brad and Chad.

a lot of/lots of/plenty of 可以用在**不可數名詞／複數可數名詞**前面

爸爸為布萊德和查德煮了很多雞蛋。

- **much** traffic（擁擠的交通）
  修飾不可數名詞
- **many** cars（許多汽車）
  修飾複數可數名詞
- **a lot of** traffic（擁擠的交通）
  修飾不可數名詞
- **a lot of** cars（許多汽車）
  修飾複數可數名詞

3

不自然用法 June got much sleep yesterday afternoon.

自然用法 June got a lot of sleep yesterday afternoon.

茱恩昨天下午睡了很多覺。

肯定句常用 a lot of/lots of/plenty of

⑴ 在**疑問句**和**否定句**裡通常用 much，也可以用 a lot of、lots of、plenty of。

- I **don't** have **much** time to make up a new rhyme.

  否定句用 much，也可以用 a lot of 或 lots of

  （我沒有多少時間去編出一首新押韻詩了。）

- Do you have to do **much** work for Lulu?

  疑問句用 much，也可以用 a lot of 或 lots of

  （你必須為露露做很多工作嗎？）

⑵ **肯定句**常用 a lot of/lots of/plenty of。

⑶ 請參見 too much/much too。

文法加油站

上面的規則不適用於下面兩種情境

① 如果句中有 **so**、**too**、**as** 或 **more**，那麼 much 就可以用在肯定句中。

② 如果是**非常正式**的文體，那麼 much 就可以用在肯定句中。

- Ann should sleep **as much** as she can.
  └─句中有 as，much 可用在肯定句中
  （安應該盡量多睡覺。）

- Kay has **too much** responsibility and not much pay.
  └─句中有 too，much 可用在肯定句中
  （凱的責任太多，而薪水卻不多。）

- I want **much more** time for my vacation at the space station.
  └─句中有 more，much 可用在肯定句中
  （我需要更多的時間在太空站度假。）

- Pollution in the ocean has already caused **much** discussion.
  非常正式，much 可用在肯定句中─┘
  （海洋的污染已經引起了很多討論。）

007 above/over 在……上方／覆蓋、超過

1

✗ Mary Red felt cold, so she put a scarf above her head.

✓ Mary Red felt cold, so she put a scarf over her head.

表示「某物覆蓋另一物」

瑪麗 · 雷德感到很冷，於是把頭巾包在頭上。

2

✗ Margo got married above seven years ago.

✓ Margo got married over seven years ago.

瑪歌結婚超過七年了。　在數字和數量前，表示「超過」

(1) above 和 over 都可以表示「**在……上方**」。

- the light above/over the mirror
  （在鏡子上方的燈）

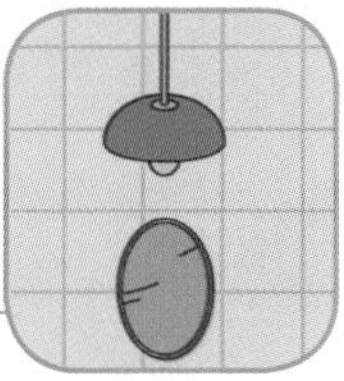

(2) 如果要表示「**某物覆蓋另一物**」，要用 over。

- a scarf over her head
  （一條頭巾披在她的頭上）

(3) 如果要表示「**越過某物；在……上空**」，要用 over。

- jump over the fence
  （跳躍過籬笆）
- Coco is flying a UFO over Tokyo.
  （可可駕駛著那架幽浮，在東京上空飛行。）

(4) 在數字和數量前，表示「**超過**」，要用 over。

- over seventy years ago
  （七十多年前〔超過七十年〕）

文法加油站

表示方位的介係詞

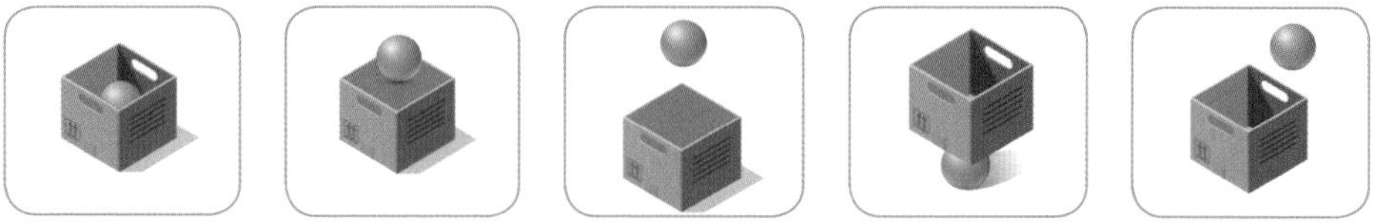

in	on	over	under	above
在……之內	在……上面	在……（正）上方	在……（正）下方	在……上方

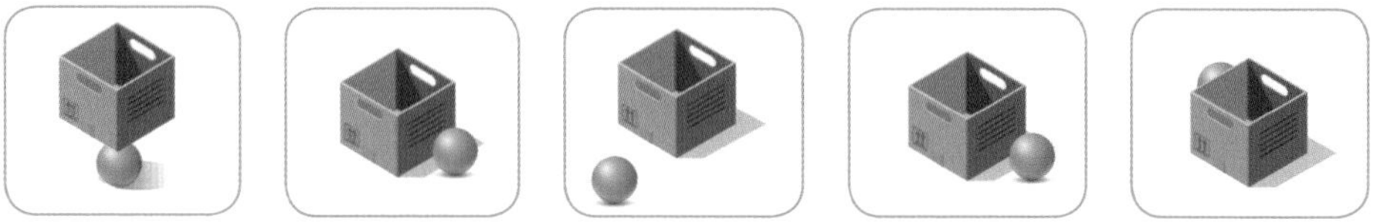

below	by/beside	near	next to	behind
在……下方	在……旁邊	在……附近	在……旁邊	在……後面

008 absent/away/out 缺席／離開／在外

1

✗ June will be absent for 20 days on a trip to the moon.

✓ June will be away for 20 days on a trip to the moon.

表度假、旅遊等原因而不在工作場所或不在家，用 **away**

茱恩要離開 20 天，去月球旅行。

2

表示「（工作、上課、會議）缺席」，用在這裡語意不通

❌ If I am absent when Tyrone calls, please tell him to call me on my cellphone.

不在家或不在工作場所，但很快就會回來，用 out

✅ If I am out when Tyrone calls, please tell him to call me on my cellphone.

如果迪龍打電話來時我不在，請他打我的手機。

⑴ 表示「**（工作、上課、會議）缺席**」，要用 absent。

- Because of her cold, Kay Gold is absent from school today. 表示上課缺席，用 absent

  （凱・戈爾德因為感冒了，今天沒有來上課。）

⑵ 如果因某人**去度假、去旅遊等原因而不在家、不在工作場所**，要用 away。

- Maybe Kay could teach my ballet classes while I am away. 表度假、旅遊等原因而不在工作場所，用 away

  （我不在時，也許凱可以教我的芭蕾舞班。）

⑶ 如果某人不在家、不在工作場所，但**很快就會回來**，要用 out。

不在家，但很快就會回來，要用 out

- Ms. Pool is usually out between 4 and 5 p.m. when she goes to pick up her children at school.

  （在下午四點和五點之間，普爾女士通常要去學校接孩子，不在家。）

009 accept/except 接受／除……以外

1

❌ Mr. Nation has excepted our invitation.

介系詞，表「不包括……；除……以外；排除……」

✅ Mr. Nation has accepted our invitation.

納欣先生已經接受了我們的邀請。

動詞，表「（樂意地）接受」

（except 的詳細用法，請參見 except。）

• Sorry, Brad, I don't **accept** expensive gifts from **any** man **except** my dad.

表概括性的字 any 之後，可以用 except，也可以用 except for

= Sorry, Brad, I don't **accept** expensive gifts from **any** man **except for** my dad.

（對不起，布萊德，除了我的爸爸，我不接受任何男人昂貴的禮物。）

010 according to 依照……

1

✗ According to me, this sailboat is an excellent deal.

✓ In my opinion, this sailboat is an excellent deal.

指資訊來自自己

我認為這帆船買得真划算。

2

✗ According to Jeff's opinion, James is not the ideal boyfriend for Liz.

✓ According to Jeff, James is not the ideal boyfriend for Liz.

指資訊來自別人或別處

✓ In Jeff's opinion, James is not the ideal boyfriend for Liz.

依傑夫的看法，詹姆斯不是莉茲理想的男朋友。

(1) 如果要表示資訊來自「**自己**」：

✗ according to me　錯誤用法

✓ in my opinion/view　正確用法

(2) 如果要表示我們的消息是從某人或某一本書中得來的，而不是來自自己，要用 according to **somebody/something**。

表示消息從時刻表得來，而非來自自己

• **According to** the **timetable**, Clem Wood's train should arrive at 10 p.m.

（根據時刻表，克勒姆・伍德的火車會在晚上十點到達。）

(3) according to 不能與 view 和 opinion 之類的字連用。

✗ according to Jeff's opinion　錯誤用法

✓ according to Jeff　正確用法

011 acoustics 聲學；音響效果

1

✗ Acoustics are a branch of physics.

✓ Acoustics is a branch of physics.

指「聲學」是**不可數名詞**，接單數動詞

聲學是物理學的一個分支。

2

✗ The meeting was unbearable, because the room's acoustics was terrible.

✓ The meeting was unbearable, because the room's acoustics were terrible.

指「音響效果、音質」是**複數**，動詞用複數

由於房間的音響效果很差，會議讓人難以忍受。

(1) 當 acoustics 的意思指「聲學」（一門學科）時，是不可數名詞；在句中作主詞時，要接**單數動詞**。

(2) 如果指房間、劇院等的「音響效果、音質」，acoustics 就是複數，**動詞也要用複數**。

(3) 請參見 politics。

012 action 行動；活動

1

✗ Our President's reaction was to take immediate actions.

✓ Our President's reaction was to take immediate action.

用在 take action 中為**不可數名詞**

我們總統的反應是，立即採取行動。

2

✗ Alice Herd's action speaks louder than her words.

✓ Alice Herd's actions speak louder than her words.

指「行為、活動」，**可數名詞**

艾麗絲 · 赫德做的比說的還好。

(1) action 指「**行為、活動**」時，是**可數名詞**。

(2) action 用在下面的片語裡，是**不可數名詞**：

- take action （採取行動；開始起作用）
- course of action （行動方針；做法）
- in action （在運轉中；在活動中）
- out of action （不運轉；不活動）

文法加油站

① in action 表示「**在運轉中**」，只能用不可數名詞 action。

② 表示「**陣亡**」，通常用 be killed in action，也可以用 be killed in an action，或 be killed in actions。比如：

- Here are the names of our sailors missing in action in the Pacific Ocean.

= Here are the names of our sailors missing in actions in the Pacific Ocean.
（這是我們在太平洋戰爭中失蹤的水手名單。）

013 advice/advise 建議；勸告

1

✗ Please give me some advices.

✓ Please give me some advice.

不可數名詞，無複數形式

請給我一些意見。

2

✗ Dennis gave Bryce a good advice.

✓ Dennis gave Bryce a piece of good advice.

不可數名詞，不能和 an/a 連用

丹尼斯給了布萊斯一個好建議。

3 ✗ Did Mr. Rice take my advise on how to kill his lice?

動詞，此處需用名詞 advice

✓ Did Mr. Rice take my advice on how to kill his lice?

關於如何消滅他身上的蝨子，賴斯先生接受了我的建議嗎？

4 ✗ Did Ms. Wise advice Eloise to study Chinese and Japanese?

名詞，此處需用動詞 advise

✓ Did Ms. Wise advise Eloise to study Chinese and Japanese?

懷斯女士建議過伊露意絲學習中文和日文嗎？

(1) advice ─ 不可數名詞，無複數形式
　　　　└ 不能和 an/a 連用

(2) advise（作動詞用時）＝ 提建議；勸告；推薦

014 affect/effect 影響／效果

1 ✗ The bad news about Gertrude effected Sue's mood.

名詞，需用動詞 affected

✓ The bad news about Gertrude affected Sue's mood.

關於葛楚德的壞消息影響了蘇的情緒。

2 ✗ Bret's dad died from the affects of smoking cigarettes.

動詞，需用名詞 effects

✓ Bret's dad died from the effects of smoking cigarettes.

布瑞特的爸爸死於吸菸所產生的後果。

affect：(1) ＝ influence ＝ produce an effect or change on
影響；對……發生作用

(2) 通常用作**及物動詞**

(3) 用法：to affect a person or thing

- The drought affected the growth of corn in Iowa and Indiana. 動詞，後面接事物
（乾旱影響了愛荷華州和印第安納州的玉米生長。）

effect：(1) =result　結果；影響；作用；效果
(2) 通常用作**名詞**

- Debbie is beginning to feel the effects of smoking cigarettes. 名詞，表結果、影響
（黛比已經開始感覺到吸菸所產生的影響了。）

文法加油站

① have an effect on = affect 影響

- The divorce had a great effect on Dawn, John, and their son Ron.
= The divorce greatly affected Dawn, John, and their son Ron.
（離婚對朵安、約翰以及他們兒子朗的影響很大。）

② effect (vt.) = bring about = achieve = make something happen
產生；造成；招致
只是**偶爾**用作動詞

- Drinking alcohol has effected a bad change in Paul.
（喝酒已經給保羅帶來了不良的變化。）

015 afraid of/afraid to 害怕

1

✗ Peg didn't jump off the wall, because she was afraid to break her leg.

✓ Peg didn't jump off the wall, because she was afraid of breaking her leg. 不希望把腿摔斷，用 afraid of doing

佩格沒有從牆上跳下去，因為她害怕把腿摔斷。

(1) 如果你**不希望做某事，不希望某件不好的事情發生**，比如：fail the exam（考試考壞）、break your leg（摔斷腿）、lose the way（迷路），那麼就要用 **afraid of doing**。這種情形不用不定詞 afraid to do。

- Kay is **afraid of losing** her way.（凱擔心迷路。）
  不希望迷路，用 afraid of doing

(2) 如果你**想做某事，但因擔心可能會有什麼不良的後果**，這種情形可以用 **afraid to do**，也可以用 **afraid of doing**。

(3) 在考試中，如果記不清楚上面兩條規則，**無論什麼情況都用 afraid of doing**，就肯定不會出錯。

- If you want to go, don't be **afraid to say** so.

= If you want to go, don't be **afraid of saying** so.
（如果你想去，就不要害怕說出來。）

「把自己的想法說出來」不是一件不好的事。可以用 afraid to say，也可以用 afraid of saying

016 after 在……之後

1

✗ I'll email Margo after I will arrive in Tokyo.
after 後不能接未來式

✓ I'll email Margo after I arrive in Tokyo.

✓ I'll email Margo after I have arrived in Tokyo.

= I'll email Margo after my arrival in Tokyo.

我到了東京後就會發電子郵件給瑪歌。

(1) after、before、until、as soon as、when、if 引導的副詞子句中，動詞不能用未來式，而要**用現在式表示未來的含意**。

- Please send a text message to Clive **as soon as you arrive**.
（你一到達就請發手機簡訊給克萊夫。）
✗ as soon as you will arrive

(2) 請參見 simple present tense/simple future tense 現在簡單式／未來簡單式。

017 afterward/later 之後／以後

1

❌ I will send you the alligator picture afterward.

✅ I will send you the alligator picture later.

我隨後再寄給你那張鱷魚的照片。

指以後；稍後（未來某時間）

(1) afterward 指「（在已經提及的某事）之後」。
美式常用 afterward，而英式更常用 afterwards。

(2) later 意思是「以後；稍後（未來某時間）；較晚地（比較已經提及過的時間，是 late 的比較級）」。

- **You worked as a shepherd last summer**, and what did you do afterward?

指已經提及的某事之後用 afterward

（去年夏天你當過牧羊人，之後你又做過什麼呢？）

文法加油站

- two days afterward = two days later （兩天後）
- three weeks afterward = three weeks later （三週後）
- Lee won the car race, and an hour afterward he had a phone call from his ex-girlfriend Liz.

= Lee won the car race, and an hour later he had a phone call from his ex-girlfriend Liz.

（李贏了汽車賽之後的一個小時，收到了前女友莉茲的電話。）

018 after/in 在……以後

1

❌ Monique's plan is to go away to college after two weeks.

✅ Monique's plan is to go away to college in two weeks.

莫妮可計畫兩週後離開去上大學。

從講話開始到未來某時，用 in+時間

(1) 從講話開始到未來某個時刻，某事要發生，需用 in + 時間，而不用 after。

從講話開始一小時後

- Mark will be back in an hour.（馬克一小時後就會回來。）

(2) after 表示「在……以後」，通常不接時間，比如：
after graduation from high school

「在高中畢業以後」，不接時間

019 ago/for 多久以前／延續多久（指時間）

1

✗ Margo Spear's mother has died for ten years.

短暫的動作，不能與 for 連用

✓ Margo Spear's mother passed away ten years ago.

✓ Margo Spear's mother died ten years ago.

瑪歌・斯比爾的母親十年前去世了。

與**過去式動詞**連用

✓ Margo Spear's mother has been dead for ten years.

瑪歌・斯比爾的母親已經去世十年了。

表示狀態，可以延續，因此可以與 **for** 連用

2

短暫的動作，不能與 for 連用

✗ Margo Wu left Moscow for two years.

✓ Margo Wu left Moscow two years ago.

瑪歌・吳兩年前離開了莫斯科。

與**過去式動詞**連用

表示狀態，可以延續，因此可以與 **for** 連用

✓ Margo Wu has been away from Moscow for two years.

瑪歌・吳已經離開莫斯科兩年了。

(1) ago 說明「某件事是在離現在多長時間以前發生的」，都是與**過去式動詞**連用，不與完成式連用。

(2) for 說明「一個動作或一種情況延續了多長時間」。

(3) die、pass away、return 和 leave 這類動詞不是延續動作，而是短暫的動作，**不能與 for 連用**。has been dead、has been away 表示狀態，可以延續，因此**可以與 for 連用**。

文法加油站

比較

- Kay and Dan returned home for a day, and then they flew to Japan.
  （凱和丹回家待了一天，然後飛往日本。）〔凱和丹回家待了一天，就離開了。〕
- Kay and Dan returned home yesterday.
  （凱和丹昨天回家了。）
- Kay and Dan have been back home for a day.
  ⊗ have returned
  （凱和丹回家已經一天了。）〔凱和丹還在家中。〕

020 ago/since 多久以前／自從

1

⊗ Clyde died since two years ago.
兩者不能同時用

✓ Clyde died two years ago.
ago 與一個過去式連用

克萊德兩年前去世了。

✓ It's been two years since Clyde died.
主要子句用完成式　since 引導的子句用過去式

克萊德已經去世兩年了。

⑴ since 和 ago，這兩者只能用其中一個，不能同時用。

⊗ since two/three/four months/years ago

⑵或者用 ago，與一個過去式連用；或者用 since，**主要子句**裡的動詞用現在完成式、現在完成進行式或過去完成式，**since 子句**裡的動詞用過去式。

ago 只和過去式連用

- Did Coco go to Jericho ten years ago?
  （可可十年前去了耶利哥〔約旦一古城〕嗎？）

主要子句用現在完成式 —— since 引導的子句用過去式

- How many years has it been since Benny met Jenny?
（班尼認識珍妮已經有多少年了？）

主要子句用現在完成進行式 —— since 接一個過去時間點

- June has been reading a romance novel since four this afternoon.（從今天下午四點起，茱恩就一直在讀一本言情小說。）

修飾整個子句，非修飾 two years ago

- Since she arrived in Chicago two years ago, Margo has been really busy managing the Bell Hotel.
（自從瑪歌兩年前來到芝加哥後，她就一直忙著管理貝爾旅館。）

021 all 全部（接單或複數動詞）

1

✗ All of Mort's friends is boring because they all talk about nothing but sports.

指「他們全部」，動詞用複數

✓ All of Mort's friends are boring because they all talk about nothing but sports.

莫特的朋友全都很乏味，因為他們只聊運動。

(1) 不定代名詞 all 可以接單數動詞和代名詞，也可以接複數動詞和代名詞，要根據它在句中的意思而決定。

(2) 如果 all 是指 all of it、everything、the only/whole thing，那麼作主詞的時候，動詞就用**單數**，意思是「全部、所有一切、唯一的事」。

- Mr. Bell said, "**All is** well."（貝爾先生說：「一切都很好。」）

  = everything，指「所有事物的總和」，要用單數動詞 is

A B C D E F G H I J K L M N O P Q R S T U V W X Y Z

(3) 但如果 all 是指 all of them、everyone、every one of，那麼動詞就要用**複數**，意思是「他們全部，每一個人，每一個」。

- I hope **all are** healthy and happy.
  = the whole number of people，指一群人中的所有人，後面接複數動詞 are；現代英語更常用 everyone/everybody

= I hope **everybody is** healthy and happy.
（我希望大家都健康、幸福。）

文法加油站

all 接形容詞子句的句型

all 後面如果有形容詞子句修飾，動詞究竟用單數還是複數動詞？

- 句型一：all＋形容詞子句＋單數動詞＋單數主詞補語
- 句型二：all＋形容詞子句＋單數動詞＋複數主詞補語

在上面的句型二中，如果補語是複數，「all＋形容詞子句」後面究竟是接單數動詞 be，還是複數動詞 be，有不同的說法。甚至一些母語是英文的人士對這一點也感到困惑。在正式用語中，用單數動詞。

- "**All** that matters **is to be happy**," explained Paul.
  單數動詞（is）；單數主詞補語（to be happy）

（保羅解釋說：「最重要的是，要快樂。」）

→ 主詞補語是不定詞片語（to be happy），看作是單數，動詞自然要用單數 is。

- **All** Lars talks about **involves cars**.
  單數動詞（involves）；複數主詞補語（cars）

= **Everything** Lars talks about **involves cars**.（拉斯只聊汽車。）

→ 雖然主詞補語是複數（cars），但我們把 cars 看成是他所談論的一切事（everything）。那 all 就是單數，後面接單數動詞。

- **All** Grace talks about **is NASA, astronauts, and space**.
  單數動詞（is）；複合主詞補語（為複數主詞補語）

（葛蕾絲只談論美國太空總署、太空人及外太空。）

022 all/not all 全部／並非全部

1

✗ "All birds cannot fly," explained Scot.

「所有的鳥兒都不會飛。」意思不對

✓ "Not all birds can fly," explained Scot.

表示「並非所有」，要用 not all 作主詞

史考特解釋說：「並不是所有的鳥兒都能飛。」

如果要表示「並非所有」，不用 all 作主詞，而用 not all 作主詞。

2

動詞是否定式，不用 all 作主詞

語意不清 Mort said, "All of the departments did not file a report."

(a) 並非所有的部門都有提交報告。
(b) 所有的部門都沒有提交報告。

語意清楚 Mort said, "Not all of the departments filed a report."

表示「並非所有」的意思

莫特說：「不是所有的部門都提交了報告。」

語意清楚 Mort said, "All of the departments failed to file a report."

表示「沒有一個」的意思

莫特說：「所有的部門都沒有提交報告。」

語意清楚 Mort said, "None of the departments filed a report."

表示「沒有一個」的意思

莫特說：「沒有一個部門提交了報告。」

023 all right/alright 好吧

1

✗ Alright, Marty, I'll go with you to the party.

錯字

✓ All right, Marty, I'll go with you to the party.

好吧，瑪蒂，我會跟你一起去參加聚會。

alright 不等於 all right，這是一個錯字，雖然有些字典有這個字，但在書寫中不要用。

024 allow 准許

1

✗ "We do not allow people smoking in the building," explained Scot.

✓ "We do not allow people to smoke in the building," explained Scot.
受詞是「人」，接不定詞

✓ "We do not allow smoking in the building," explained Scot.
沒有「人」作受詞，接 V–ing

✓ "People are not allowed to smoke in the building," explained Scot.

✓ "Smoking is not allowed in the building," explained Scot.

史考特解釋說：「在這棟大樓裡不許吸菸。」

(1) allow **someone to do** something
受詞是「人」，接不定詞

(2) allow **doing** something
沒有「人」作受詞，接 V–ing

(3) allow **something**
接名詞作受詞

- Sue will not **allow that kangaroo** in her canoe.
接名詞 kangaroo

（蘇不允許那隻袋鼠進她的獨木舟。）

文法加油站

permit/allow/let 比較

三者意思相近，用法不同

兩者用法和意思相近
permit（稍正式）　allow

let（最不正式）
→ 不接帶 to 的不定詞
→ 不用被動式
→ 句型：let sb. do sth.

① permit 的用法和意思與 allow 相近。但 permit 稍微正式一些。

- Ms. Joan Bloom doesn't permit **anyone to use** a cellphone in her classroom.

  接「sb. + 不定詞」

= Ms. Joan Bloom doesn't allow **anyone to use** a cellphone in her classroom.

（裘恩・布盧姆老師不允許任何人在她的教室裡使用手機。）

- The law doesn't permit **parking** on Neat Street.

  接「動名詞」

= The law doesn't allow **parking** on Neat Street.

（法律規定，在尼特街不允許停車。）

- I'm sorry Ms., but county law doesn't allow/permit **nudity** on this part of the beach.

  接「名詞」

（對不起，女士，這個郡的法律不允許在海灘的這一區裸露身體。）

② let 的意思與 allow、permit 相近，是三者中最不正式的字。但 let 的用法與 allow 和 permit 的用法不一樣，let 不用於被動式，通常接「不帶 to 的不定詞」，句型為：let someone do something。

接「不帶 to 的不定詞」

- Joan, please let me buy you an ice cream cone.

= Joan, please allow me to buy you an ice cream cone.

（裘恩，讓我買給你一個甜筒。）

接「帶 to 的不定詞」

- Dwight **was allowed to** go out last night.

  ✖ Dwight was let to go out last night.

（昨晚杜威特得到了許可才出門。）

③ 請參見 let。

025 alphabet/letter 字母系統／字母

1

✖ Little Andy often confuses the alphabets "b" and "d."

✔ Little Andy often confuses the letters "b" and "d."

小安迪常混淆字母 b 和 d。

alphabet 指一套完整的「字母系統」，A、B、C、D 等則是 letter（字母）。

指「字母」

- One-year-old Bret knows the 26 letters in the English alphabet.（一歲大的布瑞特認識英語字母表裡的所有 26 個字母。）

指「字母系統」

026 also/too 也

1

❌ My wife Sue loves kung fu, also. ← 不放**句尾**

✅ My wife Sue loves kung fu, too. ← 通常放**句尾**

✅ My wife Sue also loves kung fu. ← 通常放**句中**（置於一般動詞 loves 前面）

我的太太蘇也愛好中國功夫。

「也」
- → too → 通常放句尾（用逗號與前面的句子分開）。
- → also → 不放在句尾。
  通常放：**(1) 一般動詞前面。**
  (2) 助動詞、情態助動詞、be 動詞的後面。

- Sue Cook has finished reading that English storybook, too.
= Sue Cook has also finished reading that English storybook.
  在助動詞 has 後面

（蘇・庫克也讀完了那本英語故事書。）
- Kim Wu is slim, too.（金姆・吳也很苗條。）
= Kim Wu is also slim.
  在 be 動詞後面

文法加油站

also	too
可放**句首**，接一個逗號。	可放**句中**，用兩個逗號分開。

- Also, your baby was harmed by alcohol before he was born.
= Your baby was harmed, too, by alcohol before he was born.
（你的嬰兒在出生之前也受到了酒精的傷害。）

027 also/too/either 也

1

不用於否定句

✗ Heather, the truth is I don't like playboys, too.

✓ Heather, the truth is I don't like playboys either.

海瑟，事實是，我也不喜歡花花公子。

用於否定句

「也」→ also、too → 用在**肯定句**中。請參見上面的 also/too。

→ either → 用在**否定句**中（在 not、no、never、rarely、hardly 等後面）。

- Bing Ink's breath, too, smells bad because of his smoking.

= Also, Bing Ink's breath smells bad because of his smoking.（因為抽菸，賓・印克的呼吸也有臭味。）

- Heather, if you don't go, Coco won't go either.
（海瑟，如果你不去，可可也不去。）

028 although/but 雖然／但是

1

✗ Although Taiwan is small, but it's a beautiful island.

不能同時並用

✓ Although Taiwan is small, it's a beautiful island.

✓ Taiwan is small, but it's a beautiful island.

臺灣雖小，卻是一個非常漂亮的島嶼。

(1) 連接詞 although 和 but 只能用其中一個，不能同時使用。這點與中文不同。

(2) 請參見 conjunctions。

文法加油站

連接詞 although 的用法

① 連接詞 although 也不能與連接詞 yet（但是）連用。

- "Your English is good, yet it could be improved," declared Trish.

不能與 although 連用

A B C D E F G H I J K L M N O P Q R S T U V W X Y Z

= "Although your English is good, it could be improved," declared Trish.

└── 不能與連接詞 yet 連用

（翠西聲明：「你的英語雖然不錯，但可以更進步。」）

② although 可以與副詞 yet（還沒有）、nevertheless（仍然、不過）連用。副詞 yet、nevertheless 通常放在句尾。

可以與副詞 yet 連用

• Although we are planning to go to the moon, we haven't designed the spaceship yet. —— 副詞 yet 通常放在句尾

（雖然我們計畫去月球，但還沒有設計好太空船。）

• Although Tess was sick, she went with Coco nevertheless.

可以與副詞 nevertheless 連用　　副詞 nevertheless 通常放在句尾

（雖然黛絲生病了，她仍然跟可可一起去了。）

029 altogether/all together 總共／一起

1

✗ Dinah spent all together $7,000 on the trip to China.

表「一起」，在此句語意不通

✓ Dinah spent altogether $7,000 on the trip to China.

表「總共」

✓ Dinah spent $7,000 altogether on the trip to China.

表「總共」

那趟中國之旅，黛娜總共花了七千美金。

2

✗ Because of the large crowd, Heather and her friends were squeezed altogether.

✓ Because of the large crowd, Heather and her friends were squeezed (all) together. —— all 可省略，不影響意思

= Because of the large crowd, Heather and her friends were all squeezed together. —— all 和 together 也可以被其他字分開

由於擁擠的人群，海瑟和她的朋友們被緊緊地擠在一起。

比較 altogether/all together

altogether 完全；全部； 合計；總的說來	┌── = on the whole • "<u>Altogether</u>, I'm glad the play is over," declared Heather. （海瑟宣布：「**總體說來**，我很高興這場戲結束了。」） • Heather, we lost the TV picture <u>altogether</u>. = completely ──┘ （海瑟，電視畫面**完全**沒有了。）
all together 一道；一起；每 一件東西都……	• The dishwasher can wash the dishes all together. （洗碗機能**同時**把所有的盤子都洗乾淨。）

🔦030 a.m./p.m. 上午／下午

1 ❌ Ray leaves home for work at 7:30 <u>a.m.</u> in the morning
every weekday.

> a.m. **單獨使用**，不能和時間片語（in the morning）用在一起

✅ Ray leaves home for work at 7:30 a.m. every weekday.

✅ Ray leaves home for work at seven-thirty in the
morning every weekday.

雷每個工作日都是早上七點半離開家去上班。

2 ❌ Every day Clem Lock gets up at 6 <u>a.m. o'clock</u>.

> a.m. 或 p.m. 不與 o'clock 用在一起

✅ Every day Clem Lock gets up at 6 <u>a.m.</u>

> **單獨使用**，不能和時間片語或 o'clock 用在一起

✅ Every morning Clem Lock gets up at <u>six o'clock</u>.

> o'clock 的前面要把表示時間的數字**拼寫**出來

克勒姆・洛克每天都是早上六點起床。

(1) 縮寫詞 a.m. 或 p.m. 不能和時間片語 in the morning、in the afternoon、in the evening、at night 用在一起；不是用縮寫詞 a.m. 或 p.m.，就是用時間片語，兩者選一。

- 8:20 a.m. = eight-twenty in the morning（上午八點二十分）
- 4:30 p.m. = four-thirty in the afternoon（下午四點半）

(2) o'clock 只用來表示**整點**。前面要把表示時間的數字拼寫出來（如：six o'clock、ten o'clock）。

(3) 縮寫詞 a.m. 或 p.m. 不與 o'clock 連用；兩者只能用其中一個。也可以不用縮寫詞（a.m./p.m.），或是不用 o'clock（如：at five、at 5、at five in the morning）。

- 5 a.m. = five (o'clock) in the morning（早上五點）
- 9 p.m. = nine (o'clock) at night（晚上九點）
- Every morning Rick's mom gets up at **six**.
  （瑞克的媽媽每天早上六點起床。）

文法加油站

時間的表達法

- 縮寫詞 a.m. 或 p.m.

① 在書寫時，要用數字（4、5、8 等）搭配。

② 表示「整點」時，數字後面通常不需要兩個零。「00」用來表示分鐘，比如：2 a.m.、6 p.m. 等，而不是 2:00 a.m.、6:00 p.m. 。

③ 如果省略了縮寫詞 a.m. 或 p.m.，那麼「整點」就要用兩個零，如：2:00、6:00 等。

④ 也可以把時間拼寫出來，如：two、six 等。

✖	Evan told Clem, "My bookstore is always open until seven p.m."
非正式	Evan told Clem, "My bookstore is always open until 7:00 p.m."
正式	Evan told Clem, "My bookstore is always open until 7 p.m."
正式	Evan told Clem, "My bookstore is always open until 7:00."
正式	Evan told Clem, "My bookstore is always open until seven."

（伊文告訴克勒姆：「我的書店總是營業到（晚上）7 點。」）

031 among/between 在……之中／在……之間

1

❌ In her will, Honey divided her money equally among her brother and mother.

✅ In her will, Honey divided her money equally between her brother and mother. —— 在兩人之間，只能用 between

杭妮在遺囑中把錢平均分給她的弟弟和媽媽。

2

❌ Veronica Fine is between the nine best actresses in America.

✅ Veronica Fine is among the nine best actresses in America. —— 在一群人或物之中，用 among

薇若妮卡・樊恩是美國九名最佳女演員之一。

(1) 當一組人或物被看成是**群體**（group or mass）時，就用 among。在正式英語中，among 與**兩個以上的人或物**相關。某人／物在一群人或物之中，用 among。

(2) 當一組人或物被分別看成是**分離的個體**（distinct individuals or units），無論是兩個還是兩個以上的人或物，都要用 between。

表示分離的個體，即使是兩個以上的實體，也要用 between

- **Between** teaching, editing, and writing, she hasn't much time for dancing.（教學、編輯和寫作，使她沒有時間跳舞。）

(3) 如果指定了具體**兩個實體**（人或物），就只能用 between，比如 **between** her brother and mother、to choose **between** tea and coffee。

(4) between 可以指兩個（人或物），也可以指一個（人或物）與一組（人或物）。

一個人和一組人，用 between

- "There is no disagreement **between Mary** and **her three brothers**," declared Claire.

一個人（Mary）與一組人（her three brothers）

（克萊兒宣稱：「在瑪麗和她的三個兄弟之間沒有意見不一。」）

032 amount/number 數量

1

❌ Lately, Honey has come into a big amount of money.

big 不可形容 amount

✅ Lately, Honey has come into a large/huge amount of money.

large/huge 可形容 amount

杭妮最近獲得了一大筆錢。

2

❌ The number of tourists visiting our city gets bigger every year.

big 不可形容 number

✅ The number of tourists visiting our city gets larger every year.

large 可形容 number

我們市的旅遊者的數量每年都在增加。

用 large 或者 small 來描述 amount 和 number。不能用 big 和 little 來描述 amount 和 number。

3

❌ Lily has inherited a large number of money.

number 與**複數名詞**連用

✅ Lily has inherited a large amount of money.

莉莉繼承了一大筆錢。

amount 與**不可數名詞**連用

(1) amount 與「用容積來計量的東西」相關，與**不可數名詞**連用。

(2) number 與「可以數的東西」相關，與**複數名詞**連用。

(3) 請參見 number: a number of。

與不可數名詞連用

• The **amount** of **money** stolen is $5,000.
（有五千美金被偷了。）

number 與複數名詞連用

• The **number** of **electric cars** in our city is getting **larger** every week.

用 large 描述 number

（我們城市電動汽車的數量每週都在增加。）

文法加油站

下表區別了形容數量的辭彙：

• 可以用容積計量的東西 • 與不可數名詞連用	• 可以數的東西 • 與複數名詞連用
amount	number
quantity	
little	few
less	fewer
much	many

033 amused/amusing

請參見 excited/exciting。

034 and/or 和／或

1

❌ Nate's wife never skis and skates.

✅ Nate's wife never skis or skates.

內特的妻子從來不滑雪，也不溜冰。

never 後面，要用 or，不可用 and

比較 and 與 or

and	or
用在**肯定句**中，連接並列肯定詞組。	用在 no、not、never 等**否定詞**後面，連接並列否定詞組。不可用 and。
• Mort reported, "They stole my money, credit cards, and passport." = Mort reported, "They stole my money, my credit cards, and my passport." 重複 my，語氣更強烈 （莫特報告說：「他們偷了我的錢、信用卡和護照。」）	• His wife replied, "But they did not take your health, happiness, or life." = His wife replied, "But they did not take your health, your happiness, or your life." 重複 your，語氣更強烈 （他的妻子回答說：「不過，他們沒有奪走你的健康、幸福和生命。」）

文法加油站

用 and 連接，當作一個整體的字

① 如果由 **and** 連接的名詞構成一對（即，一個整體），它就可以用在 **no**、**not**、**never** 等否定詞後面。

- curry and rice（咖哩飯）
- horse and carriage（馬車）
- husband and wife（夫妻）
- knife and fork（刀叉）
- law and order（法律與秩序）
- time and tide（歲月）
- bread and butter（麵包和奶油〔抹了奶油的麵包〕／生計／謀生之道）
- Midge noted, "That law does not apply to a horse and carriage."（米姬指出：「那條法律並不適用於馬車。」）

② 這些複合名詞在句中做主詞時，通常接**單數**動詞。

- Bread and butter is my usual breakfast.（我早餐通常吃奶油麵包。）

③ 通常不要使用 and/or 這種結構。只有在商務寫作中，有時才會出現這種結構。

不適當	Margo and/or Lars are going to Mars.
適當	Margo and Lars are going to Mars, or perhaps only one of them will be able to go.（瑪歌和拉斯打算去火星，或許他們倆只有一個能夠去。）

035 and/plus 加

and 和 plus 不可同時使用

1

✗ Little Sue told Clive, "Two and plus three are five."

✓ Little Sue told Clive, "Two and three are/is five."

✓ Little Sue told Clive, "Two plus three is five."

小蘇告訴克萊夫：「二加三等於五。」

and	plus
兩者之間選一個，不能同時使用。	
two and three two and two →看成是一個整體，後面用**單數動詞 is** 或 **equals** →看成是兩個由 and 連接起來的個體，可以用**複數動詞**	two plus three two plus two →後面要用**單數動詞 is** 或 **equals** 加法用 plus 較正式

036 another/more 另外的／更多的

1

❌ Jerome has another three day to finish his paper about Rome.
應為「another + 數字 + 複數名詞」

✅ Jerome has another three days to finish his paper about Rome.
可接帶數字的複數名詞

✅ Jerome has three more days to finish his paper about Rome.
數字 + more + 複數名詞

傑羅姆還有三天時間來完成關於羅馬的論文。

another 的用法

(1) 後面要用「**單數可數名詞**」，而不用「複數名詞」，也不用「不可數名詞」。

- another house → ❌ another houses （另一棟房子）
- another piece of furniture → ❌ another furniture （另一件家具）

(2) 可以接**帶數字的「複數名詞」**，表示還有多少人或還有多少東西／事情。句型為：

another + **數字**（two/five/ten/hundred/few etc.）+ **複數名詞**

- After another few minutes, Mr. How asked again, "Can I see the cow now?"
（又過了幾分鐘，郝先生再次問：「我現在可以看一看乳牛了嗎？」）

2

只用在**單數可數名詞**之前

❌ I need another information before I can make a decision about this issue.

可用在**不可數／複數可數名詞**前

✅ I need more information before I can make a decision about this issue.

在對這個問題做出決定之前，我還需要更多的資訊。

(1) more 可以用在**不可數名詞**之前，也可以用在**複數可數名詞**之前。

(2) another 只用在**可數名詞**之前。請參見上面 another 的用法。

A B C D E F G H I J K L M N O P Q R S T U V W X Y Z

文法加油站

other 指「別的；其他的；其餘的」

句型為：**數字**（two/five/ten/hundred etc.） + **other** + **複數名詞**

- five other states（另外五個州）
- three other days（另外三天）
- ten other teams（另外十個隊）
- four other people（另外四個人）
- Lenore and I started to dance, and soon three other couples joined us on the dance floor.
  （蕾諾兒和我開始在舞池上跳舞，很快地另外三對舞伴加入了我們。）

037 antecedents 先行詞（含糊的先行詞）

1

語意不清 "If your baby doesn't want the milk now, just freeze it," suggested Ms. Silk. —— 盡量少用代名詞 it 來做指代

語意清楚 "If your baby doesn't want the milk now, just freeze the milk," suggested Ms. Silk. —— 明確陳述想表達的意思

西爾克女士建議：「如果你的嬰兒不喝牛奶，就把牛奶冷凍起來。」

(1) 中文的「它」指「物」，不指「人」，但英語的 it 可以用來指代嬰兒。在第一個句子裡，無法確認 it 是指牛奶還是指嬰兒。

(2) 要避免這種含糊的意思，就應該盡量少用代名詞 it，精確地陳述想表達的意思。

2

語意不清 After Mrs. Bell and Mr. Brooms left their hotel rooms, the cleaning worker cleaned them.

避免使用有雙重含意的先行詞指代

語意清楚 After Mrs. Bell and Mr. Brooms left, the cleaning worker cleaned their hotel rooms.

貝爾夫人和布魯姆斯先生離開後，清潔工人打掃了他們住過的旅館房間。

(1) 第一句代名詞 them 是指先行詞 Mrs. Bell and Mr. Brooms，還是指先行詞 rooms？雖然從上下文可以猜測代名詞 them 應該是指 rooms，但仍然應該避免這種有雙重含意的先行詞指代。

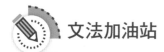

(2) 解決這類含糊先行詞指代的辦法是：**(a) 改變句型；(b) 刪除代名詞**

(3) 請參見 pronoun reference。

038 any 一些、一點、若干、任何

1

✗ **Is there any ticket** available for Fay and Janet's new ballet?

✓ **Are there any tickets** available for Fay and Janet's new ballet?

菲和珍妮特的新芭蕾舞表演還能買得到票嗎？

any 的意思是「一些；一點；若干」，用在**疑問句**、**否定句**或**附屬子句**中代替 some。句型為：

(1) any + **複數名詞**　　(2) any + **不可數名詞（單數）**

- "Are there **any** cookies left?" asked Claire.
  用在疑問句裡（no matter how many cookies）
  （克萊兒問：「餅乾還有剩嗎？」）
- Lenore tried to buy a toy rocket, but there were not **any** left in the store.
  用在否定句裡（no matter how many toy rockets）
  any 後面省略了 toy rockets
  （蕾諾兒想買一個玩具火箭，可是店裡所有的玩具火箭都賣完了。）
- If there is **any** trouble, please let Ray know right away.
  用在條件副詞子句裡
  （no matter what kind of trouble）
  （如果有什麼麻煩，請立刻讓雷知道。）

2

✗ Penny Best declared, "I am sure **any students** can pass that test."

✓ Penny Best declared, "I am sure **any student** can pass that test."

表示泛指所有人，用於**肯定句**中，後面接**單數**名詞

潘妮・貝斯特宣稱說：「我確定任何一個學生都可以通過那個考試。」

可以用 any 來表示「任何一個；每一個」，究竟哪一個不重要（one or another），泛指所有的人或所有的物（everyone 或 everything）。在這個意義上，any 用在**肯定句**中，後面接**單數名詞**。句型為：

any + 單數名詞（可數或不可數）

- Any teacher would be glad to have students like Jenny and Penny.

（任何一個老師都會很高興有像珍妮和潘妮那樣的學生。）

039 any/one 任何／一個

1

✗ Nan Sun has a van, but I don't have any.

指**單數**的可數名詞，不用 **any**

✓ Nan Sun has a van, but I don't have one.

指**單數**的可數名詞，用 **one**

南・孫有一輛休旅車，可是我沒有。

(1) 如果指單數的可數名詞，要用 one，不用 any。

(2) 指複數名詞可以用 any；與 even 連用，也可以用 one。

- Jenny has four pets, but Penny doesn't have any.
  句末省略了 pets（= doesn't have any pets）
  （珍妮有四隻寵物，可是潘妮沒有任何寵物。）
- Mr. Sun has four pets, but Ms. Done doesn't even have one.（孫先生有四隻寵物，可是多恩女士連一隻寵物都沒有。）

040 any other 其他

1

✗ Can Penny Bridge swim faster than any other female students at her college?

✓ Can Penny Bridge swim faster than any other female student at her college?

any other 後面接單數名詞

潘妮・布里奇游泳能比她大學裡的其他女生都游得快嗎？

041 anybody 任何人

1

❌ Mr. West won't hire anybody who have not passed the 12th grade reading test.

搭配單數動詞

who的先行詞是anybody，所引導的子句用單數動詞

✅ Mr. West won't hire anybody who has not passed the 12th grade reading test.

任何沒有通過 12 年級（高三）閱讀考試的人，韋斯特先生都不會聘用。

不定代名詞 anybody 要與單數動詞搭配。

- "Is anybody hurt?" asked Kurt.（「有人受傷嗎？」克特問。）

042 anyway/any way 無論如何、反正／任何方法

1

❌ Can I help you in anyway?

✅ Can I help you in any way?

我能用什麼方式幫助你嗎？

片語（兩字）任何方法，通常用在片語 **in any way** (= by any method)

2

❌ Rae is lazy, but I helped her any way.

✅ Rae is lazy, but I helped her anyway.

副詞（一字）nevertheless, in any case, anyhow 反正；無論如何；不管怎樣；不過

芮懶惰，不過我還是幫了她。

043 apartment/flat 公寓

1

美式 Vincent and Mat live in an apartment.

英式 Vincent and Mat live in a flat.

文森特和麥特住在一間公寓房子裡。

	美式	英式
（一戶）公寓房子	apartment	flat
公寓大樓	an apartment building	a block of flats
英式英語的 apartment 通常指備有昂貴家具和裝飾，專供重要人物使用或具有特殊用處的公寓房子，意思是「豪華寓所」。		

美式
- Ann Crown lives in an apartment building on the north side of town.
  （安・克朗住在城北的一棟公寓大樓裡。）

英式
- Mat's company is building a block of flats.
  （麥特的公司正在蓋一棟公寓大樓。）

044 apostrophe 撇號（'s）

1

✗ Pam's sister got 5 A on the final exams.

✓ Pam's sister got 5 A's on the final exams.

's 表複數形式

潘姆的妹妹期末考試得了五個 A。

(1) 撇號包括「省略號」（如 It's）和「所有格符號」（如 Mike's wife）。

(2) 美式：on the exams　英式：in the exams

(3) 一般不具有複數形式的**數字**（3, 10, 1999, 2016）、**大寫字母**（U, V, Y）、**大寫縮寫詞**（UFO, M.D.）以及**單字**（but, and）在用複數形式書寫時，可以用撇號，再加「s」，即「's」，比如：5's、U's、UFO's、and's。

文法加油站

A 現代英語也常不加撇號，直接加「s」

- Lee's sister Louise married Nate in the late 1990's/1990s.
  （李的姐姐露易絲在二十世紀九十年代末嫁給了奈特。）
- Dr. Chestnut's lecture about economics had too many "but's/buts."
  （切斯納特博士在經濟學的演講中，說了太多「但是」。）

- UFO's = UFOs （幽浮）
- VIP's = VIPs （重要人物）
- Ph.D.'s/Ph.D.s/PhD's/PhDs （博士）
- the three R's = the three Rs (reading, writing, arithmetic)
 （基本三會〔指初等教育讀、寫、算三要素〕）

B 正確的用法是保持一致

那麼究竟選擇「's」還是「s」，關鍵在於一致，不要同一句話裡一下用「's」，一下又用「s」。

────── 不一致 ──────
❌Some people are nostalgic for the <u>1970's</u>, and some are nostalgic for <u>1980s</u>.

────── 一致 ──────
✅Some people are nostalgic for the <u>1970's</u>, and some are nostalgic for <u>1980's</u>.

────── 一致 ──────
✅Some people are nostalgic for the <u>1970s</u>, and some are nostalgic for <u>1980s</u>.
（一些人懷念二十世紀七十年代；一些卻懷念二十世紀八十年代。）

C 字母加了「s」構成複數，如果可能與單字混淆，就最好改用「's」

✅2 U's →❌2 Us（易與受格 us 混淆）　　✅2 A's →❌As（易與連接詞 as 混淆）

D 小寫字母和小寫縮寫詞

為了清楚明瞭，小寫字母和小寫的縮寫詞應該加撇號，再加「s」，即「's」。比如：

- Mind your <u>p's and q's</u> if you don't want to get into trouble.
 └── ❌ps and qs
 （如果不想陷入困境，就得謹言慎行。）

- When my boyfriend came over this morning, I was still in my <u>pj's</u>.
 （今早我男朋友來的時候，我還穿著睡衣褲。）└── ❌pjs

045 appraise/apprise 評價／通知、告知

1　❌ Kay <u>apprised</u> my work as excellent and raised my pay.
　　　└── 表「通知」，用在這裡與句意不符

　　✅ Kay <u>appraised</u> my work as excellent and raised my pay.
　　　└── 表「評價」

凱對我的工作評價很高，還幫我加薪。

比較 appraise 與 apprise	
appraise (vt.)	(= evaluate) 估計；估量；估價；評價
apprise (vt.)	(= inform) 通知；告知

- Dawn hired lawyer Kate Knight to appraise Shawn's child support agreement.
（朵安雇用了凱特・奈特律師來估價肖恩的子女撫養費協議。）
- Kent Wise was eager to apprise me of the fact that my report was appraised as excellent.
（肯特・懷斯迫不及待地告訴我，我的報告被評價為優秀。）

046 appreciate 感激

1

❌ I would greatly appreciate if you could write a review of my book *A Tibetan Valley*.

appreciate 後要加受詞 it

✅ I would greatly appreciate it if you could write a review of my book *A Tibetan Valley*.

如果你為我的書《一個西藏山谷》寫一篇評論，我會感激不盡。

appreciate 後面要接受詞 it，然後接 if 或 when 引導的子句。
句型：appreciate + it + if/when 子句

047 approach 靠近

1

❌ Brian raised his gun and carefully approached to the angry lion.

✅ Brian raised his gun and carefully approached the angry lion.

布萊恩舉起了槍，小心翼翼地靠近那隻憤怒的獅子。

approach 後面直接接受詞（approach somebody/something），不需要介系詞 to。

048 arithmetic 算術

1 ✗ Nick is good at arithmetics. —— 後面沒有 -s

✓ Nick is good at arithmetic.

尼克的算術很好。

(1) 數學 mathematics 的拼寫後面有 -s。
(2) 算術 arithmetic 的拼寫後面沒有 -s。

049 arrangement: make(the)arrangements 安排

1 非正式 Lucy will make the arrangement for our trip to Washington, DC.

正式 Lucy will make the arrangements for our trip to Washington, DC. —— 要用複數

露西要對我們去華盛頓的旅行做些安排。

make (the) arrangements for something 為……做安排

- Margo Nation has made the arrangements for your winter vacation in Mexico.
 （瑪歌・納欣已經為你在墨西哥度寒假做好了安排。）

050 as a result of

請參見 due to/owing to。

051 as bad as or worse than 跟……一樣糟，或許更糟

1 ✗ My Chinese is as bad or worse than my English. —— as bad as 漏掉一個 as

累贅 My Chinese is as bad as or worse than my English. —— 語法正確，但語句累贅

✓ My Chinese is as bad as my English, or worse.

我的中文跟我的英文一樣糟糕，或許比英文還差。

✓ My Chinese is as bad as my English, if not worse.

我的中文如果不比英文差，至少跟英文一樣糟糕。

文法加油站

需要避免的類似句型	正確的句型
❌ as bad or worse than ❌ as good or better than ❌ as much or more than	✅ as bad as . . ., or worse（一樣糟或更糟） ✅ as bad as . . ., if not worse 　（若不是更糟……則一樣糟） ✅ as good as . . ., or better（一樣好或更好） ✅ as good as . . ., if not better 　（若不是更好……則一樣好） ✅ as much as . . ., or more（一樣多或更多） ✅ as much as . . ., if not more 　（若不是更多……則一樣多） ✅ Lenore likes me as much as she likes you, or more. 　（蕾諾兒喜歡我就像她喜歡你一樣，或許更喜歡我一些。） ✅ Lenore likes me as much as she likes you, if not more. 　（蕾諾兒如果不是更喜歡我一些，至少對你和我喜歡的程度是一樣的。）

052 as/like 好像

1

非正式　In February, like in January, it is a good time to water-ski in Hawaii.

正式　In February, as in January, it is a good time to water-ski in Hawaii.　像……一樣，**連接詞**（連接詞＋介系詞片語）

正式　February, like January, is a good time to water-ski in Hawaii.　像；如，**介系詞**（介系詞＋名詞）

二月就像一月一樣，是在夏威夷滑水橇的好時光。

(1) as 表示「像……一樣；依照」，可以作**連接詞**，後面接從屬子句，也可以接介系詞片語。

(2) like 的意思是「像；如」，是**介系詞**，通常後面接名詞或代名詞（如 like January、like you），而不接介系詞片語。在口語中常用 like 來替換 as 作連接詞，後面接從屬子句或介系詞片語，尤其是在美式英語中。但在正式文體中（考試、商務信函等），要遵循文法規則。

文法加油站

要用 as，還是用 like？

① as 和 like 都可以當作介系詞，後面接名詞。

- Jane was dressed like a queen.（珍打扮得像皇后。）
  └ 介系詞，表示「像；如同」
- Jane was dressed as a queen.
  └ 介系詞，表示「像；如同」=like →「像皇后」
  也可以表示「以……身分」→「以皇后的身分」

（珍打扮得像皇后。／珍以皇后的身分打扮好了。）

- Scot looks like his friend Mike.（史考特看上去像他朋友麥克。）
  └ 介系詞，與 feel、look、seem、sound、taste 連用，表示「好像是」
- Scot worked as an astronaut.（史考特當過太空人。）
  └ 介系詞，表示「身為；以……的身分」

② 在**正式用語**中，只有 as 當作從屬連接詞。因此，在一個從屬子句前面，要用 as 而不用 like。在**美式口語**中可用 like 引導從屬子句。

非正式	Margo likes to argue like you used to do long ago.
正式	Margo likes to argue as you used to do long ago. （瑪歌喜歡爭論，就像你很久以前那樣。）

- Talking to Lynne is not so difficult as you imagine.
  （跟琳恩談話並不像你想像那樣困難。）
  └ as 作從屬連接詞。「so . . . as」是固定片語，即使在口語中也不能用 like

053 as if/like 好像

1 美式 Judy began to kiss me as if/like we were on our honeymoon.

英式 Judy began to kiss me as if we were on our honeymoon.

裘蒂開始親吻我，就好像我們在度蜜月一樣。

like（介系詞）美式 英式	as if（連接詞）美式 英式
用於名詞或代名詞前	用於從屬子句前
美式口語裡，like = as if/as though（like + 子句）	英式英語只用「as if/as though + 子句」
• **加名詞**：Dee is like a daughter to me.（蒂就像是我的女兒。） • **加代名詞**：Monique is just like me; she works twelve hours a day and seven days a week.（莫妮可就像我一樣，她也每天工作十二個小時、每週工作七天。） • **加子句**：Sue Collins looks like she's going to have twins!（蘇・科林斯看起來好像要生雙胞胎了。）（**美式口語**：like = as if）	• **加子句**：Mother cried with joy as if she had found a long-lost sister or brother.（媽媽高興地哭了起來，好像她找到了失蹤多年的妹妹或弟弟。） • Trish Best was acting as if/as though she had already won the English speech contest.（翠西・貝斯特表現得好像她已經贏了這次的英語講演比賽。）

文法加油站

① 當 like 的意思相當於 as if 時，在非正式語中也可以和少數的形容詞連用。

- To finish the job on time, Dad worked like mad. 非正式
  （為了按時完成那份工作，爸爸拼命地工作。）

② as if/as though 常用於假設語氣，表示**與事實相反**。

- Bing talks as if/as though he **were** the king.（賓講起話來好像他是國王。）

→ 事實上賓不是國王。與現在事實相反，在 as if/as though 引導的從屬子句中要用過去式動詞的假設語氣，be 動詞通常用 **were**。

③ as if/as though 也用於**一般條件句**。

- Midge has done very well in high school, and it looks as if/as though she is ready for college.

 （米姬在高中的成績很好，看起來她已經做好了上大學的準備。）

→ 這句是事實，as if/as though 引導的從屬子句就不要用假設語氣。

054 as well as 也、和

1

✗ Sybil's dishonesty, as well as her rudeness, are going to cause her trouble.

✓ Sybil's dishonesty, as well as her rudeness, is going to cause her trouble.

單數主詞（dishonesty）；插入的額外資訊（as well as her rudeness）；單數動詞（is）

希博不誠實的行為以及粗魯會給她帶來麻煩的。

· as well as	(1) ≠ and (2) 在主詞和動詞之間插入的額外資訊並不影響動詞的數和量。主詞 Sybil's dishonesty 仍然是單數，無論你加了多少別的資訊，動詞依然用**單數動詞**。
· with · as well as · in addition to · except · together with · along with · accompanied by	(1) 所組成的片語是插入成分，連接**單數主詞**，並置於**主詞和動詞之間**時，無論這些插入成分增加了多少額外資訊，動詞依然要用**單數**形式。 (2) 動詞要與主詞本身保持一致，而不是與插入的片語保持一致。 (3) 請參見 Subjects Not in Prepositional Phrases。

- John, accompanied by his wife on the piano, was very well received at the concert last night.

 （約翰，由他夫人鋼琴伴奏，在昨晚的音樂會上受到了好評。）

文法加油站

比較下列用法：

• Dwight, with his wife and three daughters, was at the party last night.

└單數主詞 └插入的額外資訊 └用單數動詞

= Dwight, his wife, and their three daughters were at the party last night.

└用 and 連接的複合主詞是複數 └用複數動詞

（杜威特和他的夫人以及三個女兒昨晚出席了聚會。）

• Yvonne, as well as a number of her students, is running in the marathon.

└單數主詞 └插入的額外資訊 └用單數動詞

= Yvonne and a number of her students are running in the marathon.

└用 and 連接的複合主詞是複數 └用複數動詞

（伊芳和她的一些學生在參加馬拉松賽跑。）

055 ask/ask for 詢問／要求得到

1

非正式 I asked for the price of the apples.

正式 I asked the price of the apples.

└詢問資訊，用 ask

我詢問蘋果的價錢。

2

✗ Anna's mom asked a kilogram of bananas.

✓ Anna's mom asked for a kilogram of bananas.

└請求要一件東西，用 ask for

安娜的媽媽要了一公斤的香蕉。

(1) 上面第一句 I asked for the price of the apples 在口語中也許是可以接受的，但在正式的書面語中，如果你想要文法正確，那麼就不用 for，因為「價格」是對方可以告訴你的資訊。

(2) 一般來說，如果受詞是對方告訴你的什麼資訊（如價格、時間、路程等），就用 ask（不加 for），表示「詢問」。

- ask directions（詢問方向）
- ask the time（詢問時間）
- ask questions（提問）
- ask the way（問路）
- I'm going to ask that police officer the time.
（我要向那位員警詢問時間。）

⑶ 如果你要想得到的是「一件東西」（如錢、食物、飲料等），就用 ask for，表示「請求……、要求……」。

- ask for food（要食物）
- ask somebody for a loan（向某人貸款）
- Officer Thor Miller asked for help in catching the killer.
（索爾・米勒警官請求援助以便抓住殺人犯。）

文法加油站

ask 的各種用法

A 固定的片語用法

- ask too much of somebody（對某人提出過多的要求）
- ask a favor of somebody/ask somebody a favor （請求某人幫忙）

B ask money 和 ask for money 的區別

① ask money (for something)（要價／索價）

- Omar asked only $300 for his used car.
（那輛舊車，歐馬只要價三百美金。）

② ask for money (from someone)（向某人要錢）

- Ann: Are you asking for more money?
（安：你想借更多的錢嗎？）
- Dan: Yes. I am asking for $1,000 from you and $2,000 from Sue.
（丹：對。我要從你那裡要一千美金，從蘇那裡要兩千美金。）

C ask somebody 和 ask for somebody 的區別

ask somebody 向某人提問	Sybil didn't understand the school rules, so she asked the principal. （希波不懂學校的校規，於是**去問了校長**。） → 希波向校長提問。
ask for somebody 求見某人	Sybil asked for the principal. （希波**請求見校長**。） → 希波想與校長談話。

056 assure/ensure/insure 保證／確保／為……投保

1

✗ The captain of the plane assured that there was no danger.

✓ The captain of the plane assured the passengers that there was no danger.
先接人再接 that 子句

機長向乘客保證沒有危險。

(1) assure 的意思是「保證；**使某人放心**」。句型為：

assure somebody that（✗ assure that）
assure somebody of something

- The doctor **assured me that** I would feel all right in a week.
  先接人（somebody）再接 that 子句
  （醫生向我保證一週後我就會好起來。）
- Mom **assured us of** the health of Amy's newborn daughter.
  先接人（somebody）再接 of 片語
  （媽媽向我們保證艾咪的新生女兒很健康。）

(2) ensure 的意思也是「保證；確保」，但不是你向別人保證什麼，而是**確保某事**發生或完成，句型為： ensure + that 子句。

- Rose will ensure that nothing goes wrong during tomorrow's tour.（蘿絲將確保明天的旅程一切順利。）

2

❌ That scholar's house is assured for $10,000,000.

✅ That scholar's house is insured for $10,000,000.

那個學者的房子投保了一千萬美元。

insure 的主要意思是「保險；給……投保」。

- Alice decided to insure her pure gold necklace.
（艾麗絲決定給她的純金項鍊買保險。）

文法加油站

ensure/insure 美式英語和英式英語的差別

① 美式英語中，ensure 和 insure 都可以指確保某事發生或完成。

② 英式英語中，insure 只指為生命、財產損失提供保險；投保或承保。

- Jill can't ensure/insure that she'll marry her boyfriend Bill.
（潔兒不能確保她是否會嫁給她的男朋友比爾。）美式

057 attend/join 出席／參加

1

❌ Over 500 guests joined the two-day Chinese art exhibition at Saint Leo University.
（joined：參加社團、組織等）

❌ Over 500 guests attended at the two-day Chinese art exhibition at Saint Leo University.
（attended：及物動詞，後面接受詞，不接介系詞 at）

✅ Over 500 guests attended the two-day Chinese art exhibition at Saint Leo University.
（attended：參加、出席一項社會活動）

五百多位來賓參觀了聖・利奧大學舉辦的兩天中國藝術展。

(1) attend = be present：參加、出席一項社會活動或定期去某處（比如去學校讀書、去教堂做禮拜），要用 **attend**。attend 是及物動詞（vt.），後面接直接受詞（D.O.）。

- I was born in Malaysia, but I attended (vt.) a high school (D.O.) in Indonesia.
  （我在馬來西亞出生，但我在印尼念高中。）

(2) join = become a member of：參加（社團、組織等）。

- Did Ms. Chubb join your English club?
  （查布女士有加入你們的英語俱樂部嗎？）
- After graduation from high school, Amy joined the Army.
  （艾咪高中畢業後就從軍了。）

058 attention/attentions 注意／殷勤

1

✗ Did I mention how her smiles caught my attentions?

✓ Did I mention how her smiles caught my attention?

我提及過她的微笑如何引起了我的注意嗎？

(1) attention 的意思是「注意、照顧」，是**不可數名詞**，沒有複數形式。

- turn your attention to something/somebody
  （把你的注意力轉向某事／某人）
- hold/keep your attention
  （抓住／保持你的注意力）
- draw somebody's attention to something
  （把某人的注意力引到某事）
- bring something to somebody's attention
  （讓某人注意某事）
- something comes to somebody's attention
  （某事引起了某人的注意）

(2) 複數形式 attentions 的意思是「**殷勤**」，指「行為舉止表示出你對某人感興趣，愛上了某個人」。尤指男性對女性獻殷勤。

- Ann ran away to avoid the unwelcome attentions of the drunk man.
  （安跑開回避那個向她獻殷勤、令人討厭的醉漢。）

059 attitude 態度

1

❌ Olive has a positive attitude for Gertrude.

後面不接介系詞 for

✅ Olive has a positive attitude toward Gertrude.

attitude 後面接 to 或者 toward

奧莉芙對葛楚德表現出了正面的態度。

- Jane's attitude toward me was rude.
  （珍對我的態度很粗魯。）

060 attributive clauses/ adjective clauses/relative clauses 定語子句／形容詞子句／關係子句

1

❌ The woman to who/that Scot is going to get married is an astronaut.

介系詞後面不接主格 who 或 that，要用**受格 whom**

前無介系詞，口語可以代替 whom，也可省略

口語 The woman (who) Scot is going to get married to is an astronaut.

可和介系詞 to 分開，也可省略

正式 The woman (whom/that) Scot is going to get married to is an astronaut.

非常正式 The woman to whom Scot is going to get married is an astronaut.

介系詞 to 直接放 whom 前面，非常正式

史考特要娶的那個女子是一名太空人。

2

❌ The fish whom Dad bought yesterday has gone bad.

指「事物／動物」，不用 who/whom，要用 that

✅ The fish (that) Dad bought yesterday has gone bad.

that 作形容詞子句動詞 bought 的受詞，可省略

爸爸昨天買的魚肉已經壞了。

先行詞指「**人**」時，關係代名詞用 who/whom/that，先行詞指「**事物／動物**」時，不用 who/whom，要用關係代名詞 that。that 在形容詞子句中既可以是主詞，也可以是受詞，作受詞時可以省略。

3

不常用 The ballet shoes **which** I just bought last week were stolen today.

較常用 The ballet shoes **that** I just bought last week were stolen today.

我上週剛買的那雙芭蕾舞鞋今天被人偷了。

(1) **which** 和 **that** 都可以指「物」，不過限定性形容詞子句裡更常用 that。

(2) 請參見 that/which，以及第 55 頁「文法加油站」第 B 點「限定性形容詞子句／非限定性形容詞子句」的講解。

4

不自然 Penny Park is a fun place **the attractions of which** are many.

自然 Penny Park is a fun place **whose attractions** are many.

潘妮公園是一個令人嚮往、好玩的地方。

(1) 例句中的關係代名詞 **whose** 是指「地方」（the place）。whose 用在名詞前表示所屬關係，相當於（of whom, of which）。不要把關係代名詞 whose 和疑問代名詞 whose 弄混淆了。疑問代名詞 whose 只用來指代人，意思是 belong to whom。

(2) 請參見 which/whose。

5

介系詞後面不能接關係代名詞 that

✗ This is the cave <u>in that</u> Lynne Horn was born.

✓ This is the cave **which** Lynne Horn was born **in**.

✓ This is the cave **in which** Lynne Horn was born.

✓ This is the cave **where** Lynne Horn was born.

琳恩・霍恩就是在這個洞穴裡出生的。

(1) 務必注意：介系詞後面不能接關係代名詞 who 和 that。介系詞後面，只能接 **whom** 和 **which**。

(2) 指「物／地點」，可以用 that，也可以用 which。限定性更常用 **that**。但如果句中有 **this**、**that**、**these** 等，那麼最好用 **which**。

(3) that 和 which 的區別，請參見 that/which。

(4) 表示 at that place，也可以用關係副詞 where 引導形容詞子句。

6

✗ Ray remembers the day which his mom passed away.

✓ Ray remembers the day when his mom passed away.

先行詞，指時間，要用 when 引導形容詞子句　　形容詞子句

雷記得他媽媽去世的那天。

例句中的形容詞子句先行詞是 day，指時間，所以形容詞子句要用關係副詞 when 來引導，表達 at that time/on that day。

文法加油站

A 形容詞子句的用法（又稱「定語子句」或「關係子句」）

① 與「**人**」有關的形容詞子句，用關係代名詞 who/that, whom, whose 來引導。這些關係代名詞與主要子句裡的「人」有關聯。

② 與「**地方、事物、動物**」有關的形容詞子句，用關係代名詞 which, that, whose 來引導。這些代名詞與主要子句裡的「地方、事物、動物」有關。

③ where 和 when 是關係副詞，引導形容詞子句時，修飾主要子句裡表示地點或時間的字，在子句中表達 at that place 或 at that time。

④ 有時 why 也可以放在 reason 後面引導一個形容詞子句。

- Kate didn't give me a reason why she was late.
（凱特沒有告訴我她為什麼遲到的理由。）　形容詞子句

B 限定性形容詞子句／非限定性形容詞子句

① 限制性形容詞子句對句子的意義不可缺少，如果把它從子句裡刪除，句子的意思就會不清楚或不完整。限制性子句與主要子句不能用逗號分開。

- Does Nell still remember the evening when she first saw Del?
（尼爾還記得她第一次看見戴爾的那個晚上嗎？）

→ 限定性子句：如果刪除了 when she first saw Del，句子的意思是：Does Nell still remember the evening? 沒有上下文，句意不清楚是哪一個晚上。因此，這個形容詞子句是限定性的，不能刪除。

② 非限制性形容詞子句是對主要子句的意思補充說明，不是必要的。它可以從句子裡刪除而不會改變句子的基本意思。在形式上，非限定性子句被一個逗號或一對逗號（如果子句插在主要子句中間）與句子的其餘部分分開。非限定性形容詞子句用關係代名詞 who、which 和 whose，不用 that。指地點用 where，指時間用 when。

- My new gray sports car, which my dad just gave to me on Friday, was stolen today.
  （我那輛新的灰色汽車今天被偷了，那是我爸爸星期五剛送給我的。）

→ 非限定性：如果刪除形容詞子句 which my dad just gave to me on Friday，剩下的句子仍然是一個完整、清楚的句子：My new gray sports car was stolen today.（我那輛新的灰色汽車今天被偷了。）

061 average 平均

1

✗ In the average, Midge goes to visit Grandma Gear twice a year.

✓ On the average, Midge goes to visit Grandma Gear twice a year.

米姬平均一年去拜訪格爾奶奶兩次。

on the average（或 on an average）是固定片語。

- On the average, Bridget reads 200 words a minute.
  （布麗姬特平均一分鐘可以閱讀 200 個字。）

062 avoid 迴避、避免

1

✗ Kim doesn't like Tim at all, so she has tried to avoid to talk to him.
不接**不定詞**

✓ Kim doesn't like Tim at all, so she has tried to avoid talking to him.
接**動名詞**

✓ Kim doesn't like Tim at all, so she has tried to avoid him.
接**代名詞**

金姆一點也不喜歡迪姆，所以她一直盡量避免跟他說話。

avoid (doing) something 表示迴避做某事，avoid 後面要接**名詞**、**代名詞**或**動名詞**（V-ing），不能接不定詞形式。

063 a while/awhile 一會兒／片刻

1 ✗ Kyle napped for awhile.
✓ Kyle napped awhile.
✓ Kyle napped for a while.
凱爾小睡了一會。

(1) a while 和 awhile 發音相似，拼寫也相似，書寫時常被混淆。實際上，兩者不能互相替換。

(2) awhile 是**副詞**，不能放在介系詞（after、for、in 等）後面，此外，awhile 意思是 for a time，本來就包含了 for 的意思，因此前面不應該加 for。

(3) while 是**名詞**，可以用在介系詞（after、for、in 等）後面。
- once in a while （有時）
- after a while （過了一會）
- stay awhile = stay for a while = stay a while
（逗留一會）
a while 前面也可以不用介系詞

- After resting for a while in Denver, Sue drove to Salt Lake City.
= After resting awhile in Denver, Sue drove to Salt Lake City.
（在丹佛休息了一會後，蘇開車去鹽湖城。）

Kyle napped awhile/for a while.

B

064 bad/badly 壞的／壞地

1

❌ Lee drives bad. —— **形容詞**，不用來修飾動詞

✅ Lee drives badly.

李的開車技術很差。 —— **副詞**，意思是「壞地、不正確地」

2

美式

口語 Pam and Millie did bad on the math exam.

美式口語可當副詞，與特定動詞連用

正式 Pam and Millie did badly on the math exam.

這次數學考試潘姆和米莉考得很差。 —— 正式用語要用副詞 badly

(1) 一般來説，**badly** 是副詞。**bad** 是形容詞。

(2) 在美式口語中，**bad** 有時當作副詞，與一些特定的動詞連用（比如「Pam did **bad** on the math exam.」）。但在正式用語中，副詞要用 **badly**。

(3) 假若你養的小貓死了，那麼，應該説「you feel bad」還是「you feel badly」？在 **feel** 後面要用**形容詞**來表示人的感情「You felt **bad**.」（你感到傷心。）。簡言之，**感官動詞**（verbs of senses），比如 feel、smell、taste、look 等，就像連綴動詞 be 一樣，後面接**形容詞**作補語。

- Dad felt **bad**.（爸爸感覺很不好。）
  —— **感官動詞後面用形容詞**

(4) good 和 well 也應遵守同樣的規則。請參見 good/well。

065 baggage/luggage 行李

1

❌ Mort Ridge stored all his baggages at the airport.

不可數名詞，沒有複數形式

✅ Mort Ridge stored all his baggage at the airport.

莫特 · 瑞吉把他的行李都存放在機場了。

2

美式 Jane took only one piece of hand baggage to Spain.

英式 Jane took only one piece of hand luggage to Spain.

珍只隨身攜帶了一件手提行李去西班牙。

(1) baggage（美式）和 luggage（英式）是不可數名詞，沒有複數形式。

(2) 當需要表達複數意思時，用 bags、suitcases 或者 pieces of baggage/luggage。

066 ball/balls/baseball 球／睪丸／棒球

1

❌ Does Paul like to play balls?

複數指男性的睪丸

❌ Does Paul like to play with balls?

✅ Does Paul like to play basketball or football?

通常會具體說出打什麼球

保羅喜歡打籃球還是橄欖球？

✅ Does Paul want to play ball? —— 表示「打球」為不可數名詞

保羅想打（棒）球嗎？／保羅想不想合作？

(1) 當我們說打球時，通常都要說出具體打什麼球，比如，棒球、籃球、排球等。當然也可以說，play ball（在這裡 ball 是不可數名詞），或者說 play a ball game。

- Let's go to Hall Park and **play ball**.
  （我們去霍爾公園打棒球吧。） —— 美式 通常指 play baseball

⑵ 在球場上打球（play ball），自然要遵守一些球場規則，相互合作，於是這個片語 play ball 後來發展成「合作」的意思，是美國俚語。

- I tried to get Paul to help, but he refused to **play ball**.
  （我試著想讓保羅幫忙，但他拒絕合作。） —— 【美俚】合作

文法加油站

為什麼說 play balls 不恰當？

「We like to play balls!」這是學生學英語很容易犯的一個常見錯誤。因為有各種球類，學生認為喜歡打球就自然應該說 play balls。但無論你喜歡打幾種球，英語都不說 play balls，否則會引起外國人士捧腹大笑，因為 balls（複數）常用的意思是指男性的睪丸（a male's testicles）。

067 bathe/bath 洗澡

1

美式 Maybe I need to bathe the baby.

英式 Maybe I need to bath the baby

也許我需要幫孩子洗澡了。

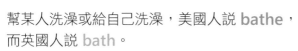

幫某人洗澡或給自己洗澡，美國人說 bathe，而英國人說 bath。

- Kay likes to bathe twice a day.（凱喜歡一天洗兩次澡。）

068 bathroom/toilet/restroom 浴室、洗手間

1

美式 Our classroom has a nice bathroom.
我們教室有一間舒適的洗手間。

英式 Janet, where's the toilet?
珍妮特，廁所在哪裡？

美式英語

(1) go to the bathroom/restroom
（需要大小便）
美式英語的 bathroom 指的是私人房子或公共大樓裡安裝有抽水馬桶（toilet）的房間。

bathroom

(2) 美國人認為 toilet 使人想到抽水馬桶，那可不是令人愉快的情景。所以，提到廁所時美國人喜歡用 bathroom（洗手間）或 restroom（休息室），這樣可以給人愉快的感覺，因為它暗示「浴缸或淋浴器」，儘管大部分公共洗手間（bathroom/restroom）裡並沒有「浴缸或淋浴器」。

(3) **私人房子裡的洗手間：**bathroom

公共洗手間：bathroom/restroom
〔指辦公大樓、體育場所、餐館裡配備了 toilet 以及洗手台的房間〕

- Anna is putting on her Halloween costume in the women's **restroom**.
（安娜正在女洗手間裡穿她的萬聖節服裝。）

指「公共洗手間」，也可以用 women's bathroom

英式英語

(4) go to the toilet
（需要大小便）
英式英語的 bathroom 指的是有「浴缸」的房間，而有些 bathroom 並沒有抽水馬桶（toilet）。

bathroom

069 because/so

請參見 although/but、conjunctions。

070 because of

請參見 due to/owing to。

071 been/gone 到過、去過／去了

1

❌ I have gone to New York's Times Square many times.

去了某地，但還沒有回來，與句意不符

✅ I have been to New York's Times Square many times.

去過某地，已經回來了

我去過紐約時代廣場多次。

當對 you 說話時，you 這個人肯定是在現場，不在別處，或者說到 I 本人時，I 肯定在現場，不在別處。上面的第一句，說話時刻「我」不在紐約時代廣場，而是在此地，因此是錯誤句子。不能說：

❌ Have you gone to . . . ?

❌ You have gone to . . .

❌ I have gone to . . .

第一人稱（I、we）和第二人稱（you）不能與 have gone 連用

說話此刻，你並不在 New York，而是在此地

- Ms. Cork, have you ever been to New York?
（科克女士，妳去過紐約嗎？）

已經返回

- May has been to the library today.（梅今天去過圖書館。）

去書店了，但還沒有回來

- Lenore has gone to the New Dawn Bookstore.
（蕾諾兒去新黎明書店了。）

072 begin/start 開始

1

❌ Margo observed, "It's beginning snowing."

begin 進行式後面不要用動名詞

✅ Margo observed, "It's beginning to snow."

瑪歌說：「要開始下雪了。」

begin 進行式後面要接**不定詞**

begin 和 start

(1)皆可接**不定詞**，也可接 **V-ing** 形式（即動名詞），意思幾乎沒有區別。

started to consider

- Midge began to consider the possibility of going abroad for college.

started considering

= Midge began considering the possibility of going abroad for college.

（米姬開始考慮去國外讀大學。）

(2) 兩者**進行式**後面，要用**不定詞**，不要用動名詞。

只能接不定詞

- Midge was beginning to consider the possibility of going abroad for college.

只能接不定詞

= Midge was starting to consider the possibility of going abroad for college.

（米姬開始考慮去國外讀大學。）

(3) 兩者後面如果是**狀態動詞**，比如 believe、understand、realize、know 等，只用**不定詞**，不用動名詞。

- I have finally begun to understand why Aunt Alice bought this palace.

= I have finally started to understand why Aunt Alice bought this palace.

（我終於開始明白了艾麗絲姨媽買這棟豪宅的原因。）

073 behavior 行為

1

✗ Such foolish behaviors must end, or we won't learn very much.

表行為舉止時，是**不可數名詞**，沒有複數形

✗ Such a foolish behavior must end, or we won't learn very much.

表行為舉止時，不能用不定冠詞 a 修飾

✓ Such foolish behavior must end, or we won't learn very much.

這樣愚蠢的行為必須終止，否則我們學不到什麼知識。

074 believe

請參見 will/would。

075 belong in 應放置在……

1

✗ Claire, the forks belong to that drawer over there.

屬於某人的財產，與句意不符

✓ Claire, the forks belong in that drawer over there.

應被放在某處

克蕾兒，那些叉子應放進那邊的抽屜裡。

- "You and your bikini **belong in** a fashion show," teased Jeannie.

表示某人或某物在這個地方正合適；應被放在某處

（「妳和妳的比基尼泳裝適合參與時裝展覽。」珍妮開玩笑說。）

076 belong to 屬於

1

✗ That elf robot on the shelf belongs in Mat.

應被放在某處，與句意不符

✓ That elf robot on the shelf belongs to Mat.

架子上的那個小精靈機器人是麥特的。

屬於某人的財產

(1) belong to somebody：

屬於某人的財產（to be owned by someone）

- This motorcycle belongs to Michael.（這輛摩托車是麥克的。）

(2) belong to something：

(a) 屬於某組織的成員

（to be a member of an organization or a club）

- Amy Tub belongs to the Astronomy Club.

（艾咪・塔布是天文學俱樂部的成員。）

(b) 是同類東西或同類人物的一部分

（to be part of a group of similar things or people）

- Sue Nation belongs to my generation.

（蘇・納欣與我是同一代的人。）

(c) 與特定的時間或地點相關

（to be related or connected to a particular time or place）

- "This gun clearly **belongs to** the American Civil War period," noted Dr. Sun.

 （孫博士指出：「這把手槍顯然是屬於美國獨立戰爭時期的。」）

077 beside/besides 在……旁邊／除……之外

1 ❌ Audrey Ride knelt down <u>besides</u> her bed and prayed for the sick and hungry.

除……之外，與句意不符

✅ Audrey Ride knelt down <u>beside</u> her bed and prayed for the sick and hungry.

介系詞，= next to, by the side of
（在……旁邊）

= Audrey Ride knelt down **next to** her bed and prayed for the sick and hungry.

奧德莉 · 賴德跪在床邊，為病人和飢餓的人祈禱。

2 ❌ <u>Beside</u> geography, she studies biology and psychology.

在……旁邊

✅ <u>Besides</u> geography, she studies biology and psychology.

除……之外

除了地理學，她也學習生物學和心理學。

(1) beside： **介系詞**，意思是 next to、by the side of（在……旁邊）。

(2) besides： ① **介系詞**，意思是「除……之外」，如 besides geography。

② **副詞**，意思是 in addition to 或 moreover （而且、加之、此外）。

- "That string bikini isn't modest enough for me; besides, it might get ripped off by a big

 = moreover

 wave," explained Jeannie.

 （珍妮解釋道：「那件細線比基尼對我來說不太端莊。此外，一個大波浪就可能把它扯下來。」）

078 besides/except 除……之外

1

✗ Everyone went to the beach besides Ms. Peach.

包括；加之，用在這裡語意錯誤

✓ Everyone went to the beach except Ms. Peach.

除……之外（皮奇女士沒有去海濱）

✓ Everyone went to the beach except for Ms. Peach.

除了皮奇女士外，大家都去了海灘。

besides	except
(a) 通常表示「包括；加之」（請參見前一條） (b) 如同 with 或 plus (+) • Besides Mark, Sue and Lulu went to the park.（除了馬克，蘇和露露也去了公園。） → 馬克去了公園。	(a) 表示「不包括」 (b) 如同 without 或 minus (−)

(1) except 或 except for 都可用在以下表概括性的字之後：

• all	• anything	• everybody	• no	• whole
• anybody	• every	• everything	• nowhere	

• We all decided not to drink any alcohol except (for) Paul.

all 後面既可用 except 又可用 except for

= Except for Paul, we all decided not to drink any alcohol.

all 前用 except for

（除了保羅外，我們大家決定一點酒都不喝。）→保羅決定喝酒

(2) 請參見 accept/except 和 except/except for。

079 better/had better 更好的／最好做……

1

✗ It's going to rain, so I better leave now with Jane.

✓ It's going to rain, so I had better leave now with Jane.

表「最好做某事」，此片語非過去式

快下雨了，我最好現在就和珍一起離開。

(1) better 是 good、well 的比較級（better at math、better pay、doing better and better）。

(2) had better do something

(a) 對具體的情況（specific situations）提建議或勸告。
意思為「最好做某事；比較有用的辦法是……」。

(b) 此片語不是過去式。

(c) **縮寫形式**：'d better do something

否定形式：had better not do something

- You'd better not say a word about this to Scot.
（關於這件事，你最好連一個字都不要對史考特透露。）

(3) 請參見 rather/would rather。

080 better/more better 更好的

1 ✗ "Is wisdom more better than strength?" asked Liz.
good 的比較級，前面不能再加比較級 more

✓ "Is wisdom better than strength?" asked Liz.
麗姿問：「智慧勝過力量嗎？」

文法加油站

比較級中的重複贅詞

• cheaper	✗ more cheaper	• heavier	✗ more heavier
• higher	✗ more higher	• noisier	✗ more noisier
• cheapest	✗ most cheapest	• heaviest	✗ most heaviest
• highest	✗ most highest	• noisiest	✗ most noisiest

081 between . . . and . . ./from . . . to . . .
在……之間／從……到……

1

between 後面**不接 to**

❌ Clem is at lunch between 12:30 p.m. to 1:30 p.m.

between 後面接 **and**

✅ Clem is at lunch between 12:30 p.m. and 1:30 p.m.

from 後面接 **to**

✅ Clem is at lunch from 12:30 p.m. to 1:30 p.m.

下午十二點半到一點半是克勒姆的午餐時間。

between	後面接 and，不接 to • between 2009 and 2029 • Between 130 and 140 people were listening to the band.（有 130 至 140 人在聽樂隊演奏。）
from	後面接 to • from 2009 to 2029

2

❌ Jane Doors searched the building between the 1st and the 5th floor.

✅ Jane Doors searched the building between the 1st and the 5th floors.

✅ Jane Doors searched the building from the 1st to the 5th floor.

珍・多羅斯搜查了這棟大樓的一樓到五樓。

between . . . and . . .	from . . . to . . .
後面接同一個單數名詞（比如 floor），如果 between 後面的名詞（floor）被省略，and 後面的名詞就要用**複數**（floors）。 • between the 1st floor and the 3rd floor = between the 1st and the 3rd floors	後面接同一個單數名詞（比如：floor），如果 from 後面的名詞（floor）被省略，to 後面的名詞仍然用**單數**（floor）。 • from the 1st floor to the 3rd floor = from the 1st to the 3rd floor

082 between you and me/ between you and I 只有你我知道

1

❌ Just between you and I, Lee is always talking on his cellphone to Amy.

介系詞，後面只能接受格代名詞 me、him、us 等，不能接主格代名詞 I、he、we 等

✔ Just between you and me, Lee is always talking on his cellphone to Amy.

告訴你一個祕密，不要告訴別人，李時時刻刻都在用手機與艾咪聊天。

(1) between 是**介系詞**，後面只能接受格代名詞 me、him、us 等，不能接主格代名詞 I、he、we 等。

(2) 這是學生常犯的一個錯誤。不過，出於習慣，英語是母語的人也常不由自主地把 you and I 放在介系詞後面。會犯這種錯誤不是屬於知識問題，而是屬於習慣問題。

(3) 當我們要告訴某人某事，而又不想讓第三者知道，就可以用 between you and me 這個片語。

083 big/old 大的／…… 歲的

1

❌ Next year Amy Gold will be big enough to join the Army.

指大小，非指年齡

✔ Next year Amy Gold will be old enough to join the Army.

指年齡要用 old

明年艾咪・戈爾德的年齡就大到可以從軍了。

big 通常指大小，不用來指年齡。

- Mike is proud of his big pig.（麥克為他的大豬感到驕傲。）

084 biscuit/cookie 餅乾

1

美式 Where are Annie's cookies?
安妮的餅乾在哪？

英式 Where are Janet's biscuits?
珍妮特的餅乾在哪？

(1) 作「餅乾」講時，美國人用 cookies；而英國人說 biscuits。

(2) 美國人用 biscuits 指小麵包、軟餅。

- I love Lee's Chinese cookies.（我愛吃李做的中國式餅乾。）

085 blood pressure 血壓

1

✗ Art has a high blood pressure and a problem with his heart.
不加冠詞和複數形

✓ Art has high blood pressure and a problem with his heart.

亞特有高血壓，心臟也有問題。

high/low blood pressure（高／低血壓）沒有冠詞 a，也沒有複數形式。

086 bored/boring

請參見 excited/exciting。

087 borrow/lend 借入／借給（他人）

1

✗ May I lend this book?

✓ May I borrow this book?

我可以借這本書嗎？ 從某人那裡借東西

2

✗ Did you borrow Omar Friend your car?

✓ Did you lend Omar Friend your car?
把東西借給某人

你把你的汽車借給了歐馬 · 弗蘭德嗎？

(1) 從某人那裡借東西，用 borrow (something from somebody)。

(2) 把東西借給某人，用 lend (somebody something/something to somebody)。

088 borrow/use 借／借用

1

✗ Ms. Bloom, may I borrow your bathroom?
　不能用在無法搬動的東西

✓ Ms. Bloom, may I use your bathroom?

布盧姆女士，我能借用一下妳的洗手間嗎？

2

✗ Janet, may I borrow your cellphone for a minute to read the news?
　要把手機帶走才用 borrow

✓ Janet, may I use your cellphone for a minute to read the news?
　只是借用，而非帶走

珍妮特，我能借用一下你的手機讀一讀新聞嗎？

比較這兩種用法的意思：

- Sue, may I use your cellphone for a minute or two?
　表示不會遠離手機主人
　（蘇，我可以借你的手機用一會嗎？）
- Sue, may I please borrow your cellphone for a day or two?
　也許會遠離手機主人

= Sue, would you please lend me your cellphone for a day or two?
　（蘇，我可以借用你的手機一、兩天嗎？）

=（蘇，把你的手機借給我使用一、兩天，好嗎？）

089 both . . . and . . . 兩者都

1

　動詞片語和名詞片語，不是相同詞類

✗ Rose was both robbed of her money and her clothes.

✓ Rose was robbed of both her money and her clothes.
　後面一定要接相同詞類的字

蘿絲的錢和衣服都被搶了。

(1) 用這個結構時，**both** 和 **and** 後面一定要接相同詞類的字，即**平行結構**。如果 both 後面是名詞片語（her money），那麼 and 後面也應該是名詞片語（her clothes）。

如果 both 後面是一個形容詞（exciting），那麼 and 後面也應該接一個形容詞（tiring），比如：

- both exciting and tiring（既興奮又疲憊）
- Mel can both run fast and shoot a gun well.
（梅爾能夠跑得很快，還能準確射擊。）
→ both + 動詞片語（run fast）；
and + 動詞片語（shoot a gun well）
- Both Jerome and I are going to move to Rome.
（傑羅姆和我都即將搬到羅馬。）
→ both + 主詞（Jerome）；and + 主詞（I）

(2) 請參見 either . . . or . . .。

文法加油站

平行結構的連接詞

下面這些結構都需要用平行結構，亦即，都要求用同一類的詞類連接：主詞與主詞（如：either Mom or I、neither he nor she)、名詞與名詞、動詞與動詞、介系詞與介系詞、形容詞與形容詞、副詞與副詞、子句與子句等。

- between . . . and . . .（在……之間）
- either . . . or . . .（不是……，就是……）
- neither . . . nor . . .（既非……，亦非……）
- not only . . . but also . . .（不只……，而且……）
- not because . . . but because . . .（不是因為……，而是因為……）
- When will Penny choose between Bennie and Denny?
（潘妮何時會在班尼和丹尼之間做出選擇？）
→ between + 名詞；and + 名詞

- Either Lenore is lying or she is still married to Theodore.
  （蕾諾兒不是在撒謊，就是她和希歐多爾的婚姻還存在。）
  → either + 獨立子句；or + 獨立子句
- Neither Claire nor Heather is there.（克萊兒和海瑟都不在那裡。）
  → neither + 名詞；nor + 名詞
- Not only does Janet want to travel into space, but she also has enough money to do it.
  （珍妮特不僅想去太空旅遊，而且她也有足夠的錢去太空。）
  → not only + 獨立子句；but + 獨立子句（主詞 + also + 動詞）
  → not only 放在句首，句子要用倒裝結構（does Janet want . . .）
- Kay is happy today not because it is Friday but because it is her birthday.
  （凱今天很高興，不是因為今天是星期五，而是因為今天是她的生日。）
  → not because + 獨立子句；but because + 獨立子句

090 both/either/neither

兩者都／（兩者之中）任一／兩者都不

1

both 不用來表示「兩者都不」

✗ Both Theodore and Thor did not want to marry Lenore.

✓ Neither Theodore nor Thor wanted to marry Lenore.

否定句中要用 neither . . . nor，表示「兩者都不」

希歐多爾和索爾都不想娶蕾諾兒。

2

✗ Olive did not buy both of the swimsuits, because they were too expensive.

否定句中，要用 either 表示「兩者之中的任何一個都不」

✓ Olive did not buy either of the swimsuits, because they were too expensive.

那兩件泳衣，奧莉芙一件也沒有買，因為太貴了。

3

❌ "Can Ray play ping-pong on Saturday or Sunday?" asked Kay.
Ray's mom replied, "He's free on either days."

作形容詞（= one or the other），後面要接單數名詞

✅ "Can Ray play ping-pong on Saturday or Sunday?" asked Kay.
Ray's mom replied, "He's free on either day."

作形容詞，指「兩者之中的任何一個」，接單數名詞

= Ray's mom replied, "He's free on both days."

作形容詞，指「兩者都」，後面接複數名詞

凱問：「星期六或星期天雷有空打乒乓球嗎？」
雷的媽媽回答：「星期六或星期天雷都有空。」

4

❌ Ms. Sun could not afford either of the dresses, so she bought the used one.

✅ Ms. Sun could not afford both of the dresses, so she bought the used one.

用「否定動詞 + both」表達「兩者之中的其中一個，但不是兩個」

孫女士沒有足夠的錢買那兩件洋裝，於是她只買了那條舊裙子。

091 bowling 打保齡球

1

❌ Joe will play bowling with his friends tomorrow.

❌ Joe will play bowling ball with his friends tomorrow.

✅ Joe will go bowling with his friends tomorrow.

打保齡球要用 go bowling

喬明天要和朋友一起去玩保齡球。

092 brake/break 煞車／破裂、暫停

1

✗ If big Jake sits on that chair, it might brake.

✓ If big Jake sits on that chair, it might break.

brake: n. 車裝置 v. 煞車

break: n. 孔；裂縫；休息；暫停 v. 分開；弄碎；破裂；使破裂

如果高大的傑克坐在那把椅子上，
椅子可能會壞掉。

這兩個字發音一樣，拼寫也很接近，常被混淆。

- Kirk tried to brake (v. 煞住) his car, but the brakes (n. 煞車) did not work.
  （柯克試圖煞住汽車，但煞車失靈了。）

- Sheriff Martie Drake heard a break (n. 暫停) in the songs, and she decided to break (v. 解散) up the wild party.
  （瑪蒂・德瑞克警長聽見歌曲中有一個間斷，於是她決定解散瘋狂的派對。）

093 breakfast 早餐

1

美式 Ming Corning is usually too busy to eat breakfast/have breakfast in the morning.

英式 Ming Corning is usually too busy to have breakfast in the morning.

明・科寧早上通常忙得沒時間吃早餐。

(1) 英國人說 have breakfast/lunch/supper/dinner，而認為 eat breakfast 等犯了文法錯誤。

(2) 美國人可以 eat breakfast/lunch/dinner/supper，也可以 have breakfast/lunch/dinner/supper。從文法角度講，美國人享受更多的自由啊！

- Kate Skinner ate a hearty dinner.
= Kate Skinner had a hearty dinner.
  （凱特・史金納吃了一頓豐盛的晚餐。）

094 bring/take 帶來／帶去

1

❌ Come and stay with us for a week, and take your granddaughters Kay and May.

come 和 bring 連用

✅ Come and stay with us for a week, and bring your granddaughters Kay and May.

帶你的孫女兒凱和梅，到我們這裡來住一週。

2

❌ Kay brought us to the zoo last Friday.

✅ Kay took us to the zoo last Friday.

上週五，凱帶我們去了動物園。

⑴ 通常 bring 表示向「說話者／聽話者／寫文章者」的方向移動（toward the speaker/hearer/writer）。
- (a) 如果你是從「到達」（arrival）的角度來看某個東西的移動方向，就用 bring。
- (b) 你帶著（bring）一個人或一件東西到「說話者／聽話者／寫文章者」所在地。
- (c) 要某人給你帶來（bring）某件東西時，come 和 bring 連用。

⑵ 通常用 take 表示向其他方向移動。離開「講話者／聽話者／寫文章者」（away from the speaker/writer/hearer）的移動方向就要用 take。
- (a) 如果你是從出發（departure）的角度來看某個東西的移動方向，就應該用 take。
- (b) 你帶著（take）一個人或一件東西離開「說話者／聽話者／寫文章者」所在地。
- (c) 你去一個地方時，就帶（take）一個人或一件東西與你一起去。故 go 和 take 連用。

come 與 bring 連用

- Andrew, when you come to see Ms. Powers, you may want to bring her some flowers.

（安德魯，你**來**探望鮑爾斯女士時，也許可以帶一些鮮花來給她。）

go 與 take 連用

- Andrew, when you go to see Ms. Powers, you may want to take her some flowers.

（安德魯，你**去**探望鮑爾斯女士時，也許可以帶一些鮮花去給她。）

→ 鮮花向哪一個方向移動？

✅ 如果是來這裡（come here），那麼你就把鮮花帶來（bring the flowers）。

✅ 如果是去那裡（go there），那麼你就把鮮花帶去（take the flowers）。

• Can you bring Sue and Lulu home from the airport by two?（你可以在兩點前把蘇和露露從機場接回家嗎？）

→ 講話者不在機場，在家中

• Is May going to take Jake home from the hospital today?（梅今天要把傑克從醫院帶回家去嗎？）

→ 講話者不在家，可能在醫院或其他地方

✏️ 文法加油站

不易判斷用 take 或 bring 的場合

難判斷的場合：在一些場合下究竟應該用 bring 還是用 take，並不那麼容易判斷。

• "What should I bring?" I asked Clyde. "Just bring yourself, please," he replied.
（我問克萊德：「我帶什麼好？」他回答道：「什麼也不要帶，你來就行了。」）

→ 講話人想像自己在何處影響 bring 和 take 的選擇。這句問話裡，「我」從主人的角度想，想像自己在主人的家，所以用 bring。

→ 用 bring 還是 take，主要取決於你想像自己的目的地在何處。

095 busy 忙碌的

1 ❌ Mort cannot go, because he is busy in preparing his book report.

✅ Mort cannot go, because he is busy preparing his book report.
└──── 後面直接接動名詞

✅ Mort cannot go, because he is busy with his book report.
└──── 後面接名詞

莫特不能去，因為他忙著（準備）他的讀書報告。

(1) be busy with something → busy with 後面接名詞
(2) be busy doing something → busy 後面接動名詞

C

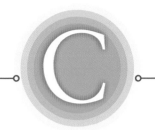

096 call/phone/ring 打電話

1 美式 英式 Dwight, did you phone/call Ms. White?

英式 Dwight, did you ring Ms. White?

杜威特，你打電話給懷特女士了沒有？

「打電話」美式用 call 或 phone。英式主要用 ring。

- give me a call = give me a ring（打電話給我）

097 called/named 叫做……

1 ✗ She lent me a book named *Common Errors in English From A to Z.* ── 意思是「給某人／生命體取名字」

✓ She lent me a book called *Common Errors in English From A to Z.* ── 用於提到某個人／東西的名字

她借給我一本書，書名是《常見的英語錯誤》。

(1) 當提到某個人的名字或某個東西的名字，通常用 (be) called。尤其是無生命的東西，人們通常不說 named，而說 called。

(2) name 的意思是「給某人或某物（通常指有生命的）取名字」。

- We named our puppy Lucky.
（我們給我們的小狗取名叫「來福」。）

- They named their baby Abby.
（他們給嬰兒取名為「艾比」。）

098 can not/cannot 不

1

非標準英語 Kim can not swim.

標準英語 Kim cannot swim. —— 正式文體中使用

標準英語 Kim can't swim. —— 縮寫詞，口語常用

金姆不會游泳。

(1) can 的否定詞 cannot 是一個字，不是兩個字。在口語中常用縮寫詞 can't。

(2) 一些美國人也把 can 的否定詞寫成兩個字 can not，但 can not 不屬於標準英語。在正式文體中請用 cannot。

(3) 注意區別：在 can not only 這一片語中，not 是與 only 搭配，不是表示否定，而是表示「不僅」。

- Lily can not only sing well, but she can also dance beautifully.（莉莉不僅唱歌唱得好，而且跳舞也跳得好。）

099 can't/mustn't 不可能／不准許

1

✗ That mustn't be Erica—she is in America. —— 指「不允許」

✓ That can't be Erica—she is in America. —— 指「不可能」

那不可能是艾芮卡。她在美國。

- You mustn't smoke around a swimming pool or anywhere around a school.
（在游泳池周圍或在學校周圍任何一個地方，都不許抽菸。）

100 capital/capitol 首府／議會大廈

1

✗ Erika asked, "Is Washington, D. C. the capitol of America?" —— n.（美國）國會大廈；州議會大廈

✓ Erika asked, "Is Washington, D. C. the capital of America?" —— n. 首都；省會／a. 為首的；最重要的；首都的

艾芮卡問：「華盛頓是美國的首都嗎？」

- Yesterday Lulu visited the Hawaiian capitol in Honolulu.
  （昨天露露參觀了位於檀香山的夏威夷州議會大廈。）

101 capitalization 字母大小寫原則

1

✗ Penny Brown is President of the company.

指職位，不需大寫

✓ Penny Brown is president of the company.

潘妮 · 布朗是公司的總裁。

(1) 指「職位、工作」的名詞不需要大寫，比如：lawyer、teacher、police officer、writer 等。

(2) 政府高官的官銜通常大寫。如果後面有修飾語時，通常也要大寫。

- The President of the United States knows that the asteroid might hit the earth in 2042.
  （美國總統知道，那顆小行星在 2042 年有可能擊中地球。）

2

✗ Vincent wrote, "We have 25 teachers in our Math Department."

有 our 修飾，組織名不大寫

✓ Vincent wrote, "We have 25 teachers in our math department."

文森特寫道：「我們數學系有二十五名教師。」

(1) 一般組織的名字，比如，物理系、廣告部、董事會、財政委員會等等，如果是作者本人所在單位（within the writer's own organization），通常都要大寫。

(2) 如果不是作者所在單位，而是別人的單位，這些組織名字就不大寫，除非是作者想特別予以強調。

(3) 如果這些字前面有 its、our、your 等修飾，就不大寫，比如上面的正確句。

- Clive wrote, "The Advertising Department will have a surprise party tonight at five."
  作者屬於廣告部，大寫
  （克萊夫寫道：「廣告部五點將舉辦一場驚喜派對。」）

- Oliver will meet you at four this afternoon in the advertising department of Wide River.

  作者不屬於「寬河」公司，小寫

  （今天下午四點奧利弗會在「寬河」公司的廣告部見你。）

3

✗ I looked at the position of the **Sun** and guessed at which direction was **West**.

通常不大寫

表方向不需大寫

✓ I looked at the position of **the sun** and guessed at which direction was **west**.

sun、moon、earth 通常小寫，前面要加 the

表方向用小寫

我望著太陽的位置，猜測了哪一個方向是西邊。

(1) 表示方向的 west、east、north、south **不需要大寫**。

(2) the sun、the moon、the earth（earth 指「大地」：the land on which we live）等世界上獨一無二的東西，要用 **the**，而且這些字通常**不大寫**。

- **The moon** was very bright on that warm night.

  moon 獨一無二，需加 the

  （在那個溫暖的夜晚裡，月亮非常明亮。）

(3) 注意：earth「地球」也有不加冠詞的用法，特別是片語 on earth。另外，earth 指「泥土」、「陸地」、「人間」時，不要冠詞。

- Miss Cower was brought back to **earth** from her daydreams of wealth and power.

  塵世，不要冠詞

  （考爾小姐從財富和權力的白日夢裡回到了現實中。）

- To tell you the truth, it was a hell **on earth**.

  人世間、世界上

  （老實告訴你，那是人間地獄。）

(4) 除非 sun、moon 以及 earth 與其他大寫的行星或天體的名字連接時，才需要**大寫**。

- Compare the sizes of **the Moon, Earth, and Neptune**.

  moon、earth 與大寫行星 Neptune 連接，需大寫

  （比較月球、地球和海王星的大小。）

(5) 有一些文法學家主張，Earth 如果是指行星（the planet that we live on）時，應該大寫。也就是說，如果內容是**天文學**，Earth 就會自豪地以大寫形式出現。而且在這種情況下，正如 Mars（火星）和 Venus（金星），Earth 也不需要定冠詞 the 修飾（尤其是片語 on Earth）。

(6) 有時為了強調「月球」，也可以大寫 Moon，尤其是片語 on the Moon。比如：water on the Moon。

文法加油站

A 下面行星（planets）的名字需要大寫：

- Mercury（水星）
- Venus（金星）
- Earth（地球）
- Mars（火星）
- Jupiter（木星）
- Saturn（土星）
- Uranus（天王星）
- Neptune（海王星）

B 恆星（stars）的名字需要大寫：

- the North Star/Polaris（北極星）

C 星座（constellations）的名字需要大寫：

- the Big Dipper（大熊星座的北斗七星）

4

✗ Mary has decided to study Biology. ——學科名不大寫

✓ Mary has decided to study biology.

瑪麗已經決定要主修生物學。

(1) 不要大寫學科名字或研究領域的名字，除非這些學科名字或研究領域的名字裡面含有專有名詞，那麼，那些專有名詞就需要大寫（比如：Chinese literature、British history）。上面例句中的 biology 是屬於學科名字或研究領域的名字，不用大寫。

(2) 特定的課程名字（specific class/course titles）需要大寫，它們實際上是專有名詞。

（注意：「課程」一詞，美語用 class ，英式英語用 course。）

School Subjects 學科	Particular Classes/Courses 特定的課程
· American literature（美國文學）	· American Literature 103（美國文學 103）
· biology（生物學）	· Biology 201（生物學 201）
· physics（物理學）	· Physics 101（物理學 101）

（注意：許多美國特定的課程用號碼表示，號碼小的課程通常是大學低年級的課程。）

- Maggie is taking one class in English and another in biology. (general subject)
  （瑪姬選修了一門英語課程和一門生物學課程。）一般學科
- Maggie is taking English 303 and Biology 103. (particular classes/courses)
  （瑪姬選修 303 英語課程和 103 生物學課程。）特定的課程

文法加油站

大寫原則：在英文裡頭，到底有哪些字是要大寫？

① 每一個**句子**的起首字第一個字母都要大寫。

- **Silently** and slowly, Joan read the lovely message on her cellphone.
  句子的起首字第一個字母 S 要大寫
  （裘恩默默地、慢悠悠地閱讀手機上那則愉快的訊息。）

② 每一個直接引語的第一個字的首字母要大寫。引語被中斷後，繼續的引語第一個字首字母不用大寫，除非那個字是一個專有名詞或專有形容詞，或者是一個新句子的開始。

- Ms. Sun said, "**She** won!"（孫女士說：「她贏了！」）
  引語的第一個字要大寫
- "I've done my best," Lenore said, "**and** I can do no more."
  不大寫，因為後面的引語是獨立子句，不是接一個新的完整句子
  （「我已經盡了全力，」蕾諾兒說，「我無能為力了。」）

- "Why worry?" asked Murray. "**Your** relationship with Liz Letter is getting better and better." └─ **Your 大寫，因為第二個引語是新的完整句子**

（「為什麼要擔心？」穆瑞問，「你和莉茲・雷特之間的關係越來越好了。」）

③ 要大寫人名、地名、語言、種族、宗教、民族、組織以及組織的成員等。

- Dr. Seuss （蘇斯博士）
- Kuala Lumpur （吉隆坡）
- the Pacific Ocean （太平洋）
- American English （美式英語）
- Indians （印度人／印地安人）
- Buddhism （佛教）
- Chinese-Americans （美籍華人）
- the Cancer Society （癌症社團）
- the Republican Party （共和黨）
- Republicans （共和黨員）

④ 地理區域要大寫。

- East Coast （東海岸）
- West Coast （西海岸）
- the North （北部）
- the South （南部）

⑤ 大寫月分和星期，但不要大寫季節。

- January （一月）
- Monday （星期一）
- spring （春天）
- winter （冬天）

⑥ 大寫歷史時期、歷史事件和節日。

- the Middle Ages （中世紀）
- World War II （二次世界大戰）
- Christmas Day （耶誕節）
- the Fourth of July （七月四號〔美國國慶日〕）

⑦ 大寫品牌名和商標名。

- Coke
- Sony
- IBM
- Apple

⑧ 大寫具體的人名、事物名、地名，但不要大寫普通名稱。

- My academic adviser spoke to the professor.
（我的學術指導老師跟那位教授談了話。） └─ 普通名稱
- My academic adviser spoke to Professor Lulu Fly.
（我的學術指導老師跟露露・弗萊教授談了話。） └─ **具體人名（專有名詞）**
- Oliver sailed on the river.（奧利弗在那條河上航行。）
└─ 普通名稱
- Oliver sailed on the Yangtze River.（奧利弗在長江上航行。）
└─ **具體地名（專有名詞）**
- Ann Best drove west.（安・貝斯特向西駕駛。）〔方向〕
- Is Ms. Best from the Midwest?（貝斯特女士是中西部人嗎？）〔特定的區域〕

⑨ 標題裡的第一個字和最後一個字需要大寫。標題裡的**實詞**（名詞、動詞、形容詞、副詞、代名詞）都要大寫。

· 標題裡的介系詞（如：of、for、in 等）不需要大寫，但介系詞有**四個或四個以上字母**（比如 about、from、with）時，就需要大寫。

· 連接詞（比如：and、or）不要大寫。

· 冠詞 a 和 an 不大寫（除非在標題的最前面）；冠詞 the 在標題最前面時，如果是**標題裡一部分**，就要大寫，如果不是，就不要大寫。

✔ Gone With the Wind《飄》〔小說名稱〕

✔ The Washington Post《華盛頓郵報》〔報紙名稱〕

✔ Hamlet《哈姆雷特》〔戲劇名稱〕

✔ Hours《小時》〔電視節目名稱〕

· read **The** Globe and Mail《環球郵報》
  └The 是報刊標題的一部分，要大寫

  Of 在標題的最後面要大寫
· **A** Love to Be Proud **Of**（值得驕傲的愛）
  └A 在標題的最前面要大寫

⑩ 請參見 mom/mum/pop/dad。

102 care about/take care of 關心／看護

1

✘ When my husband and I are at work, our maid **cares about** our twin daughters, Nan and Ann.
└表示對某人有感情，指「關心、介意」

✔ When my husband and I are at work, our maid **takes care of** our twin daughters, Nan and Ann.
└表示對某人負責或看護某人

我先生和我都在上班時，保姆照顧我們的雙胞胎女兒，南和安。

· Do you really **care about** Sue?（你真的在乎蘇嗎？）
└指「關心、介意、在意」

103 careful 小心的、仔細的

1 不常用 Be careful so that the medicine is kept away from little Abby.
be careful 通常不接 so that 子句

常用 Be careful that the medicine is kept away from little Abby.
be careful 通常接 that 子句

常用 Be careful to keep the medicine away from little Abby.
be careful 通常接不定詞

那些藥物要小心存放，不要讓小艾比拿到。

句型： be careful (not) to do something
be careful that + 子句

104 cart/trolley（裝有腳輪的）手推車

1 美式 Bart went to get a baggage cart.
巴特去取行李車了。

英式 Molly has a trolley.
茱莉有一個手推車。

表示「手推車、運貨車」，美國人用 cart，而英國人用 trolley。

105 case（片語 in case 的用法）

1 ✗ Marty will bring his best camera in case if the photographer doesn't show up at your party.
in case 後面不要用 if

✓ Marty will bring his best camera in case the photographer doesn't show up at your party.
馬迪會帶著他最好的相機，以防攝影師沒有出現在你的聚會上。

106 cattle

請參見 police。

107 check/cheque 支票

1 美式 Kitty Beck wrote a million-dollar check for that charity.

英式 Kitty Beck wrote a million-dollar cheque for that charity.

發音相同

姬蒂・貝科給那個慈善機構開了一張百萬美金的支票。

2 ✗ Kim gave Kyle a check of $50 and her best smile.

不用介系詞 of

✓ Kim gave Kyle a check for $50 and her best smile.

介系詞用 for

✓ Kim gave Kyle a $50 check and her best smile.

金姆給凱爾開了一張 50 美元的支票，還給了他最甜美的微笑。

要表示「一張面額是多少的支票」，有兩種型：

- a/an + 一筆特定數字的錢 + check
- a check for + 一筆特定數字的錢

108 check-in/check in

入住登記手續、領取登機卡手續

1 ✗ Lynn can meet Dan at the check in.

片語動詞，此處需用名詞

✓ Lynn can meet Dan at the check-in.

名詞，指到達機場或飯店時辦理手續的地方

琳恩可以在登機櫃台見到丹。

(1) at the check-in = at the check-in counter
（注意：check-in 作名詞和形容詞時，要有連字符號。）

(2) 美式 check-in counter
英式 check-in desk （登記櫃台）

- Eve's plan is to **check in** at least two hours before her flight leaves.

片語動詞，不要連字符號

（伊芙計畫至少在航班離開前兩小時辦理登機手續。）

文法加油站

checkout/check out 的用法

① checkout（結帳櫃台）／ check out（結帳離開）

1) checkout（= check-out）是名詞，指「在超級市場或大賣場付款的地方」，或指「結帳離開旅館或結帳離開旅館的時間」。

- Ms. Trout is at the checkout.（特拉特女士在結帳櫃台處。）
  checkout counter

2) check out 是片語動詞，指「結帳離開旅館或付款離開超級市場或大賣場」。

- Bing King checked out early this morning.
  （賓・金今天一大早就退房了。）

② check out（檢查）

片語動詞 check out 也有「檢查」的意思。

- Nancy carefully checks out her sailboat before she goes to sea.
  （南西出海之前仔細檢查她的帆船。）

109 child/kid 孩子

1
口語 Megan is in a special class for troubled kids.
正式 Megan is in a special class for troubled children.
梅根在一個專門為問題兒童開設的班裡。

kid 用於非正式的書面和口語中。

- Sid's wife went to pick up the kids.（席德的妻子去接孩子了。）

110 cinema/movies 電影院／電影

1
美式 I like to go to the movies with Mike.
英式 I like to go to the cinema with Mike.
我喜歡和麥克一起去看電影。

請參見下面 cinema/theater/theatre。

111 cinema/theater/theatre 電影院／劇場

1

美式 I'm in a line outside the theater for the new movie *Love Crime*.

英式拼法 theatre

英式 I'm in a queue outside the cinema for the new film *Love Crime*.

我在電影院外面排隊買《愛情罪》的電影票。

(1)

	美式	英式
電影院	theater/movie theater/movie house	cinema
劇院	theater（觀看 live performances〔表演、演出〕的地方）	theatre
電影	movie	film
排隊	line	queue

(2) 請參見 cinema/movies。

- Sue Vine told us to form a line. 美式
- Sue Vine told us to form a queue. 英式
  （蘇．弗埃恩要我們排隊。）

112 clarify/correct 闡明、澄清／糾正

1

表「對某事做更仔細的解釋，使它更容易讓人理解」，與此句句意不符

✗ Daisy decided to clarify her misleading statement that learning English was easy.

表「糾正一個錯誤的陳述、假定等」

✓ Daisy decided to correct her misleading statement that learning English was easy.

黛絲決定糾正她錯誤的陳述：學習英語很容易。

- Sue needs to clarify her relationships with Mark and Mike, because each expects to marry her.
  （蘇需要澄清她與馬克和麥克的戀愛關係，因為那兩個男人都期待與她結婚。）

113 class/classroom 班／教室

1

✗ There are two beautiful statues in our class.

「班」，指由一群學習的人組成的集體

✓ There are two beautiful statues in our classroom.

在我們的教室裡，有兩座漂亮的雕像。 「教室」，指上課的地方

(1) classroom 的意思是「教室」，是指上課的地方。

- Were you airsick on your magic broom while flying around in our classroom?
  （你騎著你的魔力掃帚在我們教室裡飛行時感到頭暈嗎？）

(2) class 的意思是「班」，是由一群學習的人組成的集體。

- Megan is in the class for three-year-old children.
  （梅根在一個為三歲兒童開設的班上讀書。）

(3) class 也可表示「課程」： 美式 class 英式 course

take a class/course in economics（選了一門經濟課程）

- I learned how to make glass flowers in my art class.
  （在藝術課裡我學會了怎樣製造玻璃花。）

114 climate/weather 氣候／天氣

1

✗ Heather does not like today's cold and windy climate.

某地區習慣性的、長期的氣候

✓ Heather does not like today's cold and windy weather.

海瑟不喜歡今天寒冷而多風的天氣。

某個特定地區在某段特定時間的天氣狀況，與氣溫、濕度、多雲等有關

- It was the cold climate of Norway that made me move to the USA.
  （正是因為挪威寒冷的氣候使我搬到美國。）

115 close/closed 關閉、附近的／關閉的

1

✗ Why is the Sunny Day Restaurant close today?

附近（= near，常與 to 連用，構成複合介系詞 close to）

✓ Why is the Sunny Day Restaurant closed today?

（形容詞）關閉的（= not open，用於談及商店、辦公室、學校等「關閉的」）

為什麼陽光日餐館今天關門？

- I have a cottage close to Lake Porridge.
（我在粥湖附近有一棟別墅。）

動詞，意思是「關閉」

- I'm going to close my eyes for a while.
（我要把眼睛閉上一會。）

116 close, open/turn off, turn on 關／開

1

✗ Tonight I won't close your bed light.

✓ Tonight I won't turn off your bed light.

關上水龍頭或電源，用 turn off

今天晚上我不關你的床頭燈。

(1) 這是學生常犯的一個錯誤。turn off/turn on 關上或打開水龍頭、電源或媒體，不用 close 或 open。（turn down、turn up 的意思是「把燈調暗一點」、「把燈調亮一點」。）

- I need to turn on my new computer and write an email to Lulu.（我需要啟動我的新電腦，寫一封電子郵件給露露。）
- Please turn on the light, Louise.
（露易絲，請開燈。）
- Please turn down the lights, Louise.
（露易絲，請把燈光調暗一點。）
- Mark, please turn up the lights, because it's getting dark.
（馬克，天快黑了，請把燈調亮一點。）

· Did Mr. Potter turn off the water?
（波特先生把水關了嗎？）

(2) 關開門窗用 close 和 open。

· Sue, please close the door behind you. （蘇，請隨手關門。）
表示「你過了門檻後隨手把門關上」

· If we open the window and shout, that bat may fly out.
（如果我們打開窗戶並大聲喊叫，那隻蝙蝠就可能會飛出去。）

117 cloth/clothes/clothing 布／衣服／服裝

1

✗ I took the clean cloths out of the washing machine.

✓ I took the clean clothes out of the washing machine.

我把乾淨衣服從洗衣機裡取出來。

(1) cloth 是不可數名詞，指做衣服、窗簾等的材料（a piece of material），或是擦洗東西的布。「一塊布」是 a piece of cloth，而不是 a cloth。

· This colorful silk cloth could be used to make a lovely skirt or a nice shirt.
（這種色彩鮮豔的絲綢布可以用來做漂亮的短裙或好看的襯衫。）

(2) clothes 指衣服，**沒有單數形式**；不能說 a clothe、a cloth、a clothes。

可用 some 修飾

· I'll take a shower, put on some clean clothes, and go for a walk around the lake.
（我要沖個澡，穿上一些乾淨衣服，然後繞著湖散步。）

(3) 但作某種特殊用途時（比如擦桌子、覆蓋桌子的布），cloth 是**可數名詞**，常用在**複合字**裡。

· a tablecloth （桌巾）
· a washcloth （毛巾、面巾）
· Sue Roth's dishcloths are all new.
（蘇·羅思的擦碗布都是新的。）

2 不常用 Mr. Fox put all his clothing into a big box.

「服裝」總稱。也可指具特殊用途的衣服

常用 Mr. Fox put all his clothes into a big box.

法克斯先生把他所有的衣服都裝進一個大箱子裡。

⑴ clothing 是「服裝」的總稱；也可以指具有特殊用途的衣服。

⑵ clothing 是不可數名詞。如果要表示單數的意思，就說 a piece/an item/an article of clothing。

- the clothing industry（服裝業）
- provide the homeless with food and clothing（為無家可歸的人提供食物和衣服）「服裝」總稱
- The Wild Thing store sells a lot of waterproof clothing.（搞怪衣物商店銷售許多防水衣。）具特殊用途的衣服

118 collective noun 集合名詞

請參見 family、pronoun agreement（文法加油站）和 subject-verb agreement（第 C 點）。

119 color/colour 顏色

1 ✗ On Friday night Lenore Chance wore white color pants.

color 不用在表示顏色的字後面

✓ On Friday night Lenore Chance wore white pants.

星期五晚上，蕾諾兒 · 錢斯穿著白色的褲子。

贅詞		正確用法
✗ red color hat	✗ red-colored hat	✓ red hat
✗ brown color eyes	✗ brown-colored eyes	✓ brown eyes
✗ white color shoes	✗ white-colored shoes	✓ white shoes

2 美式 Can you guess the color of my new dress?

-or 是美式英語的拼寫

英式 Can you guess the colour of my new dress?

-our 是英式英語的拼寫

你能猜出我新洋裝的顏色嗎？

文法加油站

許多英式英語含有 -our 的字，在美式英語中變成了 -or

美式 "Is blue your favorite color?" asked Sue.

英式 "Is blue your favourite colour?" asked Sue.

（「藍色是你最喜歡的顏色嗎？」蘇問。）

	美式	英式
顏色	color	colour
幽默	humor	humour
勞動	labor	labour

	美式	英式
恩惠	favor	favour
榮譽	honor	honour
鄰居	neighbor	neighbour

120 come/go

請參見 bring/take。

121 come with/follow 跟……一齊來／跟隨

1 ✗ Since you don't have a car, would you like to follow Lenore and me to the bookstore?

意思是「跟隨」，非「一起」

✓ Since you don't have a car, would you like to come with Lenore and me to the bookstore?

意思是「跟……一起來」

既然你沒有車，你願意跟蕾諾兒和我一起去書店嗎？

follow 的意思是「跟隨」，跟在某人或某物後面，朝著同一個方向移動。

- Lily did not know the way to the airport, so she followed my car closely.
（莉莉不知道去機場的路，於是她緊緊地跟在我的汽車後面。）

122 compare to/compare with

比喻為、比作／比較

1

❌ Mary compared her friend Cherry with a walking dictionary.
把……相比（比較同類型的兩個事物）

✅ Mary compared her friend Cherry to a walking dictionary.
把……比作（描述不同種類的兩個事物）

瑪麗把她的朋友伽麗比作一本活字典。

(1) compare . . . to 的意思是「把……比作」，用來描述**不同種類的兩個事物**（between members of different classes）之間的相似之處。上面的句子裡，人與字典是完全不同種類的，不過他們之間有相似之處。

- June says her husband often compares her to the moon.（茱恩說，她的丈夫常把她比作月亮。）
→ 人與月亮進行對比

(2) compare . . . with 的意思是「與……相比」。傳統文法規定 compare 後面用 with 來比較**同一種類的兩個事物**（between members of the same category）之間的相似處或不同之處。不過，現代習慣用法既可以用 with 也可以用 to，但更常用 with。

- Please compare the London of today with/to the London of the late 1940s.
（請把今日的倫敦與二十世紀四十年代末的倫敦進行比較。）

(3) compared to/wih 作為分詞片語置於句首時，無論是比較同類型或不同類型的事物，to 和 with 都可以用。

· Compared with/to me, Paul looks pretty tall.
人與人進行對比
（與我相比，保羅看上去就很高。）

地點與地點進行對比
· Compared with/to Chicago, San Francisco is cooler in the summer and warmer in the winter.
（與芝加哥相比，舊金山不僅在夏天更涼爽，而且冬天也更暖和。）

123 condition/conditions 狀態／環境

1

✗ Mary Gold is old, but she is still in excellent physical conditions and very bold.
conditions（**複數**）指「環境」

✓ Mary Gold is old, but she is still in excellent physical condition and very bold.
condition（**不可數**）指「健康狀態」

瑪麗 · 戈爾德雖然年老了，但她身體非常健康，而且還很大膽。

⑴ condition（單數）表示「健康狀態」（a state of health）或「情況」，用法為：

· in condition = in shape
（處於良好的健康狀況／情況好）

· out of condition = out of shape
（健康狀況不好／情況不好）

· in good/poor/terrible condition = in good/bad/terrible shape（情況或健康狀況好／壞）

⑵ conditions（複數）表示「環境、形勢」(existing circumstances)。

· conditions in the office（辦公室的環境）

· Are those physicians willing to live and work under poor and dangerous conditions?
（那些醫生願意在貧窮和危險的環境下生活和工作嗎？）

124 conjunctions

連接詞（不能同時使用從屬連接詞和對等連接詞）

兩者只能選其一

1 ✗ Even though Joe has found a job, but his salary is low.

✓ Even though Joe has found a job, his salary is low.

✓ Joe has found a job, but his salary is low.

雖然喬找到了一份工作，但他的薪水很低。

(1) 中文可以說「雖然……但是」，但英文只需要一個連接詞連接子句，不需要兩個連接詞。

(2) even though = although，請參見 although/but。

· Although/Even though Bob had good qualifications, he did not get that job. 從屬連接詞連接從屬子句

= Bob had good qualifications, but he did not get that job. 對等連接詞連接獨立子句

（雖然鮑伯有很強的能力，但他沒有得到那份工作。）

(3) 下面列表裡面的兩欄連接詞，連接子句時，只需要其中一個。

although	but
since	so
as	so

though	but
even though	but
because	so

· Because Gert was sick, she did not attend our concert. 從屬連接詞

= Gert was sick, so she did not attend our concert. 對等連接詞

（葛特因為生病了，所以沒有參加我們的音樂會。）

125 consider 考慮

1

❌ I am considering to visit Boston.

consider 不接不定詞

✅ I am considering visiting Boston.

consider 接動名詞或名詞

✅ I am considering a visit to Boston.

我正考慮去波士頓參觀。

(1) consider 後面接名詞或動名詞，而不是不定詞。句型為 consider (doing) something。

否定：consider + not + 動名詞

- Holly Wood is **considering not moving** to Hollywood.
  （霍莉・伍德在考慮不要搬遷到好萊塢。）

(2) 請參見 verb + 動名詞（V-ing 形式）／verb + 不定詞（第B點）。

126 consideration 考慮

1

❌ The UN's plan to explore Mars is under considerations by our nation.

✅ The UN's plan to explore Mars is under consideration by our nation.

不可數名詞，指「考慮」

聯合國探索火星的計畫，我國正在考慮之中。

(1) 當 consideration 指的是「考慮」（careful thought）時，是不可數名詞。

- after serious/careful consideration of something
  （認真／仔細考慮某件事後）
- for your consideration
  （供你考慮）
- give serious/careful consideration to something
  （仔細考慮某事）

(2) 當 consideration 指「需要考慮的事、動機、原因」（factors）時，是可數名詞，可以用複數。

- practical/political/security considerations
（實際／政治／安全考慮）
- Improving our nation's businesses and environment are President Jane Wu's two main considerations.
（改善我國的企業和環境，是珍・吳總統的兩個主要考量點。）

127 consist 組成

1

✗ The cake I made for Mr. Cutter last night was consisted mainly of sugar, flour, and butter.

被動語態是錯誤用法

✓ The cake I made for Mr. Cutter last night consisted mainly of sugar, flour, and butter.

consist of 片語動詞，意思是「由……構成」，用主動語態

昨晚我為卡特先生做的蛋糕主要由糖、麵粉和奶油所組成。

- Angels from far above sent us messages that consisted of hope and love.
（遠在天上的天使給我們送來了包含希望和愛的訊息。）

128 continual/continuous/constant

頻繁的／連續的／不變的

1

指「沒有間斷的」，與此句的句意不符

✗ Jim keeps on smoking despite continuous warnings from his wife that his nicotine addiction will steal ten years from his life.

表示「反覆的、多次重複」；不能用 continuous

✓ Jim keeps on smoking despite continual warnings from his wife that his nicotine addiction will steal ten years from his life.

儘管他的夫人多次重複告誡他，尼古丁上癮會使他少活 10 年，吉姆還是繼續抽菸。

(1) 雖然許多人，甚至一些字典認為 continual 和 continuous 意思是一樣的，但實際上這兩個字還是有細微的差別。

(2) continual 或 continually 指「反覆的、多次重複的動作」（happening regularly or frequently）。在這種情況下，不要用 continuous 或 continuously。

- Dan got tired of the continual arguments with Ann.
  （丹厭煩了跟安的頻頻爭吵。） 多次重複的爭吵（有間斷的）

(3) continuous 或 continuously 指「不被打斷的動作」。（going on without interruption）。

- Rose aimed the hose at Jim and sent a continuous stream of water at him. 沒有間斷的水流
  （蘿絲把水管瞄準吉姆，將水流源源不斷地向他射去。）

(4) constant 意思是「不變的、固定的」（not changing）。副詞是 constantly。

- Fay's praise and constant smile helped Max to relax. 不變的微笑
  （菲的讚揚以及她自始至終的微笑，使馬克斯變得不拘謹了。）

129 continue/continue on 繼續

1

✗ Our debate continued on for another hour.

continue 和 on 都有「繼續」之意，形成重複的累贅詞語

✓ Our debate continued for another hour.

✓ Our debate went on for another hour.

我們的辯論又繼續了一個小時。

(1) continue on 是一個疊義詞／累贅詞語（doublet phrase/wordiness），即重複同一個意思「繼續」，是多餘的，無論是口語還是書面語，都應該避免累贅詞語。

- Traffic noise from Bright Street continued all night.

= Traffic noise from Bright Street went on all night.
  （明亮街的交通喧鬧聲持續了整個晚上。）

(2) 請參見 doublets/wordiness、raise/raise up、repeat/repeat again、reply/reply back 和 return/return back。

130 cook/cooker 廚師／炊具

1

✗ Ann Look is an excellent cooker. —— 炊具，烹調器具

✓ Ann Look is an excellent cook. —— v. 烹調／ n. 廚師

安 · 盧克的烹調很棒。（安 · 盧克是一個好廚師。）

⑴ 一些動詞後面加上 -er = 做這個動作的人。

- write（v. 寫作）→ writer（n. 作家）
- drive（v. 駕駛）→ driver（n. 駕駛員）
- teach（v. 教學）→ teacher（n. 教師）

⑵ 但 cooker 不是廚師，而是用來做飯的用具，即「炊具，烹調器具」。

⑶ 烹調用的爐灶：英式 cooker　美式 stove

- Ms. Hooker bought a great gas cooker for Kate. 英式
（胡克女士給凱特買了一個大瓦斯爐。）
- Sue Sun prefers an electric stove to a gas one. 美式
（蘇 · 孫喜歡電爐勝過瓦斯爐。）

⑷ cook

① 動 烹調；做飯

- Does Andrew like to cook for you?
（安德魯喜歡為你做飯嗎？）

② 名 廚師

131 cost/price 費用、成本、代價／價格、代價

1

✗ Ann, please compare the price of living between Japan and Pakistan.

✓ Ann, please compare the cost of living between Japan and Pakistan.

安，請比較日本和巴基斯坦的生活費用。

「生活費用」，為了買日常生活中的必需品（比如：食品、衣服、住所、暖氣、交通等）所需要的錢

2 ✗ What is the cost of your best rice?
指「費用、成本」，與此句的句意不符

✓ What is the price of your best rice?
價格

你上等米的價格是多少？

cost 意思是「費用、成本、代價」，price 的意思是「價格、代價」。

- the cost of success/the price of success （成功的代價）
- at all costs/at any cost （不惜一切代價）
- the production cost （生產成本）
- health insurance costs （健康保險費）
- travel insurance price list （旅遊險價目表）
- the price of/for gasoline （汽油價格）

132 costly/expensive/dear 昂貴的

1 ✗ Olive said her new shoes were not costly. 指「代價高」

✓ Olive said her new shoes were not expensive.

奧莉芙說，她的新鞋並不貴。 指日常用品「價格高」

(1) expensive 的意思是「**價格高**」，一般暗示價格超過了物品的價值或者購買者的購買能力。**人們所需要的日常用品**（比如：書、車費、票、衣服、食品等），用 expensive 來表示昂貴，而不用 costly 來表示。

- expensive jacket（昂貴的夾克）
- expensive toy（昂貴的玩具）

(2) costly (adj.) 通常指「**代價高**」，對什麼事有嚴重的後果，需要付出很多錢或很多努力才能糾正或取代。costly 也可用來指**物品因稀少珍貴（precious, very valuable）、因精巧或豪華而價格昂貴**。

- costly victory （代價高的勝利）
- costly gems （貴重的寶石）

- Not insuring your car might prove very costly, especially if you lend it to Lily.
  （沒有投保汽車險，尤其是如果你還把車借給莉莉，也許會讓你付出很高的代價。）
- Kings often wear costly diamond rings.
  （國王常戴昂貴的鑽石戒指。）

(3) dear 指「高價的」（high-priced），**超過了正常或公平的價格**。dear 也指「珍貴的」、「在……（心中）寶貴的」（precious, much valued）。

- "Beef is so dear these days," complained Liz.
  （莉茲抱怨說：「現在牛肉的價格太高了。」）
- Both you and Lee are very dear to me.
  （你和李，我都非常珍視。）

133 couple 伴侶；兩、三個

1

✗ Kate has noticed that the young couple next door often stay up late.

✓ Kate has noticed that the young couple next door often stays up late.

couple 前面有 the，通常看成是單數，接單數動詞

凱特注意到隔壁房間的那對年輕夫婦常熬夜。

2

✗ Lenore did not notice that a couple of her friends was standing near the door.

✓ Lenore did not notice that a couple of her friends were standing near the door.

couple 前面是 a，後面有介系詞 of（a couple of = a few of），就是複數，接複數動詞

蕾諾兒沒有注意到她的幾個朋友正站在門口。

(1) couple 作主詞時候，是一個常令人困惑的字。它後面該接單數動詞，還是接複數動詞？這主要取決於 couple 這個字是指兩個個體（two individuals）還是指一個整體（a whole）。如果把它看成

是「整體」，就是單數，如果把它看成是「兩個個體」，就是複數。

(2) 簡單提示：

- 只要在 **couple** 前面有 **the**，通常就把它看成是**單數**，後面接單數動詞。
- 如果 **couple** 前面是 **a**，尤其是後面有介系詞 **of**（a couple of），它就是**複數**，接複數動詞。

(3) 片語 **a couple of** 為**複數**，指「幾個；兩個」（= a few of; two of）；**the couple** 為**單數**，指「夫婦、未婚夫妻、一對舞伴」。

- **A** nice American **couple has** moved in next door to Lenore.（一對友好的美國夫婦搬進了蕾諾兒的隔壁。）

→ 這裡 nice American couple 前面雖有 a，但仍然接一個單數動詞，因為我們把一對夫婦（a married couple）看成是**一個整體**（a whole）。

文法加油站

total 和 number：是要作單數，還是複數？

① **total** 和 **number** 既可以是單數也可以是複數。有時它們指一個集體，有時又指一個集體中的成員。

② 如果是 **the total** 或 **the number** 作主詞時，通常用**單數**動詞。

③ 如果是 **a total** 或 **a number**，尤其是後面還跟著一個 of 時，動詞用**複數**。

④ number 的用法請參見 amount/number、number: a number of 和 number: the number of。

- **The total** of the fish she caught **was** 33.（她共釣了 33 條魚。）
- **A total of** four hundred American robots **were** destroyed in that war.（在那次戰爭中，總共有四百名美國機器人陣亡。）

majority 的用法

① **a majority of** 類似 a couple of、a number of 以及 a total of，動詞應用**複數**。

• "A majority of the voters are happy with the result," stated Kitty.

不能用 is

（姬蒂說：「大多數投票者對結果滿意。」）

② the majority (of) 後面動詞可能是單數，也可能會是複數，主要取決於把這「大多數」看成是一個整體，還是看成一群單獨的個體。常見的結構：

✔ the majority（多數黨、多數派）+ **單數動詞**

選舉是由一個整體來完成的，
接單數動詞 elects、單數代名詞 it

• Mike's explanation is that the majority elects the candidate it likes.（麥克的解說是，多數黨選出其需要的候選人。）

✔ the majority of + **複數名詞** + **複數動詞**

一群被看成是個體的人；強調個體

• The majority of our employees are Chinese.
（我們多數職員是中國人。）

✔ the majority of + **單數名詞** + **單數動詞**

一群被看成是整體的人

• The majority of the Oak City public thinks that the right to eat or work in a restaurant with clean air is far more important than the right to smoke.
（橡樹市的民眾以為，享有在空氣純潔的餐廳用餐或工作的權利，比享有抽菸的權利更為重要。）

134 cut/cut out 剪、切／剪下

1

✖ I cut out the cheese into four pieces and gave them to Louise.
指「剪下文章」

指「切開」
✔ I cut the cheese into four pieces and gave them to Louise.

我把起司切成四片後給了露易絲。

2

✖ Lenore cut the colorful car ad and taped it to her door.

✔ Lenore cut out the colorful car ad and taped it to her door.
指「剪下文章」

蕾諾兒剪下色彩鮮豔的汽車廣告，把它貼在她的門上。

比較下面兩句：

= remove by cutting，指「從報紙、雜誌等剪下文章」

- Sue's dad cut out the story from the *Morning Glory News*.
  （蘇的爸爸從《牽牛花新聞》報上剪下那篇故事。）
- Sue's dad cut the story from the *Morning Glory News*.
  指「不讓這個故事在報紙上發表」
  （edit by omitting a part or parts）
  （蘇的爸爸把那個故事從《牽牛花新聞》報上刪除了。）

135 cure/treat 治癒／治療

1

✗ Is Louise being cured for a skin disease?

疾病完全治療好了才用 cure

✓ Is Louise being treated for a skin disease?

在接受治療時，用 treat（常用於被動語態）

露易絲正在接受皮膚病的治療嗎？

- (person) be treated (by doctors)（〔病人〕在接受〔醫生〕的治療）
- cure a patient（治好了病人）
- cure a disease（治好了疾病）
- cure a patient of a disease（治好了病人的疾病）
- (person) be cured of a disease（〔病人的〕病治好了）
- The medicine Jack took yesterday cured the rash on his back.
  cured a disease
  （傑克昨天吃的藥治癒了他背部的疹子。）
- "When Lily left the hospital, she was completely cured," explained Millie.
  a patient was cured
  （米莉解釋說：「莉莉出院時已經完全痊癒了。」）

D

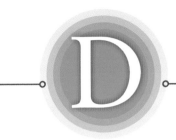

136 dad

請參見 mom/mum/pop/dad。

137 damage/hurt/injure 損害／受傷／傷害

1

❌ "Luckily, none of us was damaged," declared Lily.
談及「物」時使用

✅ "Luckily, none of us was hurt," declared Lily.
談及「人」時使用

✅ "Luckily, none of us was injured," declared Lily.
談及「人」時使用

莉莉宣布：「幸運的是，我們沒有一個人受傷。」

- My house was badly damaged during Hurricane Jane.
（我的房子遭受到颶風珍嚴重的損壞。）

2

❌ Midge saw that her car had suffered only a minor damage.
damage 作名詞用，表「損害、損失」，是不可數名詞，不和冠詞 a/an 連用，也無複數形

✅ Midge saw that her car had suffered only minor damage.

米姬看見她的車僅僅受了一點損壞。

- do damage（造成損害）
- suffer damage（遭受損害）
- serious/severe damage（嚴重的損壞）
- brain/liver damage（大腦／肝臟損害）
- permanent damage（永久的／不能挽回的損害）

文法加油站

damages 當作複數時，意思是指「賠償金」

- Kim was ordered to pay $10,000 in **damages** to the victim.

  複數指「賠償金」

（金姆被命令向受害者支付一萬美金的賠償金。）

138 dangling constructions/ misplaced modifiers

垂懸結構／修飾語錯位

何謂垂懸結構（dangling construction）？一個字、片語或子句在句中的位置放錯了，結果造成這個**字、片語或子句去修飾它不應該修飾的成分**。這樣的字、片語或子句就是垂懸結構或修飾語錯位。垂懸結構與其句中的另一個成分之間缺乏明確的句法連接。

垂懸結構是常見的錯誤，四處可見，在報紙、雜誌、網路新聞、電臺以及電視節目裡都可以發現垂懸結構。因此在口語中，尤其是在書面表達中，一定要避免垂懸結構。以下我們將分別介紹七種垂懸結構：

A. Prepositional phrases（介系詞片語）

B. Adjective phrases（形容詞片語）

C. Adverbs/Adverbial phrases（副詞或副詞片語）

D. Participial phrases（分詞片語）

E. Gerund phrases（動名詞片語）

F. Infinitive phrases（不定詞片語）

G. Clauses（子句）

A) Prepositional phrases 介系詞片語

1

語意不清　Ms. Bloom bought a cottage from an old man with no bathroom.

介系詞片語 with no bathroom 位置放錯，變成修飾 man

語意清楚　An old man sold Ms. Bloom a cottage with no bathroom.

介系詞片語 with no bathroom 修飾 cottage，應放 cottage 後面

一個老翁賣給了布盧姆女士一棟沒有洗手間的小屋。

(1) 上面第一句表達出兩種含意：

- 【從結構上看】：介系詞片語 with no bathroom 放在名詞 man 後面，表達出的含意是：「布盧姆女士從一個沒有洗手間的老翁那裡買了一棟小屋。」這意思不是有點不合邏輯嗎？
- 【從意思上看】：指「小屋沒有洗手間」。

(2) 無論在寫作或口語中都要避免這類有雙重含意的句子。**介系詞片語應放在所修飾的名詞後面**。上面第一句介系詞片語 with no bathroom 位置放錯了，修飾了它不應該修飾的名詞（man），是一個垂懸介系詞片語或錯位的介系詞片語。應該把介系詞片語 with no bathroom 放在名詞 cottage 後面，因為它修飾的是名詞 cottage。

2

✗ At the age of five, Amy's family moved to Miami.

不能用來修飾主詞 Amy's family，是垂懸介系詞片語

主詞

✓ At the age of five, Amy moved to Miami with her family.

表示年齡的介系詞片語與主詞「人」相關

✓ When Amy was five, her family moved to Miami.

可以把介系詞片語改成從屬子句

艾咪五歲那年，她們全家搬到了邁阿密。

(1) 在第一句中，主詞 Amy's family 與介系詞片語 at the age of five 相關聯，Amy's family 有五歲嗎？肯定不是。所以第一句中的 at the age of five 是垂懸介系詞片語。

(2) 注意介系詞片語 **at the age of**，不要漏了冠詞 the，不要寫成 at age of。

3

語意不清 Mike and I knew by Monday we would call for a strike.

可修飾前後的片語，造成雙重含意，是垂懸結構

語意清楚 Mike and I knew that by Monday we would call for a strike.

加 that 可使文意清楚

麥克和我明白，到了星期一我們將號召一次罷工。

語意清楚 Mike and I knew by Monday that we would call for a strike.

到星期一麥克和我就明白了，我們要號召一次罷工。

(1) 上面第一句介系詞片語 by Monday 在句中的位置給讀者留下疑問：「到了星期一麥克和我就明白了？」還是「到了星期一麥克和我將號召一次罷工？」修飾語 by Monday 的位置沒有放對。

(2) 因在句中的位置不對而造成句子有雙重含意的修飾語，被稱為**斜視修飾語**（squinting modifier），因為它好像朝兩個相反的方向看，既修飾它前面的字或片語（Mike and I knew by Monday），又修飾它後面的字或片語（by Monday we would call for a strike）。斜視修飾語也是一種垂懸結構。

4

不自然用法 Ann told, with a smile, her story to the Tibetan man.

修飾語離主詞 Ann 太遠，不自然

不自然用法 Ann told her story, with a smile, to the Tibetan man.

修飾語 with a smile 應該放在句首，靠近主詞 Ann

自然用法 With a smile, Ann told her story to the Tibetan man.

主詞靠近前面的修飾語

安微笑著把她的故事告訴了那位西藏男子。

B) Adjective phrases 形容詞片語

形容詞片語位置靠近 you，變成修飾主詞 you，語意不清

1

語意不清 So quiet and small, you'll never know the robot Claire is there!

把上面語意不清句中的形容詞片語改成 because 引導的子句，清楚指明 so quite and small 指的是 the robot Claire

語意清楚 Because the robot Claire is so quiet and small, you'll never know she's there!

因為機器人克蕾兒如此安靜、如此微小，你根本不會知道她就在那裡！

在第一個句子裡，形容詞片語 so quiet and small 與主詞 you 靠近，即形容詞片語修飾主詞 you。你很安靜、很微小嗎？也許是，也許不是。不過，從句子要表達的意思看，顯然是因為機器人克蕾兒 so quiet and small，你才看不見她。形容詞片語的位置放錯了，修飾了不該修飾的成分，是一個垂懸形容詞片語結構。

C) Adverbs/Adverbial phrases 副詞或副詞片語

1

語意不清　You will appreciate the advice Sue gives you years from now.

副詞片語靠近 the advice Sue gives you，造成雙重含意

語意清楚　Years from now you will appreciate the advice Sue gives you.

數年後，你會感激蘇給你的建議。

第一句語意不清，具有雙重含意：

- 【從結構上看】：第一句中的副詞片語 years from now 靠近名詞片語 the advice Sue gives you，是指「你會感激數年後蘇要給你的建議」。
- 【從意思看】：原句意指「從現在起數年後，你會感激蘇給你的建議」。副詞片語的位置放錯了，修飾了不該修飾的成分，是一個垂懸副詞片語結構或錯位的副詞片語。

D) Participial phrases 分詞片語

1

✗ Completely exhausted, Lenore's books fell to the floor.

動詞片語主詞與句子主詞不一致　主詞

✓ Completely exhausted, Lenore let her books fall to the floor.

動詞片語主詞與句子主詞一致　主詞

蕾諾兒累壞了，讓她的書都掉落到了地板上。

(1) 動詞片語（包括動名詞片語、分詞片語、不定詞片語）放在句首並用逗號與句子分開，**片語的主詞應該與句子的主詞一致**。

(2) 上面第一句的主詞是 Lenore's books，那麼分詞片語 completely exhausted 的主詞也應該是 Lenore's books。書怎麼可能筋疲力

盡呢？人（Lenore）才可能筋疲力盡。因此，句子的主詞應該改成 Lenore，否則這個分詞片語就是一個垂懸結構。

2

語意不清　Lee ran up to Lily breathing heavily.

分詞片語靠近先行詞 Lily，包含兩種意思，語意不清楚

語意清楚　Breathing heavily, Lee ran up to Lily.

分詞片語置於句首，片語主詞與句子主詞 Lee 一致，符合邏輯，文法也正確

李上氣不接下氣地朝莉莉跑去。

語意清楚　Lee ran up to Lily who was breathing heavily.

改用形容詞子句，可明確表達是 Lily 上氣不接下氣

李朝著上氣不接下氣的莉莉跑去。

⑴ 誰上氣不接下氣？是 Lee 還是 Lily ？第一句話包含兩種意思：

- 【從邏輯上講】：Lee 在跑步，當然是 Lee 上氣不接下氣。
- 【從結構上看】：分詞片語 breathing heavily 因靠近先行詞 Lily，好像是修飾 Lily，是 Lily 上氣不接下氣。
- 雖然這句的文法沒有錯，但英語是母語的人士會認為這樣的句子不自然（unnatural），或不清楚（unclear）。

⑵ 第二句把分詞片語 breathing heavily 放在句首，用逗號與主詞 Lee 分開。根據文法規則，分詞片語位於句首時，**分詞片語的主詞應該與句子主詞一致**，這句明確指明是 Lee 因跑步而上氣不接下氣，意思符合邏輯，文法也正確。

3

不自然用法　I ran across Andrew jogging with my wife Sue.

分詞片語位於句尾，包含兩種意思，易誤解

自然用法　Jogging with my wife Sue, I ran across Andrew.

分詞片語放句首，片語的主詞和句子的主詞保持一致（主詞都是 I），文法正確，意思合邏輯

= While jogging with my wife Sue, I ran across Andrew.

= While I was jogging with my wife Sue, I ran across Andrew.

與我太太蘇一起慢跑時，我遇見安德魯。

(1) 第一句分詞片語位於句尾，包含了兩種意思：

- 【從邏輯上講】：應該是「我和我妻子在一起跑步」。分詞片語修飾主詞 I。
- 【從結構上看】：分詞片語修飾先行詞 Andrew，相當於一個形容詞子句「I ran across Andrew who was jogging with my wife Sue.」。表達出的意思是「安德魯和我妻子蘇一起跑步時被我碰見了」。
- 【文法】：正確，但表達出的意思會引起誤解。要避免用這類意思含混的句子。

(2) **句子的主詞應該就是句首分詞片語的主詞。**是誰和我的妻子在跑步？是 I，不是 Andrew。因此句子的主詞和分詞片語的主詞都應該是 I。上面第二句的分詞片語放在句首，片語的主詞和句子的主詞保持一致（I was jogging、I ran across），文法正確，意思也符合邏輯。

文法加油站

① 分詞片語的主詞位於句首時，必須與句子的主詞一致，或必須與句子的主詞有關聯。

② 如果分詞片語的主詞與句子的主詞不一致，就必須刪除分詞片語，使用另一種句型，或者改變句子的主詞。下面的範例，把分詞片語置於句尾，然後用逗號與句子分開，請看看它是否是正確的句子？

- Lee ran up to Lily, **breathing heavily.**

→【句型結構】：句中有逗號，分詞片語不是修飾其前面的句子受詞 Lily，而是修飾句子的主詞 Lee。

【文法】：文法正確，但句型不道地、不自然、不清楚。

【正確用法】：既然跑步的是 Lee，分詞片語 breathing heavily 就需要靠近 Lee，才不會產生歧義。

③ 如果你口頭講這句話，聽者就不可能看見逗號，因此會感到疑惑。你的目的是為了有效傳達你的意思，而不是為了從理論上去論證一個文法結構。無論是口語還是書面語，都應該避免用一些文法正確但意思含混、不道地的句子。

不自然用法 Creating many new jobs, Sue and Rob's software company has grown fast. 表結果的分詞片語置於句首不自然、不符合邏輯
（產生了很多新工作，蘇和羅布的軟體公司發展很快。）

自然用法 Sue and Rob's software company has grown fast, creating many new jobs. 表結果的分詞片語最好放句尾

= Because Sue and Rob's software company has grown fast, it has created many new jobs.
（因為蘇和羅布的軟體公司發展很快，產生了很多新工作。）

這句的分詞片語 creating many new jobs 如果置於句首，反而不自然，不符合邏輯。因公司發展得快，才會產生許多新工作。表示結果的分詞片語最好放在句子的後面，才自然、流暢，如果放在句首會成了因果倒置。

E) Gerund phrases 動名詞片語

1

✖ By reading extensively last semester, Dot's English improved a lot. 主詞是 Dot's English，Dot 的英文上學期大量閱讀了嗎？當然不是！

✔ By reading extensively last semester, Dot improved her English a lot. 句子主詞應為行為者 Dot，和前面動詞片語主詞才能保持一致

✔ Because Dot read extensively last semester, her English improved a lot. 動名詞片語改成原因副詞子句

✔ Because Dot read extensively last semester, she improved her English a lot.

妲特因上學期進行了大量閱讀，她的英語進步很多。

(1) 如果句中動名詞片語的行為者（doer）不清楚，那麼與分詞片語一樣，這個動名詞片語就成了垂懸結構。要避免垂懸結構，就要指明句子裡動名詞片語的行為者。

(2) 所以應該像第二句那樣把 Dot 當作主詞，與動名詞片語 reading extensively last semester 靠在一起。Dot 既是動名詞「閱讀」（reading）也是句子的動詞「改進」（improved）的行為者（doer）。

F) Infinitive phrases 不定詞片語

1

❌ "To pass the test, more hard work is needed," said Dirk.

是 hard work 需要通過考試嗎？主詞應該是「人」，而非 hard work

非正式 "More hard work is needed to pass the test," said Dirk.

不定詞片語放句後，口語常見

正式 "To pass the test, you need to do more hard work," said Dirk.

明確指明主詞 you

德克說：「要想通過這次考試，你需要更努力用功。」

在正式用語中，需要明確指明主詞——是誰需要通過考試？上面第三句不定詞片語動詞的主詞和句子的主詞一致，都是 you：you 通過考試，you 需要更努力用功。

G) Clauses 子句

1

❌ Kitty gave some clothes to a charity that she did not need any more.

形容詞子句放 charity 後，表「她不再需要的慈善機構」，語意怪異

✔ Kitty gave some clothes that she did not need any more to a charity.

形容詞子句放 clothes 後，語意清楚

姬蒂把一些她不再需要的衣服給了一家慈善機構。

2

❌ When ten years old, my Aunt Gwen married again.

與省略子句 when ten years old 靠近，表「我的葛雯姨媽十歲時再婚了」，語意怪異

✔ When I was ten years old, my Aunt Gwen married again.

補充主詞 I 和動詞 was，把省略子句改成 when 引導的副詞子句，語意清楚

我十歲那年，我的葛雯姨媽再婚了。

垂懸結構有時會令人啼笑皆非。不過，假如人人都使用標準的英語，生活也許就會失去很多歡樂啊！

3

❌ While jogging slowly along the side of the road, a huge toad was seen.

表「a huge toad 在慢跑（jogging）」。jog（尤指健身鍛鍊身體的慢跑運動）的行為者應該是「人」

句子主詞「I」是動作「看見」（saw）和「跑步」（jogging）的行為者（doer）

✅ While jogging slowly along the side of the road, I saw a huge toad.

把被動語態改成主動語態，把 I 當作句子的主詞

沿著路邊慢跑時，我看見了一隻大癩蛤蟆。

這是一個省略子句（elliptic clause）的範例。省略子句和其他子句一樣，也應該避免垂懸結構。

文法加油站

獨立分詞片語（Independent Participial Phrases）

① **不要使用垂懸結構**：修飾語應該緊靠所修飾的成分，不要讓修飾語垂懸或錯位。分詞片語的主詞必須與句子的主詞一致。

② 請參見 participial phrases/participle clauses 分詞片語。

③ **獨立片語**：不過，一些慣用的分詞片語屬於例外，它們可以不與句子的主詞有關聯。這些慣用的獨立分詞片語以及其他一些可以垂懸的介系詞片語、不定詞片語等，被稱為「獨立片語」（independent phrase）。

・Generally speaking, Lily dances beautifully.

不是動詞 speaking 的主詞，兩者並沒有任何關聯，但這個句子仍然正確

（一般說來，莉莉跳舞跳得很優美。）

④ 下表是其他可以垂懸的獨立片語：

・strictly speaking（嚴格說來）	・after all（畢竟）
・broadly speaking（概括說來）	・judging from（由……判斷）
・supposing（假設）	・in the long run（最終）
・assuming the worst（做最壞的打算）	・considering everything（考量一切）

- given the conditions（在特定的條件下）
- on the whole（就整體而論、一般說來）
- to be frank（坦白說）
- to tell you the truth（老實告訴你）

- **To tell you the truth,** Henry is not in love with Ruth.（老實告訴你，亨利沒有與露絲相愛。）

允許使用分詞垂懸結構的句型（Some Acceptable "Misplaced Participles"）

一些錯位的分詞（misplaced participle）是可以接受的，而且常常很自然，尤其是當句子用 **it** 作主詞，或者句子是用 **there is/are** 的句型。

- **Having grown** up in Sichuan, **it**'s not surprising that Gertrude loves to eat spicy food.

= Gertrude grew up in Sichuan, so it's not surprising that she loves to eat spicy food.
（葛楚德是在四川長大的，所以她喜歡吃辛辣的食物一點也不令人驚奇。）

- **Having so little time, there was** not much that Sue could do to help Lulu.（因時間如此地少，蘇無法幫助露露。）

分詞獨立主格結構（Absolute Phrases）

分詞片語可以有自己的主詞（participial phrase with its subject）：
有時候分詞可以有自己的主詞，與句子的主詞沒有關聯。這種結構叫「分詞獨立主格結構」。

分詞 permitting 的主詞　　句子的主詞

- **Weather permitting**, **the spaceship Neptune** will take off at noon.

（如果天氣允許，海神太空船將在正午時分發射。）

過去分詞 gone 的主詞

- She explained, "With **my parents gone** from September through February, **our big house** was empty."

句子的主詞

（她解釋說：「從九月到二月，因我父母在外，我們家的大房子是空著的。」）

一些具有獨立主詞而不自然的分詞片語（Unnatural Participial Phrase With Its Own Subject）

一些分詞片語雖然具有自己獨立的主詞，文法上好像沒有錯，但非常不自然、不道地。無論是口語還是書面語都要避免這類不自然的分詞片語。

不自然用法　Jim sunbathing on the beach, a tall woman came toward him.

自然用法　While sunbathing on the beach, Jim saw a tall woman coming toward him.
（在海灘上沐日光浴時，吉姆看見一個高大的女子朝他走來。）

第一句雖然文法看起來好像沒有問題，分詞片語 sunbathing 有自己的獨立主詞 Jim，但這樣的句子非常不自然，是道地的 Chinglish（中式英語）。學習文法，不僅要學習規則和原理，更重要的是要學習文法在生活中的實際運用，這就需要大量閱讀，否則寫出來的句子雖然文法正確，卻充滿了 Chinglish。記住，每天需要閱讀 25,000 個字，才有可能成為一流的英語使用者（a first-class user of English）。

139 dare

請參見 need。

140 dead/die 死亡

1

形容詞，表示狀態。這句應該用動詞 die

✗ Jack was dead in Ocean View Hospital an hour after the shark attack.

動詞，表示動作或事件

✓ Jack died in Ocean View Hospital an hour after the shark attack.

在遭到鯊魚襲擊一小時後，傑克在海景醫院去世。

- Ted doesn't know if Clive is alive or **dead**.
（泰德不知道克萊夫是生是死。）　形容詞，表示狀態

動詞，表示動作或事件

- Uncle Tyr **died of** a heart attack last year.
（提爾叔叔去年死於心臟病發作。）

2 ✗ Clyde Spear has died for a year.

表達短暫的動作，不與表示一段時間的片語一起使用（比如：for a month、for a year、for two years）

dead 表狀態，可以與表示一段時間的片語連用

✓ Clyde Spear has been dead for a year.
= It's been a year since Clyde Spear died.

克萊德・斯比爾已經去世一年了。

141 dead/deadly 死的；非常／致命的；死一般地

1 ✗ Ted was deadly drunk and ran his bicycle over a dead skunk.

dead drunk 是慣用語，而不是 deadly drunk

✓ Ted was dead drunk and ran his bicycle over a dead skunk.

作副詞用，意為「完全、絕對、非常」

當形容詞時，意為「不再活著、死了」

泰德昨晚醉得一塌糊塗，騎著自行車從一隻死臭鼬身上輾過。

(1) dead 在有些片語裡作**副詞**用，修飾形容詞或動詞，意思是「完全；絕對；突然； 非常；直接；確切」（completely; absolutely; suddenly; very; directly; exactly）。

- dead right（絕對正確）
- dead slow（慢死了）
- stop dead（突然停下來）
- dead ahead（正前方）

(2) deadly 做**形容詞**用時，意思是「致命的；死一般的；不共戴天的；極度的」（able or likely to kill people; like death; aiming to kill; extreme）。

- a deadly weapon（致命武器）
- a deadly enemy（不共戴天的敵人）

· deadly silence（死寂）
· deadly haste（非常快）
· Why was the deadly poison given to Queen Lily?
（為什麼把那致命的毒藥給了莉莉皇后呢？）

⑶ deadly 作**副詞**用時，意思是「死一般地；極度地」（in a way suggestive of death; excessively），而不是「致命地」的意思。要表示副詞「致命地」，需要用 fatally。

· deadly dull（非常乏味）
· deadly serious （非常嚴肅）
· When he saw the dead whale, Lee turned deadly pale.
（當看見那條死鯨時，李的臉色變得死白。）

文法加油站

fatal 形 = resulting in death 致命的、生死攸關的

① deadly (adj.) 指「能夠致命的東西」，比如：deadly weapon、deadly poison。

② fatal (adj.) 指「造成或命中註定要導致死亡或可怕後果的形勢、環境或事件」。fatal 常與下面的字連用：

· fatal accident （致命的事故）
· fatal injury （致命傷）
· fatal disease/illness （致命的疾病）
· fatal blow （致命的打擊）
· fatal mistake/error （致命的錯誤）
· fatal shooting （致命的射擊）
· "Is this disease usually fatal?" asked Liz.
（莉茲問：「這種疾病通常致命嗎？」）

fatally 副 = mortally 致命地

要表示副詞「致命地」，用 fatally，而不要用 deadly（死一般地、極度地）。

· Lenore was fatally wounded in that stupid war.
（蕾諾兒在那場愚蠢的戰爭中遭受到了致命的傷害。）

142 deal in/deal with 經營／對付

1

❌ Kay, you need to deal in that rat right away.

指「經營；買賣」，與文意不合

✅ Kay, you need to deal with that rat right away.

凱，你需要馬上對付那隻老鼠。

指「處理；對付」

(1) deal with 的意思是「關於；處理；對付；與某人或某公司做生意」。

- Coco's book deals with UFOs.（可可的書談論不明飛行物。）

  關於 = be about（關於）

(2) deal in something 的意思是「經營；買賣」。

- Joan's brother is dealing in stolen cellphones.

  經營；買賣 = buy and sell（買賣）

  （裘恩的哥哥在買賣被盜的手機。）

143 decision 決定

1

❌ Kitty was making a decision of whether to move to Tokyo or Mexico City.

✅ Kitty was making a decision about whether to move to Tokyo or Mexico City.

「對……做出決定」，後面通常接 about 或 on

姬蒂要做出決定，自己究竟該搬遷去東京還是墨西哥城。

make a decision to do something 指「決定做……」，後面接不定詞。

- Kitty made a decision to go to the International Music College in Mexico City.

  （姬蒂決定去墨西哥城的國際音樂學院讀書。）

144 degree 學位

1

❌ Maggie will receive a bachelor's degree of biology.

在哪方面的學位，不用 degree of

學科名小寫

✅ Maggie will receive a bachelor's degree in biology.

小寫

在哪方面的學位，用 degree in

瑪姬將獲得生物學學士學位。

- a bachelor's degree（學士學位）
- a master's degree（碩士學位）
- a doctorate（博士學位）

(1) 也可以說：

- a Bachelor of Arts degree (a BA degree)（文學學士學位）
- a Master of Science degree (an MS degree)（理學碩士學位）
- a Master of Business Administration degree (an MBA degree)（企管碩士學位）

字母 M 的第一個發音是母音，前面要用 an（請參見 a/an。）

(2) 在文憑上的寫法是：

- Master of Arts in Education（教育碩士）
- Master of Science in Computer Science（計算機理學碩士）

介系詞小寫，其餘字的首字母大寫；不用 degree 這個字

145 despite/in spite of 雖然

1

❌ Despite of his old age, Clive is learning to drive.

despite 是介系詞，後面接名詞，不接介系詞 of

❌ Inspite of his old age, Clive is learning to drive.

in spite of 是分開寫的三個字，而不是連在一起的 inspite of

✅ Despite his old age, Clive is learning to drive.

despite something = in spite of something（雖然；儘管）

✅ In spite of his old age, Clive is learning to drive.

雖然年事已高，克萊夫還在學開車。

· In spite of having rich parents, Joan paid for her college education on her own.
= Despite having rich parents, Joan paid for her college education on her own.
（儘管父母很富有，裘恩自己支付了她的大學費用。）

146 desert/dessert 沙漠／甜點

1

❌ Gert ate her ice cream desert while looking at the Sahara Dessert.

✅ Gert ate her ice cream dessert while looking at the Sahara Desert.

葛特一邊望著撒哈拉沙漠，一邊吃著霜淇淋甜點。

	意思	如何區別
desert	「沙漠」，只有一個 s	乾燥、多沙的荒漠，只能擁有一個 s
dessert	「飯後甜點」，有兩個 ss	飯後豐富的點心，有權享有兩個 s

147 detail 細節

1

❌ The recent divorce of Annette and Bret is described in details on the Internet.
in detail 是固定片語，detail 作單數，沒有 s

✅ The recent divorce of Annette and Bret is described in detail on the Internet.
意為「詳細地」

網站上詳細地描述了安妮特和布瑞特最近的離婚事件。

(1) 含有單數 detail 的固定片語：

· attention to detail （注意細節）
· Gail usually pays careful attention to detail.
（蓋兒通常都非常注意細節。）

A B C D E F G H I J K L M N O P Q R S T U V W X Y Z

- go into **detail** about/on （詳細描述；逐一細說）
- Marta **went into great detail** about her trip to Jakarta.
  （瑪爾塔詳細地描述了去雅加達的旅程。）

(2) 如果沒有用在固定片語裡，**detail** 是可數名詞，有**複數**形式。

- the **details** of our plan（計畫的細節）
- minor **details**（枝微末節）

(3) 複數 **details** 也指「訊息」（information）。

- Many of the **details** about global warming can be found in the movie *Whales*.
  （在電影《鯨》裡可以找到關於全球氣溫上升的許多詳情。）

148 diagnose 診斷

1

diagnose 不用來診斷病人（Kim）

✗ Kim was diagnosed with lung cancer by Doctor Lancer.

✓ Doctor Lancer diagnosed Kim's health problem as lung cancer.

diagnose 用來診斷疾病（health problem）

蘭西醫生診斷金姆的健康問題是肺癌。

(1) 用 **diagnose** 來表示診斷疾病，而不是診斷病人。

(2) **常被使用的錯誤片語** diagnose somebody with a disease

標準的片語 diagnose a disease as something

- tests to **diagnose heart disease** （診斷心臟病的化驗）

149 differ 不同於

1

✗ Midge wants to get married before she finishes college. Sue and Lulu's thinking **differs to** hers over this issue.

✓ Midge wants to get married before she finishes college. Sue and Lulu's **thinking differs from hers** over this issue.

想法與想法（不同），要用 differ from

米姬想在大學畢業之前就結婚。在這個問題上蘇和露露的想法與米姬的想法不同。

(1) differ from something（與……不同）（be unlike）

(2) differ with/from someone（對某事與某人意見不一致）（disagree with someone about something）

上面例句也可以改寫成：

- Midge wants to get married before she finishes college. **Sue and Lulu** differ with **her** over this issue.

  人與人（意見不一致）

  (Sue and Lulu differ with her = Sue and Lulu differ from her)

  （米姬想在大學畢業之前就結婚。在這個問題上蘇和露露與米姬的意見不一致。）

150 different from/different than/different to 不同的

1

美式 英式 Food in Shanghai is quite different from that in Chengdu.

美式 非正式 Food in Shanghai is quite different than that in Chengdu.

英式 非正式 Food in Shanghai is quite different to that in Chengdu.

上海菜與成都菜完全不同。

在正式用語、商務用語、考試中，請用 different from。

- Sid and his identical twin brother, Trent, are very different from each other.

  （席德與他的雙胞胎弟弟崔恩特完全不同。）

文法加油站

different from 和 different than 的使用時機

① 當比較兩個事物時，最常用的片語是 different from。

② 如果 different 後面是一個從屬子句，美式非正式用語中可以用從屬連接詞 than。

非正式 美式

The true story was different than **Lori had told Lulu**.

從屬子句

正式

The true story was different from **what Lori had told Lulu**.

（蘿麗告訴露露的事與事實不符合。）

what 引導的名詞子句；名詞子句相當於一個名詞

③ 下面的例句，用 than 比用 from 更自然。

- Buzz thinks about love in a different way from the way in which Kay does. →文法正確，但不自然，顯得笨拙。
- Buzz thinks about love in a different way than Kay does.
  （巴斯對愛情的看法與凱對愛情的看法不一樣。）
  →較自然

151 difficulty 困難

1

✗ Ms. King has difficulty to walk.

不能用不定詞 have difficulty to do something

✗ Ms. King has difficulties (in) walking.

作不可數名詞時，意為「困難、艱難」，不可用 difficulties

✓ Ms. King has difficulty (in) walking.

金女士走路有困難。

正確句型為：

(1) have difficulty with something

(2) have difficulty (in) doing something

- Arty completed the test **with difficulty**.（亞提艱難地完成了測驗。）

意指「困難地、費勁地」

文法加油站

difficulty 也可作可數名詞

① difficulty 作可數名詞時，常用作複數，意思是「難事、難題、障礙、（財政）困境、反對、爭論」等。

② in difficulties = in distress, esp. financially （財政困境）

- Louise is also having some **financial difficulties**.
  作「（財政）困境」的意思時，要用複數
  （露易絲也有一些財政方面的困境。）
- Louise has had all kinds of **difficulties** since she married Vince.
  難事、難題、障礙
  （自從露易絲嫁給了文斯，她就遇上了各種各樣的困難。）

152 difficulty/problem 困難／麻煩

1

✗ Liz Wise is a single parent and has a big difficulty with her son's habit of telling lies.

片語 have difficulty/difficulties 中的 difficulty 作不可數或作複數，不與冠詞 a 連用

✓ Liz Wise is a single parent and has a big problem with her son's habit of telling lies.

可以與冠詞 a 連用

單身母親莉茲・懷斯碰到她兒子常撒謊這個大麻煩。

請參見 difficulty。

- Liz Sun is a single parent and has some difficulty in raising her son.（單身母親莉茲・孫撫養她兒子有些艱難。）

153 discourage 勸阻

1

✗ Did Dan discourage Ann to move to Japan?

後面不接不定詞

✓ Did Dan discourage Ann from moving to Japan?

discourage sb. from doing sth.：勸阻、阻擋（某人做某事）

丹勸阻過安不要搬遷到日本嗎？

- Alice was discouraged from going into business.
  （艾麗絲被勸阻不要從商。）
- Dwight discouraged Kate from staying out late at night.
  （杜威特勸告凱特不要夜裡太晚歸。）

文法加油站

encourage somebody to do something
鼓勵某人做某事

- Teddy encouraged Midge to study hard to get ready for college.
  後面要接不定詞
  （泰迪鼓勵米姬努力學習，做好上大學的準備。）

154 discuss 討論

1

✗ Neither Lenore nor Russ wanted to discuss about the war.

及物動詞，後面直接接受詞，不能接 about

✓ Neither Lenore nor Russ wanted to discuss the war.

無論是蕾諾兒還是魯斯都不願意討論那場戰爭。

discuss something (with somebody) （與某人討論某事）

- Gus loves to discuss the weather with Heather.
  （加斯喜歡與海瑟談論天氣。）

A B C D E F G H I J K L M N O P Q R S T U V W X Y Z

文法加油站

名詞 discussion 後面要接 about 或者 on

- Yesterday Fay and I had a discussion about/on ocean pollution.
（昨天菲和我討論了海洋汙染的問題。）

155 disinterested/uninterested
公正的／不感興趣的

1

不常見 Ivy's mom didn't like that movie, because she is disinterested in violent movies.
　　disinterested —— 中立的、公正的、無偏見的（impartial、neutral）

常見 Ivy's mom didn't like that movie, because she is uninterested in violent movies.
　　uninterested —— 不感興趣、厭倦（not interested、bored）

愛葳的媽媽不喜歡那部片子，因為她對暴力片不感興趣。

- Judge Liz Bloom is disinterested (公正的) but not uninterested (不感興趣) in the cases she hears in the courtroom.
（莉茲・布盧姆法官不僅關心，而且公正地處理法庭上所審理的案子。）

文法加油站

uninterested 和 disinterested 的原始及現代含意

	原始意思	現代意思
uninterested	公正的	不感興趣
disinterested	不感興趣的	主要指「公正的」；也可以指「不感興趣的」

156 divorce 離婚

1

✗ Monique divorced last week.

及物動詞，要接受詞「人」

✓ Monique divorced **Mike** last week.

及物動詞，後接受詞 Mike

✓ **Monique and Mike** divorced last week.

主詞涉及了兩個人（複合主詞），divorce 就是不及物動詞

莫妮可上週與麥克離婚了。

✓ **Monique** got divorced last week.

主詞是單數，不是複合主詞，如沒有受詞，要用 get divorced

✓ Monique got a divorce (**from** Mike) last week.

當作名詞

莫妮可上週（與麥克）離婚了。

⑴ 常用片語：end in divorce。

⑵ marry 和 get married 的用法與 divorce 和 get divorced 有點類似。請參見 marry。

157 do (auxiliary verb): missing
（遺落的）助動詞 do

1

✗ How often you visit your Aunt Lulu?

✓ How often do you visit your Aunt Lulu?

現在簡單式，疑問句通常用「助動詞 do/does + 主詞 + 原形動詞」

你多久去探望你的露露姑姑一次？

- When **did** Paul **play** volleyball?（保羅什麼時候打過排球？）

  過去簡單式，疑問句用「助動詞 did + 主詞 + 原形動詞」

- When **can** Paul **play** volleyball?（保羅什麼時候可以打排球？）

  疑問句裡有情態助動詞（can、could、may、should 等），就不要用助動詞 do、does、did 等

158 do (auxiliary verb): redundant
（多餘的）助動詞 do

1

✗ I wonder what did Sue say to Lulu.

間接疑問句中，不需要助動詞 do、does、did 等

✓ I wonder what Sue said to Lulu.

間接疑問句要用直述句的語序：主詞 + 動詞

我納悶，蘇究竟對露露講了些什麼。

直接疑問句：

- What did Sue say to Lulu?（蘇對露露講了些什麼？）

159 doublets/wordiness 疊義詞／累贅詞語

1

累贅 The fact of the matter is that Dad is tired and sad.

簡潔 Dad is tired and sad.

累贅詞語（wordiness），刪除後並不影響句子原意

爸爸疲勞又傷心。

2

疊義詞，口語常見，正式文體請避免

累贅 Each and every one of us knows what killed Clive. Never drink and drive!

簡潔 Every one of us knows what killed Clive. Never drink and drive!

簡潔 All of us know what killed Clive. Never drink and drive!

我們大家都知道克萊夫的死因。千萬不要酒後開車！

(1) each and every 是疊義詞（doublets），即一對類似字的其中一個。疊義詞把同一個意思的字重複說。無論是口語還是書面語，都應該**避免疊義詞或累贅詞語**。

(2) 令人滿意的寫作是簡潔的。如果能用 5 個字就能表達清楚你的意思，那麼就不要用 10 個字。不要使用對句子的意思沒有任何補充的多餘字或片語。

(3) 參見 continue/continue on、raise/raise up 以及 unique。

3

累贅詞語，可用單字代替　多餘，可刪

累贅　In this day and age, there are many students who are attending Hobbs High School and also have part-time jobs.

多餘，可刪

用單字代替 in this day and age

簡潔　Today many students at Hobbs High School have part-time jobs.

用 at 代替 who are attending

用單字代替 in this day and age

簡潔　Nowadays many students at Hobbs High School have part-time jobs.

用 at 代替 who are attending

如今霍布斯高中的許多學生都有兼職工作。

4

累贅詞語。尤其在書面語中，應避免使用

累贅　In my personal opinion, Ann often blames other people for her own problems and is spending really

多餘，可刪

too much of her time playing computer games.

統一用現在簡單式更協調

簡潔　Ann often blames other people for her problems and spends too much time playing computer games.

統一用現在簡單式更協調

安常把自己的問題怪罪他人，並把太多的時間用來玩電腦遊戲。

文法加油站

避免用疊義詞或多餘的修飾詞，請用必要的修飾詞

✗	✓
actual truth	truth
added bonus	bonus
advance warning	warning
advance planning	planning

✗	✓
6 a.m. in the morning	6 a.m.; six in the morning
and etc.	etc.
and plus	and; plus
anything and everything	anything; everything
at that point in time	then
at the present time	at present; now; at this time
basic fundamentals	fundamentals
because why	because; why
big in size	big
blue in color	blue
circulate around	circulate
collaborate together	collaborate
consensus of opinion	consensus
continue on	continue
each and every	each; every
end result	end; result
enter into	enter
exactly the same	the same
exactly identical	identical
famous celebrity	celebrity
first and foremost	first; foremost
free gift	gift
fundamental basis	basis
honest truth	truth
important essentials	essentials
in spite of the fact that	though; although
in the month of May	in May
in the year 2052	in 2052
in this day and age	today; nowadays
joint cooperation	cooperation

✗	✓
leave from	leave
long in length	long
lower down	lower
mix together	mix
more better	better
most ideal	ideal
most perfect	perfect
new innovation	innovation
off from/off of	off
one of the only . . . *	one of the few
over-exaggerated	exaggerated
owing to the fact that	since; because
repeat again	repeat
return back	return
round in shape	round
rules and regulations	rules; regulations
share in common	share
share together	share
the reason is because . . .	because; the reason is that . . .
there is no doubt but that	no doubt
two in number	two
unexpected surprise	surprise
very unique	unique
more/most unique	unique
wealthy millionaire	millionaire
west in direction	west
widow woman	widow

*the only 本來就意味著唯一的一個，不能與 one 同用。如果你說 one of the only，就好像是在說 one of the one。

160 doubling the final consonant

雙寫字尾子音

1

✗ Rose smiled, and her sunglasses sliped all the way down her nose.

✓ Rose smiled, and her sunglasses slipped all the way down her nose.

蘿絲微笑了，她的太陽眼鏡一直滑落到鼻子下面。

雙寫字尾子音。原因：
1) 單一的子音結尾（p）
2) 結尾子音 p 前面只有一個母音（i）
3) 只有一個音節

(1) 如果下面三種情況都存在，要先**雙寫字的結尾子音**，然後再給這個字加一個以母音開始的字尾（比如：-ing、-ed、-er 等）：

- 以單個子音結尾的字
- 結尾的子音前面只有一個母音
- 重音在最後一個音節上（或者這個字只有一個音節）

① **begin**

以一個單一的子音結尾（n）
結尾子音 n 前面只有一個母音（i）
這個字有兩個音節，重音在最後一個音節上 [bɪˋgɪn]

- 因此，要雙寫結尾子音（n），再加 -ing、-er 變成 **beginning**、**beginner**。

② **quit**

以一個單一的子音結尾（t）
結尾子音 t 前面只有一個母音（i）
這個字只有一個音節

- 因此，要雙寫結尾子音（t），再加 -ing、-er 變成 **quitting**、**quitter**。
注意：qu 被看作是一個子音（指發音），因為 q 總是與 u 連在一起。因此，quit 結尾子音 t 前面只有一個母音（i）。

③ **cook**

- 以一個單一的子音結尾（k）
- 但是結尾子音 k 前面有兩個母音（oo）
- 因此，不需要雙寫結尾子音（k），直接加 -ing、-ed、-er 變成 **cooking**、**cooked**、**cooker**。

④ **kick**

- 不是以一個子音結尾，而是以兩個子音 ck 結尾
- 因此，不需要雙寫結尾子音（k），直接加 -ing、-ed、-er 變成 **kicking**、**kicked**、**kicker**。

⑤ **motor**

- 以一個單一的子音結尾（r）
- 結尾子音 r 前面只有一個母音（o）
- 這個字有兩個音節，不過重音沒有在最後一個音節上，而是在第一個音節上 [ˋmotɚ]
- 因此，不需要雙寫結尾子音（r），直接加 -ing、-ed 變成 **motoring**、**motored**。

(2) 注意：以 l 結尾的字，即使重音落在最後一個音節上，可以雙寫 ll，也可以不雙寫。英式雙寫，美式不雙寫。

	英式	美式
travel	traveller	traveler
label	labelled	labeled

161 doubt 懷疑

1

✗ Lulu did not doubt whether the story was true.

✓ Lulu did not doubt that the story was true.

= Lulu was certain that the story was true.

露露肯定那個故事是真實的。

1) **否定句中**，doubt 後面總是接 **that** 引導的子句，表示「肯定」（sure、certain）
2) 當子句的內容是肯定的，通常 doubt 後面要接 that

(1) 在**否定句**中，doubt 後面總是接 that 引導的子句，表示「肯定、確定」（sure、certain）。

· I never doubted for a minute that hardworking Ted would move ahead.

= I **was** always **certain that** hardworking Ted would move ahead.

（我一直都堅信勤奮的泰德一定會有成就。）

(2) 在**肯定句**中，doubt 究竟是接 whether 還是 that，要看意思而定。當暗示主詞「**不信、懷疑**」（disbelief）時，後面接 that；當表示主詞「**不確定**」（uncertainty）時，後面通常接 whether（非正式語中也可以用 if）。

· I doubt that Mary wants to marry Harry.

表示「不相信」，用 that

= I **don't think that** Mary wants to marry Harry.

（我**不信**瑪麗想嫁給哈利。）

· I doubt whether Fay and Kay can go fishing with us on Saturday.

表示「不肯定」，用 whether，非正式語中可以用 if

= I **am not sure whether** Fay and Kay can go fishing with us on Saturday.

（我**不能肯定**菲和凱星期六**是否**能與我們一起去釣魚。）

(3) 比較下面的句子：

· I doubt that Clive will arrive at five.

= I **don't think that** Clive will arrive at five.

（我不相信克萊夫會在五點到達。）

· I doubt whether Clive will arrive at five.

= I **am uncertain whether** Clive will arrive at five.

（我不能肯定克萊夫是否會在五點到達。）

· Sue doubted that the story was true.

= Sue **did not believe that** the story was true.

（蘇不相信這個故事是真實的。）

・Andrew doubted whether the story was true.
= Andrew **was uncertain whether** the story was true.
（安德魯不確定這個故事是否真實。）

⑷ doubtful 的用法與 doubt 的用法一樣。

・I am not doubtful that Clive is still alive.
否定句中，doubtful 後面總是用 that，表示「肯定」（sure、certain）
= I **am sure that** Clive is still alive.
（我堅信克萊夫還健在。）

・I am doubtful whether Clive is still alive.
肯定句中，doubtful 後面用 whether，表示「不確定」（uncertain）
= I **am not sure** Clive is still alive.
（我不確定克萊夫是否還健在。）

・I am doubtful that Clive is still alive.
在肯定句中，doubtful 後面用 that，表示「不信、懷疑」（disbelief）
= I **don't think** Clive is still alive.
（我懷疑克萊夫還健在。／我認為克萊夫已經不健在了。）

162 downtown 市區

1

✗ Ms. Brown lives in an apartment in downtown.
副詞 downtown 本來就包含了 in 或 to（在、往）的意思，前面不能有介系詞 in 或 to

✓ Ms. Brown lives in an apartment downtown.
當副詞，表示「在商業區、往商業區」

布朗女士住在市區的一間公寓裡。

・Lenore often goes to a **downtown** bookstore.
（蕾諾兒常去市區的一家書店。）形容詞，表示「商業區的、市區的」

163 drink/eat/take 喝／吃／服（藥）、放

1

❌ Jane's mom likes to take beans.

✅ Jane's mom likes to eat beans.

珍的媽媽喜歡吃豆子。 「吃食品」要用 eat

2

❌ Dee eats sugar in her tea.

✅ Dee takes sugar in her tea.

蒂喝茶要放糖。 「加到食品或飲料的東西」要用 take

- Dee just drank her morning tea.（蒂剛喝了早茶。）
  「喝水、茶、牛奶、飲料」用 drink
- Jane has started taking vitamin D for her leg pain.
  （因腿疼，珍開始服用維生素 D。） 「服藥、服營養品」要用 take，這個句子不用 eating vitamin
- Lee doesn't take milk or sugar in his coffee.
  「加到食品或飲料的東西」要用 take
  （李喝咖啡不放牛奶，也不放糖。）

164 drunk/drunken 喝醉的

1

❌ Audrey was not drunken, just tired and angry.

✅ Audrey was not drunk, just tired and angry.

奧黛莉沒有喝醉，只是又疲倦又生氣。 連綴動詞（be、get、become、seem 等）後面只能用 drunk

2

美式 After Trish woke up in jail, she told herself, "My drunk driving/drunk-driving is foolish."

英式 美式 After Trish woke up in jail, she told herself, "My drunken driving is foolish."

英式 美式 After Trish woke up in jail, she told herself, "Driving while I'm drunk is foolish."

翠西從牢房裡醒過來後對自己說：「我酒後開車是非常愚蠢的。」

⑴ **連綴動詞**後面只能用 drunk 作補語，不用 drunken。

⑵ drunk 和 drunken 都可以置於名詞前用來修飾「人」，比如：

- a drunk/drunken driver （喝醉酒的駕駛員）
- a drunk/drunken sailor （喝醉的水手）

⑶ 如果修飾的名詞不是指「人」，通常要用 drunken 來修飾，表示「酒醉引起的」，比如：

- a drunken sleep （酒醉後睡著）
- a drunken fight （酒醉引起的打架）

⑷ 名詞 driving 不是指「人」，前面應該用 drunken。但美式英語卻常用 drunk driving/drunk-driving。這是美式的特殊用法。

· Marge was arrested on a drunk-driving charge.

= Marge was arrested on a drunken-driving charge.

（瑪姬因被指控酒後開車而被捕。）

165 due to/owing to 由於

1

在非正式語中，有些人把 due to 放在句首，但在考試等正式用語中，最好不要放句首

非正式 Due to global warming, the Hubble Ski Resort is in deep financial trouble.

口語 The Hubble Ski Resort is in deep financial trouble due to global warming.

口語中當複合介系詞，相當於 owing to、because of，因此可以放在句尾

正式 Owing to global warming, the Hubble Ski Resort is in deep financial trouble.

正式 As a result of global warming, the Hubble Ski Resort is in deep financial trouble.

正式 Because of global warming, the Hubble Ski Resort is in deep financial trouble.

由於全球氣溫上升，哈伯滑雪休閒度假村深陷財務困境。

(1) 在正式用語中，**due to** 片語（如：due to hard work）當作補語，放在連綴動詞 be 或 seem 等後面，意思是 caused by、resulting from。

= resulting from（起因於）

- Kirk knows that success in life is due to hard work.
  （柯克明白，生活中的成功是由於辛勤工作。）

= caused by（由……而造成）

- Paul knew the difference in his behavior was due to alcohol.
  （保羅明白，他的舉止改變都是因為酒精而造成的。）

(2) 可用 owing to、because of、as a result of、on account of 等表示「由於；因為」。這些複合介系詞在句中的位置比較靈活，放在句尾或句首都可以。

- "Owing to/As a result of/Because of the mistakes made by the new accountant, some of us received incorrect checks," Sue explained to Gus.
  （蘇對加斯解釋：「由於新會計犯的錯誤，我們一些人收到了錯誤的支票。」）
- Norm told me that our school would be closed owing to/as a result of/because of this dust storm.
  （諾姆告訴我，我們學校因沙塵暴要停課。）

(3) **due to the fact that**：有些人也喜歡用片語 due to the fact that，可是這個片語很笨拙、冗長，在正式書面語中，請用 because。請參見 doublets/wordiness。

166 during/for 在……期間／持續

1

✗ Monique's mom will be on vacation in Hawaii during three weeks.
表示「在什麼時間內發生了什麼事」

✓ Monique's mom will be on vacation in Hawaii for three weeks.
表示「這件事持續了多長時間」

莫妮可的媽媽要在夏威夷度假三個禮拜。

(1) during 表示「在什麼時間內發生了什麼事」。

「Kate 在波士頓」發生在「2008 年的春天」

・Kate was in Boston during the spring of 2008.
（2008 年的春天，凱特在波士頓。）

(2) for 表示「這件事持續了多長時間」。

「住在我家」持續了「一個月」，表達how long

・Tyr stayed with me for a month last year.
（去年提爾在我家住了一個月。）

167 during/since 在……期間／自……以來

1

✖ Tyr's hometown has changed a lot since the last 30 years.

是一段時間，不是具體的過去時間點，不能用 since，而要用表示一段時間的 during

✔ Tyr's hometown has changed a lot during the last 30 years.

指某事發生在某一段時間

近三十年來提爾的家鄉發生了很大的變化。

(1) 指某事發生在某一段時間，用 during，意思是「在……的整個期間」；「在……的某個時候」。

指在暴風雪的某個時候

・Norm was born during a big snowstorm.
（諾姆在一場暴風雪中出生。）

(2) since 的意思是「自……以來；從……至今」；通常 since 後面接一個具體的**過去時間**、特定的**過去日期**（yesterday、last month、July、2009）或接一個具體的**過去事件**（moved out in May、graduated from high school in 2016）。

since 後面接一個具體的過去時間，句子用完成式

・I haven't emailed Tyr since last year.
（自去年以來我就沒有寄過電子信件給提爾。）

since 引導的子句用過去式，主要子句要用完成式，表示從過去某個時刻開始然後持續到現在

・Scot has not seen Kay since she moved out in May.
（自從五月凱搬出去後，史考特就再也沒有看過她了。）

文法加油站

since 也有「因為；由於」的意思

since 也可以用來解釋某人做某事的原因，或者一種形勢存在之原因，意為「既然；因為；由於」。在這種情況下，since 子句中的動詞就可以用現在式。

- You should talk to Ivy since she is the director of this movie.
（既然艾薇是這部影片的導演，你就應該去找她談談。）

movie director

E

168 each 每個

1

❌ Each new days are a wonderful chance to work and play.

✅ Each new day is a wonderful chance to work and play.

each 後面接單數名詞和單數動詞

每一個新的一天，都是工作和玩耍的一個好機會。

(1) each + 單數名詞 + 單數動詞

each of + 複數名詞／複數代名詞 { + 單數動詞（ + 單數代名詞）正式 ／ + 複數動詞（ + 複數代名詞）非正式 }

each of 接複數名詞 girls，動詞要用單數

- **Each of** the **girls has** an apple and a peach.
  （這群女孩中各個都有一個蘋果和一個桃子。）

→ 在非正式用語中，可用複數動詞 have。不過，在考試中最好遵守文法規則。

(2) 複數主詞 + each + 複數動詞（ + 複數代名詞）：當 each 出現在所指的複數主詞後面時，動詞應該用複數，人稱代名詞也應該是複數。

- **Gary, Jerry, and Larry each have their** own opinion about Mary.

  each 用在複數主詞 Gary, Jerry, and Larry 後面，用複數動詞 have 和複數代名詞 their

  （蓋瑞、傑瑞和賴瑞對瑪莉都有各自的看法。）

169 each/none 每個／無一個

1

不與否定動詞（not play、never play）連用

✗ Each of the guys could not play soccer as well as Kay Sun.

✓ None of the guys could play soccer as well as Kay Sun.

表示否定，要用 none + 肯定動詞

那群小夥子中，沒有一個人踢足球能踢得比凱．孫好。

· None of the women wanted a hotdog on a bun.
（那群女子中，沒有一個願意在麵包上面放一根熱狗。）

170 each other/one another 互相、彼此

1

✗ Ever since the quarrel, Sue and her mother have stopped talking to one another.

✓ Ever since the quarrel, Sue and her mother have stopped talking to each other.

Sue、her mother 兩個人，用 each other

自從那次爭吵後，蘇和她的母親彼此就不說話了。

2

口語 Mom, her younger brother, and her three older sisters often help each other.

口語中可指「兩個」或「三個或三個以上」。正式書面語中最好遵守文法規則

正式 Mom, her younger brother, and her three older sisters often help one another.

只指三個或三個以上的人或事。即使在口語中，也不能用來指兩個人或兩件事

媽媽、她的弟弟和三個姐姐常互相幫助。

each other 指兩個人或兩件事；one another 指三個或三個以上的人或事。

171 earth

請參見 capitalization。

172 economic/economical
經濟上的／省錢的、節儉的

1

✗ India's rate of economical growth is great.

用於談論「某個東西比較便宜，某人比較節儉」，與句意不符

✓ India's rate of economic growth is great.

用於談論「一個國家或地區的經濟」

印度的經濟成長率非常理想。

(1) 當談論「一個國家或地區的經濟」時，用 economic。economic 通常放在名詞前修飾名詞。

- economic system（經濟制度）
- economic reasons（經濟上的原因）
- Britain's wind farm companies are helped out by the government's economic policies.
  （英國的風力發電廠公司得到了英國政府的經濟政策支持。）

(2) 當談論「某個東西比較便宜，某人比較節儉」時，用 economical（= thrifty）。economical 可用來放在名詞前修飾名詞，也可以放在連綴動詞後面作補語。

- an economical husband（一位節儉的丈夫）
- an economical meal （節儉的一餐）
- a modern and economical heating system
  （一種現代化、經濟的暖氣系統）
- 用在連綴動詞後作補語
  Omar says his new electric car is more economical than his old car.（歐馬說，他的新電動車比他的舊車省錢。）

(3) 請參見 historical/historic。

173 -ed form/-ing form

請參見 excited/exciting, interested/interesting。

174 efficient/effective 效率高的／有效的

1

✗ The medicine Olive took was immediately efficient.

指「效率高的，有能力的」，與句意不符

✓ The medicine Olive took was immediately effective.

奧莉芙服的藥立刻產生了效果。 指「有效果的」

(1) effective（= having the expected effect; successful），指「有效果的」：某人或某事如果 effective，那麼這人或事就起了作用，產生預期的效果。

- effective teaching methods（有效的教學方法）
- effective measures（有效措施）
- She says a daily swim is an effective way to stay healthy.（她說，每天游泳是保持健康的有效方法。）

(2) efficient（giving a relatively high output of work; capable），指「效率高的，有能力的」：某人或某事如果 efficient，那麼這人或事就最有效地利用了時間、金錢、物品等，產生出好效果。

- an efficient secretary（效率高的祕書／有能力的祕書）
- highly efficient（效率很高）
- Kirk is organized and efficient at work.（柯克工作有條理、有效率。）

175 effort 努力、力圖

1

✗ To become an expert in English takes a lot of efforts.

✓ To become an expert in English takes a lot of effort.

要想精通英語需要辛勤的努力。 指「努力」時，是不可數名詞，沒有複數形式

effort 作可數 vs. 不可數名詞

可數	不可數
(1) 指「力圖」（an attempt to do something; a hard try） (2) 指「努力的成果」（a product or result of working or trying）	指「努力」（hard work）
可用複數 efforts	沒有複數形式
可加不定冠詞 an effort	不能用冠詞 an/a 來修飾
範例： · Kate made a successful effort to lose weight. （凱特努力使體重減少了。） └ 可數名詞，意指 a hard try · "That huge grammar book is Ann's finest effort," declared Bert. └ 可數名詞，意指 an achievement （柏特宣布說：「那本厚厚的文法書是安的最佳作品。」）	**範例：** · a job requiring time and effort （需要花時間和精力的工作） · put a lot of effort into (doing) something （為了某事付出了許多辛勤的努力）

176 either 也；任一的、每一的

A) either 副 也

1

✗ Sue said, "Lorelei doesn't like to fly."
—— "I don't too," replied Eli.

✗ Sue said, "Lorelei doesn't like to fly."
—— "I also don't," replied Eli.

否定句中不能用 too 和 also

✓ Sue said, "Lorelei doesn't like to fly."
—— "I don't either," replied Eli.

✓ Sue said, "Lorelei doesn't like to fly."
—— "Neither do I," replied Eli.

作副詞時，意為「也」。**否定句**中，用 either，不用 too 和 also

蘇說：「蘿芮萊不喜歡搭飛機。」——伊萊回答說：「我也不喜歡。」

2 ❌ "Clive loves to drive." —— "I do either."

✅ "Clive loves to drive." —— "I do too."

「克萊夫喜歡開車。」——「我也喜歡。」

肯定句中，用 too 或 also，不能用 either

請參見 also/too/either。

B) either 形（兩者之中）任一的、每一的

1 ❌ "Last night I dreamed about having some lovely angels on either sides of me," said Dwight.

✅ "Last night I dreamed about having some lovely angels on either side of me," said Dwight.

當形容詞時，意為「（兩者中）任一方的」，接**單數名詞**

✅ "Last night I dreamed about having some lovely angels on both sides of me," said Dwight.

當形容詞時，意為「兩者的」，接**複數名詞**

杜威特說：「昨晚我夢見在我的左右兩邊都有幾位可愛的天使。」

(1) either 是形容詞時，意為「（兩者中）任一的、每一方的」，後面應接單數名詞，比如：either side of the street、using either hand。either 引導的主詞，其後要接單數動詞（**either + 單數名詞 + 單數動詞**）。

(2) both 當形容詞時，意為「兩者的、雙方的」，其後接複數名詞。both 引導的主詞，其後要接複數動詞（**both + 複數名詞 + 複數動詞**）。

C) either 代（兩者之中）任何一個

1 非正式 Were either of these apple pies OK with Mr. Wise?

正式 Was either of these apple pies OK with Mr. Wise?

either 後接「of + 複數名詞」時，傳統文法需用**單數動詞**

這兩個蘋果派任何一個懷斯先生都覺得不錯嗎？

正式 Were both of these apple pies OK with Mr. Wise?

這兩個蘋果派懷斯先生都覺得不錯嗎？

當代名詞 either 後面接有「of + 複數名詞／複數代名詞」的結構，傳統文法要求用單數動詞，但現在也有用複數動詞的傾向。不過，在正式用語、考試、商務英語中，請遵守傳統文法：**either of + 複數名詞／複數代名詞 + 單數動詞**。

177 either . . . or . . .

是……或是……（兩者之間選擇其一）

A) either . . . or . . . 要用平行結構

1

非平行結構：either + 動詞片語；or + 名詞

✖ Coco **either would like to live in Mexico or Morocco.**

✔ Coco would like to live in either **Mexico** or **Morocco.**

名詞　名詞

介系詞片語

✔ Coco would like to live either **in Mexico** or **(in) Morocco.**

成對連接詞 either 和 or 後面的成分應保持對稱的結構

可可想在墨西哥或者摩洛哥居住。

(1) 成對連接詞 either 和 or 後面的成分應保持對稱的結構，即主詞配主詞，名詞配名詞，動詞配動詞，介系詞片語配介系詞片語，副詞配副詞，獨立子句配獨立子句等。如果 either 和 or 後面的成分不一致，就需要把 either 的位置挪動一下，放到正確的位置上。

- Coco is going to drive to Chicago **either today or tomorrow**.

  either + 副詞（today）；or + 副詞（tomorrow）

  （不是今天就是明天，可可會開車去芝加哥。）

- To make Mark happy, **either I'll read a book to him or I'll take him to Lake Park**.

  either + 獨立子句（I'll read a book to him）；
  or + 獨立子句（I'll take him to Lake Park）

  （為了使馬克高興，我會唸書給他聽，或是帶他去湖公園。）

(2) 其他類似的對稱結構還有：

- between . . . and . . .（在……兩者之間）

- both . . . and . . .（兩者都⋯⋯）
- neither . . . nor . . .（兩者都不⋯⋯）
- not only . . . but also . . .（不僅⋯⋯而且⋯⋯）
- not because . . . but because（不是因為⋯⋯而是因為⋯⋯）

(3) 請參見以下各條：「both . . . and . . .」、「neither . . . nor . . .」、「not only . . . but also . . .」和「parallel structure」。

B) either . . . or . . .，要接單數動詞還是複數動詞？

1

✗ Either May or June are usually a good time to visit Norway.

✓ Either May or June is usually a good time to visit Norway.

either . . . or . . . 的結構裡如兩個主詞都是單數（May、June），動詞要用單數

五月或六月都是去挪威玩的好時機。

(1) 同樣道理，當「either . . . or . . .」結構裡的兩個主詞都是複數，動詞也要用複數。

兩個複數主詞 your parents、Paul's parents，動詞用複數

- **Have either your parents or Paul's parents** ever visited Crystal Falls?
  （你的父母還是保羅的父母去參觀過水晶瀑布城嗎？）

(2) 比較下面兩個例句：

用 both 強調「兩者都」

- **Have both** Lorelei **and** Eli visited you in Sydney?

用 both . . . and . . . 連接的複合主詞（Lorelei and Eli），動詞用複數

≒ **Have** Lorelei **and** Eli visited you in Sydney?
（蘿芮萊和伊萊都去雪梨看過你嗎？）

用 either 強調「兩者中任一」

- **Has either** Lorelei **or** Eli visited you in Sydney?

用 either . . . or . . . 連接兩個單數主詞（Lorelei or Eli），雖是複合主詞，但表示「兩者之間任何一個」，動詞要用單數

≒ **Has** Lorelei **or** Eli visited you in Sydney?
（蘿芮萊還是伊萊去雪梨看過你嗎？）

2

❌ Either Lars or his assistants has that information about Mars.

or 後面是複數名詞（assistants），動詞要用複數形式，不用單數形式

✅ Either Lars has or his assistants have that information about Mars.

重複動詞，一個用單數動詞，另一個用複數動詞（**較累贅**）

✅ Either Lars or his assistants have that information about Mars.

複數主詞放在 or 的後面，靠近動詞，動詞自然就用複數（**最佳**）

不是拉斯，就是他的助手們，手上有關於火星的那條資訊。

✅ Either his assistants or Lars has that information about Mars.

單數主詞放在 or 的後面，靠近動詞，動詞要用單數

不是拉斯的助手們，就是拉斯，手上有關於火星的那條資訊。

(1) 在 either . . . or . . . 結構裡，如果其中一個主詞是單數，而另一個是複數，**動詞應與靠最近的主詞一致**，即動詞單複數形取決於第二個主詞的單複數。

(2) 最佳辦法是把複數主詞放在 or 的後面，靠近動詞，動詞自然就用複數。比如上面的第 3 句（or his assistants have）。

(3) 請參見 neither . . . nor . . .。

文法加油站

either 的結構用法

① 注意 either 的以下四個結構：

- either + 單數動詞
- either + 單數名詞 + 單數動詞
- either + 名詞（可以是複數，也可以是單數）+ or + 單數名詞 + 單數動詞
- either + 名詞（可以是複數，也可以是單數）+ or + 複數名詞 + 複數動詞

② 類似 either . . . or . . . 的結構還有：

- both . . . and . . .（兩個都……）
- neither . . . nor . . .（既不……也不）
- not only . . . but also . . .（不僅……而且）

178 electric/electrical

請參見 historical/historic。

179 elder/older 年齡較大的

1

✗ Amy is three years elder than me.

elder 或 eldest 只能用在它所描述的名詞前面，不能置於連綴動詞 be 後面與 than 用在一起

✓ Amy is three years older than me.

艾咪比我大三歲。

older 和 oldest 可以用在連綴動詞 be 後面與 than 連用

2

oldest 或 older 也可以用在名詞前作修飾語

美式 Is Emily the oldest child in her family?

英式 Is Emily the eldest child in her family?

eldest 或 elder 只能用在名詞前面作修飾語

愛蜜莉是家中最大的孩子嗎？

比較人的年齡

美式 用 older 和 oldest（older brother/oldest brother）

英式 用 elder 和 eldest（elder brother/eldest brother）

180 elevator/lift 電梯

1

美式 Ms. Swift exclaimed, "There is an alligator in the elevator!" —— 美式「電梯」說法

英式 Ms. Swift exclaimed, "There is an alligator in the lift!" —— 英式「電梯」說法

斯威夫特女士驚叫：「電梯裡有一條鱷魚。」

也可以當動詞用，意為「舉起、升起、抬起」

- Paul **lifted** Sue up to the top of the wall.
 （保羅把蘇舉起到牆頭上。）

A B C D E F G H I J K L M N O P Q R S T U V W X Y Z

181 emigrate/immigrate 移居出境／移居入境

1

❌ Sue immigrated from Britain to the U. S. in 2016.
　　搬進並定居一個新國家或地區

✅ Sue emigrated from Britain to the U. S. in 2016.
　　離開你的國家或地區到別的地方去定居

蘇在 2016 年從英國移居到美國。

　　從一個國家移出

- Lars emigrated from Britain in 2015, and after spending five months in India, he immigrated to Australia.

　　移進另一個國家

（2015 年拉斯移民離開了英國，在印度生活了 5 個月後，他移民到了澳洲。）

文法加油站

emigrant 和 immigrant

① emigrant 和 immigrant 意思雖然都是「移民」，但它們之間是有區別的。兩者 的區別與 emigrate 和 immigrate 之間的區別是一樣的。

② emigrant（移居他國的移民），是指那些離開自己的國家而前往另一個國家定居的移民，而在他們的新國家，他們就被稱呼為 immigrant（外來移民），即 immigrant 是一個從別的國家移居進一個新國家的移民。

③

emigrant	immigrant
去（going）／出去（exiting）	來（coming）／進入（entering）

emigration 和 immigration

名詞 emigration（移民出境；〔總稱〕移民）和 immigration（移居入境；〔總稱〕外來移民）的區別也是一樣的。

集合名詞，總稱「外來的移民」

- The large Irish immigration into America included many people who couldn't read English.
  （大量移居美國的愛爾蘭移民中有許多人看不懂英文。）

移民出境

- Last year's wave of emigration out of Italy included Lily and her family.
  （去年移民高峰時期，莉莉和她一家也離開了義大利。）

182 emphasis/emphasize 強調

1

及物動詞 emphasize 後面不接 on

✗ Dr. Sun emphasizes on that you learn vocabulary by reading extensively for fun.

及物動詞 emphasize 後面可接 that 子句

✓ Dr. Sun emphasizes that you learn vocabulary by reading extensively for fun.

孫博士強調靠大量趣味閱讀來掌握辭彙。

及物動詞 emphasize 後面可接名詞

✓ Dr. Sun emphasizes the importance of extensive reading for fun.

名詞 emphasis 後面要用 on

✓ Dr. Sun puts emphasis on the importance of extensive reading for fun.

孫博士強調大量趣味閱讀的重要性。

emphasis n./emphasize vt.（強調）。句型為：

- emphasize + 名詞
- emphasize + that 子句
- put emphasis on + 名詞

183 encourage 請參見 discourage。

184 end/end up 結束／以……告終

1

❌ If Gail continues to steal, she will **end** in jail.

✅ If Gail continues to steal, she will **end up** in jail.

片語動詞「以……告終」，指「做了某事後或因做了某事，而陷入了某地方或某狀態」

如果蓋兒繼續偷竊，她最終會進牢房。

2

❌ Tyr's marriage to Midge **ended up** after only two years.

✅ Tyr's marriage to Midge **ended** after only two years.

動詞「終結、了結」，指「到達一個終點」

提爾和米姬的婚姻只持續了兩年就結束了。

185 enjoy 使過得快活；欣賞

1

❌ Sue seems to **enjoy at** everything she tries to do.

及物動詞，後面一定要有受詞

✅ Sue seems to **enjoy herself** at everything she tries to do.

enjoy oneself 表示「嬉笑、玩得痛快」

蘇無論嘗試做什麼事，好像都會從中得到樂趣。

(1) **enjoy something** （欣賞、喜歡）

- **enjoyed** Chinese food（喜歡中國菜）
- **enjoy** good health（享有健康）
- Our room at the Peach Hotel **enjoys a lovely view** of Clearwater Beach.
  （從我們的「桃子飯店」房間望出去，可以觀賞清水海灘美麗的景象。）

(2) **enjoy oneself** （嬉笑、玩得痛快）

- The elf gave us a welcoming smile and said, "Relax and **enjoy yourself**."
  （小精靈微笑著歡迎我們，並且說：「放鬆吧，盡情地玩。」）

186 enjoy doing 喜歡做……

1

✗ Roy didn't enjoy to travel with that goat in his boat.

只能接 V-ing 或名詞

✓ Roy didn't enjoy traveling with that goat in his boat.

和船上的那頭山羊一起旅遊，羅伊玩得不開心。

enjoy 後面不能接 to 不定詞，應該接動詞 -ing 形式或名詞；我們通常說 enjoy doing something 或者 enjoy something。

187 enough 足夠的、足夠地、足夠

A) enough 形 副 代

1

✗ Mandy has enough of pizza for Candy, Andy, and Randy.

enough 後面的字如果是名詞（如 pizza），要用「enough + 名詞」結構，不加 of

✓ Mandy has enough pizza for Candy, Andy, and Randy.

作**形容詞**時，直接放在名詞前

曼蒂有足夠的披薩讓坎蒂、安迪、蘭迪吃。

- enough food （足夠的食物）
- enough water（足夠的水）

2

✗ Is Liz enough wise to figure out that Roy Huff is a playboy?

✓ Is Liz wise enough to figure out that Roy Huff is a playboy?

作**副詞**的 enough 應該放在副詞或形容詞後面

莉茲是否夠聰明，能看出羅伊 · 赫夫是一個花花公子呢？

enough 放在副詞後面

- carefully enough （夠小心）
- fast enough （夠快）
- well enough （夠好）

enough 放在形容詞後面

- good enough （夠好）
- foolish enough （夠愚蠢）
- serious enough （夠嚴重）

3

❌ Mr. Wise has had enough Lorelei's lies.

名詞前有限定詞 Lorelei's，enough 後面要接 of，此時 enough 是**代名詞**

✅ Mr. Wise has had enough of Lorelei's lies.

懷斯先生已經聽夠了蘿芮萊的謊言。

形容詞 enough	代名詞 enough，後面要接 of
直接放在名詞前面（enough lies、enough money）	名詞前面有一個限定詞，如 Lorelei's、the、this、that、my、his

注意： enough of 後面必須接一個「限定詞 + 名詞」。如果沒有限定詞，就不能用 enough of。enough of 後面也可以接代名詞 her、it、them 等，比如：enough of it、enough of her。

B) enough（代名詞作補語或形容詞作修飾語）

1

主詞是名詞，enough 不能作 be 動詞的補語

❌ The time wasn't enough for Claire to cut my hair.

改變句子結構，使用 there wasn't 的句型，enough 後面接名詞

✅ There wasn't enough time for Claire to cut my hair.

克蕾兒沒有足夠的時間幫我剪頭髮。

(1) 只有當主詞是代名詞（that、this、it 等）時，enough 才可以放在連綴動詞 be 後面作補語。

主詞是代名詞 that；enough 在連綴動詞 be 後作補語

- That's enough, Mr. Huff. Thank you.
（夠了，赫夫先生。謝謝你。）

(2) 當主詞是名詞（如 beer、money、time、bread 等）時，enough 就不能作 be 動詞的補語了。我們得改變句子結構，比如上面範例，使用 there wasn't 的句型，然後把 enough 當修飾語使用，後面接一個名詞。

- "There is enough food for everyone," said Claire.

❌ The food is enough for everyone.

（克蕾兒宣布：「有足夠的食物夠大家吃。」）

188 enter/enter into 進入、參與／簽訂、參與

1

✗ Bret waved goodbye and then entered into his jet.

進入「房間、建築物、飛機」等，要用 enter

✓ Bret waved goodbye and then entered his jet.

= enter

= Bret waved goodbye and then went into his jet.

布瑞特揮手告別，然後進入他的噴射機。

(1) 進入「房間、建築物、飛機」等，要用 enter（= go into）。

- enter a building（進入一棟大樓）

(2) enter 作及物動詞時，意思為「進入、參加、開始從事、登錄」。

- enter the space age（進入太空時代）
- enter the software market（進入軟體市場）
- enter a competition（參與一場競賽）

(3) 片語動詞 enter into something 指「參與一次官方討論或其他正式的活動；簽訂正式協定或合約」。

- enter into a dialog with the governor（與州長交換意見）
- enter into negotiations（開始談判）
- enter into/enter politics（從政）
- Sue Wu is going to enter into a five-year contract with that company in Bangkok.
（蘇・吳打算與曼谷的那家公司簽訂一份五年的合約。）

189 enter/join 參與／加入

1

✗ Ann West joined last week's reading contest.

加入政黨、團體、俱樂部才用 join

✓ Ann West entered last week's reading contest.

參與競賽（a contest、a competition）要用 enter（= take part in）

= Ann West took part in last week's reading contest.

安・韋斯特參加了上週的閱讀比賽。

加入政黨、團體、俱樂部（a political party、an organization、a club）等用 join

· Ms. Tubb, we hope you'll **join** our reading club.

（塔布女士，希望你加入我們的閱讀俱樂部。）

190 entitle/title 給……權力／給……題名

1

❌ Who titled Sue Pound to boss us around?

給……稱號、給……題名，不用來表示「給……權力」

✅ Who entitled Sue Pound to boss us around?

賦予某人權力或資格去擁有某物或做某事

是誰賦予了蘇・龐德權力，讓她對我們發號施令？

· Dwight **entitled** his new picture "Moonlight."

要表示「給……稱號、給……題名」，可以用 title，也可以用 entitle

= Dwight **titled** his new picture "Moonlight."

（杜威特給他的新畫取名為「月光」。）

191 envelope/envelop 信封／裹住

1

❌ Did Hope address the envelop and bring her telescope?

沒有結尾 -e，表**動詞**，意思是「**裹住、環繞**」

✅ Did Hope address the envelope and bring her telescope?

有結尾 -e，表**名詞**，意思是「**信封**」

荷普在信封上寫好了收件人姓名和地址，並帶來了她的望遠鏡嗎？

名詞，指信封

· The envelope contained a letter filled with words of hope.

（信封裡裝有一封信，信裡的辭彙充滿了希望。）

· I'll develop a story about why a lot of flies began to envelop Mr. Wise.

動詞，指環繞

（我將寫一個為什麼許多蒼蠅開始圍著懷斯先生的故事。）

192 equipment 設備

1 ✖ Vincent lent me some camping equipments.

不可數名詞，沒有複數形式

✔ Vincent lent me some camping equipment.

文森特借給我一些野營用具。

- all kinds of equipment （各種設備）
- two pieces of equipment （兩件設備）

文法加油站

總稱或泛指的名詞

① equipment（設備）是泛指「為了某個特定目的所需要的材料」（anything kept, furnished, or provided for a specific purpose）。這類泛指的名詞通常是不可數名詞。

② 類似的 furniture（家具）、fruit（水果）等名詞都是總稱或泛指，這類表示總稱的名詞都是不可數名詞。

③ 與這些不可數名詞相應的是具體名詞，例如 machine、tool、desk、chair、bed、apple、pear，而具體名詞通常都是可數名詞。

193 escape from school/skip school 翹課

1 ✖ Reed often escapes from school because he can't read.

「翹課」不是 escape from school，這是學生常犯的錯

✔ Reed often skips school because he can't read.

因為不識字，里德常翹課。

skip school/class = cut school/class （翹課）

194 especially/specially 尤其／專門地

1

❌ Lily likes to talk a lot, specially when we go to bed early.

指「專門地」，表示「為一個特殊或特定的原因或目的」（for a special reason or purpose），與句意不符

✅ Lily likes to talk a lot, especially when we go to bed early.

表「尤其、格外、特別」，多用在介系詞片語或從屬子句前

莉莉喜歡不停地說話，特別是當我們早早上床睡覺的時候。

- especially at night（特別是在晚上）
- especially careful（特別小心）

尤其、格外、特別 = particularly, mainly

- Kitty's mom doesn't like to drive, especially in big cities.
（姬蒂的媽媽不喜歡開車，尤其不喜歡在大城市開車。）

特意地、專門地 = purposely

- This blue dress was specially made for Bess.
（這條藍色的裙子是專門為貝絲做的。）
- *Trish Made a Wish and Caught a Fish* was specially written for children who are learning English.
（《翠西許了一個願，釣到了一條魚》是專門為學英語的兒童寫的。）

195 even/even though/even if 甚至／儘管／即使

1

❌ Daisy will help us, even she is feeling lazy.

even 是**副詞**，不是連接詞，不能用 even 來連接子句

✅ Daisy will help us, even though she is feeling lazy.
(Daisy is feeling lazy.)

用 even though 連接主要子句和從屬子句

儘管黛絲此刻感到無精打采，但她仍然會幫助我們。

用 even if 連接主要子句和從屬子句

✅ Daisy will help us, even if she is feeling lazy.
(Daisy may or may not be feeling lazy.)

即使黛絲此刻感到無精打采，她還是會幫助我們。

副詞，修飾副詞 more

- I like Mike **even more** than I like Steven.
（我喜歡麥克勝過喜歡史蒂文。）

196 even though/but 雖然／但是

1

在同一個句子裡，不要同時使用從屬連接詞 even though 和對等連接詞 but，兩者只能選其一

✗ Even though Bob had good qualifications, but he did not get that job.

= although

✓ Even though Bob had good qualifications, he did not get that job.

✓ Bob had good qualifications, but he did not get that job.

雖然鮑伯有很強的能力，但他沒有得到那份工作。

· 請參見 although/but 和 conjunctions。

197 every day/everyday 每天

1

形容詞，不能用來修飾動詞

✗ Kay does some exercise everyday.

✓ Kay does some exercise every day.

each day, daily（每天、天天）。表達時間的**副詞片語**，要分開寫成兩個字

凱每天都做一點運動。

2

✗ Kay and Trish study every day English every day.

✓ Kay and Trish study everyday English every day.

routine, usual（每天的、日常的、常見的、平常的）。**形容詞**，直接放在其修飾的名詞之前

表達時間的**副詞片語**，兩個字

凱和翠西每天學日常英語。

無論是母語是英語的人士，還是把英語作為外語學習的人，幾乎每天（every day）都會混淆這兩個表達法。

形容詞	副詞片語
· everyday clothes（便裝）	· laugh every day（每天笑）
· everyday worries（日常的憂慮）	· jog every day（每天慢跑）

198 every one/everyone 每個／每一個人

1

✗ Why is Lorelei Sun ignored by every one?

✓ Why is Lorelei Sun ignored by everyone?

= everybody，意思是「人人、大家」

為什麼大家都不理會蘿芮萊・孫呢？

2

everyone 後面不能接 of，正如 everybody 後面不能接 of

✗ Everyone of us gave Ms. Tower a flower.

✓ Every one of us gave Ms. Tower a flower.

≠ everybody
= each one; each single one，意思是「每一個」；every one 後面常接 of（如：every one of them）

我們每人都給了陶爾女士一朵鮮花。

(1) everyone（= everybody）：意思是「人人、大家」。只要能用 everybody 代替，那就應該是 everyone。everyone 後面不能接 of，正如 everybody 後面不能接 of。

Everybody（人人、大家）

・Everyone enjoys the sunshine and fun.
（大家都喜歡陽光和娛樂。）

(2) every one（= each one; each single one）意思是「每一個」。凡是不能用 everybody 來代替的，就應該是 every one。every one 後面常接 of。

each room in the Drake Hotel
（德瑞克旅館裡的每一個房間）

・Does every one of the rooms in the Drake Hotel have a good view of Sun Lake?
（從德瑞克旅館的每個房間望出去，都能清楚地看到太陽湖嗎？）

199 every thing/everything 每件事、一切事物

1

everything 是一個字，不能寫成兩個字

❌ Every thing Trish likes is either dangerous or simply foolish.

everything 作句中主詞時，動詞要用單數

❌ Everything Trish likes are either dangerous or simply foolish.

= all the things, activities, etc.，意思是「每件事、事事、一切事物」，動詞用單數

✅ Everything Trish likes is either dangerous or simply foolish.

翠西所喜歡的一切，不是很危險，就是很愚蠢。

作句中主詞時，動詞用單數

· In Green Village, **everything is** very clean.
（綠色村莊裡的一切都是乾乾淨淨的。）

200 every time/everytime 每次

1

❌ I want to cry everytime I say goodbye.

✅ I want to cry every time I say goodbye.

每次我說「再見」時，就想哭。

意為「每次」。兩個字，不能寫成一個字

· Kirk feels sleepy every time he does his homework.
（柯克每次一做家庭作業就想睡覺。）

201 evidence 證據

1

❌ The blood on the knife and the mud on her shoes are strong evidences against your wife.

不可數名詞，不加 s

✅ The blood on the knife and the mud on her shoes are strong evidence against your wife.

那把刀上的血以及她鞋上的泥漿，都是對你夫人很不利的證據。

evidence 意為「證據」，是不可數名詞。

- a piece of evidence （一項證據）
- a lot of evidence （許多證據）
- give evidence （作證）
- in evidence （明顯的）

202 except 除……之外

A) except 介

1

❌ Everyone in the family has been to Italy except Amy and I. — except 作**介系詞**，後面不接主格代名詞 I

✅ Everyone in the family has been to Italy except Amy and me. — except 作**介系詞**，後面接受格代名詞 me

除了艾咪和我，家裡其他人都去過義大利。

(1) except 在這裡是介系詞，不是連接詞，意思是「除了……之外；排除之外」，相當於「with the exclusion of 或者 other than」。介系詞後面應該接受格代名詞 me、him、her、us、them ，而不應該接主格代名詞 I、he、she、we、they。

(2) except 和 besides 的區別請參見 besides/except。

B) except 連

1

❌ Jane did nothing except sleeping while she was on the airplane.

作**連接詞**，後面不接 V-ing

✅ Jane did nothing except sleep while she was on the airplane.

作**連接詞**，前面如有 nothing 、anything 這類字，後面接**不帶 to 的不定詞**

珍在飛機上除了睡覺，什麼也沒做。

(1) **except** 也可以作**連接詞**，後面接 that 子句，意思是「除了；要不是、但是」。

- The representative of the shipping line had nothing to tell us **except that** the ship had been delayed.

  作連接詞，後面接 that 子句，表「除了」

  （航運公司的代表除了告訴我們船延誤了，什麼也沒有告訴我們。）

  作連接詞，後面接 that 子句，表「要不是、但是」

- I could have played in that volleyball game, **except that** I overslept.

  （我本來可以參加那場排球賽，但是我睡過了頭。）

(2) 作**連接詞**用的 **except** 也可以接不定詞（except to do something/except do something），意思是「除了、除此之外」（otherwise than）。

① **except do something**：在連接詞 except 前面如果有 nothing、anything 這類字，except 後面通常接**不要 to 的不定詞**（比如上頁的正確例句），而不接 V-ing 形式（即動名詞）。

② **except to do something**： 在連接詞 except 前如沒有 nothing、anything 這類字，except 後接帶 to 的不定詞

- Eve doesn't leave home **except to** visit Steve.

  （伊芙除了去探望史蒂夫，否則都不會離開家門。）

(3) 比較下面句子：

連接詞 except 前面有 nothing，後面接不帶 to 的不定詞 walk、talk

- Yesterday afternoon we **did nothing except walk** and **talk**.

  （昨天下午我們除了散步和聊天外，就什麼也沒有做。）

  except 是介系詞，後面接動名詞

- We **spent** a whole day **doing nothing except talking** and **eating**.

  → 這句是平行結構：「spent + 時間 + 動名詞（doing）+ except + 動名詞（talking、eating）」

  （除了聊天和吃東西外，我們一整天什麼也沒有做。）

203 except/except for 除……之外

1

❌ Except Room 604, Lenore cleaned all the rooms on the sixth floor.

all 在句子的後面，句首就要用 except for

✅ Except for Room 604, Lenore cleaned all the rooms on the sixth floor.

除了 604 房間，蕾諾兒打掃了六樓的所有房間。

2

❌ Paul cleaned the third floor except the meeting hall.

句中沒有 all、every、nobody、anybody 這類字，用 except for

✅ Paul cleaned the third floor except for the meeting hall.

除了會議廳，保羅把三樓的其他地方都打掃了。

(1) except = except for：在 all、every、no、everything、anything、anybody、everybody、nowhere、whole 等表概括性的字之後，既可以用「except + 名詞／代名詞」，也可以用「except for + 名詞／代名詞」，兩者可以互換。

在 nobody 後面既可用 except，又可用 except for

・ **Nobody** listened to me **except for** Amy.
= **Nobody** listened to me **except** Amy.
（除了艾咪以外，沒有人聽了我的話。）

(2) except ≠ except for：但如果 all、every、nobody、anybody 這類字在句子的後面，那麼，句首就要用 except for，不能用 except，比如上面第一組的正確例句。

nobody 在句子的後面，句首要用 except for

・ **Except for** Ms. Tool, **nobody** dove into the swimming pool.（除了圖爾女士外，沒有人跳進游泳池。）

(3) except ≠ except for：如果句中沒有 all、every、nobody、anybody 這類字，用 except for，不用 except，比如上面第二組的正確例句。

(4) except ≠ except for：在從屬子句和介系詞片語前用 except。except for 後面只能接名詞或代名詞。

在連接詞（when）引導的子句前用 except，而不用 except for

- Yesterday Lily did not laugh **except when she saw the giraffe**.
（昨天莉莉看見長頸鹿時才笑了笑，其餘時間都沒有笑過。）

(5) except ≠ except for：不定詞前用 except。

在 nothing、anything 這類字後面，except 接不帶 to 的不定詞（except complain）

- Jane did **nothing except complain** all the time on our train trip to Spain.
（在我們搭火車去西班牙的路途中，珍除了抱怨，什麼也沒有做。）

(6) except ≠ except for：

① except for + 名詞（要不是由於）（= if it were not for; but for）

要不是由於 = but for= if it were not for

- Annie would travel around the world **except for** a lack of money.（要不是因為缺錢，安妮會去環遊世界。）

② except + that 子句（要不是、但是）口語（請參考 167 頁 except 連接詞用法的第一條）。

204 excited/exciting 激動的／令人激動的

1

人感到激動

✗ Lori told an excited adventure story.

某件事／某個東西令人激動

✓ Lori told an exciting adventure **story**.

蘿麗講的冒險故事令人激動。

2

某件事／某個東西令人激動

✗ Omar is exciting about his new car.

人感到激動

✓ Omar is excited about his new car.

歐馬對他的新車感到非常興奮。

- 請參見 interested/interesting。

文法加油站

過去分詞當形容詞的「-ed」（感到……的）

現在分詞當形容詞的「-ing」（令人……的）

(1) 用「-ed」形式描述一個人的感覺。

(2) 用「-ing」形式表示引起這種感覺的人、事、情景、事件。

-ed（感到……的）	-ing（令人……的）
amused（被逗樂的）	amusing（引人發笑的）
bored（厭倦了的）	boring（令人生厭的）
convinced（確信的）	convincing（令人信服的）
entertained（開心的）	entertaining（使人得到娛樂的）
tired（疲倦的）	tiring（令人疲倦的、累人的）
exhausted（精疲力竭的）	exhausting（使人精疲力竭的）
interested（感興趣的）	interesting（引起興趣的、有趣的）
surprised（感到驚訝的）	surprising（令人驚訝的）
an amazed reader（感到詫異的讀者）	an amazing girl（令人驚嘆的女孩）
a confused student（感到困惑的學生）	a confusing question（令人困惑的問題）
a frightened boy（受了驚的孩子）	a frightening story（令人驚恐的故事）
a surprised expression（吃驚的表情）	surprising news（驚人的消息）

① That dancing toy robot is quite amusing.
（那個會跳舞的玩具機器人很逗人發笑。）

Coco was amused by my story of how I bought that used UFO.
（我如何購買那架舊幽浮的故事把可可逗樂了。）

② The bicycle trip from Amsterdam to Berlin was tiring but exciting.
（從阿姆斯特丹到柏林的自行車旅行很累人，但也很刺激。）

Bret was tired from his exciting trip to Tibet.
（在令人興奮的西藏之旅後，布瑞特感到疲勞。）

③ "The book *Life in São Paulo* is interesting," commented Brooke.
（布露可評論說：「《在聖保羅的生活》這本書很有趣。」）

I am interested in the novel you wrote while you lived on your sailboat.
（我對你住在帆船上時寫的那本小說很感興趣。）

F

205 face/in the face of 面臨／面對、不顧

1

❌ The coach knew the reason that he and his NBA team were in the face of their third defeat this season.

指「不顧、面對」〔主英〕，不能用在連綴動詞 be 後面作補語

National Basketball Association（全美籃球協會）

✅ The coach knew the reason that he and his NBA team were facing their third defeat of the season.

及物動詞 = confront，指「面臨、正視」

教練知道他和他的 NBA 籃球隊正面臨該季的第三次失敗的原因。

= in the presence of（面對）

- In the face of the terrible storm, Ray began to pray.
  （在這場可怕的風暴面前，雷開始祈禱。）

= in spite of（不顧）

- Grace Brown won in the face of tough competition from all over the town.
  （儘管有來自全鎮的激烈競爭，葛蕾絲・布朗依然獲勝了。）

文法加油站

與 face 有關的片語

- be/get in my face（惹怒我）
- get out of my face（不要惹怒我）
- lose face（丟臉）
- save face（不丟臉、保面子）
- pull a long face（愁眉苦臉）
- make a face（做鬼臉）
- "Don't get in my face!" yelled Grace.（葛蕾絲叫喊：「不要惹怒我！」）

206 family 家庭

1 美式 My family is going to Italy to visit Aunt Lily.

被看成「一個整體、一個單位」。作主詞時，後面接單數動詞

英式 My family are going to Italy to visit Aunt Lily.

被看成「一群人」，後面接複數動詞

我們家要去義大利探望莉莉姑姑。

2 美式 My family is waiting for Lily.

被看成「一個整體、一個單位」。作主詞時，後面接單數動詞

英式 美式 My family members are all waiting for Lily.

意指「家庭中的個體」。如要強調一組人中的個體，常在集合名詞後面補充 members 等類的字，動詞就用複數

英式 My family are all waiting for Lily.

意指「一群人／家庭成員」。把一個集合名詞看作一群人，後面要接複數動詞

我全家都在等莉莉。

⑴ 常見的集合名詞有：audience、class、company、committee、crowd、corporation、enemy、family、government、group、public staff、team、union 等。

⑵ 請參見 stuff、subject-verb agreement（第 C 點）。

3 ✗ The Short family are planning to press its case against Mort in court.

複數動詞應與複數代名詞搭配

✗ The Short family is planning to press their case against Mort in court.

單數動詞應與單數代名詞搭配

美式 The Short family is planning to press its case against Mort in court.

單數動詞與單數代名詞搭配

英式 The Short family are planning to press their case against Mort in court.

複數動詞與複數代名詞搭配

肖特家打算堅持對莫特的起訴。

207 farm 農場

1

❌ In our wind farm in Inner Mongolia, horses race at dawn.
不與 in 連用

✅ On our wind farm in Inner Mongolia, horses race at dawn.
與介系詞 on 連用，表示「在農場裡、在農莊裡」

黎明時分，駿馬在我們的內蒙古風力發電廠奔馳。

- on a tree farm （在林場裡）
- on a pig farm （在養豬場裡）
- on a honey farm （在養蜜蜂場裡）
- on a dairy farm （在牛乳製品農場裡）

208 farther/further (farthest/furthest)

更遠的（地）／進一步的（地）

1

❌ Are we going to get farther instruction about how to do CPR?
本句指「進一步的」，不能用 farther（更遠的）

✅ Are we going to get further instruction about how to do CPR?
通常指「進一步的（地）、深層次的（地）」

會向我們進一步講授如何進行心肺復甦術嗎？

2

英式 美式 Lulu walked farther than you.
通常用 farther 和 farthest 來指距離

英式 Lulu walked further than you.
英式英語中 further 和 furthest 也可用來指距離

露露走得比你遠。

far 的比較級和最高級：farther/further ; farthest/furthest。

209 fatal/fatally

請參見 dead/deadly。

210 father-in-laws/fathers-in-law

請參見 mother-in-laws/mothers-in-law。

211 faucet/tap 水龍頭

1

美式 Ms. Potter turned on the faucet to get some water.

英式 Ms. Potter turned on the tap to get some water.

波特女士打開水龍頭取些水。

212 favorable/favorite

有利的、適合的；贊同的、稱讚的／特別喜愛的

1

✗ Grace thought that the cool weather seemed favorite for her long race.

✓ Grace thought that the cool weather seemed favorable for her long race.

表「有利的、適合的；贊同的、稱讚的」

葛蕾絲認為，這樣涼爽的天氣適合她長跑比賽。

2

✗ Liz Winger is my favorable singer.

✓ Liz Winger is my favorite singer.

表「特別喜愛的」

我最喜歡的歌手是莉茲．溫爾。

- receive a favorable review（贏得了好評）
- favorable to your proposal（贊同你的提議）
- favorite subject（最喜歡的學科）
- my favorite vegetable（我最喜歡的蔬菜）

213 fee 費用

1

✗ He paid one-dollar parking fee.

✓ He paid a one-dollar parking fee. —— **可數名詞**，單數要用不定冠詞 a 修飾，複數形為 fees

= He paid his one-dollar parking fee.

= He paid the one-dollar parking fee.

他付了一美元的停車費。 —— **複合名詞**，在此為形容詞，置於名詞前

- an admission fee（入場費）
- a doctor's fee（付給醫生的酬金）
- legal fees（訴訟費）
- the passport application fee（護照申請費）

214 fellow/other

請參見 other/similar。

215 few/a few 很少的／一些

1

✗ I had to sell my two old lamps to get the money to buy few stamps. —— 具否定含意，在這裡與句意不符

✓ I had to sell my two old lamps to get the money to buy a few stamps. —— 具肯定含意，意思更接近 some

為了有錢買幾張郵票，我不得不賣掉我的兩盞舊燈。

- Jim is a bit odd, **and** few people like him. —— 指「很少的」
（吉姆有點古怪，沒有幾個人喜歡他。）
- Jim is a bit odd, **but** a few people like him. —— = some people
（吉姆雖有點古怪，但還是有幾個人〔一些人〕喜歡他。）

216 few/little (a few/a little) 很少的（一些）

1

✗ In Bob's village, there are too many people and too little jobs.
需與不可數名詞和單數代名詞連用

✓ In Bob's village, there are too many people and too few jobs.
需與複數名詞和複數代名詞連用

在鮑伯的村子裡，人口太多而工作太少。

(1) a few/few 與複數詞連用（a few people、a few of us）。

(2) a little/little 與單數詞（通常是不可數名詞）連用（a little money、a little of it）。

修飾不可數名詞 juice，具有肯定含意，相當於 some

・May Bruce drink **a little** of your apple **juice**?
（布魯斯可以喝一點你的蘋果汁嗎？）

修飾不可數名詞 juice，具有否定含意，表示「甚少的」

・OK, Mr. Heft, but there is very **little** left.
= OK, Mr. Heft, but there is very **little juice** left.
（可以，海弗特先生，不過剩下很少了。）

217 fewer/less 較少的

1

✗ Less UFOs were seen in February than in January.
指「體積、容積」或「量」，是不能數的，與**不可數（單數）名詞**連用

✓ Fewer UFOs were seen in February than in January.
指「數」（可以數的物品或人），與**複數名詞**連用

二月所見的不明飛行物比一月來得少。

less 修飾不可數名詞	fewer 修飾複數名詞
・less salary（更低的薪水）	・fewer dollars（更少的美元）
・less strength（更小的力氣）	・fewer people（更少的人）

A B C D E F G H I J K L M N O P Q R S T U V W X Y Z

2

✗ Tom borrowed fewer than twenty dollars from Mom.

✓ Tom borrowed less than twenty dollars from Mom.

湯姆從媽媽那裡借了不到 20 元美金。

└ less than + 一定數量的錢

(1) less than 用在表示數或量的名詞前面，可以接**不可數名詞**，也可以接**可數名詞**。

- less than **10% fat**（不到 10% 的脂肪）
  └ less than 接不可數名詞
- less than **a gallon of paint**（不到一加侖的油漆）
  └ less than + 表「量」的可數名詞，又如：less than two gallons of paint

(2) less than 放在**複數名詞**前面指的是「一段時間、一定數量的錢、一段距離」，這種情況不能用 fewer than，比如上面例句的 twenty dollars 是一個單一的數量，一次付款額。

- in less than **sixty seconds**（不到六十秒）
  └ 被看成是一個整體，表示「一段時間」
- for less than **50 cents** a day（每天花費不到 50 美分）
  └ 表示「一定數量的錢」
- drove less than **50 miles**（駕駛了不到 50 英里）
  └ 表示「一段距離」
- Margo said, "Less than **a hundred people** came to our puppet show in Chicago."
  └ 看成一個「整體」

= Margo said, "Fewer than **a hundred people** came to our puppet show in Chicago."
  └ 看成分開的個體

（瑪歌說：「來芝加哥觀看我們木偶表演的人不到一百個。」）

→ less than a hundred people 比 fewer than a hundred people 更常見，也更自然。

(3) 片語 no less than（多達）以及 or less 也可以與**複數名詞**連用。

- No less than **20 of our classmates** voted for Margo.
  （多達 20 個同學投票選了瑪歌。）
- Tell me why you like Bess in **20 words** or less.
  （用 20 個或少於 20 個字告訴我，你為什麼喜歡貝絲。）

(4) 請參見 amount/number。

218 fill/fill in/fill out 任職／填寫／填寫

1

❌ Please fill the form, and give it to Norm.

fill 指「任職」，與本句意思「填寫」不符

✅ Please fill in the form, and give it to Norm.

英式英語用 fill in a form

✅ Please fill out the form, and give it to Norm.

美式英語用 fill out/fill in a form

請把表格填寫好，然後交給諾姆。

2

❌ Jill Nation is the most qualified person to fill in that position.

fill in 指「填寫」，與句意不符

✅ Jill Nation is the most qualified person to fill that position.

指「任職」

吉兒 · 納欣是填補那個職缺最合格的人選。

219 finally/at last 最後／終於

1

指拖延了很長時間才發生的事，與句意不符

❌ At last, I'd like to talk about why Penny West would be the best president for our company.

指「結論」

✅ Finally, I'd like to talk about why Penny West would be the best president for our company.

最後，我要談談為什麼潘妮 · 韋斯特將會是我們公司最好的總裁。

(1) finally 指「結論」（in conclusion）。在介紹「演講、論文、報告」等的最後一個專案時，要用 finally，不用 at last。

(2) 介紹某件拖延了很長時間才發生的事，用 at last，也可以用 finally。

· At last Lily Mast began to run fast.
= Lily Mast finally began to run fast.
（莉莉 · 馬斯特終於開始快跑起來。）

220 fish/fishes 魚

1

✗ To find out if they were fresh, Trish smelled those fishes.

✓ To find out if they were fresh, Trish smelled those fish.

翠西聞了聞那些魚，看看牠們是否新鮮。

fish 的複數形式有兩種：

fish（與單數同形）	fishes
1. 指同種類的魚或泛指「魚」時，單複數都用 fish，不用 fishes。 2. 用於強調多種不同種類的魚（常用 fish > fishes）。	用於強調多種不同種類的魚。

- Mike ate six kinds of fish, and there wasn't one kind he didn't like.
  指多種不同種類的魚時仍然更常用 fish
  （麥克吃了六種魚，沒有哪一種是他不喜歡的。）

- Those two kinds of fishes are served on different types of dishes.（那兩種魚放在不同的餐具裡端上了桌。）
  強調多種不同種類的魚時可以用 fishes

221 fit/suit/match 適合

1

✗ That style of swimsuit doesn't fit Kyle.
指衣服尺碼合適，不大不小，不用來指款式適合

✓ That style of swimsuit doesn't suit Kyle.
指衣服穿在身上好看（something you wear looks good on you），款式和顏色都很合適

那種泳衣的款式不適合凱爾。

fit 和 suit 這兩個字易混淆，因中文意思都是「適合」。但實際上它們的意思不同。

- That **skirt** didn't fit Gert.（那裙子葛特穿不合身。）
  指衣服尺碼合適（the right size）
- Bright **colors** suit Ms. Boot.（鮮豔的顏色適合布特女士。）
  指衣服的顏色合適

2 ✗ That dress really matches Tess.
✓ That dress really suits Tess.
→ Tess looks good wearing that dress.
黛絲穿上那件洋裝真好看。
✓ That dress really fits Tess.
→ That dress is the right size for Tess.
那件洋裝穿在黛絲身上真合身。

表示褲子與他的上衣相配
- Vance is wearing **a jacket** that matches his **pants**.
（萬斯穿著一件與褲子很搭的上衣。）

222 floor （樓房的）層

1 美式 Lenore has an office on the first floor.
英式 Lenore has an office on the ground floor.
蕾諾兒在一樓有一間辦公室。

	美式英語	英式英語
一樓	the first floor	the ground floor
二樓	the second floor	the first floor
三樓	the third floor	the second floor
四樓	the fourth floor	the third floor

223 food/foods 食物

1 ✗ The prices for foods and makeup have gone up.
✓ The prices for food and makeup have gone up.
泛指食品，通常作不可數名詞
食品及化妝品的價格已經上漲了。

food 當指特定的、具體的某種食品時，才可以用複數 foods，但即使指具體的某種食品，單數 food 仍然更常見。

- food and drink（食品和飲料）
- food for thought（〔俚〕引人深思的事）
- sweet food/sweet foods（甜食）
- baby food/baby foods（嬰兒食品）

A B C D E F G H I J K L M N O P Q R S T U V W X Y Z

224 forbid 禁止

1

通常不與 from 連用，forbid somebody from doing something 不是正式英語

非正式 Ming says the law forbids anyone from smoking inside any public building.

和不定詞（to）連用，句型為 forbid somebody to do something

正式 Ming says the law forbids anyone to smoke inside any public building.

如果後面沒「某人」，直接跟一個動詞，就用 V-ing 形式，句型為 forbid doing something

正式 Ming says the law forbids smoking inside any public building.

敏說，法規禁止在任何公共大樓裡吸菸。

forbid 的三時態：forbade/forbad, forbidden, forbidding。

- Mom **forbade** me **to** go out with Tom.

  過去式 forbade 比 forbad 更常用

= Mom **forbad** me **to** go out with Tom.
（媽媽禁止我跟湯姆出去。）

文法加油站

prevent（阻止；妨礙）的用法

- prevent something（阻止某事）
- prevent doing（阻止做某事）
- prevent something/someone from doing something
  （阻止某事／人做某事）
- Did the noise from the highway prevent Dwight from sleeping last night?
  （從高速公路傳來的噪音使杜威特昨晚無法入眠嗎？）

225 forget 忘記

1

❌ Don't forget telling Joan to turn off her cellphone.

✅ Don't forget to tell Joan to turn off her cellphone.

不要忘記告訴裘恩要關手機。

(1) forget + V-ing 指「忘記已做的事或已發生的事」。

- Sue forgot mailing the gift to Scot.

  蘇已經寄了禮物，不過她忘記了她已經做過這件事

= Sue forgot that she had mailed the gift to Scot.
（蘇忘記了她已經把禮物寄給了史考特。）

(2) forget + to do 指「忘記要做的、該做的事」。

  史考特沒有把書寄給布露可。史考特仍然需要把書寄給布露可

- Scot forgot to mail the book to Brook.
（史考特忘記要把書寄給布露可。）

(3) remember 的用法是一樣的。請參見 remember。

226 forget/leave 忘記／丟下

1

❌ Sorry, Lulu! I forgot your camera at the zoo.

✅ Sorry, Lulu! I left your camera at the zoo.

  有具體的地點要用 leave 來表示

露露，對不起！我把你的相機忘在動物園了。

(1) 如果有具體的地點，我們不用 forget，要用 leave 來表示。
句型為：leave something at/in some place。

(2) forget 的用法請參見上面 forget。

- Oh, no! I forgot to bring my magic arrow!
（噢，糟糕！我忘了帶我的魔箭！）

227 forth/fourth 向前／第四

1 ❌ "Is that your **forth** hamburger today?" asked Liz.

 ✅ "Is that your **fourth** hamburger today?" asked Liz.

莉茲問：「那是你今天吃的第四個漢堡嗎？」

⑴ 表示數目的 **fourth**（第四）裡有 **four**（四）。這一提示可幫助區分
fourth 和 forth。

⑵ 如果與數目無關，就用 **forth**。

 · Janet said, "Humans will soon go <u>forth</u> to explore the
 <u>fourth</u> planet."
 └──── 與數目無關用 forth
 └──── 與數目有關用 fourth

 （珍妮特說：「人類將很快前往探索第四顆行星。」）

文法加油站

① fo**u**r（四）、fo**u**rteen（十四）、fo**u**rth（第四），→包含字母 u。

② forty（四十）→沒有包含字母 u。

 · June North will complete her **forty-fourth** year of teaching by
 the end of this afternoon.
 （到今天下午為止，茱恩・諾思就教書滿四十四年了。）

228 forward/foreword 向前／前言

1 ❌ Our meeting with Ms. Flower has been moved <u>foreword</u>
 an hour.
 指一本書的「前言」(= preface)──┘

 ✅ Our meeting with Ms. Flower has been moved <u>forward</u>
 an hour.
 指「向前」──┘

我們與弗勞爾女士的會面提前了一個小時。

指書開始時介紹性的陳述。陳述就要含有 words，既然 foreword 是一種陳述，那麼這個字裡就要含有 word

· In this book's foreword, June Hill says we will move forward and soon begin to live on the moon.

朝前面移動（toward the front）。記住 toward 和 forward 都以 ward 結尾

（茱恩・黑爾在這本書的前言中說，我們會向前邁進，很快就會開始在月球居住。）

229 friendly 友善的

1

✗ Today Amy talked to me very friendly.

形容詞，非副詞，不能用來修飾動詞 talked

✓ Today Amy talked to me in a very friendly way.

✓ Today Amy was very friendly while talking to me.

今天艾咪非常友好地跟我說話。

形容詞 friendly 用在連綴動詞後面作主詞補語

· Lily **is** usually **friendly** toward Millie.
（莉莉通常對米莉都很友好。）

· **Friendly Millie** smiled at Billy.（友善的米莉對比利微笑。）

形容詞 friendly 用在名詞 Millie 前面作修飾語

文法加油站

以 -ly 結尾的形容詞

以 -ly 結尾的形容詞，還有 deadly、likely、lonely、lovely、silly、ugly 等。

· deadly silence（死一般的寂靜）
· a lovely view （一片宜人的景色）
· a lonely widow（一位孤獨的寡婦）
· an ugly building （一棟難看的大樓）

230 from . . . to . . .

請參見 between . . . and . . .。

231 fulfill/fulfil 執行、履行

1

✗ Jill will fullfill the conditions set out in the contract with Bill.

第一個音節結尾只需要有一個 l

美式主要使用

✓ Jill will fulfill/fulfil the conditions set out in the contract with Bill.

英式專用（美式有時用）

吉兒會遵守與比爾簽訂合約裡的條件。

232 fun 開心、有趣的人或物

1

✗ Yesterday was a great fun because of Kate and Kay.

不可數名詞，不能和 a 連用

✓ Yesterday was great fun because of Kate and Kay.

由於有凱特和凱，昨天很好玩。

(1) fun 是不可數名詞，不能和不定冠詞 a 連用。

- have fun/great fun/a lot of fun/lots of fun （玩得開心）
- be full of fun （充滿了樂趣）
- for fun/for the fun of it/in fun （鬧著玩的）
- make fun of （取笑；開玩笑）
- sound like fun （聽起來很有趣）

(2) fun 在美式非正式英語裡也可以是形容詞，用來形容某物、某事或某人是有趣的。

- Eli is a witty and fun guy.（伊萊是一個機智、風趣的人。）

形容詞，用來形容某人是有趣的

文法加油站

比較：funny 指某件事情、某人令人發笑

- Joan is the funniest woman I have ever known.
  （裘恩是我認識的人當中最有趣的女人。）

233 further/furthest

請參見 farther/further (farthest/furthest)。

G

234 garbage/trash/rubbish

垃圾；廢話；無聊作品

1 美式 Midge asked Tish to take out the garbage.

美式英語用 garbage/trash

英式 Midge asked Tish to take out the rubbish.

米姬要蒂西把垃圾拿出去。

garbage、trash 和 rubbish 都是不可數名詞，**沒有複數形式**。

- Midge collects things that other people call garbage.
  （米姬收集人們稱為「垃圾」的東西。）
- Sid just walks away from anyone who talks trash or says anything stupid.
  （如果有人說廢話或蠢話，席德就會轉頭就走。）
- Foolish Trish often says things that are just rubbish.
  （傻乎乎的翠西常常說一些廢話。）

235 garden/yard 菜園、花園、庭院

1 美式 Eli says the bush in the back yard is too high.

back yard = backyard

英式 Eli says the bush in the back garden is too high.

伊萊說，後院的灌木叢長得太高了。

	yard	garden
英式英語	指被混凝土或其他堅硬材料覆蓋的院子，不能生長花草。	長有草、花和樹的地方。
美式英語	(1) 指「**庭院**」，與房子相連，是人們用來坐、玩耍、栽種植物的地方。它可以是被混凝土覆蓋的，也可以是長有草、樹和花的庭院。 (2) 美式英語裡的 yard 通常在英式英語裡就是 garden。	指「**果園、菜園、花園**」，通常在房子附近，專門用來種花、蔬菜、水果、裝飾用的灌木叢或樹木等。

236 gas/petrol 汽油

1

美式 Did Ivy put some gas in my RV?

美式用 gas/gasoline

英式 Did Ivy put some petrol in my RV?

愛葳幫我的休旅車加油了嗎？

- After the police officer caught the thief near the gas pump, Eli breathed a sigh of relief.
（警官在加油站附近抓住了小偷後，伊萊如釋重負地鬆了口氣。）

237 get 獲得

1

美式 Omar has just gotten an electric car.
= Omar has just bought an electric car.

美式 Omar just got an electric car.（常用過去簡單式）

英式 Omar has just got an electric car.

歐馬剛買了一輛電動汽車。

(1) 要表示「剛獲得什麼」（have/has acquired or obtained）：

美式 have/has gotten; got（更常用過去簡單式）
動詞三態：get → got → gotten

英式 have/has got

動詞三態：get → got → got

(2) 要表示「收到、成為、捕獲、染上疾病」（receive、become、catch）等含意，美式英語的過去分詞也用 gotten。

- have gotten a letter = have received a letter（收到了一封信）
- have gotten better = have become better（好一些了）
- have gotten the flu = have caught the flu（感染了流行性感冒）
- Lenore has gotten all that she **ever hoped** for.

= Lenore has obtained all that she **ever hoped** for.

→ 強調現在（主要子句用現在完成式，子句用過去式）

≒ Lenore got all that she **had ever hoped** for.

→ 強調過去（主要子句用過去式，子句用過去完成式）

（蕾諾兒得到了她想要的一切。）

→ 美式英語的「已經獲得」has gotten = has obtained。也可以用過去式 got，等於 obtained。

文法加油站

get 的非正式用語：不得不；擁有

① have/has got 在口語中用來表示「必須、不得不」（must、have to）或「擁有」（possess、own）。在這兩種情況下，have、has 常用縮寫形式（'ve got、's got）。

② 請參見 have/have got。

口語　I've got to go with Margo.

　　　口語常用 have got to，表示「必須、不得不」

正式　I have to go with Margo.

　=　I must go with Margo.

　　　（我得跟瑪歌一起走了。）

口語　I've got a master's degree in biology.

　　　= I possess，表示「擁有」

正式　I have a master's degree in biology.

　　　（我有生物學碩士學位。）

口語　She's got a new sports car.
正式　She has a new sports car.
指目前所「擁有」

（她有一輛新跑車。）

③ 由上述說明可知，美國人一直在用 have got（擁有）和 have gotten（獲得），不過這兩個動詞片語的意思不同。這並不意味著美國人使用不標準的英語，而是意味著美國人使英語更加豐富多彩了。比較下面的例句：

(a) · 口語　Lulu and Scot have got the flu.
正式　Lulu and Scot have the flu.
= Lulu and Scot are suffering from the flu.
（露露和史考特得了流感。）
→ 強調狀態，表示「因流感而感覺不舒服」

· You and Sue have gotten the flu.
= You and Sue have caught the flu.（你和蘇感染上流感了。）
→ 強調動作，表示「感染上流感」

(b) · 口語　Bob's got a new job.
正式　Bob has a new job.（鮑伯有了一個新工作。）
→ 強調狀態，指目前所「擁有」

· Bob has gotten a new job.
= Bob has obtained a new job.（鮑伯獲得了一份新工作。）
→ 強調動作「獲得」，而不是強調狀態「擁有」

238 get down from/get off/get out of
下（馬、公車、汽車、船）

1

❌ I am going to get down from the bus at the next stop and go to the park to meet Gus.

✅ I am going to get off the bus at the next stop and go to the park to meet Gus.

下一站我就要下公車，然後去公園見加斯。

下馬、下自行車，用 get down from；下公車，要用 get off

· get off a bike, bus, plane, ship, or train
（下〔自行車、公車、飛機、船或火車〕）

· get off or get out of a boat（下船）

· get out of a car or taxi（下汽車或下計程車）

· get down from or get off a horse or bicycle（下馬或下自行車）

· I helped Ms. Morse get down from the horse.

= I helped Ms. Morse get off the horse.
（我幫助莫爾斯女士下了馬。）

get off a bus

239 go/come

請參見 bring/take。

240 go into

請參見 enter/enter into。

241 go jogging/go for a jog 去慢跑

1

✗ Ming goes to jog every morning.

✓ Ming goes jogging every morning.

= Ming goes for a jog every morning.

敏每天早上都要慢跑。

go + V-ing（= engage in）：go 後面接**動名詞**（不接不定詞）表示「**從事某活動**」。

· go camping（去露營）
· go climbing（去爬山）
· go fishing（去釣魚）
· go jogging（去慢跑）
· go running（去跑步）
· go shopping（去購物）
· go skiing（去滑雪）
· go swimming（去游泳）

go jogging

242 gonna (= going to) （俚語）將要

1 俚語 When is Lynne gonna fly to Berlin?

正式 When is Lynne going to fly to Berlin?

琳恩什麼時候要飛往柏林？

243 good 好的

1 ✗ Paul is good in football and baseball.

應該用 be good **at**，不用 in

✓ Paul is good at football and baseball.

= Paul is good at playing football and baseball.

保羅擅長打橄欖球和棒球。

(1) 如果你在哪方面強，應該說：be good at something 或 be good at doing something（不用 in）。

(2) 能夠很好地應付某人或某事，或能夠很好地利用某東西，用 good with somebody/something。

- good with one's hands （手靈巧）
- Louise has always been good with monkeys.
  （露易絲總是知道如何訓練猴子。）

(3) 如果要表示「具有必要的品質」或「方便」、「合宜」，用 good for something。

- good for a laugh（能引人發笑）

244 good/well 好

1 ✗ Little Marty behaved good at the party.

形容詞，不可修飾動詞（behaved）

✓ Little Marty behaved well at the party.

小瑪蒂在聚會上表現很好。

副詞，可修飾動詞（behaved）

A B C D E F G H I J K L M N O P Q R S T U V W X Y Z

(1) good 是形容詞，well 是副詞。

- Is Midge getting good grades in college?
  形容詞，修飾名詞 grades
  （米姬在大學裡成績優良嗎？）
- Mel didn't do very well.（梅爾做得不太好。）
  副詞，修飾動詞 do
- Elwood felt good, because Trish understood his English.
  形容詞，用在感官動詞 felt 後面
  （埃爾伍德感覺不錯，因為翠西聽懂了他的英語。）

(2) well 也可用作形容詞，但常用來指人的健康狀況。

- Just now Del threw up, and he is not feeling very well.
  也可用作形容詞，但常用來指人的健康狀況，用在連綴動詞 look、feel 等後面
  （戴爾剛才嘔吐了，現在他覺得身體不太舒服。）

文法加油站

bad 和 badly 的用法

①在美式非正式用語裡，有時 bad 當副詞取代 badly，與一些特定的動詞連用。但在正式用語中（包括考試、商務信函、商務會談等）要遵守文法規則：bad 是形容詞，而 badly 是副詞。

② 請參見 bad/badly。

非正式	Sam did bad on yesterday's English exam.
正式	Sam did badly on yesterday's English exam.

（山姆昨天的英語考試考得很差。）

245 got/gotten

請參見 get。

246 got/have

請參見 get。

247 graduate 畢業

1

❌ Monique graduated college last week.

後面要接 from

✅ Monique graduated from college last week.

莫妮可上週大學畢業了。

2

美式 Tyr was graduated from Harvard last year.

美式 英式 Tyr graduated from Harvard last year.

提爾去年從哈佛大學畢業。

在美式英語裡，was graduated from/graduated from 都可以，意思區別不大，前者用於及物動詞的被動式（被准予……畢業），後者用於不及物動詞，不過後者比前者更常見。英式英語 graduate 只用作不及物動詞。

- 「**研究生**」說法：美式 graduate student
  英式 postgraduate

248 grateful/thankful 感激的／欣慰的

1

❌ Jake is very grateful that he survived the earthquake.

對「某人友好的行為」表示感謝，與句意不符

✅ Jake is very thankful that he survived the earthquake.

因一件不好的事（死亡）沒有發生而感到欣慰

傑克從地震中逃生，感到非常欣慰。

(1) grateful 意為「感激的、感謝的」，對「**某人的好意、友好的行為**」表示衷心感謝。常見句型如下：

- would be grateful + if 子句
  （此結構用來正式並禮貌地請求某人做某事）
- grateful + when/that 子句
- grateful (to somebody) for something（為某事感謝〔某人〕）

(2) 請參見 will/would。

- Ms. Hubble is grateful to her friends who are always there when she is in trouble.
  （哈伯女士很感激她的朋友們，每當她有困難時，他們總是幫助她。）
- My wife and I are grateful to you for saving our daughter's life.（你救了我們女兒的命，我和我妻子非常感激你。）

(3) thankful 也表示「感激的、感謝的」，對「**某個恩人或仁慈的上帝**」表達感謝。還常包含了「欣慰的、寬慰的」的含意。

對「上帝」表達感謝

- Dee is thankful that God gave her a healthy body.
  （蒂非常感激上帝賦予了她一個健康的身體。）

(4) thankful 接 that 子句時，指**一件好事情發生**後，感到寬慰和高興；或指因**一件不好的事沒有發生**而感到欣慰。

(5) 指「不好的事沒有發生」，通常用 thankful，不用 grateful，比如範例中的例句。

- thankful for something
- thankful to do
- thankful + that 子句

好事情發生後，感到寬慰和高興

- Ms. Nation is thankful that she had a long vacation.
  （納欣女士因為度了一個長假而感到很高興。）
- My mother is thankful to have been able to find her long-lost brother.

  好事情發生後，感到寬慰和高興

  （能夠找到失散已久的兄弟，我媽媽感到非常欣慰。）
- Jane faces some health problems, but she is thankful that her body is free from pain.

  因不好的事情（pain）沒有發生而感到欣慰

  （雖然珍面臨一些健康問題，但她非常欣慰她的身體沒有什麼疼痛。）

(6) grateful 的反義詞是 ungrateful（忘恩負義的、不領情的）。
thankful 的反義詞是 thankless（不感謝的、吃力不討好的）。

- a thankful smile（寬慰的微笑）
- a thankless task（吃力不討好的任務）
- a thankless/ungrateful child（忘恩負義的孩子）

H

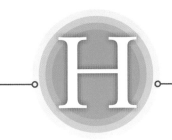

249 hair 頭髮

1 ✗ Claire has red hairs. —— 長在頭上的毛髮是**不可數名詞**，沒有複數形式

✓ Claire has red hair.

克蕾兒的頭髮是紅色的。

(1) 長在身上或頭上的毛髮是不可數名詞，沒有複數形式（hairs），也不能與不定冠詞 a 連用（a hair）。

(2) 能數的頭髮才是可數名詞，這時才能說 hairs 或 a hair。

- Jake, there is a hair on my cake!
（傑克，我的蛋糕上有一根頭髮！）
- Brooke found four blond hairs in the book.
（布露可發現書裡有四根金黃色頭髮。）

2 ✗ Claire: "Hi, Kate! Your hair looks great."
Kate: "Thank you, Claire. I just cut my hair in the shop over there."

在理髮店剪頭髮，常見的片語是 have one's hair cut 或者 have/get a haircut

✓ Claire: "Hi, Kate! Your hair looks great."
Kate: "Thank you, Claire. I just had my hair cut in the shop over there."。
= Kate: "Thank you, Claire. I just had a haircut in the shop over there."

克蕾兒：「嘿，凱特！你的頭髮看起來很好看。」
凱特：「謝謝，克蕾兒。我剛在那邊的那家美髮院剪了頭髮。」

如果你自己剪頭髮，就可以說 cut my hair。指明「誰」剪你的頭髮，可以用 somebody cut my hair。

- "I just cut my hair," said Eli.（伊萊說：「我剛自己剪了頭髮。」）
- Claire just cut my hair.（克蕾兒剛幫我剪了頭髮。）

250 hanged/hung 吊死／懸掛

1

✗ June noted, "That terrible king was hung today at noon."
指「將人絞死」時，過去分詞須用 **hanged**

✓ June noted, "That terrible king was hanged today at noon."

茱恩說：「那個可怕的國王今天正午時被絞死了。」

2

✗ Audrey hanged those colorful lights on the Christmas tree.
指「把某物掛起來」時，過去式須用 **hung**

✓ Audrey hung those colorful lights on the Christmas tree.

奧德莉把那些彩燈掛在聖誕樹上。

(1) hang 表示「把某物掛起來」，過去式和過去分詞是 hung。

- hang → hung → hung (例如：a picture)

(2) 當指「人」時，過去式和過去分詞就用 hanged（吊死／絞死）。

- hang → hanged → hanged (例如：a person)

251 hardly 幾乎不；剛

1

✗ I can't hardly wait to see Kate.
can't 和 hardly 都表示否定，兩者只能用一個

✓ I can hardly wait to see Kate.
≒ I can't wait to see Kate.

我迫不及待地想見到凱特。

hardly、scarcely 以及類似的副詞本來就含有否定的意思，如果要保留句子否定的含意，就不要與另一個否定詞 not 連用。兩者只能用其中一個。

2 ✖ Coco had hardly arrived home than it began to snow.

後面接從屬子句時，表示「剛……就」，需要用 when 來引導子句，不用 than

✔ Coco had hardly arrived home when it began to snow.

= Hardly had Coco arrived home when it began to snow.

可放句首，此時主句要用倒裝結構（had Coco arrived）

可可剛到家，就開始下起雪了。

252 have（擁）有

1 美式 英式 "Does Joan have a new cellphone?"
—"No, she doesn't."

英式 不常用 "Has Joan a new cellphone?"
—"No, she hasn't."

英式 常用 "Has Joan got a new cellphone?"
—"No, she hasn't."

「裘恩有新手機了嗎？」——「沒有。」

(1) 在美式英語中，have/has 在句中如果是實義動詞，表示「擁有」，在**疑問句**和**否定句**中，需要助動詞 do 或 does 的幫助。許多英國人也用美式的這種句型。

- "Does your mother have a brother?" —"Yes, she does."
（「你媽媽有兄弟嗎？」——「有。」）

(2) 在英式英語中，則可以將 have/has 直接提前構成一般**疑問句**，這是一種很正式的疑問句形式，現在使用得不多了。在**否定句**中，在 have/has 後面用否定詞 not（have not/haven't、has not/hasn't）。

· "Has your mother a brother?"—"Yes, she has."

(3) 不過，英式英語的疑問句更常用「have/has + 主詞 + got」的句型。

· "Has your mother got a brother?"—"Yes, she has."

(4) 請參見下面條目 have/have got。

253 have/have got（擁）有

1 美式 英式

口語 Sue has got a menu.

正式 Sue has a menu.

在肯定句中，美式和英式都可以用 have/has got 表示「擁有」

蘇有菜單。

2

doesn't have = hasn't got，兩者選一

✗ Ann doesn't have got a friend called Dan.

英式 口語 Ann hasn't got a friend called Dan.

正式 Ann doesn't have a friend called Dan.

安沒有一個叫丹的朋友。

(1) 在**英式口語**中常用 I have got、we have got、he has got 這樣的結構代替 I have、we have、he has 等表達「擁有」之意。但 have/has got 只能用來表示現在式。這裡的 got 並不是 get 的過去式。

· I have got = I have
· she hasn't got = she doesn't have
· have you got? = do you have?

(2) 在 have/has got 的結構裡（表達「擁有」之意），在**疑問句**和**否定句**中 do/does 和 got 不能搭配在一起。

✗ I don't have got	✓ I have not got
✗ he/she doesn't have got	✓ he/she has not got
✗ do you have got?	✓ have you got?
✗ does he/she have got?	✓ has he/she got?

口語 We've got a cat named Eve and a dog named Steve.

正式 We have a cat named Eve and a dog named Steve.

（我們有一隻叫伊芙的貓和一條叫史蒂夫的狗。）

口語 "Has Gus got a bus?" — "Yes, he has, and so has Tess."

正式 "Does Gus have a bus?" — "Yes, he does, and so does Tess."

（「加斯有公車嗎？」——「他有，黛絲也有一輛公車。」）

254 have to 必須

1

片語 have to 是「必須」的意思，中間不能插入別的字

✗ Trish will have also to read a lot of English novels if she is going to teach English.

✓ Trish will also have to read a lot of English novels if she is going to teach English.

如果翠西想教英語，她還必須閱讀許多英語小說。

have to 的否定式為 do not have to，而不是 have not to。

- Mary does not have to cross any busy streets to go to the city library.
  （瑪麗去市立圖書館不用穿過繁忙的街道。）

255 health 健康

1

✗ Ms. Wise has a good health, because of her proper diet and regular exercise.

不可數名詞，不能與 a 連用

✓ Ms. Wise has good health, because of her proper diet and regular exercise.

由於適當的飲食和規律的運動，懷斯女士身體很健康。

- health care（衛生保健）
- public health（公共衛生；公共衛生設施）
- mental health（心理健康）

💡256 healthful/healthy 有益健康的／健康的

1 ❌ Dee is wealthy, but her teeth aren't very <u>healthful</u>.

　　　　　　　　　　　有益健康的、不生病的 ⌐

　✅ Dee is wealthy, but her teeth aren't very <u>healthy</u>.

蒂雖然富有，但她的牙齒卻不太好。　健康的、沒有病的、運轉良好的

(1) **healthy** 的反義字是 unhealthy、ill、diseased。

(2) **healthful** 不能指「健康的」，但 **healthy** 可以指「有益健康的」，
　 與 healthful 同義。不過，healthy 的這種用法仍然遭到一些人反
　 對。因此，在考試中，表示「有益健康的」，最好用 healthful。

　 healthful 有益健康的：
　 · healthful country air
　　 （有益健康的鄉村空氣）
　 · a healthful food（健康食品）
　 · a healthful climate（有益於健康的氣候）
　 · a healthful diet（有益健康的飲食）
　 · healthful recreation（有益健康的娛樂）
　 · Violet needs to move to a more healthful climate.
　 = Violet needs to move to a healthier climate.
　　 （維莉特需要搬到一個氣候更有益於健康的地方去。）

　 → 雖然 healthy 可以取代 healthful，不過用 healthful 更常見。

　 healthy 健康的、運轉良好的：
　 · healthy appearance（健康的外貌）
　 · a healthy appetite（胃口好）
　 · a healthy body（健康的身體）
　 · a healthy mind（健康的頭腦）
　 · a healthy person（健康的人）
　 · a healthy business（生意興隆）
　 · a healthy industrial economy（繁榮的工業經濟）

257 heat/heating 暖氣；加溫

1

美式 The Crown Hotel clerk asked, "How is the room temperature, Ms. Brown?"
"It's too warm, and I'd appreciate it if you would turn the heat down." replied Ms. Brown.

英式 The Crown Hotel clerk asked, "How is the room temperature, Ms. Brown?"
"It's too warm, and I'd appreciate it if you would turn the heating down." replied Ms. Brown.

皇冠旅館的職員問：「布朗女士，室溫還可以嗎？」
布朗女士回答：「太暖和了。如果您能把暖氣調低一些，我會非常感激。」

(1) heat 和 heating 可以指「暖氣設備」，也可以指「加熱、溫度」。

(2) 美國人說 turn the heat up/down/on/off。

(3) 英國人說 turn the heating up/down/on/off。

美式 · The heat was on when Dirk returned from work.

英式 · The heating was on when Dirk returned from work.

（德克下班回到家時，暖氣是開著的。）

· Pete has a solar heating system（暖氣系統） that provides his house with both hot water and heat（熱度）.

（彼特的房子用太陽能暖氣系統來取熱水和取暖。）

258 hear 聽見

1

✗ Kit heard you to say it.

✓ Kit heard you say it. 接不帶 to 的不定詞，或接 V-ing

姬特聽見你說過那些話。

(1) hear 意思是「聽見」，後面接不帶 to 的不定詞，或接 V-ing。

hear somebody do something

・Lenore, did you hear someone knock on the door?

接不帶 to 的不定詞表示發生過某動作

（蕾諾兒，你聽見有人敲門了嗎？）

hear somebody doing something

・I heard Dwight singing at nine last night.

接 V-ing 強調動作的進行

（昨晚九點時，我聽見杜威特在唱歌。）

(2) 請參見下一則條目：hear/listen。

259 hear/listen 聽說；聽見／聽從；傾聽

1

✗ Sue Hubble heard her parents and therefore didn't get into trouble.

沒有「聽從」這個意思，與句意不符

✓ Sue Hubble listened to her parents and therefore didn't get into trouble.

可以表示「聽從」（take advice）

蘇・哈伯聽從了她父母的話，因此沒有遇到麻煩。

2

✗ Have you listened to that Eli is learning how to fly?

沒有「聽說、得知」的意思，與句意不符

✓ Have you heard that Eli is learning how to fly?

可表示「聽說、得知」（be informed of、be told）

你聽說伊萊在學習飛行了嗎？

listen to 還表示「傾聽」，hear 表示「聽見」。請看下面「文法加油站」。

A B C D E F G H I J K L M N O P Q R S T U V W X Y Z

文法加油站

感官動詞：Look、Listen、See、Hear

① look 和 listen 以及 see 和 hear 都屬於感官動詞，都表示「看、聽」。但 look 和 listen 與 see 和 hear 並不相同。

② look 和 listen 意味著（有意識的）努力或專注地（make a conscious effort）去「看」或「聽」；而 see 和 hear 沒有這種「努力」的含意，只是具有 complete 的含意，強調動作的完成，指「看見」或「聽見」，即強調動作的結果（result）。

③ look 和 listen（看、聽）強調動作的過程，所以可以用進行式，而 see 和 hear「看見、聽見」具有終結性含義，強調動作的結果，所以不能用進行式。

- As Ming was listening to the VOA at ten last night, she heard a bird singing.
  was listening to：強調動作的過程
  heard：強調動作的結果；這裡不能用 was hearing
  （敏昨晚 10 點聽美國之音時，聽見了一隻小鳥唱歌。）
- Lorelei is looking at the blue sky. → 這句不能用 is seeing
  （蘿芮萊正望著天空。）
- She saw her kite land on the top of the tree.
  → 這句不能用 was seeing
  （她看見自己的風箏掉落在樹頂上。）

260 help 幫助

1

✗ Vicky, can you help me carrying this monkey?

✓ Vicky, can you help me carry this monkey?

help 後面須接**帶 to** 或**不帶 to** 的不定詞

✓ Vicky, can you help me to carry this monkey?

薇姬，你能幫我抬這隻猴子嗎？

261 hers/her/her's 她的

1

❌ Ann often sends text messages to a friend of **her** in Japan.

❌ Ann often sends text messages to a friend of **her's** in Japan.
沒有 her's 這種表達形式

✅ Ann often sends text messages to a friend of **hers** in Japan.
she 的獨立所有格形式（又稱「所有格代名詞的名詞形式」，即名詞性的所有格代名詞），相當於「her + 名詞」

✅ Ann often sends text messages to **her** friend in Japan.
she 的受格或所有格；作所有格時，後面要接名詞

安常發手機簡訊給她在日本的一個朋友。

their's、him's、our's 等，這些字都是錯誤的。正確的獨立所有格形式應該是 **theirs**、**his** 以及 **ours**。

262 high/tall 高

1

描述人的高度時，一定要用 tall，不能用 high

❌ Glen and Paul are **high** men.

✅ Glen and Paul are **tall** men.

葛蘭和保羅是高個子男人。

2

❌ Paul thought that the old tree was very **high**.

✅ Paul thought that the old tree was very **tall**.

保羅認為那棵老樹很高。
形容樹高，要用 tall，不用 high

(1) tall 形容（高度與直徑成對稱）樹、植物、人、建築物或動物，及狹窄筆直的東西。

(2) 也有一些人用 high building，但用 **tall** 來描述 building 更常見。

- **tall** buildings（高樓）
- **tall** chimneys（高聳的煙囪）
- **tall** grass（深草）
- a **tall** woman（一位高個子女子）

(3) high 形容「相對而言某個遠處地面上方的東西；高出地面之上體積巨大的東西」。

(4) 雖然有時也會聽到 tall mountain 或 tall hill，這在口語中是可以接受的，但在正式用語中，最好用 high mountain 或 high hill。

- high mountains（高山）
- high ceilings（高天花板）
- high walls（高牆）
- high-rises（超高層的大樓）

→ high-rises 比 tall buildings 高，但比 skyscrapers（摩天大樓）矮。在 23 m 到 150 m 高度之間的大樓是 high-rises，高於 150 m 的大樓是 skyscrapers。

263 hire/rent 雇用／租用

1

美式 I want to rent a big balloon for a day and float high in the sky.

英式 I want to hire a big balloon for a day and float high in the sky.

我想要租用一天大氣球，高高飄浮在天空中。

(1) 在英式英語中，rent 指「長時間的租用某物」(rent something)。
- How long has Margo rented your house in Chicago?
（瑪歌租借你在芝加哥的房子有多長時間了？）

(2) 在英式英語中，hire 指「短期租用某物或短期雇用某人」（hire a thing/hire a person）。
- hire a bike for a day（租一天自行車）
- hire a temporary maid（雇用一位臨時的女僕）

(3) 在英式英語中，如果需要長期雇用某人，就用 employ（somebody）。
- We have employed that maid for over a decade.
（我們雇用那位女僕已經十年多了。）

(4) 在美式英語中，無論是長時間還是短時間的出租某物，都用 rent。也請注意，rent 可以指「租用、租入」，也可以指「租出」。

- Oliver is going to rent an electric boat and explore the Trent River. ── 這句英式用 hire 表示短期租用

 （奧利弗打算租用一艘電動船，探索崔恩特河。）

⑸ 在美式英語中，無論是長期雇用還是短期雇用某人，都可以用 hire 或 employ。

 這句美式也可以用 employ

- I hired an interpreter during my last business trip to Buenos Aires.

 （最近一次在布宜諾斯艾利斯進行商務旅行期間，我雇用了一名翻譯。）

⑹ 請參見 let/rent。

264 his/her 他的／她的

1

性別歧視 "A good captain is always ready to teach his sailors," explained Elwood.

含意是「凡是好船長都是男性」，具性別歧視意味，應避免使用

累贅多餘 "A good captain is always ready to teach his or her sailors," explained Elwood.

沒有性別歧視，也沒有文法錯誤，但卻不流暢

笨拙 "A good captain is always ready to teach his/her sailors," explained Elwood.

常見但文法錯誤 "A good captain is always ready to teach their sailors," explained Elwood.

their 包括男性和女性，避免了性別歧視，但主詞是單數 a good captain，後面代名詞用複數 their，與單數主詞不相配，文法不正確

最佳 "Good captains are always ready to teach their sailors," explained Elwood.

最佳用法是主詞改成複數 captains，後面用複數人稱代名詞

埃爾伍德解釋：「好船長隨時樂意教水手。」

如何避免代名詞的性別歧視，也請參見 one 以及 sexist language。

文法加油站

his or her 或 his/her 結構

① 應該儘量改變句型以避免性別歧視語言，也要儘量避免多餘而笨拙的 his or her 或 his/her 結構。更要避免用複數人稱代名詞（their）搭配單數不定代名詞（someone、everyone 等）。

非正式	Everyone was clean after taking their shower.
性別歧視	Everyone was clean after taking his shower.
累贅多餘	Everyone was clean after taking his or her shower.
最佳	Everyone was clean after taking a shower. （沖澡後，大家都很乾淨。）

② 在無法改變句型的情況下，寧願用 his or her 或者 his/her 的結構，也不要用 their。上面及下面的非正式例句，在考試中務必要避免。

非正式	Nobody really understands humankind or even their own mind.
正式	Nobody really understands humankind or even his or her own mind. （沒有人真正瞭解人類，甚至不瞭解自己的心靈。）

③ 請參見 one 以及 sexist language。

單數不定代名詞與單數人稱代名詞

① 人稱代名詞應該與它的先行詞一致。下面單數不定代名詞後面通常不用複數人稱代名詞 they、them、their 和 theirs 替代。

- anybody
- everyone
- somebody
- anyone
- nobody
- someone
- everybody
- no one

② 即使一些文法書說我們可以在 anybody、somebody、nobody、one、everybody 等後面用 they 或者 their，但在正式用語中，比如考試、商務信函、商務會談、學術報告等，我們還是應該嚴格遵守文法規則，避免這種不標準的用法。

265 historical/historic 歷史的／具有歷史意義的

1

✖ Mr. King will take one of the historic tours of Athens.

✔ Mr. King will take one of the historical tours of Athens.
與歷史有關的

金先生將參加一次認識雅典歷史的遊覽活動。

2

✖ September 11, 2001 was a historical date that I will always remember.

✔ September 11, 2001 was a historic date that I will always remember.
具有歷史意義的

2001 年 9 月 11 日是我將永遠不會忘記、具有歷史意義的一天。

(1) 具有歷史意義的事物，要用 historic 來描述。

- the historic first voyage to the moon
（歷史上著名的第一次去月球的太空旅行）
- a historic building
（具有歷史意義的建築物）
- historic victories
（具有歷史意義的勝利）
- a historic site
（值得紀念的歷史遺跡）

(2) 與歷史有關的事物（無論這些事是否有重要性），就要用 historical 來描述；意思是「歷史的、史學的、有關歷史的」。

- historical clothing（歷史衣服）
- a historical character（歷史人物）
- a historical novel（歷史小說）
- historical research（史學研究）

(3) 雖然這兩個字有區別，但有時可以互換，比如：historical/historic times（歷史時期）。

文法加油站

比較：electric 和 electrical

① electric 意指「用電的／電動的；導電的」。

- an electric blanket（電熱毯）
- an electric iron（電熨斗）
- an electric razor（電動刮鬍刀）
- an electric toy（電動玩具）
- an electric outlet（電源插座）
- an electric plug（電源插頭）
- an electric cord（電源電線）

② electrical 意指「與電有關的；電氣科學的」；也可以用在泛指的名詞（equipment、appliance）前面，意指「用電的」。

- an electrical fault（電氣故障）
- an electrical engineer（電氣工程師）
- electrical equipment（電氣設備）

③ 請參見 economic 和 economical。

266 holiday/vacation 假期

1

美式 Sue Long plans to spend her vacation in Hong Kong.

英式 Sue Long plans to spend her holiday in Hong Kong.

蘇・龍計畫在香港度假。

(1) 美式英語中，離開學校或離開工作去休息一段時期（假日、休息日），用 vacation。美國人去度假是用 go on (a) vacation，而不是 go on holiday。

- Eve Nation is on vacation.（伊芙・納欣正在度假。）

  也有人用 on a vacation，但用 on vacation 更常見

- Did Paul go on a five-week vacation to Nepal?
  （保羅去了尼泊爾度過他的五週假期嗎？）

(2) 英式英語卻用 holiday(s) 指假日、休息日。即英式英語的 holiday 就等於美式英語的 vacation。英國人去度假是用 go on holiday，而不是 go on vacation。

- Monique is going on holiday next week.
（莫妮可下週要去度假。）
- Where is Ray going for his two weeks' holiday?
（雷要去哪裡度過他的兩週假期？）

(3) 對比美式和英式片語的用法：

	美式	英式
在休假中	on vacation	on holiday
度假期	spend one's vacation	spend one's holiday(s)
三週的假期	a three-week vacation	three weeks' holiday
兩個月的暑假	a two-month summer vacation	two months' summer holiday(s)

文法加油站

假期與節日的說法

① 美式英語中的 holiday 指的是美國法定或國定節日（legal holidays throughout the year）。美式通常說 a public holiday。（英式英語更常用 a bank holiday。）

② 當美國人說 the holiday season 或 the holidays 時，指的是包括耶誕節（Christmas）、光明節（Hanukkah）、新年（New Year's Day）的節日假期。

- Does Rae's brother have any plans for the holidays?
（芮的哥哥假日有任何計畫嗎？）
- I will be in Norway for the Christmas holiday.
（我要在挪威度過耶誕假期。）

③ 美國一年中的法定節日有：

- the Fourth of July（國慶日）
- Labor Day（勞動節）
- New Year's Day（新年）
- Presidents' Day（總統日）
- Martin Luther King Day（馬丁・路德・金節）
- Christmas Day（耶誕節）
- Thanksgiving Day（感恩節）
- Memorial Day（陣亡將士紀念日）
- Veterans Day（退伍軍人節）

④ 特殊祝賀語：

- Merry Christmas!（聖誕快樂！）（注意：不是 Happy Christmas!）
- Happy holidays!（節日快樂！）

267 home 在家、回家、到家

1

✗ Tomorrow Jerome is flying to home.

✓ Tomorrow Jerome is flying home.

在此片語中是副詞，前面不能加介系詞 to

傑羅姆明天飛回家。

(1) 在 fly home、go home 等片語中，home 是一個副詞，前面不能用介系詞 to。

- go/come/return/walk/drive/fly home

(2) 如果 go/come/return/walk/drive/fly 後面是名詞，不是副詞 home，要用介系詞 to。

- Next Tuesday Jerome is flying to Rome.
（下星期二傑羅姆要飛往羅馬。）

268 homework 家庭作業

1

✗ Annette, finish your homeworks before you surf on the Internet.

不可數名詞，沒有複數形式

✓ Annette, finish your homework before you surf on the Internet.

安妮特，完成家庭作業後再上網。

269 homework/housework
家庭作業／家務事

1

✗ Dirk has two chapters to read for housework.

家務工作（如打掃、做飯、洗衣等），與句意不符

✓ Dirk has two chapters to read for homework.

家庭作業；在家完成的計件工作

德克的家庭作業包括閱讀兩個章節。

- Lenore Burk hates housework even more than she hates homework.
  （蕾諾兒・伯克討厭做家務事甚於討厭做家庭作業。）

270 hope 希望

1

✗ We hope our mayor Dawn Peach could solve the problem of the pollution on the beach.

✓ We hope our mayor Dawn Peach can solve the problem of the pollution on the beach.

✓ We hope our mayor Dawn Peach will solve the problem of the pollution on the beach.

✓ We hope our mayor Dawn Peach will be able to solve the problem of the pollution on the beach.

hope 用現在式時（hope/hopes），通常後面接 can/will，不接過去式 could/would

✓ We hope our mayor Dawn Peach solves the problem of the pollution on the beach.

在 I/We hope 後面，經常用現在簡單式來表示未來

我們希望市長朵安・皮奇能解決海灘汙染的問題。

請參見 will/would。

文法加油站

比較：wish 後面用 would 或 could，表示假設語氣

- I wish I could catch a fish.（但願我能釣到一條魚。）

請參見 hope/wish。

2

❌ I don't hope he'll marry Cherry.
not 不能放在 hope 前面

✅ I hope he won't marry Cherry.
在否定句中，not 放在 hope 之後（hope . . . not）

我希望他不要娶伽麗。

文法加油站

英語的轉移否定句

比較：not 放在動詞 think/suppose/expect/believe/imagine 之前，表示轉移否定，即結構上否定主句，但意思上否定的是子句。

- not . . . think/suppose/expect/believe/imagine
- I don't think Bill will climb that hill.

→ I don't think ≒ I don't suppose/expect/believe/imagine
（我想／認為／期待／相信／猜想比爾不會爬那座山。）

271 hope/wish 希望／祝願

1

❌ I hope Bess Reed every success.

✅ I wish Bess Reed every success.
接人 + 名詞

✅ I hope Bess Reed will succeed.
接 that 子句，that 常省略

我祝貝絲・里德成功。

⑴ wish 意思是「祝福」，句型為：「wish + somebody + noun」。

⑵ hope 也可以表示「祝福」，但後面接 that 子句（常省略連接詞 that）。

- Kay and I wish you (somebody) a happy birthday (noun).

= Kay and I hope (that) you will have a happy birthday. (that 子句)

（凱和我祝你生日快樂。）

272 hospital 醫院

1

美式 Fay was admitted into the hospital yesterday.

英式 Fay was admitted into hospital yesterday.

菲昨天住院了。

⑴ 在美式英語中，無論是表示「住院、在醫院看病」還是表示「在醫院探望病人」，hospital 前面都需要 the。

⑵ 請參見 the 以及 a/an。

⑶ 英式英語在 hospital 前，有時用 the 有時不用 the，兩者意思有區別。如以下例句：

- Liz Whittle is in hospital.（莉茲・惠特爾在住院治療。）
  - 莉茲・惠特爾是病人
- Liz Whittle is in the hospital.（莉茲・惠特爾在醫院裡。）
  - 莉茲・惠特爾在這所特指的醫院裡，也許在探望一個病人，也許在看醫生

273 hot 熱的；燙的；性感的

1

美式 英式 Margo Scott said, "Oh, it's so hot!"

瑪歌・史考特說：「哎，好熱啊！」

Margo Scott said, "Oh, I'm so hot!"

英式 瑪歌・史考特說：「哎，我好熱啊！」

美式 瑪歌・史考特說：「哎，我好性感啊！」

(1) 如果想表示「熱的」，最好說「It is hot.」。

(2) hot 還可以表示「性感的」，尤其在美式英語中。因此，「I'm hot.」包含兩個意思，除了表示「我感覺很熱」，也可以表示「我很性感，讓人想入非非」。

- Dot is really hot!（達特好性感啊！）

(3) 注意，英式英語中的「I'm hot.」主要指「熱」。

274 how/what 怎麼／什麼

1

✗ How did the fish Mike cooked taste like?

✓ What did the fish Mike cooked taste like?

詢問一個人或者一個物品像什麼樣子

麥克做的魚味道怎麼樣？

2

✗ Trish, what's your English like?

✓ Trish, how's your English?

詢問某人的進步（how 的後面沒有 like）

翠西，你的英語如何？

(1) 一個人或者一個物品像什麼樣子，或者對人和事物的性質提問「持久的特性」，用 what . . . like ，而不用 how。

詢問一個人像什麼樣子，持久的特性

- What's Pete Pike like? — Pete is short, dark skinned, well-organized, and sweet.
（彼特・派克是怎樣的一個人？—— 彼特個子矮小、皮膚微黑、做事有條不紊，而且很和藹。）

(2) how 用來問候某人的健康，或詢問某人的進步（如：How's your English?），詢問變化的事物（如暫時的情況和情緒等）。請注意：在 how 的後面沒有 like。

問候某人的健康

- How's your sister Lenore? — She's fine.
（你的妹妹蕾諾兒好嗎？——她很好。）

(3) **how** 也用來詢問「人們對所經歷過的事有什麼反應、感覺、印象」。

詢問對經歷的事有什麼感覺

- June, **how** was your honeymoon? — Heavenly!
  （茱恩，你的蜜月怎樣？——棒極了！）

(4) 注意下面的細微區別：

詢問對方對電影的反應或感覺（問觀影後對電影的感受）。意為「你看了那部愛情電影，有些什麼感受？」

- Ivy, **how** was that love movie? — Both Brigitte and I liked it.
  （愛葳，那部愛情電影怎麼樣？——布麗姬和我都很喜歡。）

請對方對電影作描述並評論（問電影本身演的是什麼）。相當於「What was that movie about?」

- **What** was that movie **like**? — It was a scary movie, because some giant spiders from outer space were trying to destroy the human race.
  （那是一部什麼樣的電影？——那是部恐怖片，描述來自外太空的一些巨大蜘蛛試圖毀滅人類。）

(5) 用來詢問天氣時，**how** 和 **what** 兩者沒有什麼區別。

- "**What**'s the weather **like** today?" asked Heather.
  = "**How**'s the weather today?" asked Heather.
  （海瑟問：「今天天氣如何？」）

在 how 的後面沒有 like

(6) **how about . . .** 和 **what about . . .** 之間沒有任何區別，都是用來提建議。

- Glen inquired, "When do you want to meet Pete?"
  — Kay replied, "**How/What about** 7 p.m. on Sunday."
  （葛蘭問：「你希望何時見彼特？」——凱回答：「星期天晚上七點怎麼樣？」）

(7) **how** 錯誤用法例句：

⊗ **How do you think of** Lulu?

✔ **What do you think of** Lulu?（你怎樣看待露露？）

275 however/but 然而／但是

1

✗ Olive bought a nice house, however it was too expensive.

副詞 however 不是用來連接兩個獨立子句

✓ Olive bought a nice house, but it was too expensive.

奧莉芙買的房子雖好，但太貴了。

副詞 however 用在第二個句子裡

- I understand your financial difficulties. However, I can't do anything to help you.
（我理解你的財務困境。可是，我無法幫助你。）

276 hundred 一百

1

✗ Jane Ash reported that over two hundreds people were injured in the train crash.

前面如還有另一數詞（five、ten 等），不使用複數形

✓ Jane Ash reported that over two hundred people were injured in the train crash.

珍・亞許報導，在這次火車相撞事故中，有兩百多人受傷。

(1) 數詞 hundred、thousand 和 million 前面如果還有另一個數詞（five、ten 等），就不用複數形式，比如：five hundred people（五百人）、six thousand people（六千人）、two million people（兩百萬人）。

(2) 不表示確切的幾百、幾千，而表示數以百計或數以千計時，這些字要用其複數形式，這時前面不能有其他數詞修飾，後面要接 of。比如：

- hundreds of people（數百人）
- thousands of people（數千人）
- millions of people（數百萬人）

I

277 I 我

1

❌ I and my brother are going to fly to Vancouver in July.

應該把自己（I）放最後

✅ My brother and I are going to fly to Vancouver in July.

出於禮貌，人們通常最後才提及自己（I）

我和哥哥七月時要飛往溫哥華。

2

❌ Why don't I and you go and watch the International Space Station travel across the sky?

✅ Why don't you and I go and watch the International Space Station travel across the sky?

為什麼你和我不去觀看國際太空站的空中之旅？

出於禮貌，人們通常最後提及自己，即把自己（I 或 me）放在後面，比如：you and I（主格），you and me（受格），she and I（主格），Jerry and I（主格），Amy and me（受格）。而中文較多的是「我和……」，注意中英文表達順序的區別。

文法加油站

下面是常見的成對代名詞

Subject 主格	Object 受格
he and she	him and her
he and we	him and us
she and I	her and me

Subject 主格	Object 受格
she and they	her and them
we and they	us and them
they and I	them and me

278 ideal/perfect 理想的／完美的

1

❌ Today's weather is the most ideal for having a picnic at Lake Heather.

ideal 和 perfect（完美）不需要用 most、very 這類字修飾

❌ Today's weather is very perfect for having a picnic at Lake Heather.

✅ Today's weather is ideal for having a picnic at Lake Heather.

✅ Today's weather is perfect for having a picnic at Lake Heather.

今天的天氣非常適合在海瑟湖舉行野餐。

2

❌ Little Lily is dancing the most perfectly.

✅ Little Lily is dancing perfectly.

小莉莉跳得很完美。

(1) ideal 和 perfect 意思是「完美」。我們說某人／某事 ideal 或 perfect，就意味著這人或這事是「最好」的。不需要用 most/more/rather/very 這類字修飾。

(2) 請參見 doublets/wordiness。

279 if 如果

1

if 子句表示未來，if 子句裡通常不用 will

❌ If Ann and I will have enough money next year, we will go on a tour of Afghanistan.

if 子句表示未來，if 子句裡通常用現在式

✅ If Ann and I have enough money next year, we will go on a tour of Afghanistan.

如果明年安和我有足夠的錢，我們就要去阿富汗旅行。

(1) 表示未來時，if 子句通常用現在式。請參見 simple present tense/simple future tense 以及 after。

(2) 當 **if** 具有與 **whether** 大致相同的意思時，if 之後可以跟 will。

這句 if 可以用 whether 來代替

- Jane will let us know soon **if** she **will** be able to come to Spain.
（珍很快就會讓我們知道她是否能來西班牙。）

(3) 如果 if 子句表示意願、願望或堅持的意思（不表示將來），if 子句裡可以用 will。比較下面兩個例句：

if 子句表示未來，子句裡通常不用 will 而用現在式

- **If** Lars **calls**, tell him I have moved to Mars.
（如果拉斯打電話來，告訴他我已搬去火星了。）

如果 if 子句表示意願、願望或堅持的意思（不表示未來），if 子句裡可以用 will

- **If** you **will** come right now, I can take you to the UFO.

= **If** you are **willing** to come right now, I can take you to the UFO.
（如果你願意現在就來，我可以帶你去看那架不明飛行物。）

→ 這句的 if 子句裡也可以用現在式：**If you come right now . . .**

文法加油站

if 子句與主要子句的文法結構

① 如果**某事總是事實**，在 if 子句和主要子句中都用**現在簡單式**。

if + 現在式；主要子句 + 現在式（某事總是事實）

- **If** I **eat** too much cake, I **get** a stomachache.
（只要吃太多蛋糕，我的胃就會痛。）

② 如果 if 子句表達的是一個**未來可能發生的事**，在 if 子句中要用**現在簡單式**，在主要子句中要用 **will**。

if + 簡單現在式；主要子句 +will（未來有可能發生的事）：她明年很可能有足夠的錢

- **If** Ann **has** enough money next year, she **will** go to Japan.
（如果安明年有足夠的錢，她就要去日本。）

③ 如果 if 子句表達的是一個**過去可能發生過的事情**，在 if 子句中和主要子句中都要用**過去簡單式**。

if 可以與 even 連用，表示讓步，意指「即使」。even if + 過去式（過去可能發生過的事情）：他昨天可能在學校；主要子句 + 過去式

- **Even if** Jim **was** in our school yesterday, I **did not see** him.
（即使吉姆昨天在我們學校，我卻沒有看見他。）

④ 如果 if 子句表達的是一個現在或未來不可能發生的事，或**與現在或未來事實相反的事**，在 if 子句中用**過去簡單式**（if 子句中的 be 動詞一律用 were；英式非正式用語也可以用 was），而在主要子句中用 **would/might/could**。這種句型是**假設語氣**，表示與現在或未來事實相反的假設。

if+ 過去簡單式；主要子句 +would/might/could（未來不可能發生的事；與未來事實相反的事）：我明年很可能沒有足夠的錢

- **If** I **had** enough money next year, I **would** go to visit Brad and Stan in Pakistan.
（假如我明年有足夠的錢，我就要去巴基斯坦找布萊德和斯坦。）

⑤ 如果 if 子句表達的是過去某件沒有發生的事情，或**與過去事實相反的事**，if 子句裡用**過去完成式**，主要子句裡用 **would have done**、**should have done**、**could have done** 或 **might have done**。這種句型也是**假設語氣**，表示與過去事實相反的假設。

if+ 過去完成式；主要子句 +would+ 現在完成式（與過去事實相反的事）：事實上昨天他不在辦公室，我也沒有看見他

- **If** Jim **had been** in the office yesterday, I **would have seen** him.
（假如吉姆昨天在辦公室，我就會看見他。）

280 if/in case 如果／以防

1

✗ Gus drove slowly if someone suddenly stepped in front of his bus.

表示「以防、免得」

✓ Gus drove slowly in case someone suddenly stepped in front of his bus.

加斯開車很慢，以防有人突然出現在他的公車前面。

2

✗ Sue and I will stop by to see you in case we pass through Seoul.

意思是「如果」，表示「條件」

✓ Sue and I will stop by to see you if we pass through Seoul.

如果蘇和我經過首爾，我們就會順便去看你。

in case 和 if 不是同一個意思。in case 用來談論預防措施，意思是「以防、免得」。if 表示「條件」，意思是「如果」。用 if 和 in case 所表示的事情發生的先後次序不一樣。

表示「發生嚴重問題後打電話（在美國打 911）」

· Harlem will call 911 if there's a serious problem.
（如果發生嚴重的問題，哈林會打 911。）

表示「失火之前給房船保險」

· Ms. Wire, you should insure your houseboat in case there's a fire.（崴爾小姐，你應該給你的房船保險，以防發生火災。）

281 ill/sick 生病的

1

美式 Jill Brick is sick.

表示健康狀況不好，美式常用 sick。sick 既可放在連綴動詞 be 後面作補語，也可放在名詞前作修飾語

英式 Jill Brick is ill.

吉兒 · 布里克生病了。

表示健康狀況不好，英式連綴動詞 be 後面用 ill 作補語，但 ill 不能放在名詞前作修飾語，而 sick 卻可放在名詞前作修飾語

2

✗ My brother is taking care of our ill mother.

表示健康狀況不好，ill 不能放在名詞前作修飾語

✓ My brother is taking care of our sick mother.

我的哥哥在照顧生病的母親。

sick 可以放在名詞前面作修飾語

(1) sick/ill 放在連綴動詞後面作補語。

美式 am/is/are/was/were sick

英式 am/is/are/was/were ill

(2) sick 還可以表示「噁心的」。比如：feel sick（感覺想嘔吐）。

(3) sick 可以用在名詞前作修飾語。

· a sick person（一個病人） · a sick tree（一棵病樹）

282 import/export 輸入；進口商品／輸出；出口商品

1

✗ The imports of beer from Russia increased last year.

「進口量」是**不可數名詞**，沒有複數形

✓ The import of beer from Russia increased last year.

表示「從國外購買商品，然後帶進國內」

✓ The amount of imported Russian beer increased last year.

俄國啤酒進口量去年增加了。

(1) import「進口、輸入（額）」，是**不可數名詞**，沒有複數形。表示「從國外購買商品，然後帶進國內」。反義詞是 export「出口、輸出（額）」。

(2) import「進口商品」，是**可數名詞**。反義詞是 export「出口商品」。

- "Is tea a major export of China?" asked Dee.
（蒂問：「茶是中國的一種主要出口商品嗎？」）

- Mort's company will buy fifty electric trucks to reduce its reliance on oil imports.
（莫特的公司要購買 50 輛電動卡車，目的是為了降低對石油進口產品的依賴。）

(3) import 和 export 也可以用作**動詞**。

- the import of American cars（美國汽車進口）
- to import American cars
= to import cars from America（進口美國汽車）
- the export of coffee（咖啡出口）
- to export coffee（出口咖啡）

283 important (essential/desirable/necessary/vital)

重要的

1

✗ June said it was important that you came to the hospital soon.
需用原形動詞

✓ June said it was important that you come to the hospital soon.

茱恩說，你有必要盡快來醫院。

(1) 在「it is/was important/essential/desirable/necessary/vital + that 子句」的結構中，句子的主要子句表達「重要、必要、要求、強烈的請求」，無論主要子句的動詞是現在式還是過去式，無論 that 子句的主詞是單數還是複數，動詞都要用原形動詞的假設語氣〔美式〕，而英式英語常在原形動詞前加 should。

(2) 當然在口語中，你會常聽見一些人無視這條規則。比如「It was important that you came to the hospital soon.」，這句在口語中是可以接受的，但並不是標準英語。這種錯誤如此常見，有時候聽上去好像很順耳。但在考試中、商務信函和其他正式文體中，請記住要用「**原形動詞**」的假設語氣或用「**should + 原形動詞**」。

(3) 類似的形容詞如下：

· advised · important · proposed · urgent
· desirable · mandatory · recommended · vital
· essential · necessary · required
· imperative · obligatory · suggested

(4) 同樣道理，一些表示「**必要、建議、要求**」的動詞和名詞（**demand, insist, requirement, suggestion**）後面接 that 子句時，無論主要子句的動詞是現在式還是過去式，無論 that 子句的主詞是單數還是複數，要直接用**原形動詞〔美式〕**，或用「**should + 原形動詞**」〔英式〕。

美式 **Lily** insisted that **Millie** go to Italy immediately.
主要子句和子句的主詞不同

英式 Lily insisted that Millie should go to Italy immediately.
（莉莉堅持要米莉立刻去義大利。）

· Pat ignored her doctor's suggestion that she (should) eat less fat.（蓓特無視醫生要她少攝取脂肪的建議。）

(5) 請參見 request 和 suggest 的用法。

284 in/on 在……時候／在……某天

1

✗ In July 7, Ron and I will fly to Jerusalem.

✓ On July 7, Ron and I will fly to Jerusalem.
表示某個特定的一天發生了某事，要用 on。on 與 day 或 date 連用

七月七號，我和朗要飛往耶路撒冷。

2

✗ On May next year, Rae will visit Norway.

✓ In May next year, Rae will visit Norway.
用 in 表示在某個特定的時候某事發生了，常與 month/year/season 連用

明年五月芮要去挪威旅行。

(1) 表示某個特定的一天發生了某事，要用 on，不用 in。on 與 day 或 date 連用。

- on Friday（在星期五）
- on the previous day（在前一天）
- on June 3（在六月三號）
- on National Day（在國慶日）
- On Friday Eve will leave Tel Aviv.
（星期五伊芙要離開〔以色列〕特拉維夫市。）

(2) 用 in 表示在某個特定的時候某事發生了，常與 month/year/season 連用。

- in April（在四月）
- in 2038（在 2038 年）
- in (the) spring（在春天）
- in (the) summer（在夏天）
- in (the) winter（在冬天）
- in the fall（在秋天）〔在這個片語裡必須用 the〕
- Clive learned to dive in 2016.（克萊夫在 2016 年學會了跳水。）

285 in/since/on 在……時候／自從……以來／在……某天

1

✗ Since March Trish started to study English.

✓ In March Trish started to study English.

翠西從三月開始學習英語。

(1) since 可以作連接詞（後面接從屬子句），也可以作介系詞（後面接名詞），用來表示從過去某一點開始，持續到現在或持續到另一個過去的時間點。主要子句裡的動詞通常用**現在完成式**，或**過去完成式**，或**完成進行式**（不用過去簡單式）。有時在主要子句裡用現在簡單式。

(2) 請參見 since。

句子的動詞用現在完成進行式（has been working）

- Mary has been working as a waitress in a Chinese restaurant since January.

介系詞 since 後面接名詞，since 表示從過去某一時間點開始持續到現在

（瑪麗從一月起，就一直在一家中式餐館當女服務生。）

主要子句用過去完成式（hadn't seen）。連接詞 since 引導的從屬子句用過去式（went）。since 表示從過去某一時間點開始持續到另一個過去時間點。

- I hadn't seen Ann since she went to live in Japan.
（自從安去日本定居，我就再也沒有看見過她。）

It is = It has been。主要子句用現在簡單式（is）或現在完成式（has been），since 子句用過去式（saw）。since 表示從過去某一時間點開始持續到現在。

· **It is** five years **since** I last **saw** Clive.
（自從我上次見到克萊夫後，已經過了五年了。）

(3) 有介系詞 in 和 on 的句子裡，可以用現在式、未來式或過去式。（in 和 on 的區別請看上一個條目。）

· In the winter Lake Rover freezes over.
（羅維湖在冬天結冰。）**現在式**

· Will June go downtown in the afternoon?
（下午茱恩會去市區嗎？）**未來式**

· Evan started reading novels in English in the fall of 2007.
（伊文從 2007 年的秋天開始閱讀英文小說。）**過去式**

· Mary Wu's birthday is on the 19th of January.
（瑪麗 · 吳的生日是一月十九號。）**現在式**

· Ray is going to Las Vegas on Monday.
（雷星期一要去拉斯維加斯。）**未來式**

· Rae and I first met on a stormy day last May.
（芮和我是在去年五月的一個暴風雨天相識。）**過去式**

286 in school/at school 在學校

1

✗ Last year Ann Lime worked in a hotel, but now she is at school full time.

at school 表示講話的此刻正在學校上課。**in** school 才是指「在校生」

✓ Last year Ann Lime worked in a hotel, but now she is in school full time.

表示在校接受教育（participation in education），意為「在校生」

去年安 · 萊姆在一家旅館工作，而現在她是全日在校生。

(1) at school：指具體的地理位置（physical location），表示講話的此刻正在學校上課。

(2) in school = at school：也可以指具體的地理位置（physical location），表示講話的此刻正在學校上課。

- Ann: Where is Claire McCool?
  Dan: Claire McCool is at/in school. 指具體地理位置；講話的此刻克萊兒正在學校上課

  （安：克萊兒・麥可庫爾在哪裡？
  丹：克萊兒・麥可庫爾在學校上課。）

(3) in school ≠ at school：表示在校接受教育（participation in education），指「在校生」。

- Claire McCool took a year off to work in Europe, but now she's back in school. 表示在校接受教育；克萊兒・麥可庫爾是在校生

  （克萊兒 ・ 麥可庫爾休學去了歐洲工作一年，現在她回到學校讀書了。）

(4) 談論過去時態，at school 和 in school 沒有什麼區別。

- Brice: Louise, where did you learn your Chinese?
  Louise: I learned it at/in school from Mr. Pool. 談論過去時態，at school 和 in school 可以互換

  （布萊斯：露易絲，你在哪裡學的中文？
  露易絲：我在學校跟普爾先生學的。）

287 indirect speech/reported speech
間接引語

1

✗ Joe, just tell me what do you want to know?

間接疑問句不用助動詞 do 和問號

✓ Joe, just tell me what you want to know.

喬，告訴我你究竟想知道什麼。

整個句子是祈使句，句尾用句號，不用問號

2

✗ Mort, could you please tell me how can I get to the airport?

間接疑問句的語序應該要和直述句的語序一樣

✓ Mort, could you please tell me how I can get to the airport?

莫特，可以請你告訴我怎樣去機場嗎？

間接疑問句中，情態助動詞（can、could、may、should 等）要放在主詞 I 後面，與直述句的語序一樣

(1) 請參見 do（auxiliary verb）。

(2) 上面兩個例句都是特殊疑問句的間接引語。特殊疑問句從直接引語變間接引語時，仍保留原來的疑問詞（what、how）引導。

3

直接 Lorelei asked Buzz, "**Who is that guy**?"

間接 Lorelei asked Buzz **who that guy was**.

蘿芮萊問巴斯那人是誰。

保留直接引語的疑問詞

特殊疑問句的間接引語用原疑問詞 **who** 引導；直接引語的連綴動詞現在式 is 在間接引語中改為過去式 **was**，並放在主詞 that guy 後面，與直述句語序一樣。

4

直接 Trish asked, "**Are you** fond of English?"

間接 Trish asked **me whether I was** fond of English.

翠西問我是否喜歡英語。

(1) 直接引語如果是一般疑問句，變為間接引語時，要用連接詞 **whether** 或 **if** 引導。間接引語用直述句的語序，動詞置於主詞後面（I was）。

(2) 主句動詞 **asked** 後面需要補充受詞（me、him、us 等）。

(3) 直接引語的代名詞 **you** 在間接引語中要變為 **I**。**現在式**（Are you）也要變為**過去式**（I was）。時態變化請參見下頁。

5

✗ Dee said that she **will** never forgive me.

✓ Dee said that she **would** never forgive me.

蒂說她永遠也不原諒我。

在間接引語中，原直接引語中的 will 要改成 would

在一個表示說話的過去式動詞或表示報導的過去式動詞（比如 said、stated、reported）後面，在間接引語中需要改變直接引語中的動詞時態。

直接 Kate said, "Nate, you **look** great."

間接 Kate told Nate he **looked** great.

（凱特告訴內特，他看起來好極了。）

文法加油站

時態改變參考表

直接引語	間接引語	直接引語	間接引語
· am/are/is	→ was/were	· 現在簡單式	→過去簡單式
· have/has	→ had	· 過去簡單式	→過去完成式 （有時需要保留過去簡單式）
· will	→ would	· 現在進行式	→過去進行式
· can	→ could	· 現在完成式	→過去完成式
· do/does	→ did		

直接引語變間接引語，有些字需要做相對應的改變

① 在表示「說、講」等動詞的過去式（比如 said、stated、reported）後面，我們有時需要對副詞以及其他的一些字進行變動。改變的原因是因為在轉述的時候，時間、地點、講話人不同了。

直接引語	間接引語
here	→ there
tomorrow	→ the next day or the following day
yesterday	→ the day before or the previous day
today	→ that day
now	→ then
this	→ that
next week	→ the next week
come	→ go

· Rae said, "I am working today."（芮說：「我今天在上班。」）

· Rae said she was working that day.（芮說她那天在上班。）
　作者／轉述者在轉述這句話時，時間已經變化了，不在同一天

· Rae said she was working today.（芮說她今天在上班。）
　作者／轉述者在轉述這句話時，時間是相同的，在同一天

· Rae said she is working today.（芮說她今天在上班。）
　由於時間相同，仍然在同一天，也可以不改變時態；用 is working 表示動作或狀態仍在繼續

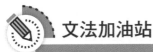

② 間接命令或請求（Indirect Commands or Requests）用「**ask/tell/order/beg/warn 等動詞 + 受詞 + 帶 to 的不定詞**」，來表達某人要我們或他人做什麼（what people want(ed) us or others to do）。總之，直接引語變為間接引語時，要注意人稱、時態、語序上的變化。

(a) "Read 25,000 English words every day," said Rae.
（芮說：「每天要閱讀 25,000 個英語字彙。」）

Rae asked us to read 25,000 English words every day.
（芮要我們每天閱讀 25,000 個英語字彙。）

(b) "Ted, don't smoke anywhere on this ship," said Skip.
（史基普說：「泰德，不要在這艘船上任何一個地方抽菸。」）

否定詞 not 要置於不定詞 to 前面

Skip asked Ted not to smoke anywhere on this ship.
（史基普要泰德不要在這艘船的任何一個地方抽菸。）

288 infinitive 分離不定詞

1

不自然 Lily has learned how to wisely spend money.

不定詞一般來說不分開

自然 Lily has learned how to spend money wisely.

莉莉已經學會了如何明智地花錢。

(1) 一般來說，不要把不定詞分開。

(2) 但有時候，堅持這一規則，反而會造成句子含混不清楚或不自然。在這種情況下，就不要遵守這條規則了。

語意不清 My family decided to discuss further Kay's plan to study in Japan.

分不清是修飾 Kay's plan 還是修飾動詞 discuss

語意清楚 My family decided to further discuss Kay's plan to study in Japan.

不定詞分開反而使句子更清楚

（我家人決定進一步討論凱去日本讀書的計畫。）

(3) 如果不得不把不定詞分開，最好只用一個單字來分開。

✗ Mom decided **to put quickly little Ted** to bed.

✓ Mom decided **to quickly put little Ted** to bed.
副詞 動詞 受詞

用這種分離不定詞結構，動詞和受詞就不會被一個副詞分開

（媽媽決定馬上把小泰德放到床上睡覺。）

(4) 請參見 try not to/try to not。

289 infinitive form/-ing form

請參見 avoid, consider, forget, practice, regret, remember, spend, stop, suggest 和 try to do/try doing。

290 infinitive without "to"

請參見 let 和 make。

291 inform 通知

1

✗ I regret to **inform that** Arty and I cannot attend your birthday party.

✓ I regret to **inform you that** Arty and I cannot attend your birthday party.

我很抱歉通知你，亞提和我不能參加你的生日聚會。

2

✗ Mabel, please **inform me your decision** as soon as possible.

✓ Mabel, please **inform me of/about your decision** as soon as possible.

美博，請儘快告知我你的決定。

(1) **inform somebody that**：inform 後面先接某人，然後再接 that 子句。

(2) **inform somebody of/about something**：inform 後面接某人，再接介系詞 of 或 about，然後接某事。

292 information 資訊

1

✗ Why did you tell Jane Nation the wrong informations?

不可數名詞，沒有複數形式，也不能與不定冠詞 an 連用

✓ Why did you tell Jane Nation the wrong information?

指「消息、報導、諮詢、資訊」，**不可數**

你為什麼要把那條錯誤的資訊告訴珍・納欣？

- a piece of information（一則消息）
- a lot of information（許多資訊）

293 -ing form/-ed form

請參見 excited/exciting 和 interested/interesting。

294 injure 傷害

1

✗ Paul injured while playing basketball.

✓ Paul was injured while playing basketball.

injure 是**及物動詞**，常用於被動式 be injured

保羅在打籃球時受傷了。

- be seriously/badly/severely injured（嚴重受傷）
- Kay injured her back while practicing ballet today.（凱今天在練習芭蕾舞時傷了背。）

295 injure/wound 受傷

1

✗ "Were you wounded during the car accident," asked Sue.

用於「在打架或戰爭中」受刀傷或槍傷

✓ "Were you injured during the car accident," asked Sue.

用於「在事故中受了傷」

蘇問：「你在車禍中受傷了嗎？」

(1) 人們「在事故中受了傷」，用 they are injured，不用 they are wounded。

(2) 人們「在打架或戰爭中」（in a fight or battle or war）受刀傷或槍傷，通常用 they are wounded (by guns, knives, etc.）。

(3) 如果某人 is wounded，那麼這個人就是受到了暴力的傷害，有時也可以用 is injured 來表示這個意思。

· Kay said, "Five of our soldiers were wounded today."

這句也可以用 were injured

（凱說：「今天我們有五個士兵受傷。」）

(4) the wounded = people who are wounded, especially in warfare（傷兵、受傷者）。

296 inside 在……裡面

1

非正式 Mark and his friends played all day inside of the park.

美國人有時會用來代替 inside，但正式用語中不可加 of

正式 Mark and his friends played all day inside the park.

意為「在……的裡面」，是介系詞，後面接名詞，不與 of 連用

馬克和他的朋友們在公園裡玩了一整天。

(1) 有些美國人有時會用 inside of 來代替 inside。但在正式用語中，介系詞請用 inside，不要用 inside of。

(2) inside 也可以作名詞，意思是「內部、裡面」（= the inner part of something）。不要把當介系詞 inside 與當名詞的片語 the inside of 混淆。

· Skip explored the inside of the huge spaceship.

這裡的 inside 是名詞，因此後面可以接 of

（史基普探索了那艘巨大太空船的內部。）

297 insist 堅持要求；堅持認為

1

❌ Ann insisted me to accept her plan.

後面不接不定詞

✅ Ann insisted that I accept her plan.

安堅持要我接受她的計畫。

insisted + that 子句（用原形動詞）

⑴ insist 後面不接不定詞。句型為：

insist that somebody (should) do something

（〔某人〕堅持主張／堅持要求〔另一個人〕做某事）

→ 受詞子句的動詞要用原形動詞 美式

或 should+ 原形動詞 英式

· Ms. Fish insisted that we use our cellphones and MP4 players to learn English.

（費許老師堅持要我們使用手機和 MP4 播放器來學習英語。）

insist on doing something（一定要）

· If Dawn Sun insists on acting like a spoiled child, we will treat her like one.

（如果朵安・孫一定要表現得像一個被寵壞的孩子，那麼我們就把她看作是一個被寵壞的孩子。）

⑵ 當 insist 的意思是「堅持認為」（to assert firmly）的時候，insist 後面的受詞子句就**不用原形動詞**。

· Coco insisted that she saw a UFO.

（可可堅持認為她看到一個不明飛行物。）

298 interested 對……感興趣的

1

❌ Is Gus interested to go for a swim with us?

「對做某事感興趣」，通常不用不定詞 be interested to do something

✅ Is Gus interested in going for a swim with us?

「對做某事感興趣」（be interested in doing something），介系詞用 **in**

加斯有興趣跟我們一起去游泳嗎？

(1) be interested in doing something：表示「對做某事感興趣」（willing or eager to do something），指將要或可能發生的事。通常不用不定詞 be interested to do something。

- Dinah is interested in teaching in Taiwan.
  （黛娜對去台灣教書感興趣。）

(2) be interested＋不定詞： be interested to 後面通常接**特定的一些動詞**，表示「對他人所瞭解的事或經歷過的事感興趣」（want to know about something），表示出自「好奇、關心」（showing curiosity, fascination, or concern）。

- be interested to hear/know/learn/note/read/see something
- I am interested to learn if Grace has won the sailboat race.（我很想瞭解葛蕾絲是否贏了那場帆船比賽。）
- Jill is interested to hear the latest news about Bill.
  （吉兒很想〔有興趣〕聽到關於比爾的最新消息。）
- I am interested to know who was on the phone with Coco.

= I want to know who was on the phone with Coco.
（我很想〔有興趣〕知道剛才誰在跟可可通電話。）

299 interested/interesting 感興趣的／有趣的

1

✗ Brooke lent me an interested book.

✓ Brooke lent me an interesting book.

布露可借給我一本有趣的書。

interesting：意思是「引起興趣的、令人關注的、有趣的」

(1) interesting 的意思是「引起興趣的、令人關注的、有趣的」。請參見 excited/exciting。

(2) interested 的意思是「感興趣的、關心的」。請一定要記住 interested 表示「感興趣的」時，只能用來描述人，不用來描述事物，比如，不能說 an interested story 或 a story is interested。

(3) interested 還可以表示「有利害關係的、利益相關的、當事的」。

(4) interested 的反義詞是 uninterested（不感興趣的；無利害關係的）。

- an interesting person（有趣的人）
- interested members（感興趣的成員們）
- an interesting talk（有趣的談話）——這裡不能用 interested
- an interested party（當事人）—— 意思是「利益相關的」
- Lori was not interested in that love story.
  （蘿麗對那個愛情故事不感興趣。）

(5) 某人是否「對故事感興趣」，一定得用 be interested in。假若 Lori 是這個故事裡的一個人物，而這個人物很乏味，那麼，就可以說 Lori was not interesting in that love story.。意思是，「在那個愛情故事裡，蘿麗是一個乏味的人物」。

300 into/in to

1

✗ Nancy Bell walked in to the fancy hotel.

✓ Nancy Bell walked into the fancy hotel.

南西・貝爾走進那家豪華旅館。 —— 含意是「進入」（entry），作**介系詞**

(1) into 的含意是進入（entry），用作**介系詞**。

- Last week Amy went into the Army.

= Last week Amy joined the Army.（上週艾咪從軍了。）

(2) 那麼 in to 的含意是什麼呢？ in 通常是某片語動詞的一部分，to 則為介系詞或不定詞的一部分。

in 是片語動詞 sent in 的一部分；to 是介系詞

- All crime reports should be sent in to Police Chief Hall.
  （所有的犯罪報告應當送交給警長霍爾。）

in 是片語動詞 came in 的一部分；to 是不定詞 to see 的一部分

- To our delight, Mayor Gus White came in to see us.
  （使我們高興的是，加斯・懷特市長走進來見我們。）

301 inversion 倒裝結構

請參見 not only . . . but also . . .。

302 irregardless/regardless 不管怎樣

1 ✗ Irregardless of what I say, Kate is going to date that playboy Nate.

✓ Regardless of what I say, Kate is going to date that playboy Nate.

不管我說什麼，凱特也要跟那個花花公子內特約會。

有些字典列舉了 irregardless 這個字，但實際上根本就沒有 irregardless 這個字。irregardless 不僅是錯誤的，而且也是累贅的。字尾 -less 已經使 regard 具有否定含意，不需要再加一個字首 ir- 使這個字雙重否定。

303 its/it's 它的／它是

1 ✗ Its Joan surfing the Internet on her cellphone!

= of it，意思是「它的」，與句意不符

✓ It's Joan surfing the Internet on her cellphone!

= It is 的縮寫形式

是瓊在用手機上網！

什麼時候應該用 its，什麼時候又應該用 it's。這兩個小小的字很多聰明的人感到頭痛。只需記住兩點，你就可以輕而易舉解決這個問題，不會混淆這兩個字：

(1) it's 是 it is 或者 it has 的縮寫形式。如果你能用 it is 或者 it has 來取代，那麼就應該選擇 it's，而不是 its。

(2) 而 its = of it，是 it 的所有格形式，就像 my、his、her、ours、theirs 等。its 的意思是「它的」，後面接一個名詞。

= It has

- It's been a long time since I last visited Hong Kong.
  （自從我上次去香港玩，已經過了很長的時間了。）

  = of it，意思是「它的」

- We love Hungary because of its charm and beauty.
  （我們愛匈牙利，因它美得迷人。）

J

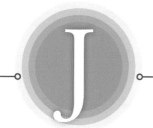

304 jewel/jewellery/jewelry 寶石／珠寶首飾

1

❌ Before her divorce, Claire always wore jewelries in her hair.
珠寶首飾總稱，為**不可數名詞**，沒有複數形式

✅ Before her divorce, Claire always wore jewelry/jewellery in her hair.
英式的拼寫，比美式多兩個字母 -le

克萊兒離婚前頭上常戴珠寶首飾。

(1) jewelry 指珠寶首飾，是 rings（戒指）、brooches（女用胸針）、bracelets（手鐲）、necklaces（項鏈）等的總稱，為不可數名詞，沒有複數形式，也不用不定冠詞 a 修飾。

(2) jewel 是可數名詞，指「寶石」、「寶石飾物」、「珍貴的東西；難得可貴的人」等具體的東西。

- Dan: Does Rose have a jewel on the pin in her nose?
  Ann: Yes, and that jewel is on her nose everywhere she goes.
  （丹：蘿絲鼻子的飾針上有一顆寶石嗎？
  安：有啊，無論她走到哪裡，那顆寶石都在她的鼻子上。）

305 journey/tour/voyage 旅遊

1

❌ Gus went on a journey around the city by bus.

❌ Gus went on a voyage around the city by bus.

✅ Gus went on a tour around the city by bus.

加斯搭公車環城遊覽。

(1) 如果我們搭公車參觀許多地方，應該是：a bus tour/a tour by bus。tour 通常表示一種為了娛樂的遊覽，有時也可以表示一種為了工作的旅行。

(2) journey 尤指「特別長的旅行」，有專門的目的，從一處旅行到另一處。

- Annie's job as a train engineer means she has been on many long journeys.
（安妮是一名火車駕駛員，這意謂著她有過多次長程旅行的經驗。）

(3) voyage 指「搭船旅行、航海」（a long journey by ship）。

- Jane is going on an around-the-world voyage that starts and ends in Spain.
（珍妮要搭船環遊世界，從西班牙起航然後回到西班牙。）

306 just 剛才

1

美式 June just landed on the moon.

意思是「剛才」(a moment ago) 時，美式常用於**過去式**中

英式 June has just landed on the moon.

意思是「剛才」(a moment ago) 時，英式常用於**現在完成式**中

茱恩剛登陸了月球。

307 just/only 僅僅

1

✗ The only information Tess had was just Ted's email address.

only 意思等於 just，表示「僅僅」。兩者只能用一個

✓ The only information Tess had was Ted's email address.

黛絲掌握的唯一資訊是泰德的電子信箱帳號。

- Sue is just teasing you. = Sue is only teasing you.
（蘇不過是在跟你開玩笑。）

請參見 continue/continue on、doublets/wordiness、other/similar、raise/raise up、reason、repeat/repeat again、reply/reply back 和 return/return back。

308 just now/right now 剛才／目前

1

❌ Ms. How, please start searching for that information just now. = a moment ago「剛才」，需用於**過去式**中

✅ Ms. How, please start searching for that information right now. = right away, at once, immediately, or at the present time「馬上；立刻；現在；目前」，用於**現在式**中

郝先生，請立刻開始在網路上搜索那條資訊。

- My new cow **arrived** just now. = a moment ago；arrived：過去簡單式
  （我的新乳牛剛到。）
- Right now she **is indeed searching** for the information we need. Right now = at present；is indeed searching：現在進行式
  （她的確現在正在網路上搜索我們需要的那條資訊。）

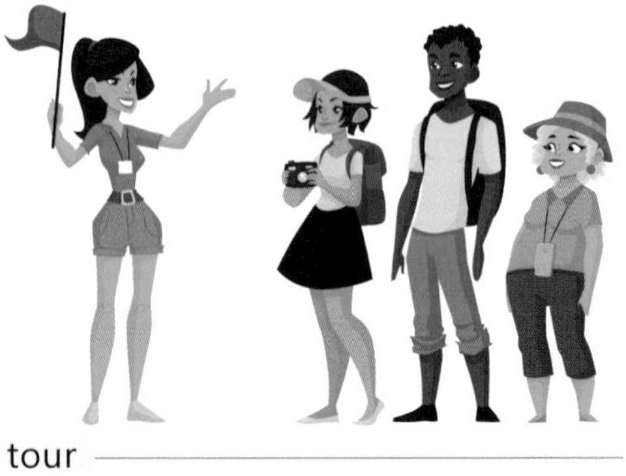

K

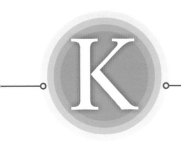

309 keep/put 存放／放

1 ✗ After Ed finished reading the book, he kept it on the bed.
指「存放」，與句意「放、擺」不符

✓ After Ed finished reading the book, he put it on the bed.
讀完那本書後，艾德就把它放到床上。 指「放、擺」

(1) keep 相當於 store（存放），把東西放在特定的地方，以便知道它在何處。

- Where does Dwight usually keep his flashlight?
（杜威特通常把他的手電筒放在哪裡？）

(2) 如果沒有 store（存放）的含意，就用 put（放、擺），意思相當於 place、set。

- Dwight put his flashlight in the tent last night.
（昨晚杜威特把他的手電筒放在帳篷裡。）

310 kind of 類型

1 ✗ I felt bored with that kind of a silly talk, so I used my cellphone to call Joan.
接不帶 a 或 an 的單數名詞（可數或不可數）

✓ I felt bored with that kind of silly talk, so I used my cellphone to call Joan.
我對那種愚蠢的談話厭倦了，於是我用手機打電話給裘恩。

2

✗ "That kind of cellphones are out of stock," declared Mort. ── 接不帶 a 或 an 的單數名詞（不接複數名詞）

✓ "That kind of cellphone is out of stock," declared Mort. ── 單數結構作主詞時，動詞用單數

莫特宣稱：「那個型號的手機已經沒貨了。」

單數結構 kind/sort/type of 後面要接**不帶 a 或 an 的單數名詞**（可數名詞或不可數名詞），前面是 this 或 that 或 what。這種單數結構作主詞時，動詞自然用**單數**。

- What kind/type/sort of robot did you buy for Eli?
  （你買給伊萊的是哪種機器人？）
- Pocket computers of that sort are being used at the spaceport. ── 這句主詞是複數 computers，動詞要用複數 are
  （那類袖珍電腦正在太空站使用。）

文法加油站

「these kinds of + 複數名詞」還是「these kind of + 單數名詞」？

古英語／非正式 Jake often makes these kind of mistake.

正式 Jake often makes these kinds of mistakes.
（傑克常犯這些類型的錯誤。）

正式 Jake often makes this kind of mistake.
（傑克常犯這類錯誤。）

① 一些文法書說我們應該用「these kind of + singular noun」才是正確的。these kind of mistake 看起來不是怪怪的嗎？ these 是複數，而 kind 和 mistake 是單數，這種組合究竟是否正確？

② 這種句型屬於古英語，主要出現在莎士比亞等古時候作家的作品裡。在現代英語中，尤其是正式用語中，these、those、all、many 和 different 後面應接複數 kinds/sorts/types of，然後再接複數可數名詞或（單數）不可數名詞。

③ 當然「these kind of + singular noun」的結構依然存在，尤其在英式英語非正式的口語和寫作中，但請不要在正式語中使用這類句型。

④ class、type 和 sort 也是同樣的用法。

⑤ 提示：堅持用**對稱形式**，複數對複數，單數對單數，那麼就不會出錯。

- this/that kind of+ 單數名詞（+ 單數動詞）
- these/those/all/many/different kinds of + 複數名詞／不可數名詞（+ 複數動詞）
- all kinds of cellphones（各種手機）
- many kinds of robots（很多種機器人）
- different types of furniture（不同類型的家具）
- these types of chocolates（這些類型的巧克力）

kind of 和 sort of：有點兒

① kind of/sort of + 形容詞／動詞：這個片語的意思是「有點兒、稍微」。

② 這種意義不能用 type of。

③ 這種片語只用在口語中。正式書面語中請用 rather 或 somewhat。

用在動詞前

口語　I sort of guess she likes me.

正式　I guess she likes me.

（我猜測她喜歡我。）

用在形容詞前，表示程度

口語　Millie thinks I am kind of silly.

正式　Millie thinks I am rather silly.

正式　Millie thinks I am a little silly.（米莉認為我有點傻。）

311 knock me up/wake me up

使我懷孕、叫醒我／叫醒我

1

美式 英式　Please wake up Ms. Dix at six.
請在六點叫醒迪克斯女士。

英式 口語　Please knock up Ms. Dix at six.
請在六點叫醒迪克斯女士。（英式／口語）
請在六點讓迪克斯女士懷孕。（美式／俚語）

(1) knock up someone 是常見的美國俚語，其意思是「使女人懷孕」，等於 get a woman pregnant。

(2) 英式英語的 knock up someone 用在口語中，原本是天真無邪的「敲門叫醒某人」 之意，但一到了美國人口中，意思就完全變了。上面這個例句提醒我們，有時候女皇英語和山姆大叔的英語之間區別真大啊！

312 know 知道、認識

1

表示認知意義的動詞，不用於進行式

❌ Is Margo knowing which way is up and which way is down and which way she wants to go?

✅ Does Margo know which way is up and which way is down and which way she wants to go?

瑪歌知道哪條路是前進的路，哪條路是後退的路，而她想走哪一條路嗎？

know（知道）是表示認知意義的動詞，不用於進行式，其他還有 recognize、identify 等。

2

❌ Kay knows Ray for two years, and they're going to get married today.

表示認識某人已有多長時間，know 用現在完成式，不用現在簡單式

✅ Kay has known Ray for two years, and they're going to get married today.

凱認識雷已有兩年，他們今天就要結婚了。

313 know/get to know 認識／瞭解

1

❌ It will take a few weeks for Sue to know the ship's crew.

✅ It will take a few weeks for Sue to get to know the ship's crew.

蘇需要數週的時間才能熟悉船上的船員。

首先要 get to know（瞭解）一個人或事物，然後你才 know（認識、熟悉）這個人或事物。

- It will take a few weeks for Skip to get to know the ship.
（史基普需要數週的時間才能熟悉這艘船。）

- Del knows that ship very well.
（戴爾對這艘船非常熟悉。）

314 knowledge 知識、瞭解

1

❌ Does Bart have some knowledges on art?

不可數名詞，沒有複數形式

knowledge 後面不接 on

✅ Does Bart have some knowledge of/about art?

巴特對藝術有所瞭解嗎？

knowledge 後面接 **of** 或 **about**

A B C D E F G H I J K L M N O P Q R S T U V W X Y Z

L

315 lack 缺少

1 動詞 lack something

✗ Mitch lacked of honey, so instead he made a cheese sandwich.
（lacked of：**及物動詞**，不能接 of，需直接接受詞）

✓ Mitch lacked honey, so instead he made a cheese sandwich.
（lacked：**及物動詞**，指「缺少、沒有、不足」，直接接受詞）

米奇缺少蜂蜜，於是他沒有做蜂蜜三明治，而是做了一個乳酪三明治。

- lack ability（沒有能力）
- lack the necessities of life（缺少生活的必需品）

2 be lacking in + 名詞

✗ I'm lacking courage and don't want to cross that shaky old bridge.
（lacking：不能直接用在名詞前）

✓ I'm lacking in courage and don't want to cross that shaky old bridge.
（lacking in：與 in 連用。be lacking in 是片語，意為「缺少某品質」等）

我沒有勇氣，不想過那座搖搖晃晃的舊橋。

316 last 緊接前面的；最後的；過去的

1 ✗ The last week was a difficult time for Monique.

過去的一週（包括現在），需與現在完成式連用

✓ The last week has been a difficult time for Monique.

對莫妮可來說，過去的這一週很艱難。

✓ Last week was a difficult time for Monique.

上週（與這週無關係），只能用過去式

對莫妮可來說，上週很艱難。

(1) last week：上週（與這週無關係），只能用**過去式**。

- Ann stated that last year was the hottest on record for Japan.（安鄭重地說，去年是日本有史以來最熱的一年。）

(2) the last week：過去的一週（包括現在），與**現在完成式**連用。

during the last five（six、ten 等）years（days、weeks 等），要用完成式

- During the last five years, Hawaii has made great progress in developing solar energy.
（在過去的五年裡，夏威夷在開發太陽能方面有了很大的進展。）

(3) the last year、the last month、the last week 等表示「過去的一年／一個月／一週」，通常不用於過去式中，但如果表示「最後的那年／那個月／那週」，可以與過去式連用。

七月的最後一週已經過去了

- I wondered why the last week of July seemed to fly by.
（我納悶為什麼七月的最後一週好像飛逝地就過去了。）

317 last/latest 最後的／最近的、最新的

1 ✗ Joan always has the last and best cellphone.

指「最後的」

✓ Joan always has the latest and best cellphone.

指「最新的；最近的」

裘恩總是擁有最新、最好的手機。

A B C D E F G H I J K L M N O P Q R S T U V W X Y Z

(1) latest（= most recent or most up-to-date）：意思是「最新的；最近的」。反義詞是 old、out of date（舊的；過時的）。

- the latest scientific discoveries（最新的科學發現）

(2) last（= after all others）：意思是「最後的」。反義詞是 first、foremost（第一的；最前的）。

- the last chocolate in the box（盒子裡最後一顆巧克力）
- The last two things I did before my retirement were to fire Millie and hire Lily.
（我退休之前做的最後兩件事就是解雇了米莉，雇用了莉莉。）

318 later/latter 後來／後面的

1

✗ These two babies are called Ed and Ted. The first is our son, and the later is our grandson.
later：意思是「後來；以後」，與句意不符

✓ These two babies are called Ed and Ted. The first is our son, and the latter is our grandson.
the latter：與 the 連用，意思是「後者」

那兩個寶寶叫艾德和泰德，前一個是我們的兒子，後一個是我們的孫子。

(1) latter 形 = second in a series of two：意思是「兩者中後一個的；後面的」，與 the 連用，意思是「後者」。反義詞是 former（兩者中前者的；在前的；前者）。

(2) later 形 副 = after some time：意思是「後來；以後」。反義詞是 earlier（早先的；早先的時候）。

- I'll see you later, Alligator.（再見。）

319 lay/lie 放／躺

1

✗ Kit was quietly crying while laying on her blanket.
laying：意思是「放；鋪設；砌（磚）；下蛋」，**及物動詞**，必須接受詞

✓ Kit was quietly crying while lying on her blanket.
lying：意思是「躺；（東西）被平放」，**不及物動詞**，不能接受詞

姬特躺在毯子上輕聲地哭泣著。

(1) lie (vi.) = to recline, rest, or stay：意思是「**躺；（東西）被平放**」；屬**不及物動詞**，不能接受詞，是一個不規則動詞，即其字尾變化是不規則的（**lie/lay/lain/lying**）。

過去式

- A huge snake lay hidden near sleepy little Kay.
（一隻大蛇躲著躺在昏昏欲睡的小凱身旁。）

過去分詞

- Claire thought, "How long has that big snake lain there?"
（克萊兒想：「那條大蛇躺在那裡已有多長時間了？」）

現在分詞

- Kay's cake was lying on the plate near the snake.
（凱的蛋糕平放在蛇附近的盤子上。）

原形動詞

- Claire wondered, "Will that snake continue to lie there?"
（克萊兒納悶：「那條蛇會不會繼續躺在那裡呢？」）

(2) lay (vt.) = place or put：意思是「**放；鋪設；砌（磚）；下蛋**」；這個動詞是**及物動詞**，必須接受詞，是一個規則動詞（**lay/laid/laid/laying**）。

- Claire laid down **her hat** and reached for her baseball bat.
（克萊兒放下帽子，伸手去拿她的棒球球棒。）
- Laying **her steady hands** on the bat, Claire felt ready.
（克萊兒鎮靜地把手放在球棒上，感到一切準備就緒了。）
- She was laying out **her plan**, and the snake would not be staying.（她擬定了計劃，絕不會讓那條蛇留在那裡。）
- Claire would have laid **a blow** to protect Kay, but the snake moved away.
（克萊兒本來可以為保護凱而狠狠地給牠一擊，可是那條蛇滑走了。）

文法加油站

A 比較 lay（放）和 lie（躺）的動詞時態變化

及物動詞 lay 的過去式

- I laid down the rules to Wade.（我對韋德制定了規則。）

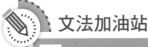

及物動詞 lay 的過去分詞

- Jade had laid the note beside Wade.
  （潔德把便條放在了韋德旁邊。）

不及物動詞 lie 過去式

- Margo lay down about an hour ago.（一小時前瑪歌躺了下來。）

不及物動詞 lie 的過去分詞

- Wayne had just lain down when it began to rain.
  （韋恩剛躺下來，就開始下雨了。）

及物動詞 lay 的過去式

- Ed laid down the magazine he had read. He shook his head and then lay down on his bed.

不及物動詞 lie 的過去式

（艾德放下剛看過的雜誌。他搖搖頭，然後上床躺下來。）

B lie (vi)「撒謊」，屬於規則動詞（lie/lied/lied/lying）

- I lied to Clyde.（我對克萊德撒了謊。）
- Ming said to Sue, "You are lying! You have lied to me ever since I met you."
  （敏對蘇說：「妳在撒謊！從我第一次遇見妳開始，妳就在對我撒謊。」）

320 learn 學會

1 美式 Have you learned how to milk a cow?

英式 Have you learnt how to milk a cow?

你學會了如何幫乳牛擠奶嗎？

(1) 請注意美式英語和英式英語的拼寫區別。

美式 learn, learned, learned

英式 learn, learnt, learnt

(2) 美式英語在 learn 的後面只需加上 -ed 就變成了過去式和過去分詞，不像女皇英語（Queen's English）那樣把它當成特殊的動詞，還得費力去記它的特殊過去式和過去分詞形式 learnt。規則化的動詞形式 learned 不是很容易記住嗎？

文法加油站

過去式動詞的美式和英式差異

下面是英式英語中以 -t 結尾的動詞；美式英語中以 -ed 結尾的動詞：

① dreamed/dreamt（夢）

美式 "I dreamed of being a butterfly," said Lorelei.
英式 = "I dreamt of being a butterfly," said Lorelei.
（蘿芮萊說：「我夢見我變成了一隻蝴蝶。」）

② spelled/spelt（拼寫、招致）

美式 Lulu loved to do things that spelled trouble for her sister Sue.
英式 = Lulu loved to do things that spelt trouble for her sister Sue.
（露露喜歡做一些給妹妹蘇帶來麻煩的事。）

321 learn/study 學習

1

✗ "When does Louise learn Japanese?" asked Ben.
"She learns Japanese every weekday at three," replied Dee.
（learn：意思是「學會」，與句意不符）

✓ "When does Louise study Japanese?" asked Ben.
"She studies Japanese every weekday at three," replied Dee.
（study：用功學習）

班問：「露易絲每天什麼時候學習日語？」
蒂回答說：「她每個平日的下午三點學習日語。」

2

✗ Five-year-old Clive has studied to dive.
（studied：指「為了獲得知識、獲得技術、理解某學科等而**用功學習或研究**」）

✓ Five-year-old Clive has learned to dive.
（learned：指「透過經驗、練習、閱讀、上課等而**掌握了知識**」）

五歲的克萊夫已經學會了跳水。

(1) 這是兩個常混淆的字。中文有時都翻譯成「學習」，但兩個英語字意思並不相同。

(2) learn 指「學會／掌握一門語言或者技術」。learn something 指「透過經驗、練習、閱讀、上課等而掌握了知識」。

(3) study 指「為了獲得知識、獲得技術、理解某學科等而用功學習或研究」；當你 study 的時候，你在做出努力（通常是透過上課、閱讀或研究）去掌握一門學科等。

- Midge studied music at college.（米姬在大學時學音樂。）
 └── to take a course in school（學習課程）

- She learned dancing from Dee.（她跟蒂學會了跳舞。）
 └── to acquire a skill by instruction（學會；掌握）

3 ❌ Lynn's mom is learning jet engines.

✅ Lynn's mom is learning about jet engines.
 │ 指「為了掌握某學科或某方面
 │ 的知識，努力學習和研究」
✅ Lynn's mom is studying jet engines.
琳恩的媽媽在研究噴射機引擎。

為了掌握某學科或某方面的知識（acquire knowledge of subjects），要努力學習和研究，應該用 learn about 或 study。

- learn about/study French culture
 （瞭解／研究法國文化）

- Jerome wants to learn about life in ancient Rome.
= Jerome wants to study life in ancient Rome.
 （傑羅姆想研究古代羅馬的生活。）

文法加油站

learn 與 study 的區別

① 指學習語言時，可以用進行式 learning（後面不接 about），這時 learn 的意思和 study 差不多。

- Liz Bench is learning French. = Liz Bench is studying French.
（莉茲 · 班奇在學法語。）

② 當 learn 當「學習」用時，通常用於下列片語：

- learn from . . .（向……學習）
- learn (how) to do something （學會如何做……）
- learn fast/quickly/rapidly （學得很快）
- learn slowly（學得很慢）
- learn something by heart (= memorize)（背熟）
- Ivy Porter learns fast, and she is an excellent TV reporter.
（愛葳 · 波特學東西很快，她是一位傑出的電視記者。）
- Learn from Mr. Sun, who works hard and gets things done.
（向孫先生學習，他總是努力工作，完成任務。）

③ 下面的段落可以清楚地表明 study 和 learn 這兩個字之間意思上的區別：

What is the most efficient way for you to study English? To learn English well, you should study interesting material. Read and listen to about 25,000 English words every day. If the books you study average more than two new words on a page, you'll probably get confused and too tired to learn much of anything. Easy and fun books and magazines with recordings can help you do the amount of reading and listening that you need to do. If the material you study is difficult and boring, you won't learn English well.

學習（study）英語最有效的方法是什麼？如果你想學好（learn）英語，就應該學習（study）趣味材料，每天閱讀和收聽 25,000 個英語辭彙。如果你學習（study）的書中，平均每頁生字多於兩個，那麼你就可能被搞糊塗，感到疲倦，結果學（learn）不到多少東西。配有錄音、簡易的趣味書籍和雜誌可以幫助你有效達到你所需要的閱讀量和收聽量。如果你學習（study）艱深、乏味的資料，那麼你就學不好（learn）英語。

322 learn about/learn of

學到、瞭解／得知、獲悉

1

表「間接獲得什麼資訊」，在這裡與句意不符

✗ Skip's work for NASA helped him learn a lot of American spaceships.

表「透過個人的經歷或努力而瞭解到什麼資訊」

✓ Skip's work for NASA helped him learn a lot about American spaceships.

斯基普在美國國家航空太空總署的工作，使他對美國太空船瞭解甚多。

(1) 透過個人的經歷或努力而獲得什麼資訊，用 learn about 而不是 learn of。

- learn about weather（瞭解天氣）
- learn about stocks（瞭解股票）

(2) 當間接獲得什麼資訊，比如得知、聽說、獲悉（become informed; hear），更常用 learn of，也可以用 learn about。

- I learned of Rae and Ron's marriage yesterday.
  （我在昨天獲悉芮和朗結婚的消息。）

323 leave 離開（動詞）；休假、許可（名詞）

1

表示「離開某處」時，後面直接接表示「地方」的名詞，不要接 from

✗ On Friday evenings, Clive normally leaves from his office at six twenty-five.

✓ On Friday evenings, Clive normally leaves his office at six twenty-five.

= go away from

星期五晚上克萊夫通常六點二十五分離開辦公室。

只有當提及的旅程「從某處出發」時才使用

- Dee, your plane to Hawaii **leaves from** Gate 3.
  （蒂，你去夏威夷的航班從三號登機口出發。）

2

後面要接 for；go 後面才接 to

❌ Joe is leaving to Chicago tomorrow.

表示「動身去（某地）」，與 go to a place 意思一樣

✅ Joe is leaving for Chicago tomorrow.
= Joe is going to Chicago tomorrow.

喬明天去芝加哥。

3

❌ Eve has come back from her sick leaves.
✅ Eve has come back from her sick leave.

不可數名詞， 沒有複數形式

伊芙休病假已經回來了。

leave 作名詞時為「**休假（期）、准假、許可**」，通常為**不可數名詞**，沒有複數形式。

- on leave（在休假中）
- go on leave（去休假）
- return from leave（休假回來）
- absent without leave（曠課、曠工）
- by somebody's leave（獲得某人的許可）
- ask for sick leave（請病假）
- take time off for maternity leave（休產假）
- 美式 be entitled to six weeks of annual leave
  英式 be entitled to six weeks' annual leave
  （每年可以享受六週休假）
- 美式 take a month of unpaid leave
  英式 take a month's unpaid leave
  （休一個月的無薪假）
- Steve is not in the office; he is on leave.
  （史蒂夫不在辦公室；他在休假。）

324 let 讓

1

✗ "You let Sue to do whatever she wants to do!" declared Lulu.

後面接不要 to 的不定詞，即原形動詞

✓ "You let Sue do whatever she wants to do!" declared Lulu.

= "You allow Sue to do whatever she wants to do!" declared Lulu.

allow 後接帶 to 的不定詞

露露宣布：「蘇想做什麼你就讓她去做吧！」

(1) let 的過去式和過去分詞都是 let（let/let/let）。

(2) let someone do something（讓某人做某事）

- Margo dropped her cellphone and shouted, "Let me go!"
  （瑪歌扔下手機，大喊了一聲：「讓我走吧！」）

(3) allow someone to do something（允許某人做某事）
allow 後接帶 to 的不定詞。

(4) 請參見 allow。

文法加油站

① 動詞 hear、let、make、see 等後面通常接不帶 to 的不定詞。

② 請參見 hear。

- Yesterday Lee **heard** his sister Margo **cry** loudly, "**Let** me **go**!"
  用不帶 to 的不定詞 cry 強調動作的完成

≒ Yesterday Lee **heard** his sister Margo **crying** loudly, "**Let** me **go**!"
  用 crying 強調動作的進行

  （昨天李聽見妹妹瑪歌大叫：「讓我走吧！」。）

- Lee tried to **make** Margo **laugh** and **forget** about the phone call from Joe.
  接不帶 to 的不定詞

  （李試圖使瑪歌笑起來，並忘記喬打來的電話。）

325 let/rent 出租

1 美式 英式 Coco has rented her cottage to a woman from Mexico.

英式 Coco has let her cottage to a woman from Mexico.

可可把別墅出租給一個來自墨西哥的女人。

(1) rent 動（出租；租借）
(2) rent 名（租金；出租）

	美式	英式
出租房子或房間	rent it/rent it out	
		let it
某個東西可以用來出租	for rent	for let/to let

- 美式／英式 rent out mountain bikes（出租登山自行車 ）
- 英式 a flat to let/a flat for let（一間要出租的公寓）
- 美式 an apartment for rent（一間要出租的公寓）
- pay one's rent（付房租費）
- I can rent you an affordable **cozy** apartment in a convenient location near the downtown police station.（我可以租給你一間價格不貴、舒適的公寓，位置方便，就在市中心警察局旁邊。）
  美式拼寫 cozy，英式拼寫是 cosy

326 let's/let us/let me 讓我們／讓我

1 ✗ Let's/Let us to watch a TV show with Margo.

let's/let us 後面不接帶 to 的不定詞和 V-ing 形式；要接不要 to 的不定詞（即原形動詞）

✗ Let's/Let us watching a TV show with Margo.

✓ Let's/Let us watch a TV show with Margo

let us 的縮寫（口語中較常用），通常兩者意思沒有區別，可互相替換

我們跟瑪歌一起看電視節目吧。

2

❌ Let me to tell you a story about Lori and Bret.

let me 後面不接帶 to 的不定詞和 V-ing 形式；
要接不要 to 的不定詞（即原形動詞）

❌ Let me telling you a story about Lori and Bret.

✅ Let me tell you a story about Lori and Bret.

讓我告訴你一個關於蘿麗和布瑞特的故事。

⑴ let us = let's：「let's/let us + 原形動詞」句型用來表達向講話者以及聽者提建議或下達命令。

⑵ 用「let me + 原形動詞」句型：用來向自己作指示，意思是「allow me to do something」。也可以用來請求對方讓「我」做某事。

文法加油站

let us 和 let's 的差異

let us ≠ let's：在有些情況下 let's 和 let us 不能相互替換。如果句中含 有第二人稱（you），那麼 let us 中的 us 就只包括說話者一方的群體（the speaker's group），不包括對方（the listener）。這種情境就不用 let's。

- Lulu and Wayne decided to give a gift to Jane. Lulu said to Jane, "Let us buy you a plane ticket to Spain."

  （露露和韋恩決定給珍一個禮物。露露對珍說：「讓我們買給妳一張去西班牙的機票吧。」）

  → 這句從上下文可以看出 us 只包括 Lulu 和 Wayne（即說話者一方的群體），而不包括對方（Jane = listener）。

- My twin sisters, Midge and Margo, wanted to go to college. Midge asked Mom, "Please let us both go to Newbridge College."

  （我的雙胞胎姐妹米姬和瑪歌想上大學。米姬請求媽媽：「請讓我們兩個都去新橋大學。」）

  → 這句從上下文可以看出實際主詞是 you，即「媽媽」（you let us），因此 us 並不包括 listener，只包括說話者一方的群體，Midge 和 Margo。

327 Let's/Let us . . ., shall we?

讓我們……好嗎？

1

✗ Let's/Let us swim in the sea, will we?

✓ Let's/Let us swim in the sea, shall we?

讓我們在海裡游泳，好嗎？

在 let's 和 let us 後面，附加問句通常用 shall we?

在多數情況下，let's 等於 let us（請參見上面條目）。在 let's 和 let us 後面，附加問句通常用「shall we?」。這個附加問句結構英式英語比美式英語更常用。

文法加油站

① 在一些特殊的情況下，let us 後面的附加問句也可以用「will you?」：

- Dad, please **let us** go to see Lulu dance, **will you?**

let 主詞是 you，即「爸爸」

受詞 us 並不包括對方（Dad），所以要用 let us

在這種情境中，附加問句可以用 will you?

（爸爸，請讓我們去看露露跳舞，好嗎？）

無論是英式還是美式，這種附加問句「 let us . . . will you? 」在實際生活中很少見，即 native speakers of English 很少使用這種句型。

② 在考試中究竟選擇「will you?」還是「shall we?」，這取決於句子的意思。記住，一般在 let's/let us 後面都是用「shall we?」。除非像上述情況，意思是 you let us 時，才可能用「will you?」不過，英美考試中幾乎不可能出現這類選擇題。

③ 請看下面這道題目：

- Let us go, _______ ?　(a) shall we　(b) will you

→ 這道題如果沒有上下文（context），就可以有兩種含意

(a) Let us go. = Let's go.（我們走吧。）

那麼，附加問句要選擇「shall we?」。

A B C D E F G H I J K L M N O P Q R S T U V W X Y Z

(b) 也可能在請求對方，表示「(You) Let us go.」。（你讓我們走吧。）那麼，附加問句就可以選擇「will you?」。

→ 這道選擇題（Let us go, shall we?/will you?）有歧義，答案不只一個，題目的設計不合理，應當避免設計這種題目

328 license/licence 許可證、執照、特許

1

美式 Jerome lost his driver's license while he was in Rome.

英式 Jerome lost his driver's licence while he was in Rome.

傑羅姆在羅馬遺失了他的駕照。

(1) 在美式英語中，無論是動詞還是名詞都是 license。

- Olive Gold used her creative license and was bold. 名
  （奧莉芙 · 戈爾德行使她的創作自由，而且作風大膽。）

(2) 在英式英語中，名詞寫成 licence，而動詞是 license。

- Lynne is licensed to practice medicine. 動
  （琳恩有行醫的執照。）

(3) 注意 licence 和 license 的發音是一樣的。

(4) 這又是美式英語簡單化，而女皇英語規則太多的一個典型例子！

329 like to do/like doing 喜歡做……

1

美式 Jake likes to eat/eating chocolate cake.

談論「樂趣、愛好」（enjoyment），動詞 like 後可用**不定詞**或 **V-ing** 形式

英式 Jake likes eating chocolate cake.

= Jake enjoys eating chocolate cake.

強調「樂趣、愛好」（enjoyment），用 V-ing 形式；強調「選擇和習慣」（choices and habits），用**不定詞**形式

傑克喜歡吃巧克力蛋糕。

・ Nancy likes to swim in the sea.

= Nancy likes swimming in the sea.（南西喜歡在海裡游泳。）

談論「愛好」，在美式英語中兩者沒有區別；英式只用 likes swimming

強調習慣，英式和美式都常用不定詞（有時接不定詞還可以表示具體動作、具體的選擇）

・ When Nancy is making milk tea, she likes to add a little bit of chocolate and instant coffee.

（南西泡奶茶時，常愛加一點巧克力和即溶咖啡。）

330 like to do/like doing/ would like to do

喜歡做……／想做……

1

✗ "Would you like dancing?" Andrew asked Sue.

would like = want，後面不能接 V-ing 形式

✓ "Would you like to dance?" Andrew asked Sue.

意思是「想要、希望」，後面接**不定詞**

= "Do you want to dance now?" Andrew asked Sue.

安德魯問蘇：「你想跳舞嗎？」

(1) would like（= want）：意思是「想要、希望」，後面接不定詞，不能接 V-ing 形式。

(2) like 意思是「喜歡、愛好」，美式英語後面可以接不定詞，也可以接 V-ing 形式。請參見上面 like to do/like doing。

・ Sue exclaimed to Mitch, "I'd like to be rich!"

= Sue exclaimed to Mitch, "I want to be rich!"

（蘇大聲對米齊說：「我想致富！」）

・ Mike Wall declared, "I like being/to be tall!"

= Mike Wall declared, "I enjoy being tall!"

（麥克 · 沃爾宣稱：「我喜歡個子高大！」）

331 like/want/wish 喜歡／想／希望

1

❌ Heather liked to know if I liked the hot weather.

當轉述某人的問題時（某人想知道），不用 like

✅ Heather wished to know if I liked the hot weather.

當轉述某人的問題時，用 wish/want to know

✅ Heather wanted to know if I liked the hot weather.

海瑟想知道我是否喜歡炎熱的天氣。

like to do 的用法請參見上面兩則條目。

332 likely 可能的

1

不自然 Tomorrow is Sunday, so Lynne will likely sleep in.

作**副詞**用時，通常不單獨使用

自然 Tomorrow is Sunday, so Lynne will most likely sleep in.

= probably（很可能），作**副詞**用時，與 **most**、**quite**、**very** 連用

自然 Tomorrow is Sunday, so Lynne is likely to sleep in.

作**形容詞**，用於 be likely to do 的句型中

明天是星期天，因此琳恩很可能會睡懶覺。

上面的第一句也許常聽見人們在口語中說，但在正式文體中請用標準的文法。

形容詞，在連綴動詞 is 後面作補語

- Heather says tomorrow **is likely to** have some really cold weather.
  （海瑟說明天天氣可能會很冷。）

副詞，與 quite 連用，修飾動詞片語 is going to take

- My wife smokes, and her smoking is **quite likely** going to take ten years off her life.
  （我太太抽菸，她吸菸的習慣很可能會使她少活十年。）

333 line/queue 行列；排隊

請參見 cinema/theater/theatre。

334 litter 廢物；把……弄得亂七八糟

1

✗ The babysitter picked up all your litters.

不可數名詞，沒有複數形式

✓ The babysitter picked up all your litter.

保姆把你所有的垃圾都收拾乾淨了。

litter 也可以用作動詞。

- Round pieces of paper and empty cans littered the ground.
（地上丟滿了圓形紙片和空罐頭。）

335 live/stay 居住／暫住

1

✗ Lily lived for three days in Italy.

✓ Lily stayed for three days in Italy.

指（作為客人或訪問者）**暫住**，不用來指長久或永久的居住

莉莉在義大利逗留了三天。

2

✗ My sister Fay now stays in the U.S.A.

✓ My sister Fay now lives in the U.S.A.

指長久或永久的居住

我的妹妹菲現在住在美國。

336 look/see

請參見 hear/listen。

337 look forward to 盼望

1

✗ Andrew and I are looking forward to see you.
是介系詞，不是不定詞，不能接原形動詞

✓ Andrew and I are looking forward to seeing you.
介系詞，接名詞或動名詞

安德魯和我盼望見到你。

look forward to (doing) something：這個片語動詞裡的 to 是介系詞，不是不定詞，所以不能接原形動詞，而應該接名詞或動名詞。

- "We all **look forward to** the **future** of solar energy," declared Lee. ── look forward to + 名詞
（李宣稱：「我們大家都很期待太陽能發電的未來。」）

338 loose/lose/loss
寬鬆的、散漫的／丟失、損失／遺失

1

✗ A baby pig ran lose in the yard, chasing after a big goose.

✓ A baby pig ran loose in the yard, chasing after a big goose.
副詞，意思是「鬆散地」

一頭小豬在院子裡亂跑，追趕一隻大鵝。

2

✗ Did Oliver loose his shoes near the rive?

✓ Did Oliver lose his shoes near the river?
動詞，意思是「丟失、 損失」

奧利弗在河邊掉了鞋子嗎？

3 ✗ Michael Moss has suffered from a lose of memory since he fell off his bicycle.

✓ Michael Moss has suffered from a loss of memory since he fell off his bicycle.

名詞，意思是「損失、遺失」

麥克・莫斯從自行車上摔下來後，就喪失了記憶。

(1) loose（= not tight; free）：是形容詞，意思是「鬆的；未控制的」；既然是「鬆散的」，那麼這個字的中間就有足夠的空間容納兩個 -o。注意 loose 與 goose 押韻。

(2) loose 也可作動詞，意思是「解開；釋放」。也可作副詞，意思是「鬆散地」，如上面第一組例句。

(3) lose（= to become unable to find; to suffer from the loss of）：是動詞，意思是「丟失、損失」。記住，丟失了一個字母 o，那麼這個字的中間就只剩下一個 -o 了。lose 中間只夠裝下一個 -o。lose 與 news、shoes、Sue's 和 use 押韻。

- Margo says the word lose has room for only one o.
（瑪歌說，單字 lose 只有裝下一個 o 的空間。）

(4) 記住這兩個特點（loose 因為鬆散，需要兩個 -o，而 lose 因為丟失了一個 -o，就只能裝下一個 -o 了），就可以幫助你牢記它們的拼寫。

- Pete Rugs always loses his friends because he uses street drugs.
（彼特・魯格斯因使用毒品而總是失去朋友。）
- Mr. Card loosed his dog from the fenced-in yard.
（卡德先生把他的狗放出有柵欄的院子。）

(5) loss（= disadvantage from losing; something lost）是名詞，意思是「損失、遺失」（比如：a loss of memory）。

339 lower 放下、降低

1

❌ Joyce made the smart choice to lower down her voice.

lower 本身就包含 down 的意思，沒有
必要在 lower 後面再加上 down

✅ Joyce made the smart choice to lower her voice.

喬伊絲選擇降低她的音量，這是明智的。

請參見 continue/continue on、doublets/wordiness、other/similar、raise/raise up、reason、repeat/repeat again、reply/reply back 和 return/return back。

lower one's voice

M

A B C D E F G H I J K L M N O P Q R S T U V W X Y Z

340 majority

請參見 couple。

341 mail 郵政、郵件

1

✗ Can a female bird carry airmails faster than a male whale can carry sea mails? —— **不可數名詞**，沒有複數形式

✓ Can a female bird carry airmail faster than a male whale can carry sea mail?

母鳥傳送航空信，會比公鯨傳送海運信來得更快嗎？

(1) 在美式英語中，mail 比 post 更常見。在英式英語中，post 比 mail 更常見。

(2) e-mail（= email）電子郵件，可以是**不可數名詞**，也可作**可數名詞**，有複數形（e-mails），可以與 an 修飾（an e-mail）。

342 make 使……做

1

✗ I told a lie that made Lorelei to cry.

使役動詞，在主動語態裡，後面的動詞要用原形動詞，不接帶 to 的不定詞或 V-ing 形式

✗ I told a lie that made Lorelei crying.

✓ I told a lie that made Lorelei cry.

我說了一個謊，使蘿芮萊哭了起來。

⑴ make somebody/something do something：make 是使役動詞，在主動語態裡，後面的動詞要用原形動詞，不接帶 to 的不定詞或 V-ing 形式。

- Ms. King made Jade and Wade stop fighting.
  （金女士〔金老師〕讓潔德和韋德停止了打架。）

⑵ be made to do something：作被動語態時，make後面的to要保留。

- Jade and Wade were made to stop fighting, and then they had to say sorry to Ms. King.
  （潔德和韋德的打架被阻止了，然後他倆不得不向金女士〔金老師〕道歉。）
- Jade and Wade were each given a broom and made to sweep the dining room.
  （潔德和韋德每人得到一把掃帚，被要求去打掃餐廳。）

343 made of (made out of)/made from
由……製成的

1

非正式 "The juice is mainly made of grapes," said Bruce.
表示能從成品中直接看見原材料

正式 "The juice is mainly made from grapes," said Bruce.
表示很難從成品中直接看見原材料，只是間接瞭解原材料

布魯斯說：「這果汁主要是由葡萄做成的。」

⑴ 某物是由某材料製造成的，究竟應該是用「made of/made out of」還是用「made from」？一般來說，用 made of/made out of 表示能從成品中直接看見原材料，而用 made from 表示很難從成品中直接看見原材料，只是間接瞭解原材料。

⑵ 從 juice 裡面已經不能直接看見 grapes 了。因此上面例句最好用 made from。

- a desk made of/made out of wood（木製桌子）
- a hammer made of/made out of steel
  （由鋼鐵做成的鎯頭）

· Elwood made some toy animals out of wood.
（埃爾伍德用木頭做了一些玩具動物。）

· Olive oil is made from olives.（橄欖油是由橄欖製成的。）

344 marry 結婚

1

✗ Claire married with a hard-working millionaire.

及物動詞，後面不接 with 或 to，要直接接受詞

✗ Claire married to a hard-working millionaire.

✓ Claire married a hard-working millionaire.

someone marries someone else：某人與另一個人結婚

克萊兒嫁給了一個勤勞的百萬富翁。

2

✗ Scot and Monique married last week.

✓ Scot and Monique got married last week.

前面是**複合主詞**，就要用 be/get married

史考特和莫妮可上週結婚了。

如果 marry 前面是複合主詞，或複數代名詞 we、they 等，就要用 be/get married。

文法加油站

注意下面兩個結構：

① Is **Liz Reed married**?（莉茲 · 里德結婚了沒有？）

這句是單個主詞，用形容詞 married（已婚的），反義詞是 single（單身的）

② **Kate** spent many years protecting wildlife and **married** late in life.
（多年來凱特都在保護野生生物，她很晚婚。）

這句的 married 前面只有一個主詞（Kate），用作不及物動詞

A B C D E F G H I J K L M N O P Q R S T U V W X Y Z

3 ✗ Two weeks later, Lulu got married with Andrew.

與某人結婚用 be/get married to somebody；要用 to，不用 with

✓ Two weeks later, Lulu got married to Andrew.

✓ Two weeks later, Lulu was married to Andrew.

= Two weeks later, Lulu married Andrew.

兩週後露露嫁給了安德魯。 主詞 + marry + 受詞；marry 作及物動詞

(1) 與某人結婚用 be/get married to somebody；要用 to，不用 with。

- I have been married to Jade for more than a decade.
  （我與潔德結婚已經有十多年了。）

(2) 與某人住在一起用 live with somebody；要用 with。

- Brad is a grown-up, but he is still living with his mom and dad.
  （布萊德是一個成人了，但他還跟他的父母住在一起。）

(3) 名詞 marriage 後面通常接 to。另外請參見 divorce。

- My marriage to Evan is a happy match made in heaven.
  （我和伊文的婚姻是上帝安排的幸福婚姻。）

345 math/maths 數學

1 美式 Studying math with Liz Sun is a lot of fun.

英式 Studying maths with Liz Sun is a lot of fun.

跟莉茲．孫一起學習數學很有趣。

美國人和英國人也用 mathematics。

- Felix loves mathematics.（菲力克斯熱愛數學。）

文法加油站

① mathematics 和英式英語的 maths 形式上雖是複數，但意義上是單數，作主詞時，動詞用單數。

② 類似的字有 politics、physics（表示學科的名詞），headquarters 等。這些字都是複數形式單數意義。

③ 請參見 news 和 politics。

346 may be/maybe 也許

1

✗ May be Kay will have her baby in May.

意思是「也許是」，may 是一個**情態助動詞**，過去式是 might

✓ Maybe Kay will have her baby in May.

副詞，相當於 perhaps「大概、或許、可能」

凱也許會在五月生孩子。

人們常常混淆這兩個簡單的字，一些母語是英語的人士也分不清楚 maybe 和 may be 之間的區別。

- Hurricane Jayne may be a little weaker when it gets to Spain.
（颶風珍襲擊西班牙時可能威力會減弱一些。）

347 me/I

請參見 between you and me/between you and I 和 myself/I/me。

348 means 方式、手段、工具

1

✗ Is a cellphone a useful mean of getting on the Internet?

means 單複數結尾都是 s

✓ Is a cellphone a useful means of getting on the Internet?

= method「方法、手段、工具」，後面常接 of，但也可接 for、to、toward

手機是上網的一種有用工具嗎？

- a **means for** transmitting sound（傳送聲音的一種工具）
- a **means to** an end（到達目標的一種手段）
- a **means toward** achieving equality（實現平等的一種方式）
- "There **are** several **means** of solving this problem," said Claire.
  └ 這句的 means 是複數，動詞用複數形式 are
  （克萊兒說：「解決這個問題有好幾種方法。」）
- **Is** there **an** easy **means** to get Joan to switch off her cellphone?
  └ 這句的 means 是單數，動詞用單數形式 is
  （有沒有一個簡單的方法能使裘恩關掉她的手機？）

文法加油站

與 means 相關的片語

- by all **means** = certainly; at any cost（當然；無論如何）
- by **means** of = with the help of（用；依賴）
- by no **means** = not at all（決不）

349 media/medium 媒體

1

✗ Reports in the medias say she is a poor girl from India.

指「新聞界」，用 the media，不用 the medias

✓ Reports in the media say she is a poor girl from India.

新聞報導說，她是來自印度的一個窮女孩。

(1) **the media** 當集合名詞，與其他集合名詞一樣，根據其含意，既可以接複數動詞，也可以接單數動詞。注意不要用 medias。

(2) **the media** 指組成通訊業和形成傳播媒介職業的新聞工作者等**團體**（the aggregate of journalists and broadcasters），相當於**新聞界**（the press）。這種含意的 media 通常被看成是單數，在句中作主詞用時，**動詞用單數**。

= the press，用單數動詞 has

- Lori says **the media has** shown a huge interest in covering that UFO story.
  （蘿麗說，媒體對報導那個不明飛行物表現出了極大的興趣。）

(3) **the media** 也指各種大眾**傳播媒介**（all the means of communication），比如報紙、雜誌、電臺、電視以及網際網路。the media 在句中作主詞時，傳統文法用**複數動詞**，但現在傾向於用**單數動詞**。

傳統　**Have** the **media**, especially the Internet, scared Maria?

現代　**Has** the **media**, especially the Internet, scared Maria?
（新聞媒介，尤其是網際網路，使瑪麗亞感到恐懼嗎？）

(4) **media** 傳統上是 **medium** 的複數形式，只能接**複數動詞**。然而語言是不斷變化的，media 這個傳統的複數字現在越來越常用，並且常被看成是**單數**。（注意：單數 medium 指「媒介、手段」時，不能用作集合名詞表示「新聞界、媒體」。）

- The Internet is an important **medium** of mass communication for every nation. ← 正式
- = The Internet is an important **media** of mass communication for every nation. ← 非正式
  （網際網路對每一個國家來說，都是一種重要的大眾傳播媒介。）

- Maria said, "Radio is a part of **the media**." ← 這句不用 the medium
  （瑪麗亞說：「無線電是傳播媒介的其中一部分。」）

350 mind 介意、反對

1

✗ Rich, would you mind to make me a cheese sandwich?

> **mind doing something**：mind 意為「介意」時，常用在疑問句和否定句中，後面接 V-ing 形式，不接不定詞

✓ Rich, would you mind making me a cheese sandwich?

瑞奇，可以為我做一個起司三明治嗎？

A B C D E F G H I J K L M N O P Q R S T U V W X Y Z

351 million

請參見 hundred。

352 mirror 鏡子

1

❌ Ms. Gold won't look at herself at a mirror, because smoking has made her look tired and old.

> **look at oneself in a mirror**：
> 用介系詞 **in**，而不用 at

✅ Ms. Gold won't look at herself in a mirror, because smoking has made her look tired and old.

戈爾德女士不願照鏡子，因為抽菸使她看起來又疲倦又蒼老。

353 miss/lose 發現遺失／丟失

1

❌ Brook, I am sorry that I missed your cookbook.

> = to notice the absence or loss of。意思是「**發現某物／某人不見了**」，強調「注意到」，並不表示「找不到了」

✅ Brook, I am sorry that I lost your cookbook.

> lose 表示「**丟失**」了什麼物品（unable to find）。lose 的過去式和過去分詞是 lost

布魯克，對不起，我把你的食譜弄丟了。

- a missing child（失蹤的孩子）
- When Claire suddenly missed her purse, she immediately called the store but was told it was not there.
  （當克萊兒突然注意到她的皮包不見了，就立刻打電話給商店，但被告知皮包不在那裡。）

文法加油站

miss 的其他用法

① miss（= to be without; lack）：可以指「遺漏」，此意只用於現在分詞 missing。

- Page's English textbook was missing ten pages.
（佩吉的英語課本缺了十頁。）

② miss（= to fail to meet, reach, catch, see, hear, understand, etc.）：指「未擊中、未到達、未得到、未看見、未聽到、未領會、未出席、未趕上、錯過」。

- miss an appointment（錯過了約會）
- miss the plane（沒有趕上班機）
- miss a target（未擊中目標）
- miss my meaning（沒有領會我的意思）
- Erika won't miss this chance to go to school in America.
（艾芮卡絕不會錯過去美國學校讀書的這個機會。）

③ miss（= to feel or regret the absence or loss of）指「想念、惦記」。

- Andrew will miss you and Sue.（安德魯將想念你和蘇。）

354 mistake 弄錯；誤解

1

✗ Lee often mistakes me as my twin sister, Amy.

✗ Lee often mistakes me into my twin sister, Amy.

mistake somebody/something for：意思是「把……誤認為是」，要用 **for**，不要用 into 或 as

✓ Lee often mistakes me for my twin sister, Amy.

李常把我誤當成了我的雙胞胎妹妹艾咪。

355 mom/mum/pop/dad 媽媽／爸爸

1 美式 Mom has some other male friends besides Tom Plum.

在口語中，美語常用 mom 和 pop，也常用 dad（爸爸）

英式 Mum has some other male friends besides Tom Plum.

英式英語常用 mum 和 dad

除了湯姆 · 普盧姆外，媽媽還有一些別的男性朋友。

2 ✗ His Mom is a lawyer, and so is his wife, Liz Sawyer.

前面有所有格 his 限定時，通常須用小寫形式

✓ His mom is a lawyer, and so is his wife, Liz Sawyer.

他的媽媽是律師，他的妻子莉茲・索耶也是律師。

(1) 當 mom/dad/pop/grandpa/grandma/father/mother 等前面有所有格 his、my、their、your、Karen's 等限定時，通常用小寫形式。

(2) 如果這些字前面沒有限定詞，或者後面接有人名，這些字就用大寫形式。

(3) aunt、uncle 和 cousin 的用法請參見 uncle。

Aunt + 名字（first name），需要大寫

- Do you think **Grandma Tree** and **Aunt Amy** will want to go sailing with me?

grandma 前面沒有所有格限制，後面還接有姓，需要大寫。英語的外婆和奶奶都是 grandma。要想表明究竟是母親的媽媽，還是父親的媽媽，就得在 grandma 後面加上姓

（你認為崔奶奶和艾咪姨媽會想跟我一起去航行嗎？）

- My brother Chad phoned Dad.

（我兄弟查德打了電話給爸爸。）

前面沒有所有格代名詞限制，需要大寫

- Brad phoned his dad.（布萊德打了電話給他爸爸。）
- I guess Mom admires Wes.

= I guess my mom admires Wes.（我猜媽媽欣賞韋斯。）

356 moral/morale 道德；寓意／士氣

1

指的是集體的「士氣」或個人的「鬥志」，與句意不符

✗ What is the morale in this brief story about teaching oral English to a thief?

意味「寓意；品性；道德規範」

✓ What is the moral in this brief story about teaching oral English to a thief?

教一個小偷口語英語，這個簡短的故事寓意是什麼？

2

✗ Shall we look for a leader that can improve our moral and help us dig this canal?

✓ Shall we look for a leader that can improve our morale and help us dig this canal?

我們找一個能增進我們的鬥志，並幫助我們挖河渠的指揮者，好嗎？

(1) **moral** 形 名 [ˈmɔrəl] 與「**正確和錯誤**」相關，意味「講道德的；教訓的；品性端正的」；「寓意；品性；道德規範」。moral 作形容詞時只用在名詞前（a moral woman）。moral 與 oral（口頭的）和 choral（聖歌）押韻。

(2) **morale** 名 [məˈræl] 指的是集體的「士氣」或個人的「鬥志」。morale 與 canal、pal、shall 等押韻。

- Sue's previous video was about oral English and moral values.（蘇先前的錄影節目是關於口語英語和道德價值。）
- Sue's new video is about building this canal and should be able to lift our morale.（蘇新錄影的節目是關於修建這座河渠，它應該能夠提高我們的士氣。）

357 most/mostly 最／大部分地

1

✗ That research was most done by Mat.

much 的最高級，意為「最」，可作形容詞，也可作副詞。與此句句意「主要地」不符

✓ That research was mostly done by Mat.

只作副詞，意為「大多數地；大部分地；主要地」（in most cases; for the most part; chiefly）

那份研究工作主要是由麥特完成的。

most 和 mostly 都是副詞，但兩者意思和用法都有區別。

- Amos knew that the places where the boat moved the most quickly down the river were the most dangerous.
  （阿摩司明白，船沿著河行駛最快的地方，也就是最危險的地方。）

358 mother

請參見 mom/mum/pop/dad。

359 mother-in-laws/mothers-in-law

婆婆

1

❌ Some daughter-in-laws do not like their mother-in-laws.

✅ Some daughters-in-law do not like their mothers-in-law.

一些媳婦不喜歡她們的婆婆。

複合字作複數時，s 應加在中心字或者字根上面；這兩個複合字的中心字是 daughters 和 mothers

(1) 有些字很複雜。如果你的配偶有兩個兄弟，那麼他們是你的「brothers-in-law」還是「brother-in-laws」？

(2) 如果一個字是複合字，無論是連字號（hyphen）連接的複合字，還是沒有連字號的複合字，作複數時候，s 應加在中心字或者字根上面。

- **fathers-in-law**（公公、岳父）
- **ladies-in-waiting**（侍女、宮女）
- **commanders-in-chief**（統帥、總司令）
- **sisters-in-law**（嫂子、小姑、大姑）
- **courts-martial**（軍事法庭）
- Does Princess Ming often read novels to her **ladies-in-waiting**?（敏公主常唸小説給她的侍女聽嗎？）
- President Lenore Gore and eight other **commanders-in-chief** want to avoid a war.
  （蕾諾兒·戈爾總統以及其他八個國家的總司令都想避免戰爭。）

文法加油站

注意由 general 構成的複合字

- attorneys general（首席檢察官）
- consuls general（總領事）
- major generals（少將）

① attorneys general 和 consuls general 裡的 general 不是字根，複數沒有 s，而是主要的字 attorney 和 consul 帶 s。

② major generals 裡的 general 是軍銜（title），是該複合字的中心字，所以複數應該有 s。

- Grace Wu was the rocket pilot that flew the two major generals into space.
  （把兩名少將送進太空的火箭飛行員，就是葛蕾絲・吳。）

360 Mr. 先生

1

✗ May I speak to Mr. Andrew?

Mr./Mrs./Ms. 後面不能只接名字（first name）

✓ May I speak to Mr. Andrew Meek?
我可以跟安德魯 ・ 米克先生說話嗎？

可用 Mr.+ 名（first name）+ 姓（last name)

✓ May I speak to Mr. Meek?
我可以跟米克先生說話嗎？

可用 Mr.+ 姓（last name）

✓ May I speak to Andrew?
我可以跟安德魯說話嗎？

可單獨用名字，此時前面不能用稱號 Mr./Mrs./Ms.

這是學生常犯的錯誤。正確的方式是：

(1) Mr.「先生」。

- Mr. + 名（first name）+ 姓（last name)
  例如：Mr. John Gore
- Mr. + 姓（last name）
  例如：Mr. Gore

(2) **Mrs.「夫人」用於已婚女性的夫姓。**

- Mrs. + 名（first name）+ 夫姓（last name）
  例如：Mrs. Jane Gore
- Mrs. + 夫姓（last name）
  例如：Mrs. Gore

(3) **Ms.「小姐／女士」用於未婚女性或已婚女性的姓。**

- Ms. + 名（first name）+ 姓（last name）
  例如：Ms. Lily Gore
- Ms. + 姓（last name）
  例如：Ms. Gore

(4) 注意：在「Mr./Mrs./Ms.」後面不能只接名字（first name）。
也就是說，單獨用名字時，前面不能用稱號「Mr./Mrs./Ms.」。

2

✗ Good morning, Wood. —— 不能直接稱呼姓

✓ Good morning, Mr. Elwood Wood.
非常正式 埃爾伍德 · 伍德先生，早安。
可用 Mr. + 名（first name）+ 姓（last name)

✓ Good morning, Mr. Wood.
伍德先生，早安。
稱呼姓時要加上 Mr.、Mrs.、Ms.、Professor、Doctor 等稱號

✓ Good morning, Elwood.
埃爾伍德，早安。
可以直接稱呼名字。如果你是 Elwood 的朋友，他希望你直接稱呼名字，就可以不用 Mr. 稱號

361 much/very 很

1

✗ That exam was much difficult for Sam.
much 通常用在形容詞的比較級前面

✓ That exam was very difficult for Sam.
那場考試對山姆來說很困難。
在形容詞的原級前面，要用 very

(1) **much** 通常用在形容詞的比較級前面。

形容詞的比較級 more difficult 前面用 much

- The last question about the sun was **much more difficult** than the first one.
  （關於太陽的最後一個問題比第一個問題難得多。）

⑵ 如果修飾過去分詞，也要用 much。

- much improved results（大有改善的結果。）
- Our dog Lily is a much loved member of the family.（我們的狗狗莉莉是深受我們喜愛的家庭成員之一。）

362 mum

請參見 mom/mum/pop/dad。

363 music 音樂

1

✗ Would a music cheer up Elwood?

不可數名詞，不能用冠詞 a 作修飾

✓ Would a piece of music cheer up Elwood?

聽一曲音樂會使埃爾伍德高興起來嗎？

✓ Would some music cheer up Elwood?

聽一些音樂會使埃爾伍德高興起來嗎？

注意下面片語的意思：

- face the music（勇敢地面對困難；接受應得的懲罰）
- set to music（為……譜曲）

364 must/should 必須；一定是／該；應當

1

✗ Since our ship is moving fast, we must arrive in Spain before Hurricane Jane.

用 must 對現狀或過去做推論，用在這裡與句意不符

✓ Since our ship is moving fast, we should arrive in Spain before Hurricane Jane.

用 should 來對未來做預測

既然我們的船行駛很快，我們應該能在颶風珍來之前到達西班牙。

⑴ 用 should 來做預測（如上面的例句），或建議什麼是應當做的。

⑵ 用 must 來做推論，或談論什麼是必須做的。

(3) must 和 should 是情態助動詞，後面應該接原形動詞。

應當

· Should I tell Ruth the truth about Elwood?
（我應當把關於埃爾伍德的事，實話實說地告訴露絲嗎？）

必須

· Clem must be in bed by 9 p.m.
（克勒姆必須在晚上九點前上床睡覺。）

對現在狀況的邏輯推論：我肯定葛蕾絲・納欣很愉快

· Grace Nation must be very happy about her life on the space station.
（葛蕾絲・納欣對她在太空站的生活一定感到非常愉快。）

365 myself/I/me 我

1

✗ Sue and myself are going to Seattle.

✗ Sue and me are going to Seattle.

不要用反身代名詞和受格代名詞作句子的主詞

✓ Sue and I are going to Seattle.

用主格代名詞作句子的主詞

蘇和我要去西雅圖。

(1) 如果「我」要獨自去西雅圖，肯定不會說 「Me is/am going to Seattle.」，而是說「I am going to Seattle.」。由此可知 「Sue and me are going to Seattle.」 是錯誤的。

(2) 同樣道理，肯定不會說 「Myself is/am going to Seattle.」，而是說 「I am going to Seattle.」。由此可知 「Sue and myself are going to Seattle.」是錯誤的。

(3) 如果和 Sue 一起去，那麼就應該說 「Sue and I are going to Seattle.」。

(4) 注意，通常為了禮貌，第一人稱 I、me 要放在另一個人的後面（Sue and I, Sue and me）。

(5) 比較下列例句：

I will go for a swim in Lake Sky.（我要去天空湖游泳。）

不能用受格代名詞 me 和反身代名詞 myself

Lorelei and I will go for a swim in Lake Sky.
（蘿芮萊和我要去天空湖游泳。）

2 ❌ Is this chocolate tea for Amy or myself?

❌ Is this chocolate tea for Amy or I?

✔ Is this chocolate tea for Amy or me?

在介系詞 for 後面只能用受格 me

巧克力茶是要給艾咪的，還是要給我的？

(1) 如果講話者不清楚該用 for Amy or me 還是 for Amy or I 時，於是就選擇 Amy or myself，這樣行嗎？答案是「不行」！

(2) 這裡既不能用 for Amy or myself，也不該用 for Amy or I。在介系詞 for 後面只能用受格 me。

(3) 請參見 between you and me/between you and I。

3 ❌ Our parents' divorce upset both Amy and I.

不能作動詞（upset）的受詞

❌ Our parents' divorce upset both Amy and myself.

意思是「親自」，或用來指代主詞 I，而這裡沒有「親自」的含意，這裡的主詞不是 I，而是 divorce，因此 myself 在這裡不能作動詞的受詞

✔ Our parents' divorce upset both Amy and me.

受格 me 在這裡作動詞的受詞

我們父母的離婚使艾蜜和我都心煩意亂。

myself 的用法請看下面的「文法加油站」。

文法加油站

反身代名詞 -self（Reflexive Pronouns）

① myself、yourself、himself、herself、itself、ourselves、yourselves 以及 themselves 都是反身代名詞。它們不能取代普通代名詞 I、me、you、he、him、she、her 等。

② 請參見 -self。

③ 反身代名詞只能用在下面兩種情況下：

(a) 用以加強語氣，表示「親自；本人」。

- Eli himself is the one who told that lie.
（那個謊言就是伊萊本人講的。）
- **I myself** have never met an elf.
只有在同一個句子裡已經用過 I 時，後面才能用 myself
（我自己也從來沒見過小精靈。）

(b) 反身代名詞，用來指代主詞（主詞和受詞是指同一個人）。

- If **you** believe in **yourself**, you should ignore that dishonest elf!
反身代名詞 yourself 指代主詞 you
（如果你信任自己，就應該不理睬那個不誠實的小精靈！）
- **I** have been teaching **myself** English by using a simple storybook that has an MP3 recording.
反身代名詞 myself 指代主詞 I
（我使用簡易故事書和配套的 MP3 錄音在自學英語。）

it's I 與 it's me

根據傳統文法，在 be 動詞後面要用主格代名詞 he、she、they 等，應該說「It is I.」，而不是「It is me.」。但在簡略回答時，「It is me.」為正確用法。

- Claire asked, "Who's there?" —— "It's **me**," replied Lee.
在這裡簡略回答 It's me 比 It is I 更常見
（克萊兒問：「是誰在那裡？」——李回答：「是我。」）

Stock Phrase "by oneself"

固定片語：by oneself（獨自）

- by myself
- by herself
- by yourself
- by himself
- by ourselves
- by yourselves
- by themselves

- I'm an old elf, and I like to count my gold coins by myself.
（我是一個老精靈，我喜歡獨自一人數我的金幣。）

N

366 name 名字的用法

1

❌ My name is Dame. —— 通常自我介紹時，不能只提到姓（family name/last name）

✅ My name is Lorelei Dame.

我叫蘿芮萊・戴姆。

通常自我介紹時，應介紹自己的名和姓

✅ My last name is Dame, and my first name is Lorelei.

我姓戴姆，我的名字是蘿芮萊。

- I am **Lorelei**.（我是蘿芮萊。）
- My **name** is **Lorelei**.（我的名字是蘿芮萊。）

在非正式的情況下，可以只提名字（first name）

2

❌ Hello, King. This is Liz Paris.

不能直接稱呼**姓**（last name），在姓前面應該加一個**禮貌稱謂**（Mr.、Mrs.、Ms.、Professor 等）

✅ Hello, Mr. King. This is Liz Paris.

你好，金先生。我是莉茲・帕里斯。

- Hi, **Eli**!（嗨，伊萊。）

可以直接稱呼名（first name），名字前不需要禮貌稱謂

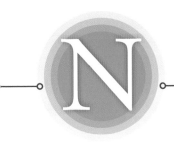

3 ❌ It's not yours. It's Ms. Lenore's.

Lenore（first name）是女性的名字，不是姓。名字不能用在 Mrs.、Professor、Doctor 等後面。要避免這樣的錯誤，應該先弄清楚是名還是姓

✅ It's not yours. It's Ms. Lenore Gore's.

那不是你的。那是蕾諾兒・戈爾女士的。

✅ It's not yours. It's Lenore's.

那不是你的。那是蕾諾兒的。

請參見 281 頁的 Mr. 條目。

Sun 是姓（last name），前面用禮貌稱謂 Mrs.

Tess 是名（first name），不用稱謂

- **Mrs. Sun** gave her lovely wedding dress to **Tess**.
（孫太太把她漂亮的結婚禮服送給了黛絲。）

4 ❌ Teacher Nancy felt pleased with what we had done.

Teacher + First Name 是典型的中式英語（Chinglish），應避免使用

❌ Our teacher, Ms. Nancy, felt pleased with what we had done.

✅ Our teacher, Ms. Nancy Sun, felt pleased with what we had done.

我們的老師，南西・孫女士，對我們所做的事感到滿意。

✅ Our teacher, Ms. Sun, felt pleased with what we had done.

我們的老師，孫女士，對我們所做的事感到滿意。

文法加油站

如何構成名字的複數形式？

❌ In Ms. Christmas's class, there are four Cherries, three Annie's, and two Amos's.

✅ In Ms. Christmas's class, there are four Cherrys, three Annies, and two Amoses.

（在克里斯特莫斯女士的班上，有四個伽麗、三個安妮和兩個阿摩司。）

① 名字用複數時，無論是姓還是名，直接加 -s 就行了，比如，
Annie → Annies。

② 如果是以 s、sh、ch、x、z 結尾的，就加 -es，比如，
Amos → Amoses。

③ 以 y 結尾的名字，不要改成 -ies，只在 y 後面加 -s，比如，
Cherry → Cherrys。

④ 總之，不要改變名字的原拼寫，也不要加省略符號（'s）。

單數形	複數形
· Anna (first name)	five Annas 五個安娜
· Ted (first name)	two Teds 兩個泰德
· Cory (first name)	three Corys 三個寇里
· Cory (family name)	the Corys = the Cory family 寇里家
· James (first name)	two Jameses 兩個詹姆斯
· James (family name)	the Jameses = the James family 詹姆斯家
· Lindberg (family name)	the Lindbergs = the Lindberg family 林德伯格家
· Shaw (family name)	the Shaws = the Shaw family 蕭家
· Wayne, Jane, and Zane Brown	the Browns 布朗家 （家中有三口人）
· Mr. and Mrs. Goodman	the Goodmans 古德曼夫婦 （✖ the Goodmen）
· Mr. and Mrs. Wolf	the Wolfs 伍爾夫夫婦 （✖ the Wolves）

367 necessary

請參見 important (essential/vital/necessary/desirable)。

368 need 需要

A) need 情態助動詞／及物動詞

1

✗ Dee needs not worry about me.
情態助動詞的字尾不加 -s

✗ Dee need not to worry about me.
情態助動詞後面不接帶 to 的不定詞

✓ 情態助動詞 Dee need not worry about me.
作**情態助動詞**時，不需要因主詞的單複數而改變動詞的形態，後面接原形動詞（用於疑問句、否定句和條件句）

✓ 及物動詞 Dee doesn't need to worry about me.
作**及物動詞**（即一般動詞）時，後面接帶 to 的不定詞。在否定句中需要用助動詞 do/does/did

蒂不必為我擔心。

(1) need 既可以作情態助動詞（如 can 或 may），也可以作一般動詞（如 want 或 try）。

(2) need 作情態助動詞時，常用於**現在式**的**疑問句**、**否定句**和**條件句**，不需要因主詞的單複數而改變動詞的形態，後面接原形動詞，在疑問句和否定句中不需要助動詞 do。不過，美式英語比較少用情態助動詞 need，而較常用及物動詞 need。

(3) need 作及物動詞（即一般動詞）時，後面接帶 to 的不定詞；在否定句和疑問句中需要用助動詞 do/does/did；在肯定句中，現在簡單式單數第三人稱要用 needs。

・Need Pam take the English exam? 情態助動詞，用於疑問句
= Does Pam need to take the English exam? 及物動詞
（潘姆需要參加這次英語考試嗎？）

・No, Jill need not take a sleeping pill. 情態助動詞，用於否定句
= No, Jill does not need to take a sleeping pill. 及物動詞
（不，吉兒不需要服安眠藥。）

情態助動詞，用於 if 從屬子句
・Jerome wants to know if he need **hurry** back home.
= Jerome wants to know if he needs **to hurry** back home.
（傑羅姆想知道他是否需要趕緊回家。） 及物動詞

肯定句中需要用及物動詞 need；
現在式單數第三人稱用 needs

‧ Lars needs **to be** on Mars, but June needs **to go** to Neptune.
（拉斯得去火星，但茱恩得去海王星。）

文法加油站

dare（敢）的用法

dare 的用法一樣，既可以作情態助動詞（常用於現在式的疑問句、否定句和條件句），也可以作一般動詞（及物動詞）。

‧ Dare you tell Ruth the truth about Claire? 情態助動詞
用在現在式的疑問句中
= Do you dare to tell Ruth the truth about Claire? 一般動詞
（你敢告訴露絲關於克萊兒的真相嗎？）

‧ Dwight dare not go out fishing at night. 情態助動詞
用在現在式的否定句中
= Dwight doesn't dare to go out fishing at night. 一般動詞
（杜威特晚上不敢出去釣魚。）
→ dare 作一般動詞時，有些人常省略助動詞 do/does/did 以及 to
比如：Dwight dares not go out fishing at night.
但這不是標準英語。正式用語中需要避免。

‧ If Gwen dare talk about it, I'll never speak to her again. 情態助動詞
用在現在式的條件子句中
= If Gwen dares to talk about it, I'll never speak to her again. 一般動詞
（如果葛雯敢談論那事，我將永遠不再跟她講話。）

‧ Did anyone dare to argue with Sue?（有沒有人敢跟蘇爭論？）
過去式 dare 只用作及物動詞，不作情態助動詞

‧ I dare Amy to argue with me.（諒艾咪也不敢與我爭論。）
當 dare 表示「挑戰」（challenge）時，dare 只用作及物動詞

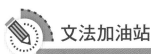

B) need 名詞

1

不能說：it's no need to do something

❌ It's no need to hide the truth from Ruth. She is strong and won't be upset for very long.

句型：there is no need (for somebody) to do something

✅ There is no need to hide the truth from Ruth. She is strong and won't be upset for very long.

句型：it is not necessary (for somebody) to do something

= It's not necessary to hide the truth from Ruth. She is strong and won't be upset for very long.

沒有必要對露絲隱瞞真相。她很堅強，不會傷心很久的。

2

❌ Our country's need of clean energy can be met by wind and solar power.

(there is a) need for something：need 後面用 for，不要用 of

✅ Our country's need for clean energy can be met by wind and solar power.

可以透過風力和太陽能來滿足我們國家對無汙染能源的需求。

- a need for fresh air（對新鮮空氣的需求）
- a need for social pressure（需要社會壓力）

369 negative infinitive 不定詞的否定式

請參見 try not to/try to not。

370 neither 兩者都不

A) 形容詞 形

1

❌ Neither movies were interesting to Ivy.

✅ Neither movie was interesting to Ivy.

用作形容詞，意思是「兩者都不」，句型為：**neither + 單數名詞 + 單數動詞**

這兩部電影都沒有引起愛葳的興趣。

- Neither idea seems proper to Maria.
（對瑪麗亞來說，兩個主意好像都不妥當。）

B) 代名詞 代

1

複數名詞前有 the/his/her/their 等作修飾時，neither 用作代名詞：**neither of + the/his/her/their + 複數名詞**

❌ Neither her parents understood that reading for fun was how Midge would gain the vocabulary needed for college.

代名詞（neither of her parents）

✅ Neither of her parents understood that reading for fun was how Midge would gain the vocabulary needed for college.

形容詞（neither parent）

= Neither parent understood that reading for fun was how Midge would gain the vocabulary needed for college.

米姬的父親和母親都沒有意識到米姬要獲得上大學所需要的辭彙量，就得靠趣味閱讀。

文法加油站

neither 的用法

neither of + the/his/her/their, etc. + 複數名詞 + 複數動詞（非正式）／單數動詞（正式）

非正式	Neither of the Swedish girls speak Spanish.
正式	Neither of the Swedish girls speaks Spanish. （那兩個瑞典女孩都不會講西班牙語。）

① 在正式文體中，「neither of + 複數名詞／複數代名詞」用作主詞時，通常後面接單數動詞。因為傳統文法認為，實際主詞是代名詞 neither，而不是介系詞 of 後面的複數名詞（比如 girls），所以動詞應該用單數。

② 但在非正式文體中，「neither of + 複數名詞／複數代名詞」用作主詞時，動詞可以用複數，因為靠近動詞的名詞（比如上面例句的 girls）是複數，那麼該動詞也用複數。

③ 考試遇見這種情況，還是要遵守傳統文法規則，選擇**單數動詞**。

④ none 和 either 的用法也一樣。請參見 none 或 either。

- **Neither dress fits** Anna Montana.
  - Neither —— 形容詞
  - fits —— 這句只能用單數動詞
- **Neither of the dresses fit** Anna Montana. 非正式
  - Neither —— 代名詞
- **Neither of the dresses fits** Anna Montana. 正式

（兩件洋裝都不適合安娜・蒙塔納穿。）

371 neither/none 兩者都不／無一個

1

❌ Dee and Lori smiled, but none understood the story.

談到「三個以上（包括三個）」時，才用 none，這裡只談到兩個人

❌ Dee and Lori smiled, but none of them understood the story.

✅ Dee and Lori smiled, but neither understood the story.

談到「兩個人／兩件事／兩種行為／兩個主意」時，要用 neither

✅ Dee and Lori smiled, but neither of them understood the story.

蒂和蘿麗笑了，但她倆都沒有聽懂那個故事。

- **None** of Ben's **friends** talked to my son.

（班的朋友中沒有一個跟我的兒子說話。）

372 neither/nor/so 也不／也

1

❌ Bob **did not have** a job, and so did Rob.

當前面獨立子句中的動詞是否定形式，後面獨立子句應該用 neither 或 nor，不用 so

並列句的第二個獨立子句副詞 neither 前面要用連接詞 and

✅ Bob did not have a job, **and neither did Rob**.

✅ Bob did not have a job, **nor did Rob**.

用 nor 時，不用連接詞 and，因為 nor 本身就是一個連接詞

鮑伯沒有工作，羅伯也沒有工作。

當前面獨立子句的動詞是肯定形式時，後面獨立子句就應該用 so；副詞 so 前面用 and 連接兩個獨立子句

- Jim **had** eaten lots of food, **and so** had Kim.
  （吉姆吃了很多食物，金姆也吃了很多。）

373 neither . . . nor . . . 不是……也不是

1

✗ **Neither** the manager **nor** the owner **were** willing to help Lenore.

neither . . . nor . . . 的結構在句中作主詞時，由 neither 和 nor 連接的成分如果都是單數，動詞也應該是單數

✓ **Neither** the **manager** **nor** the **owner** **was** willing to help Lenore.

neither、nor 後面的名詞是單數 manager、owner，所以動詞應該用單數 was

無論是經理還是老闆，都不願意幫助蕾諾兒。

(1)「neither . . . nor . . .」的結構在句中作主詞時，由 neither 和 nor 連接的成分如果都是單數，動詞也應該是單數。

(2) 同樣道理，由 neither 和 nor 連接的成分如果都是複數，動詞也應該是複數。

主詞包含兩個複數名詞，因此動詞用複數

- **Neither** the **workers nor** the **managers were** willing to help her.（無論是工人們還是經理們，都不願意幫助她。）

2

正確 **Neither** my two sisters **nor** my friend **Daisy is** lazy.

動詞與靠得最近的名詞一致

較佳 **Neither** my friend Daisy **nor** my two **sisters are** lazy.

把複數名詞放在 nor 的後面，靠近動詞，動詞自然就要用複數，此用法更自然

我的朋友戴西和我的兩個姐妹都不懶惰。

(1) 由 neither 和 nor 連接的成分如果一個是單數名詞而另一個是複數名詞，**動詞應該與靠得最近的名詞一致**。

(2) 最好的辦法是把複數名詞放在 nor 的後面，靠近動詞，動詞自然就要用複數，聽起來更自然一些。

・Neither Ambrose nor his lies are acceptable to Rose, so out the door he goes!
（蘿絲既不接受安布羅斯也不接受他的謊言，於是他從門口滾出去了！）

⑶「either . . . or . . . 」也適用這條規則，詳細解釋請參見「either . . . or . . .」。

文法加油站

neither 常用的結構總結

① neither（代名詞）+ 單數動詞

② neither（形容詞）+ 單數名詞 + 單數動詞

③ neither of+ 複數名詞 + 單數動詞（正式）或複數動詞（非正式）

④ neither + 單數名詞 + nor + 單數名詞 + 單數動詞

⑤ neither + 複數名詞 + nor + 複數名詞 + 複數動詞

⑥ neither + 名詞（單數或複數）+ nor + 單數名詞 + 單數動詞

⑦ neither + 名詞（單數或複數）+ nor + 複數名詞 + 複數動詞

3

✗ Mr. Porter neither is a writer nor a newspaper reporter.
→ 非平行結構：neither+ 動詞（is）；nor+ 名詞（reporter）

✓ Mr. Porter is neither a writer nor a newspaper reporter.
→ 平行結構：neither+ 名詞（writer）；nor+ 名詞（reporter）

波特先生既不是作家也不是報刊記者。

⑴ 這個結構應注意「對稱」，即在 neither 和 nor 後面的成分應該一致。

⑵ 請看下列結構：

(a) neither + 名詞；nor + 名詞	(b) neither + 獨立子句；nor + 獨立子句
(c) neither + 動詞；nor + 動詞	(d) neither + 形容詞；nor + 形容詞
(e) neither + 副詞；nor + 副詞	(f) neither + 介系詞；nor + 介系詞

(3) 類似這樣的對稱結構還有：「both . . . and . . . 」，「either . . . or . . . 」和「not only . . . but also . . .」。

(4) 請參見「both . . . and . . . 」，「either . . . or . . . 」，「not only . . . but also . . . 」和 parallel structure（第 E 點）。

374 never 從未

1

✗ I never have and never will forget Jill and Bill.

= never have (forget)，文法錯誤

✓ I never have forgotten Jill and Bill and never will.

never will 放在後面，省略的部分（forget Jill and Bill）因在句子最後，雖不是標準的文法，但不算是犯錯，聽起來還能接受

我從未忘記吉兒和比爾，也永遠不會忘記他們。

(1) 原句為 「I never **have forgotten** Jill and Bill and never **will forget** them.」，不過這個句子不簡潔，用同一個動詞的不同形式重複了動詞（have forgotten、forget）。

(2) 任何句子與 never have and never will 連用，要想避免重複動詞，都很難用標準的文法來解決，因為沒有一個動詞可以與（完成式的）助動詞 have 和（未來式的）助動詞 will 同用。比如上面的例句：have 要求接過去分詞 forgotten，而 will 卻要求接原形動詞 forget。

(3) always have and always will 也具有同樣的問題。

(4) 請參見 parallel structure 中第 G 點「動詞的平行結構」。

(5) 只有當重複的動詞是同形的（比如 could forget and would forget），我們才能省略第一個（forget）來避免重複。

這一句 could 後面省略了 forget，以避免重複：I never could (forget) . . .

- I **never could** and **never would forget** Jill Wood.
  （我從來不可能也永遠不會忘記吉兒・伍德。）

這一句 could 後面省略了 give up，以避免重複：Bill never could (give up) . . .

- Bill **never could** and **never would give up** on finding Jill.
  （比爾絕對不可能放棄尋找吉兒，也永遠不放棄。）

375 news 新聞

1

❌ I have a good news about Ming's diamond rings.

news 因為是以 s 結尾，看起來像複數，實際上是**不可數名詞**，前面不能有不定冠詞 a

✅ I have good news about Ming's diamond rings.

✅ I have some good news about Ming's diamond rings.

✅ I have a piece of good news about Ming's diamond rings.

要表示單數意義，用 **a piece of** news

✅ I have a good piece of news about Ming's diamond rings.

關於敏的鑽石戒指，我有好消息喔。

2

❌ The news about Sue's nasty dragon are bad news.

news 是不可數名詞，不可用複數動詞

✅ The news about Sue's nasty dragon is bad news.

news 在句中當主詞時，動詞要用**單數**

關於蘇的那頭可惡的龍的消息，不是好消息。

3

news 是不可數名詞，不能用數量詞 three 修飾；要表示複數意義，用 two pieces of news、three pieces of news 等

❌ Those are three good news about Rose.

good 修飾 news，指消息是好的，不是壞的，good news 與 bad news 相反

✅ Those are three pieces of good news about Rose.

✅ Those are three good pieces of news about Rose.

good 修飾 three pieces。例如記者找到了三條對報社來説是重要的消息，消息本身可能是好消息，可能是壞消息。但對報社來説，有用的消息，就是好消息

那是三條關於蘿絲的好消息。

請參見 math/maths 和 politics。

文法加油站

看起來像複數的單數名詞

可數名詞，單複數同形
- a crossroads（一個十字路口）
- a means（一個方法）
- a series（一套、一系列）

- economics（經濟學）
- mathematics（數學）
- the United Nations（聯合國）

376 night/evening 夜晚

1

✗ We are staying home <u>this night</u> to dine by candlelight.

沒有 this night 這種說法

✓ We are staying home **tonight** to dine by candlelight.

✓ We are staying home **this evening** to dine by candlelight.

我們今晚要待在家裡，在燭光下用餐。

2

意思是「**晚安；再會**」，用於夜晚向人道別，尤其是在睡前

✗ <u>Good night</u>, Elwood. May I introduce you to my friend Kay?

意思是「**晚安**」，用於傍晚見面時向人打招呼

✓ <u>Good evening</u>, Elwood. May I introduce you to my friend Kay?

埃爾伍德，晚安！我可以把你介紹給我的朋友凱嗎？

- Dwight: **Good night**, Elwood!（杜威特：晚安，埃爾伍德！）

  Elwood: **Good night**, Dwight! Sleep tight.

  （埃爾伍德：晚安，杜威特！祝你好眠。）

3

❌ What time does Dwight usually go to bed in the evening?

通常指晚上六點到睡前的夜晚活動時間，可以看電視、做作業等

✅ What time does Dwight usually go to bed at night?

指晚上九點以後，上床睡覺要在此時

杜威特晚上通常什麼時候上床睡覺？

- Bing plays computer games in the evening.
  （賓晚上玩電腦遊戲。）

4

❌ Did you go to visit Bing and Dwight yesterday night?

錯誤用法。不要用 yesterday night、last evening

✅ Did you go to visit Bing and Dwight yesterday evening?

✅ Did you go to visit Bing and Dwight last night?

你昨晚去拜訪過賓和杜威特嗎？

377 no body/nobody 沒有一個群體／沒有人

1

❌ Mort landed his small jet and found out there was no body at the remote airport.

body 單獨使用時，指「群體、組織、團體」。
no body 指「沒有群體」（no group）

✅ Mort landed his small jet and found out there was nobody at the remote airport.

指「沒有人」（no person 或 no one）

莫特把他的小噴射機降落在那個偏僻的機場上，發現那裡一個人都沒有。

- the student body（全體學生；學生會）
- a corporate body（法人團體）
- No body of dancers has ever had anyone as tall as Margo.
  （舞蹈團體中，沒有哪個團體曾有過像瑪歌那樣高大的舞者了。）

378 no one/noone 沒有人

1

與 anyone 和 someone 不同，no one 總是拼寫成兩個字，不能寫成一個字

❌ Lenore Grimes looks great, and noone can believe that she has given birth four times.

意思相當於 not one person 或 nobody

✅ Lenore Grimes looks great, and no one can believe that she has given birth four times.

蕾諾兒・格萊姆斯看起來很不錯，沒人相信她生過四個孩子。

379 noisy/noisome 吵鬧的／有惡臭的；有害的

1

❌ Lily and her noisome group of happy friends cheered loudly.

意思與 noisy 完全不同。noisome 的意思是「有惡臭的、（味道）有害的」

✅ Lily and her noisy group of happy friends cheered loudly.

意思是「喧鬧的、嘈雜的、吵吵嚷嚷的」

莉莉和她那群喧鬧、快樂的朋友高聲喝彩。

一些人以為 noise 是吵鬧，那麼加 -some 字尾就成了形容詞，如同 trouble（麻煩）和 troublesome（麻煩的）。實際上，與 noise 相應的形容詞是 noisy。

- Sue Spear smelled noisome after she threw up her beer.
  （蘇・斯比爾把啤酒嘔吐出來後，她的氣味很難聞。）

380 none 一點也沒；一個也沒

1

美式 口語 None of us are called Gus.

正式 None of us is called Gus.

等於 no one（沒有一個）或 not one（沒有任何一個），後面應該接**單數動詞**和**單數代名詞**

我們當中沒有人叫作加斯。

(1) 正式（傳統）：許多人曾經都學過，none 相當於 no one（沒有一個）或者 not one（沒有任何一個），因此當「none of + 複

數名詞／複數代名詞」的結構作主詞時，後面應該接**單數動詞**和**單數代名詞**，比如「None of us **is** perfect.」。

・None of the selfish children on the bus was willing to give up his or her seat for old Uncle Gus.

正式語：用單數動詞 was，單數代名詞 his or her

（公車上那些自私的孩子，沒有一個願意讓座給加斯老伯伯。）

(2) 口語／非正式文體：但也有許多人認為（尤其是美國人）none 的意思更接近於 not any (of them)。所以他們認為 none 在「none of+ 複數名詞／複數代名詞」的結構中是複數，應該接複數動詞，比如「None of us **are** perfect.」。

口語／非正式文體：用複數動詞 want

・None of my classmates want to play a game of chess with Tess.（我的同學中沒有一個想跟黛絲下西洋棋。）

(3) 假若考試遇見這種情況，還是需要遵守傳統文法規則，選擇單數動詞。

(4) neither of 的用法一樣。請參見 neither of。

文法加油站

① 當 none 明確地指 not one（一個也不）時，只能用單數動詞。

・Of all my books, none has received more attention than my latest one.

（在我的所有書中，沒有哪本比最新的這本更吸引人。）

② 當「none of + 不可數名詞／單數代名詞」的時候就只能用單數動詞，因為其意思是 none of it。

要用單數 is，不用複數 are

・**None of** the economic **news is** going to please Liz.

（這些財經新聞中沒有哪條會使莉茲高興。）

③「almost none of + 複數名詞」後面只能接複數動詞。

要用複數 were，不用單數 was

・**Almost none of** the **people** on the bus were friendly to us.

（公車上幾乎沒有一個人對我們友善。）

④ 在「**none + but + 複數名詞**」的結構中，動詞只能用複數。

- **None but** her close friends **believe** her story about Lori Sun.
  （除了她親密的朋友外，沒有人相信她關於蘿麗・孫的傳聞。）

381 not only . . . but also . . . 不僅……而且

1

✗ Lily is not only proud of her wealth but also of her health.

not only 後面接形容詞（proud），but also 後面也要接形容詞（proud）

✗ Lily is not only proud of her wealth but also is proud of her health.

✓ Lily is **not only proud** of her wealth **but also proud** of her health.

✓ Lily is proud **not only of** her wealth **but also of** her health.

not only 後面接介系詞（of）片語，but also 後面也應該接介系詞（of）片語

莉莉不僅為她的財富感到自豪，也為她的健康感到自豪。

(1) 由「**not only . . . but also . . .** 」連接的兩個成分在文法上要求用**對稱結構**，即 not only 和 but also 後面要用同樣的詞性。

(2) 請參見「both . . . and . . . 」；「either . . . or . . . 」；「neither . . . nor . . . 」。

2

✗ **Not only** Bruce **ate** my pizza, **but he also** drank all of my orange juice.

not only 放在句首，子句要用倒裝結構；but also 引導的子句不倒裝

✓ **Not only did** Bruce **eat** my pizza, **but he also** drank all of my orange juice.

布魯斯不僅吃了我的披薩，還喝光了我的柳橙汁。

在「**not only . . . but also . . .**」的句子中，not only 放在句首，獨立子句要用倒裝結構：**助動詞 + 主詞 + 一般動詞**；but also 引導的獨立子句不倒裝，結構為：**but + 主詞 +also+ 動詞**。

文法加油站

倒裝結構（inversion）

① neither、nor、seldom、rarely、never、「hardly/scarcely . . . when」、「no sooner . . . than」以及含有「only . . . 」的片語和含有「 . . . no . . .」的片語放在句首時，句子也要用倒裝結構：「助動詞 + 主詞 + 一般動詞」（一般動詞可以是**過去分詞**或**原形動詞**）或「連綴動詞 + 主詞」。這種倒裝句主要用於非常正式的文體中。

助動詞（have）+ 主詞（I）+ 過去分詞（heard）

- Seldom **have I heard** so many songs from Ms. Bird.
（我很少聽到伯德女士唱那麼多歌。）

助動詞(does）+ 主詞(Mr. Wise）+ 原形動詞（criticize）

- Rarely **does Mr. Wise criticize** Lily.（懷斯先生很少批評莉莉。）

助動詞（had）+ 主詞（Janet) + 過去分詞（finished）

- Hardly **had Janet finished** fixing her bike when Bridget showed up and asked to borrow it.
（珍妮特才剛把她的自行車修好，布麗姬特就跑來借自行車了。）

連綴動詞（was）+ 主詞（Kirk）

- No sooner **was Kirk** home **than** he discovered he had left his cookbook at work.
（柯克剛一到家就發現自己把食譜留在了工作地點。）

only + 介系詞片語（after two months . . .）+ 倒裝句：助動詞（did）+ 主詞（Rob）+ 原形動詞（Know）

- Only after two months of working at the bank **did Rob** really **know** how to do his job.
（羅伯在銀行工作兩個月後，才對自己的工作真正有所瞭解。）

助動詞(are)+ 主詞 + 過去分詞(allowed)

- Dirk explained to Sue, "On no account **are you allowed** to smoke at work."
（德克對蘇解釋：「工作時絕對不准抽菸。」）

② so 在句首，句子也要倒裝。請參見 neither/nor/so。

- Our methods of transporting people have changed, and so **have our ways** of making a living.

  助動詞（have）+ 主詞（our ways . . .）+ 過去分詞（changed）；過去分詞 changed 被省略

  （我們載送人的方式已經變了，我們謀生的方式也變了。）

③ 請參見 word order（第 4 個範例）。

382 number: a number of 一些

1

✗ A number of my friends thinks that Dan and I should visit Japan.

= some。這個片語與**複數名詞**或**代名詞**連用，後面的動詞也用**複數**

✓ A number of my friends think that Dan and I should visit Japan.

= some of my friends

我的一些朋友認為我和丹應該去日本遊覽。

383 number: the number of 數目

1

這個片語與**複數名詞**或**代名詞**連用，後面的動詞卻要用**單數**，因為意思是「⋯⋯的數量」

✗ The number of kicks Grace landed on the terrorist were enough to make him fall on his face.

✓ The number of kicks Grace landed on the terrorist was enough to make him fall on his face.

葛蕾絲用腳踢恐怖分子多次，足以把他打得撲倒在地。

請參見 amount/number 和 couple。

384 numerical expressions
以數字表達的片語

1

✗ Three miles are a long way to jog in the fog.

✓ Three miles is a long way to jog in the fog.

看成一個整體（一段距離），動詞通常用**單數**

在霧中慢跑三英里路是很長的一段路程。

2

✗ Eight dollars are not enough for my date with Kate.

✓ Eight dollars is not enough for my date with Kate.

看成一個整體（一筆錢），動詞通常用**單數**

八美元不夠我和凱特的約會使用。

(1) 當我們談到「錢、距離、時間、重量」時，如果我們把它看成是一個整體（一筆錢、一段距離、一段時間），而不是三個、五個分開的東西，這些名詞雖是複數（eight dollars、three miles、two years），但作主詞時，動詞通常用單數，與之有關的代名詞和指示形容詞也用單數。

(2) 但如果把這些表達數字的片語當成是一組個體單位、一些分開的數目（a group of individual components、a number of individual units），而不是一個整體（a unit、a total amount），作主詞時，動詞就要用複數。

(3) 請參見 time（時間表達法）以及 subject-verb agreement 的第 N 點（測量）。

單數動詞 is，因為這裡的 four years 指一段時間（一個整體）

(a) · **Four years is** a long time for you to wait for Lenore.
（你要等蕾諾兒四年，那時間太長了。）

這裡談論的 four years 不是指一個整體，而是指「分開的四年時間」（four individual years），因此要用複數動詞 have passed

· **Four years have** passed since I last kissed Lenore.
（自從我上次親吻蕾諾兒後，已經四年過去了。）

用單數動詞 is，因為這裡的 a hundred dollars 指一個價格（one price）

(b) · **A hundred dollars is** the price for that big bag of rice.
（那一大袋米的價格是一百美元。）

用複數動詞 were，因為這裡的 a hundred dollars 顯然指一組個體單位（more than one piece of money）

· **A hundred dollars were** spread out on the table in front of Ted.（在泰德面前的桌上放了一百美元。）

用單數動詞 is，因為這裡把 two miles 看成是一個整體單位，一段距離

(c) · "**Two miles is** not too far to walk," noted Sue.
（蘇指出：「步行兩英里並不算太遠。」）

用複數動詞 are，因為這裡的 four miles 指在一個更長距離中的一些個體單位（一英里、兩英里、三英里、四英里）

· "**Four miles are** behind us, and **four** more **are** ahead of us," said Gus.
（加斯說：「我們已經走完了四英里了，我們的前面還有四英里。」）

seven plus four 被看成是一個總數。主詞是單數 seven，介系詞片語 plus four 只是額外增加的成分。無論介系詞片語額外增加了多少成分，動詞都應該與主詞的數一致。注意，用 plus 時，用單數動詞。請參見 Subjects Not in Prepositional Phrases

(d) · Seven **plus** four **is** eleven.（七加四等於十一。）

seven and four 是由兩個數目組成，兩個個體單位。由連接詞 and 連接起來的主詞是複合主詞，或稱「並列主詞」，動詞通常用複數。但在加法中，也可以把這種複合主詞看成一個整體，動詞也可以用單數（Seven and four is eleven.）

· Seven **and** four **are** eleven.（七加四等於十一。）

O

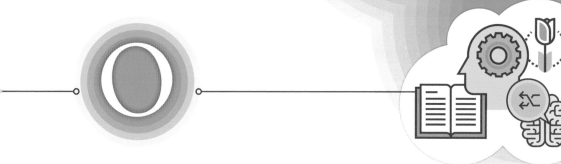

385 object 反對

1

✗ Lulu objects to be lied to.

✓ Lulu objects to being lied to.

露露討厭別人對她撒謊。

> object to (doing) something：「反對做什麼事」，to 在這裡是介系詞，後面接名詞、受格代名詞或動名詞

· Jane objected to the idea of walking home in the rain.
（珍反對冒雨走路回家的提議。）

386 off/off of/off from 從……掉下

1

✗ Paul, do not jump off of the wall.

> 用 off 就足夠了，不要用 off of 或 off from

✗ Paul, do not jump off from the wall.

✓ Paul, do not jump off the wall.

保羅，不要從牆上跳下來。

請參見 doublets/wordiness。

387 . . . old ……歲（的）

1 ✗ A girl of about seven years old was looking at the huge pearl.
不用在介系詞 of 後面

✓ A girl of about seven was looking at the huge pearl.
of 後面接數字（a girl of + 數字）

✓ A girl who was about seven years old was looking at the huge pearl.
通常用在連綴動詞 be 後面

一位大約七歲的小女孩正看著那顆巨大的珍珠。

（請參見 year。）

388 on one's own/by oneself/all alone 獨自、靠自己

沒有 by one's own 這個片語存在

1 ✗ I can't carry Amy by my own; she is too heavy for me.

✓ I can't carry Amy on my own; she is too heavy for me.

= I can't carry Amy all alone; she is too heavy for me.

= I can't carry Amy by myself; she is too heavy for me.

我無法獨自抱起艾咪，她太重了。

如果沒有人幫助你，只好 do things on your own 或 by yourself 或 all alone。

389 one 任何人；一個

A) one 任何人

1 性別歧視 Whichever ocean one looks at, he will find some pollution.

美式 Whichever ocean one looks at, he or she will find some pollution.

英式 Whichever ocean one looks at, one will find some pollution.

美式 英式 Whichever ocean you look at, you will find some pollution.
常可以用 you 來代替 one ，泛指「任何人」

無論你觀看哪一片海洋，都會發現有些汙染。

2 非正式 "Can **one** watch this war movie without having **their** emotions stirred?" asked Dan.

美式英語中，句首用了不定代名詞 one，後面需要重複這個 one 時，就改成 he or she 和 his or her

正式 美式 "Can one watch this war movie without having his or her emotions stirred?" asked Dan.

在英式英語中，不定代名詞 one 後面接 one/one's/oneself

正式 英式 "Can one watch this war movie without having one's emotions stirred?" asked Dan.

正式 美式 英式 "Can **we** watch this war movie without having **our** emotions stirred?" asked Dan.

丹問：「觀看這部戰爭片，我們能不動容嗎？」

(1) 在美式英語中，句首用了不定代名詞 **one**，後面需要重複這個 one 時，過去常用 he、him、his 和 himself 等來代替，以迴避重複彆扭的字 one。但近年來為了避免性別歧視（sexist）語言，就改成 **he or she** 和 **his or her**。還有些人用一種特殊的形式 he/she 和 his/her 來代替。

(2) 在口語和非正式語中，有些人用複數代名詞 they、them、their 來搭配單數不定代名詞 one。這種用法受到許多文法學家、編輯或嚴謹的作家反對，因為文法規則規定，**單數不定代名詞**（one、everybody、anybody、each 等）要搭配**單數動詞**和**單數人稱代名詞**。因此，在商務信函、學術報告、考試中，要遵守文法規則，使用正式用語。**類似上面範例中的第一句，在考試中務必避免**。

(3) 上面的所有形式（重複 one、he、he or she、he/she 等），都顯得笨拙或不自然，不太令人滿意。用複數人稱代名詞 they、their，又不符合文法規則。最好用別的辦法來解決這個問題。

(4) **one** 在這裡泛指「**人們；任何人**」。無論是在口語中還是在正式的文體中，用 one 來泛指人都顯得**很不自然**。因此，越來越多的人選擇使用 **you** 或者 **we**，這樣既可以避免性別歧視語言，又迴避了彆扭的 one 和笨拙的 he or she 等，而且還可以避免用複數 they、their 搭配單數代名詞 one，使文法也完全正確。比如上面範例中第一組和第二組的最後一句。

(5) 請參見 his/her 和 pronoun agreement。

B) one 一個（代替上下文中的名詞或名詞片語）

1

✗ Mr. Burr buys Jade clothes made from artificial **fur**. He'll never get her anything made from a real **one**.

只能代替可數名詞，不能用來代替不可數名詞

✓ Mr. Burr buys Jade clothes made of artificial **fur**. He'll never get her anything made of real **fur**.

如果是不可數名詞時，就需要重複那個名詞，或者有時省掉

伯爾先生買人造皮草的衣服給潔德。他從來不給她買任何真皮製品。

(1) **one** 用來代替前面已經提及的某個名詞，目的是為了避免重複那個名詞。**one** 的複數形式是 **ones**。

(2) **one** 只能代替**可數名詞**，不能用來代替不可數名詞。如果是不可數名詞時，就需要重複那個名詞，或者有時省掉。

- Rose told Rich, "Claire's sister just bought twenty-five pounds of **pears**."

  "Which kind did she buy?" asked Rich.

  pear 是可數名詞，可以用 one 來代替以避免重複。因為是複數 pears，所以用複數 ones 來代替。

  "Big **ones** like those over there," replied Rose.

  （蘿絲告訴瑞奇：「克萊兒的妹妹剛買了 25 磅的梨子。」
  瑞奇問：「她買哪一種梨子？」
  蘿絲回答：「就像那邊的那一種大梨子。」）

teacher 是可數名詞，
可以用 one 來代替以避免重複

- Your English **teacher** Ms. Sun seems to be a good **one**.
（你的英文老師孫女士看起來是一個好老師。）

- The store on Silk Island didn't have any fresh **milk**, so I bought some canned **milk**.

= The store on Silk Island didn't have any fresh **milk**, so I bought some cans of **milk**.

此句中的 milk 是不可數名詞，
不能用 one 來代替，只能重複 milk

（絲綢島上那家商店沒有新鮮牛奶了，所以我買了一些罐頭牛奶。）

C) one of those who（其中）一人、一個

1

✗ Is Lily one of those people who often goes to work early?

who 的動詞應該用複數 go

關係代名詞 who 的先行詞，複數名詞

✓ Is Lily one of those people who often go to work early?

莉莉屬於那些總是早早就去上班的人之一嗎？

(1) 這可是其中一個使我們頭痛的文法規則（Here's one of the grammar rules that drive/drives us crazy）。動詞到底應該是單數還是複數？是用 drive 還是用 drives ？

(2) 片語 one of those people who 和 one of the grammar rules that 後面應該用複數動詞（go 和 drive），因為關係代名詞 who、that 與先行詞 those people 和 the rules 相關連。

(3) 文法規則是：在 one of those（+ 複數名詞）who（或 that 或 which）結構中，who 的先行詞被認為是靠近 who 的複數名詞或複數代名詞 those，因此 who/that 引導的**從屬子句的動詞**應該用複數。

- Was Felix one of the runners that were in last year's Olympics?
（菲力克斯是參加去年奧林匹克運動會的跑者之一嗎？）

D) the only one of . . . who 其中唯一一個

1 ❌ Is Kay the only one of Liz Potter's daughters who phone her every day?

在「one of . . . who/that/which」結構中，如果 one 之前有 the only，關係代名詞 who、that、which 後面的動詞就一定要用單數

✅ Is Kay the only one of Liz Potter's daughters who phones her every day?

莉茲・波特的女兒中，唯有凱每天打電話給她嗎？

- Jane is the only one of my classmates who has visited Spain.（在我的同學中，唯有珍去西班牙旅遊過。）

文法加油站

one 的用法

① 對比「the only one of . . . who」和「only one of . . . who」。

用單數動詞 loves，因為只有一個人（Sue King）愛讀書

- Sue King is the only one of my students who loves reading.
（在我的學生中，只有蘇 ・ 金喜歡閱讀。）

用複數動詞 love，因為我的學生中不只 Sue King 一人愛讀書，許多學生都愛讀書

- Sue King is only one of my students who love reading.
（在我的學生中，蘇 ・ 金只不過是喜歡閱讀的學生之一。）

② one 作主詞。

如果 one 在句中或關係從屬子句中作主詞，動詞與單數主詞 one 保持一致，要用單數。在非正式用語中，有時用複數動詞搭配單數代名詞 one。不過，百分之九十以上的語言專家都認為要用單數動詞。

這句的主詞不是 us（複數），而是 one（單數），所以動詞應用單數

- One of us has to tell Gus.（我們之中有個人得告訴加斯。）

A B C D E F G H I J K L M N O P Q R S T U V W X Y Z

· Ming cried, "One of my friends is dying."
（敏哭喊道：「我的一個朋友快死了。」）

③ one or more 或 one or two 的結構後面一定要用**複數動詞**。

· One or more cars are parked illegally on Clay Street every day.
（每天都有一輛或更多的汽車非法停在克萊大街上。）

· Kitty said, "One or two students from my school have won scholarships to Yale University."
（姬蒂說：「我學校有一、兩個學生〔幾個學生〕獲得了美國耶魯大學的獎學金。」）

④ one + 分數。

(a) 如果 one 後面接有一個分數（**one + and + 分數 + 複數名詞**），動詞通常用**複數動詞**。

· One and a half years have passed since I last saw Vince.
（自從我上次看見文斯後，已經過了一年半了。）

(b) 但是，當「one + and + 分數 + 複數名詞」的結構被看成是一個單一的實體（一個整體）時，就要用**單數動詞**。

一個整體，用單數動詞 is

· One and a half cups of coffee is enough for me.
（一杯半的咖啡足夠我喝了。）

(c) 如果「one + and + 分數」的結構前面是由不定冠詞 a/an 取代 one（**a + 單數名詞 + and + 分數**），動詞通常要用**單數**。

由不定冠詞 a 引導，
結構為「a+ 單數名詞 +and+ 分數 + 單數動詞」

· A year and a half has passed since I last studied English with Trish.
（自從我上次跟翠西一起學習英語後，已經過了一年半了。）

390 oneself

請參見 myself/I/me。

391 only 僅有的、唯一的

1 語意不清 According to Kay, learning a large vocabulary is only possible if you read for fun every day

如果 only 的位置放錯了，就會造成意義混淆

語意清楚 According to Kay, learning a large vocabulary is possible only if you read for fun every day.

only 應放在所要修飾的字、片語或從屬子句前面才能使意思明確

據凱的看法，只有每天趣味閱讀，才可能學到大量的辭彙。

only 修飾主詞 Joe Land；沒有其他人舉了兩次手

- In English class today, **only** nice Joe Land raised his hand twice.（今天的英語課上，只有可愛的喬・蘭德舉了兩次手。）

only 修飾動詞 raised；可愛的喬・蘭德只是舉了手，但什麼也沒有說

- In English class today, nice Joe Land **only** raised his hand twice.（今天的英語課上，可愛的喬・蘭德只是舉了兩次手。）

only 修飾受詞 his hand；可愛的喬 ・ 蘭德舉了手，沒有舉起手指或手肘等

- In English class today, nice Joe Land raised **only** his hand twice.（今天的英語課上，可愛的喬・蘭德只舉起了手兩次。）

only 修飾副詞 twice；可愛的喬 ・ 蘭德沒有舉手超過兩次

- In English class today, nice Joe Land raised his hand **only** twice.（今天的英語課上，可愛的喬・蘭德舉手只有兩次。）

392 onto/on to

1 ✗ Sue climbed on to the huge stone statue.

on to 中的 on 往往是某片語動詞的一部分，而 to 是介系詞或是引導不定詞的字

✓ Sue climbed onto the huge stone statue.

介系詞，意思是朝著某個方向運動，然後上去

蘇爬上那座巨大的石雕像。

(1) 儘管有些字典說這兩者是一樣的，實際上它們的意思並不相同。

(2) 請參見 into/in to。

- The big duck hopped onto the truck.
（一隻大鴨子跳到卡車上。）

on 是片語動詞 go on 的一部分；
to 是一個介系詞

- Then Ann will go **on to** the video about her trip around Japan.（然後，安將要放她在日本旅行的錄影帶。）

on 是片語動詞 went on 的一部分；
to 是不定詞 to discuss 的一部分。

- Heather went **on to** discuss the strange weather.
（海瑟接著談論奇怪的天氣。）

393 open

請參見 close。

394 open/opened 營業的

1

✗ Was The Chocolate Cafe opened yesterday?

商店、餐館、銀行等在某段時間營業用形容詞 open，不用 opened

✓ Was The Chocolate Cafe open yesterday?

形容詞 open 意為「營業的，辦公的」，用在連綴動詞 be 後面作補語，強調狀態

昨天「巧克力咖啡廳」有開門營業嗎？

(1) 形容詞 open 的反義詞是 closed。

(2) 動詞 open 意為「打開」，強調動作。其過去式和過去分詞是 opened。

形容詞，意為「營業的，辦公的」，
用在連綴動詞 be 後面作補語，強調狀態

- The Great Gate Cafe **is** usually **open** at 7 a.m., but this morning it **didn't open** until 8:00.

這裡是動詞用法，強調動作

（「大門咖啡店」通常早上 7 點營業，但今天早上到八點才開門。）

395 opposite 相反的；對立面；在……對面

A) 對面的；相反的 形

1 ✗ Jim noticed that the opposite old woman was staring at him.

✓ 英式 Jim noticed that the old woman opposite was staring at him.

英式英語中，作為形容詞的 opposite 意為 facing「面對說話的人」時，就該放在所修飾的名詞後

吉姆注意到他對面的那位老婦人正盯著他。

(1) 在英式英語中，當作為形容詞的 opposite 意思是 facing「面對說話的人」的時候（someone or something that is on the other side of a street, corridor, room, or table from yourself），就應該放在所修飾的名詞後面。

(2) 表示「在……對面」，美式英語常用介系詞 across (from) 來代替 opposite。

美式 the house across the street

英式 = the house opposite

美式 英式 = the house on the opposite side of the street

（在街對面的房子）

美式 Lily noticed that the young man across from her was friendly.

英式 Lily noticed that the young man opposite was friendly.

（莉莉注意到她對面的那位年輕男人很友善。）

2 ✗ Jill turned and walked in the direction opposite, because she didn't want to talk to Bill.

✓ Jill turned and walked in the opposite direction, because she didn't want to talk to Bill.

當意思是「相對立的；相反的」，作形容詞的 opposite 應放在所修飾的名詞前面

吉兒轉過頭，朝相反的方向走，因為她不想跟比爾說話。

當意思是「相對立的；相反的」，作形容詞的 **opposite** 應放在所修飾的名詞前面。

- the **opposite** sex（異姓）
- **opposite** meanings（相反的意思）
- the **opposite** effect（相反的效果）
- on the **opposite** side of the road（在馬路的對面）
- Sue's two sisters have **opposite views** on many political issues.
  （蘇的兩個妹妹在許多政治議題上持相反的觀點。）

B) 對立面、對立物 名

1

✗ Beth said, "The opposite to 'life' is 'death.'"

片語應該是 the opposite of，而不是 the opposite to

✓ Beth said, "The opposite of 'life' is 'death.'"

貝絲說：「生命的相反是死亡」。

(1) **opposite** 當名詞用時，意思是「對立面、對立物」，指兩個完全不同的東西。

(2) 名詞 **opposite** 前面要有冠詞 **the**。片語應該是 **the opposite of**，而不是 the opposite to。

- Nine opinions about your art were **the opposite of** mine. （名詞）
  （關於你的藝術，共有九個人的看法與我的看法相反。）

C) 在……對面 介

1

✗ For hours, Mother and I sat opposite of each other.

opposite 在這裡當作介系詞，意思是「在……對面」，後面接名詞，不需要加 of 或 to

✓ For hours, Mother and I sat opposite each other.

我和我媽面對面坐了有幾個鐘頭之久。

整個介系詞片語（opposite each other）修飾動詞 sat

· the bus stop opposite the school（學校對面的公車站）

介系詞片語 opposite the school 修飾複合名詞 bus stop

· the bank opposite the supermarket（超級市場對面的銀行）

介系詞片語 opposite the supermarket 修飾名詞 bank

396 other/similar 其他的／相似的

1

✗ Jake's robot often makes other similar mistakes.

不是標準英語。在正式文體中，other 不能與其他含有 other 意思的字（similar）同時使用。

✓ Jake's robot often makes similar mistakes.

傑克的機器人常犯一些類似的錯誤。

✓ Jake's robot often makes other mistakes.

傑克的機器人常犯一些其他錯誤。

(1) 類似的還有：

- almost/nearly
  → almost 含有 nearly 的意思，不能說 nearly almost。
- fellow passengers
  → fellow 含有 other 的意思，不能說 other fellow passengers。
- return/back
  → return 含有 back 的意思，不能說 return back。
- repeat/again (repeat = to say or write again)
  → repeat 已經包含有 again 的意思，不能說 repeat again。

(2) 請參見 continue/continue on、doublets/wordiness、lower 及 repeat/repeat again。

P

397 parallel structure/parallelism

平行結構

A) 平行結構的定義

在一個列表裡或在一個句子中，由對等連接詞連接，或用逗號分開的系列片語或辭彙，要用統一的文法形式，即同一個詞性。

B) 一系列辭彙或片語的平行結構

平行結構要求一個系列裡的所有項目在文法形式上要一致，即形容詞與形容詞平行，名詞與名詞平行，不定詞與不定詞平行，子句與子句平行等。

1

✗ Daisy says her divorce makes her feel sad, bitter, and like a crazy person.

不相同的文法形式：連綴動詞（feel）+ 兩個形容詞（sad、bitter）和一個介系詞片語（like a crazy person）

✓ Daisy says her divorce makes her feel sad, bitter, and crazy.

平行形容詞（parallel adjectives）：用了相同的文法形式，連綴動詞（feel）+ 三個形容詞（sad, bitter, crazy）

黛絲說，離婚使她傷心、痛苦、瘋狂。

2

❌ Skating, skiing, and to run are Mort's favorite sports.

不相同的文法形式：兩個動名詞和一個不定詞

✔ Skating, skiing, and running are Mort's favorite sports.

平行主詞（parallel subjects），用了**相同的形式**，三個動名詞並列作主詞

溜冰、滑雪以及跑步，是莫特最喜歡的運動。

3

❌ Ted came back home, took a quick shower, and going to bed.

不相同的形式：兩個動詞和一個 V-ing 形式

✔ Ted came back home, took a quick shower, and went to bed.

平行動詞（parallel verbs），用了**相同的形式**，三個動詞並列

泰德回到家，迅速地沖了個澡，就上床睡覺去了。

4

❌ What matters to Sue Storm is not what you look like but your performance.

不相同的形式：一個是名詞子句，一個是名詞

✔ What matters to Sue Storm is not what you look like but how you perform.

平行主詞補語（parallel subject complements），用了**相同的形式**，兩個名詞子句並列作主詞補語

對蘇・斯托姆來說，你的表現更重要，而不是你的外表。

5

❌ The movie ended with Fay climbing into her jet, waving goodbye to her son, and she flew away.

不相同的形式：兩個動名詞和一個獨立子句

✔ The movie ended with Fay climbing into her jet, waving goodbye to her son, and flying away.

平行介系詞受詞（parallel objects of a preposition），用了**相同的形式**，介系詞 with 後面接三個動名詞片語

在影片的結尾，菲爬進噴射機，對兒子揮手告別，然後飛走了。

C) 列表裡各個項目需要平行結構

在列表、食譜、用法說明、提綱等的各個項目應該按照平行結構排列，這樣會看起來流暢、引人注目。

1

❌ Working at a gym last summer was important for Kim.
1. She earned enough money for college.
2. Some job experience.
3. Exercise.

不是平行結構：一個簡單句，一個片語，一個單字

✅ Working at a gym last summer was important for Kim.
1. She earned enough money for college.
2. She gained some job experience.
3. She had time to exercise.

平行結構：三個簡單句

去年夏天在體育館工作對金姆來說非常重要。
1. 她賺夠了上大學的錢。
2. 她獲得了一些工作經驗。
3. 她有時間鍛鍊身體。

D) to、a、an、his 或 their 在平行結構裡的用法

(1) 如果一系列的項目（平行結構的辭彙或片語）需要與 to、a、an、his 或 their 這類字搭配，可以把這類字只放在第一個項目之前，同時應用於其後的其他項目。也可以在每一個項目之前重複這類字。

(2) 如果決定要重複這類字，請務必要在每一個項目之前都要放進這類字，不能一些項目前用，而另一些項目前又不用。

1

❌ All I expect is a chance to smile, laugh, sing, and to dance.

✅ All I expect is a chance to smile, to laugh, to sing, and to dance.

✅ All I expect is a chance to smile, laugh, sing, and dance.

我所期待的不過是一個可以微笑、大笑、唱歌和跳舞的機會。

2

✗ Bud saw a truck, a jeep, and motor scooter stuck in the deep mud.

✓ Bud saw a truck, a jeep, and a motor scooter stuck in the deep mud.

✓ Bud saw a truck, jeep, and motor scooter stuck in the deep mud.

巴德看見一輛卡車、一輛吉普車、一輛小摩托車陷在深泥坑裡。

3

語意不清 I slowed down when I saw an enormous toad and lovely deer on the road.

因 deer 的單複數同形，讓人不清楚是指一頭鹿還是一頭以上的鹿？需要 (1) 補充 a，清楚指明是一頭鹿。(2) 複數應該在名詞前面用數字（two、three、four 等）或 some

語意清楚 I slowed down when I saw an enormous toad and a lovely deer on the road.

enormous toad 前面要用 an，而 lovely deer 前面要用 a，這種情況最好在每一個項目前都要有冠詞

當看見路上有一隻碩大的癩蛤蟆和一頭可愛的鹿，我的車速慢了下來。

語意清楚 I slowed down when I saw an enormous toad and two lovely deer on the road.

當看見路上有一隻碩大的癩蛤蟆和兩頭可愛的鹿，我的車速慢了下來。

E) 相關連接詞／成對連接詞與平行結構

(1) 下面的相關連接詞（即「成對連接詞」）應該用平行結構，也就是說成對連接詞連接的內容在文法形式上要一致，亦即，兩者都是子句，或都是不定詞，或都是介系詞片語，或都是相同詞性的字等。

- not only . . . but also . . .
- either . . . or . . .
- neither . . . nor . . .
- whether . . . or . . .
- between . . . and . . .

(2) 請參見 both . . . and、either . . . or、neither . . . nor 和 not only . . . but also。

後面是一個名詞片語

1

❌ Vincent has neither the patience to ride an elephant nor does he have the wisdom to ride an elephant.

後面是一個獨立子句，此句不是平行結構

neither 和 nor 後面都是名詞片語（the patience . . . , the wisdom . . .）

✅ Vincent has neither the patience to ride an elephant nor the wisdom to ride an elephant.

這句雖是平行結構，但因重複了不定詞片語 to ride an elephant 而顯得累贅

後面都是名詞，這句既是平行結構又簡潔

✅ Vincent has neither the patience nor the wisdom to ride an elephant.

不定詞片語 to ride an elephant 修飾前面兩個名詞 the patience、the wisdom

文森既沒有耐心也沒有智慧騎在一頭大象上。

F) 比較級的平行結構

(1) 同類事物才能進行比較。

(2) 比較的對象在邏輯上要一致。比如，不能把 John's English 和 Jane 進行比較（一個是語言，另一個是人）。John's English 必須與 Jane's English 進行比較。

(3) 比較的對象常用 that（單數）of 和 those（複數）of 表示，以避免重複名詞。

(4) 如果不重複名詞，就一定不要把 that 和 those 漏掉，否則就是不合乎邏輯的比較。

1

❌ Scot Bend's salary is a lot less than his girlfriend.

與 girlfriend 對比，不是合乎邏輯的比較，不平行

✅ Scot Bend's salary is a lot less than his girlfriend's.

後面省略了 salary；薪水和薪水對比，是平行結構

史考特・本德的薪水比他的女朋友低得多。

2

❌ The schools in this pretty town are better than Brown City.

把學校與城市對比，不是合乎邏輯的比較，不平行

✅ The schools in this pretty town are better than the schools in Brown City.

重複名詞 the schools

✅ The schools in this pretty town are better than the ones in Brown City.

代替 the schools 來避免重複名詞

✅ The schools in this pretty town are better than those in Brown City.

代替 the schools，避免重複名詞

在這座美麗城鎮裡的學校，比布朗城裡的學校好。

G) 動詞的平行結構

一個句子裡如果有一個以上的動詞，這些動詞要用平行結構，不要隨意變換時態和語態（被動／主動）。

1

現在完成式要用助動詞 has + 動詞的過去分詞（has trusted），過去分詞 trusted 在此處不能省略

❌ Dear sweet Kim has in the past and will next year continue to trust Tim.

不定詞 to trust 是接在 will continue 後面，不應該接在構成完成式的助動詞 has 後面（❌ has to trust）

✅ Dear sweet Kim has trusted Tim in the past and will next year continue to trust him.

可愛的金姆過去信任過迪姆，明年也會繼續信任他。

✅ As dear sweet Kim has trusted Tim in the past, she will continue to trust him next year.

因為可愛的金姆過去信任過迪姆，所以明年她將繼續信任他。

A B C D E F G H I J K L M N O P Q R S T U V W X Y Z

(1) 第一個句子裡如果刪除了 and will next year continue，結果會變成下面錯句：

✖ Dear sweet Kim has in the past to trust Tim.

(2) 請參見 never。

2

主動語態

✖ Liz approved of Joe's new plan, and then her own schedule was revised so that it matched his.

不是平行結構

被動語態

莉茲**贊成**喬的新計畫，然後她自己的日程安排表**被修正**了，以便與喬的行程表一致。

兩個動作是由同一個行為者（Liz）完成，而兩個動詞都是主動語態，保持了平衡

主動語態　　主動語態

✔ Liz approved of Joe's new plan and then revised her own schedule so that it matched his.

莉茲**贊成**喬的計畫，然後**修正**了她自己的日程安排表，以便與喬的行程表一致。

(1) 如果兩個動作（approved of 和 revised）或多個動作是由同一個行為者（Liz）完成，就要避免在同一個句子裡混合使用主動（approved of）和被動（was revised） 兩種語態。比如上面第一個句子的寫法在文體上就不合適（bad writing style）。

(2) 在第二句裡，approved of 是主動，revised 也是主動；兩個動作是由同一個行為者（Liz）完成，而兩個動詞都是主動語態，保持了平衡。

H) 結構要平行，意義也要平行

平行片語和子句如果沒有表示平行的意思，句子可能會顯得很不自然或令人誤解。

1. **結構上是平行結構**：動詞 wants 後面接了兩個不定詞結構（to move、to earn）
2. **句意上不是平行**：從 Margo「搬遷」（to move）轉移到 Margo「賺足夠的錢」（to earn enough money），讀起來彆扭

1

不自然　Margo **wants to move** to Chicago and **to earn** enough money to do so.

瑪歌想搬到芝加哥，想賺到足夠的錢搬遷。

不僅結構平行，意思也平行

合理　Margo **wants** to move to Chicago and **hopes** to earn enough money to do so.

瑪歌想搬到芝加哥，並希望能賺夠足夠的錢以便搬遷。

不僅結構平行，意思也平行

合理　Margo **wants** to move to Chicago but **needs** to earn enough money to do so.

瑪歌想搬到芝加哥，但她需要賺到足夠的錢才能搬遷。

wants 的受詞

表「目的」的不定詞片語，表示賺足夠錢的目的是要搬去芝加哥

合理　Margo **wants to earn** enough money **to move** to Chicago.

瑪歌想賺到足夠的錢，以便搬到芝加哥。

2

語意不清　Brad **never gets** angry **and criticizes** anyone who gets mad.

重複副詞 never 意思表達更清楚

語意清楚　Brad **never** gets angry **and never** criticizes anyone who gets mad.

把連接詞 and 改成 or，才不會產生歧義。並列否定要用連接詞 or 表示「也不」

語意清楚　Brad **never** gets angry **or** criticizes anyone who gets mad.

布萊德從來不生氣，也從來不批評任何一個發脾氣的人。

第一個句子結構上是平行結構，句子由 and 連接兩個動詞（gets、criticizes）。可是表達的意思含糊，不是平行的，造成下面兩種完全不同的意思：

- Brad never gets angry, and he criticizes anyone who gets mad.
（布萊德從來不生氣，對任何發脾氣的人他會進行批評。）
- Brad never gets angry, and he never criticizes anyone who gets mad.（布萊德從來不生氣，也從來不批評任何一個發脾氣的人。）

文法加油站

平行結構的使用

使用**平行結構**會使表達流暢有力，請欣賞下面名人演説中的著名平行結構：

① John F. Kennedy declared, "Ask not what your country can do for you; ask what you can do for your country."
約翰 F. 甘迺迪宣稱：「不要問國家能為你做什麼；而要問你能為國家做什麼。」

② Martin Luther King, Jr. explained, "With this faith we will be able to work together, to pray together, to struggle together, to go to jail together, to stand up for freedom together, knowing that we will be free one day."
馬丁・路德・金解釋道：「知道我們終究有一天會獲得自由，抱著這個信仰，我們就能夠一道工作、一道祈禱、一道奮鬥、一道坐牢、一道捍衛自由。」

③ Dr. Martin Luther King said, "We will not resort to violence. We will not degrade ourselves with hatred. Love will not be returned with hate."
馬丁・路德・金博士說：「我們不會付諸於暴力。我們不會因仇恨而降低自己的人格。愛不會以仇恨來回報。」

④ "We observe today not a victory of party but a celebration of freedom—symbolizing an end as well as a beginning—signifying renewal as well as change," noted President John F. Kennedy.
約翰 F. 甘迺迪總統說：「今天我們慶祝的不是政黨的勝利，而是自由的頌揚 ——象徵一個開端也象徵一個結束——意味著變化也意味著更新。」

⑤ Franklin D. Roosevelt said, "I believe that I interpret the will of the Congress and of the people when I assert that we will not only defend ourselves to the uttermost but will make it very certain that this form of treachery shall never again endanger us."
佛蘭克林 D. 羅斯福說：「我保證我們將確保自身的安全，確保這種背信棄義的行為永不再危害我們，我相信這話表達了國會和人民的意志。」

398 participial phrases/ participle clauses 分詞片語／分詞子句

1

Liz Burr 是本句的主詞，但如果也是分詞 shipping 的主詞，意思就不通順了，因為不是顧客 Liz Burr 寄貨給自己，而是賣主寄貨，顧客收貨

✗ Will Liz Burr be charged for all the fur jackets if only shipping a partial order to her?

此分詞片語的用法錯誤

主要子句動詞 be charged 的主詞

✓ Will Liz Burr be charged for all the fur jackets if only a partial order is shipped to her?

從屬子句動詞 is shipped 的主詞

此句把分詞片語改成從屬子句，符合邏輯

如果只寄給莉茲・伯爾部分的皮夾克，那她也要付全部訂單的錢嗎？

分詞片語的主詞和句子的主詞應一致。句子裡的動詞（包括句子動詞以及分詞片語裡的動詞）所表達的動作應該由同一個主詞來完成，這種分詞片語的用法才是正確的。

既是動詞 entered 的主詞，也是分詞片語 encouraged by her initial success 的主詞（Trish Best felt encouraged）

- **Encouraged** by her initial success, **Trish Best entered** another English speech contest.
（首戰告捷後，翠西・貝斯特受到鼓舞，於是又參加了另一場英語演講比賽。）

動詞 saw 和現在分詞 looking 的行為者（Lenore looked north on the busy street; Lenore saw the two suspects）

- **Looking** north on the busy street, **Lenore saw** the two suspects going into the store.
（蕾諾兒在繁忙的大街上朝北望去，看見那兩個嫌疑犯走進商店。）

文法加油站

① 總結：

(a) 分詞片語的主詞必須與句子的主詞一致，即，必須與句子的主詞有關聯。

(b) 如果分詞的主詞與句子的主詞不一致，就必須**刪除分詞片語**，**改變句子結構**，或者**改變句子的主詞**。

② **獨立分詞片語**不受這條文法規則限制：下面的片語是獨立分詞片語，其邏輯主詞不需要與句子的主詞一致。

- assuming the worst（考慮最壞的情況）
- concerning（關於）
- considering everything（考慮一切情況）
- judging from（由……判斷）
- supposing（假設）

分詞片語 generally speaking 不需要與句子的主詞「I」相關連，不是我在「大體上來說」

- **Generally speaking**, I like the weather in San Francisco.
（大體上來說，我喜歡舊金山的天氣。）

③ 有時候分詞片語還可以有它自己的主詞（稱作「**分詞獨立主詞**」）。

分詞片語 living in New York City 有自己獨立的主詞（her husband）

- With **her husband, Lee, living in New York City** for most of the year, **Ann's life** on the farm often seems lonely.

= Because **her husband, Lee, lives** in New York City for most of the year, **Ann's life** on the farm often seems lonely.
（由於她丈夫李一年中大部分時間都居住在紐約，安在農場的生活顯得很孤獨。）

④ 請參見 dangling constructions。

399 pass/passed/past 經過

1

✗ Gus drove slowly as he **went pass** us.

✓ Gus drove slowly as he **went past** us.（past 介）

介系詞片語 past us 修飾動詞 went

✓ Gus drove slowly as he **passed** us.（passed 動）

動詞 pass 的時態變化：pass/passed/passed/passing

加斯開著車緩慢地從我們身邊經過。

2

✗ Flight attendant Jim Murray smiled as he watched the last of the passengers **hurry passed** him.

✓ Flight attendant Jim Murray smiled as he watched the last of the passengers **hurry past** him.（past 介）

空服員吉姆 · 穆瑞微笑地望著最後一個乘客匆匆從他身邊走過。

(1) 如果涉及的是**動作**，就不要用 past，而要用 **pass**、**passed** 或 **passing**。動詞 **pass** 意思是「經過、及格、傳遞、通過、被批准」。

- Because she read lots of easy novels in English, Annie Best **passed** every grammar test.
  動 考試成功
  （因為安妮 · 貝斯特閱讀了大量的簡易英語小說，每次文法考試她都及格了。）

- Davy, please **pass** me the navy beans and gravy.
  動 傳遞
  （大衛，請把白豆〔海軍豆〕和肉汁遞給我。）

- After a three-week delay, a powerful new law against smoking **was passed** today.
  動 批准議案、法律等
  （耽誤了三週後，今天通過了一項強烈反對吸菸的新法律。）

(2) 如果涉及的是**時間**或**距離**，而不是動作，就要用 **past**。past 作介系詞、副詞、名詞和形容詞。

· five past four 介（四點過五分）
· watch the people hurry past 副（看著人們匆匆經過）
· in the past 名（在過去）
· for the past two days 形（在過去的兩天）

400 passive voice 被動語態

A) 不自然的被動語態結構

1

被動／不自然 A chicken leg was eaten by Peg.

一根雞腿被佩格吃了。

文法沒有錯誤，但不是道地的英文句子，實際生活中沒有人使用這樣的被動結構

主動／簡明自然 Peg ate a chicken leg.

佩格吃了一根雞腿。

主動語態聽起來不僅正確而且自然、簡潔

一些非英語國家編寫的課本或文法書單純地為了示範被動語態，而過多使用了一些不自然的被動句子，這些被動句子無論在口語還是書面語中都應該避免使用。

2

被動／不自然 A piano was bought for Margo by me two days ago.

兩天前，一台鋼琴被我買來給瑪歌。

主動／簡明自然 Two days ago I bought a piano for Margo.

兩天前，我為瑪歌買了一台鋼琴。

3

被動／不自然 Our evening movie *Heaven Loves Evan* will have been finished by 11:00.

主動／簡明自然 Our evening movie *Heaven Loves Evan* will finish by 11:00.

主動／簡明自然 Our evening movie *Heaven Loves Evan* will end by 11:00.

我們晚上要看的影片《天堂疼愛伊文》將在十一點鐘結束。

B) 不應該用於被動語態的動詞

1

✗ Lori is a writer, and in college she was specialized in European history.

不及物動詞（如 specialize、die 等）只用在主動語態句子中，不用於被動語態

✓ Lori is a writer, and in college she specialized in European history.

蘿麗是作家，在大學時她專門研究歐洲歷史。

意思是「專攻、專門研究、專門從事」，是**不及物動詞**。除非 specialize 的意思是「使專門化；使特殊化」，才作及物動詞

只有及物動詞，即可以帶受詞的動詞，才能用在被動語態句子中。

2

✗ Lily declared, "I am perfectly suited by this pair of blue jeans."

意思是「與……相配」時，不能用於被動語態

✓ Lily declared, "This pair of blue jeans suits me perfectly."

表狀態的動詞，只用於主動語態

莉莉聲稱：「這條藍色牛仔褲我穿非常合適。」

(1) 有些含特定動詞的主動語態句子不能轉換成被動語態句子。這類動詞多數是狀態動詞，即表狀態而非表動作的動詞。have（擁有）是這些動詞中最典型的一個。

(2) 一些含有介系詞的片語動詞（phrasal verb）主要用於主動語態，不能用於被動語態。

(3) 有連綴動詞（比如：taste、appear、look）的句子也不能用於被動語態。

3

✗ A small jet airplane is had by Jane.

✓ Jane has a small jet airplane.

have/has 雖是及物動詞，但表「狀態」，不表「動作」，因此只能用於**主動語態**。

珍有一架小型噴氣式飛機。

4

✗ The UFO was walked into by Margo.

✓ Margo walked into the UFO.

片語動詞 walked into 雖然接受詞，但只能用於**主動語態**

瑪歌進入了那架幽浮。

文法加油站

總結：下面的句子不能轉換成被動語態：

(a) 含有不及物動詞的句子。
(b) 含有連綴動詞的句子。
(c) 含有「be 動詞 + 形容詞」的句子。
(d) 含有「be 動詞 + 副詞」的句子。
(e) 含有「be 動詞 + 名詞」的句子。
(f) 含有類似 agree with、walk into、become、fit、have、suit 等特定狀態動詞或一些片語動詞的句子。

401 past perfect tense/present perfect tense (had done/have done)

過去完成式／現在完成式

1

形容詞子句是現在式

子句都與現在有關聯，主句動詞就應該用現在完成式，而不用過去完成式

✗ Even Wayne, who smokes heavily, had recently admitted that cigarette smoke does a lot of damage to the brain.

that 引導的受詞子句是現在式

✓ Even Wayne, who smokes heavily, has recently admitted that cigarette smoke does a lot of damage to the brain.

連老菸槍韋恩最近也承認了吸菸會嚴重損害大腦。

⑴ 如果指的時間是「直到現在」，通常要用現在完成式。現在完成式常與 already、ever、never、just、recently、yet 連用。
- Chet has not arrived yet.（切特還沒有到達。）

⑵ 現在完成式的用法另見 simple past tense/present perfect tense (did/have done)。

⑶ 當我們已經在談論過去，要用過去完成式追溯過去之前（go back

even further），表示在我們談論的這個過去時間之前某事已經發生了。所以過去完成式通常要和過去簡單式連用。

(4) 過去完成式也請參見 past perfect tense/simple past tense (had done/did)。

- By the time I arrived in that out-of-the-way village, my friend Kay had already waited for half a day.

  過去動作「等待」發生在「到達」這個過去動作之前。更早的過去要用過去完成式，與一個過去動作（arrived）搭配

≒ By the time I arrived in that out-of-the-way village, my friend Kay had already been waiting for half a day.

  一個更早的過去動作也可以用過去完成進行式表示。過去完成進行式強調過去某事正在持續進行時，另一件事發生了

（當我到達那個偏僻的村莊時，我的朋友凱已經等待了半天。）

402 past perfect tense/ simple past tense (had done/did)

過去完成式／過去簡單式

1

✗ Kate had worked in Berlin in April 2017.

談論過去發生的事，需用**過去簡單式**

✓ Kate worked in Berlin in April 2017.

凱特 2017 年 4 月在柏林工作過。

2

✗ Before Meg arrived with Peg, Dad already broke his leg.

「had broken his leg」這個動作發生在過去動作「arrived」之前

✓ Before Meg arrived with Peg, Dad had already broken his leg.

過去完成式通常要和**過去簡單式**連用

在梅格和佩格到達之前，爸爸已經摔斷了腿。

A B C D E F G H I J K L M N O P Q R S T U V W X Y Z

(1) 談論過去發生的事，要用過去簡單式（比如：worked in April 2017）。

(2) 過去完成式（比如：had broken）的基本意義是「更早的過去或過去的過去」以及「在過去某一個特定時間之前已經完成的行為動作」。所以過去完成式通常要和過去簡單式（比如：arrived）連用。

- I enjoyed the play *Door in the Floor* even though I had seen it before.
（雖然我以前就看過戲劇《地板上的門》，但我還是很喜歡看。）

(3) 過去簡單式的用法也請參見 simple past tense/present perfect tense (did/have done）。

(4) 過去完成式的用法也請參見上面條目 past perfect tense/present perfect tense (had done/have done）。

3

✗ When Dr. Eve Nation **arrived**, the train bound for Chicago **had already left** the station. Eve wondered, "What time had the train left?"

指發生在過去動作 arrived 之前，是過去完成式的正確用法

「火車離開的時間」是指過去的時間。只表示「**過去某時發生了某事**」，應該用**過去簡單式**，而不是過去完成式

✓ When Dr. Eve Nation arrived, the train bound for Chicago had already left the station. Eve wondered, "What time did the train leave?"

伊芙•納欣醫生到達車站時，前往芝加哥的火車已經離開了車站。
伊芙納悶：「火車是什麼時候離開的？」

403 patience/patient/patients
耐心／耐心的；病人／病人

1 ✗ Dr. Prudence Scott usually has a lot of patients when talking to her patience.

不可數名詞，意思是「耐心」

作可數名詞時，意思是「病人」

✓ Dr. Prudence Scott usually has a lot of patience when talking to her patients.

patients（病人）是 patient 的複數形式

✓ Dr. Prudence Scott is usually very patient when talking to her patients.

作形容詞時，意思是「有耐心的」

普魯登絲・史考特醫生與她的病人談話時通常都很有耐心。

不可數名詞，意思是「耐心」

- My teacher Ms. Door has a lot of **patience**, and she often reminds us not to leave garbage on the floor.
  （我的老師多爾女士很有耐心，她常提醒我們不要把垃圾丟在地板上。）

404 pavement/sidewalk 路面／人行道

1 美式 "I planted some flowers by the sidewalk," explained Eli.

英式 "I planted some flowers by the pavement," explained Eli.

伊萊解釋道：「我在人行道旁邊種了一些花。」

(1) **人行道：** 美式 sidewalk　英式 pavement

- I saw a mouse on the sidewalk in front of my house.
  （我看見一隻老鼠在我家門前的人行道上。）美式

(2) **鋪過的路面：** 美式 pavement　英式 roadway

- Vincent lost control of his bicycle on the icy pavement.
  （文森的自行車在冰凍的路面上失去了控制。）美式

405 pay/pay for 付（錢）

1

❌ I need a little more money to pay my trip to Mexico City.
買東西付款，要用介系詞 for

✅ I need a little more money to pay for my trip to Mexico City.
為某樣東西支付一筆費用

我還需要再多一點的錢才能支付去墨西哥市的旅程。

(1) 買東西付款要用介系詞 for（You have to pay for something when you buy it.）。

(2)「酬報他人為你提供的服務或給你提供的商品」用下面的片語：

- pay (an amount of money) for something
  （為某樣東西支付一筆費用）
- pay (someone) for something
  （為某樣東西付錢給某人）
- Lulu paid over $300 a day for her hotel room in Honolulu.
  （露露每天要花三百多美金來支付檀香山的旅店房間。）
- Yesterday Kirk paid me for my work.
  （昨天柯克付了我的工錢。）

2

❌ Jill's brother will help her pay for the medical bills.
付帳單，不要介系詞 for

✅ Jill's brother will help her pay the medical bills.

吉兒的哥哥會幫她付醫療費。

付給人家錢、付帳單、還債務、交學費，付幾筆款項或稅額（pay a bill、debt、tuition、fee、tax），用 pay（後面不接 for）。因為你不買 bill、debt、tuition、fee、tax 等。

- pay taxes（繳稅）
- pay the debt（還債）
- Midge is broke and cannot afford to pay her daughter's tuition for college.（米姬破產了，付不起女兒上大學的學費。）

3 ✗ Every time we eat at the Green Pizza Shop, Gertrude and Gus pay our food.

買東西付款要用介系詞 for

✗ Every time we eat at the Green Pizza Shop, Gertrude and Gus pay us for the food.

意為「因我們吃飯而付錢給我們」，與句意不符

✓ Every time we eat at the Green Pizza Shop, Gertrude and Gus pay for our food.

買東西付款用介系詞 for

✓ Every time we eat at the Green Pizza Shop, Gertrude and Gus pay for us.

替某人付錢用介系詞 for

每次我們去綠色披薩餐館吃飯，總是葛楚德和加斯替我們付錢。

⑴ **替某人付錢：**pay for somebody

⑵ **因某事／某物而酬報他人：**pay somebody for something（如：pay her for her work)

⑶ 上面範例中第二句文法正確，但意思是「每次我們去綠色披薩餐館吃飯，葛楚德和加斯總是因吃飯而付錢給我們。」如果每次去餐廳吃飯，某人都要為我付飯錢還要付錢給我，那我肯定非常樂意每天都帶這人去餐廳用餐啊！

406 pay/buy 付（錢）／買

1 ✗ I'll pay Jake a chocolate shake.

當我們說「出錢請人喝飲料或吃飯」的時候，通常用 buy 或 pay for，不用 pay

✓ I'll buy Jake a chocolate shake.
= I'll pay for Jake's chocolate shake.

我來給傑克買一份巧克力奶昔。

407 pay/salary 薪水

1

✗ Mary Day gets a good pay.

✓ Mary Day gets good pay.

不可數名詞，不能用冠詞 a 修飾

✓ Mary Day gets a good salary.

可以用冠詞 a 修飾，也可以有複數形式 salaries

瑪麗・戴的薪水優渥。

408 peace/piece 和平／一（個／張／片／塊）

1

✗ Do those geese want to have some pea soup and then live in piece? —— 意思是「一片；一塊；一張」等

✓ Do those geese want to have some pea soup and then live in peace? —— 意思是「和平；平靜」

那些鵝想喝點豌豆湯，然後和睦相處嗎？

2

✗ I gave Lorelei a peace of apple pie.

✓ I gave Lorelei a piece of apple pie.

我給了蘿芮萊一片蘋果派。

⑴ piece 意思是「一片；一塊；一張」等。記住片語 a piece of pie，就能記住這個字的正確拼寫，因為 a piece of something 中的 piece 就是以 pie 開頭的。

· Why did you take my piece of blueberry pie?
（你為什麼要拿走我的那片藍莓派？）

⑵ peace 意思是「和平；平靜」，是 war（戰爭）的反義詞。peace 的前三個字母是 pea。我們先享受一些豌豆湯（pea soup），然後再談論和平（peace）。

· Did the Olympic Games in Greece encourage world peace?
（希臘舉行的奧林匹克運動鼓勵世界和平嗎？）

→ 注意：Greece 與 peace 押韻。

409 percent/percentage 百分之幾／百分率

1

意思是「百分比；比例」，並不指具體的數據，從**不和數字連用**

❌ Over thirty percentage of these plates hasn't been cleaned properly and is still dirty.

作主詞時，動詞單複數要與動詞前面的名詞（即介系詞 of 後的複數名詞 plates）單複數一致，因此動詞要用複數 haven't 和 are

❌ Over thirty percent of these plates hasn't been cleaned properly and is still dirty.

意思是「百分之幾」，符號是「%」，指**具體的數據**（如：fifty-eight percent）

✅ Over thirty percent of these plates haven't been cleaned properly and are still dirty.

這些盤子中 30% 以上的盤子還沒有清洗乾淨，還很髒。

(1) percent 也可以表示「百分比；比例」，可以和 percentage 互換，前面沒有數字（a large percentage/percent of the land）。但這種情況，percentage 更常見。

這句也可以用 percent，但用 percentage 更常見

- Paul always spends a large percentage of his pay on alcohol.（保羅總是把大部分的薪水花在喝酒上面。）

(2) 如果 percentage of 前面有定冠詞 the，動詞要用單數。如果前面是不定冠詞 a，那麼，動詞要與 of 後面的名詞單複數一致。

the percentage of + 名詞（複數或單數）+ 單數動詞

- "The percentage of college students who love to read is large," explained Midge.
（米姬解釋說：「喜歡閱讀的大學生比例很高。」）

a percentage of+ 複數名詞（students）+ 複數動詞（are）

- "Only a small percentage of our high school students are serious readers," added Paul.
（保羅補充說：「我們高中學校裡只有一小部分的學生是酷愛讀書的人。」）

a percentage of + 單數名詞（class）+ 單數動詞（is）

- "A large percentage of my class is trying to do a lot of reading," noted Marge.
（瑪姬說：「我班上大部分同學都在努力大量閱讀。」）

410 permit

請參見 allow。

411 person/people 人

1

談到一大群人時要用 people。本句顯然是指一大群人，要用 people

✗ Of all the persons in our company, why did I end up sitting next to Ming at that meeting.

✓ Of all the people in our company, why did I end up sitting next to Ming at that meeting?

在那次會議上，在我們公司所有的人中，我怎麼就坐在了敏旁邊？

用 person 來指一個人；如果提到不止一個人，persons 和 people 都能用（比如：three persons/three people），但通常 people 比複數形式 persons 聽起來更自然。

kind of 後面接單數名詞。請參見 kind of

- Mike is the **kind of person** whom I respect and like.
（麥克是值得我尊重和喜歡的那種人。）

412 personal/personnel 個人的／員工、人事部門

1

（=one's own; private）個人的；私人的

✗ Nell, please take this file to our personal department and give it to Del.

✓ Nell, please take this file to our personnel department and give it to Del.

（= the employees in a business）人事
注意：personnel 與 bell、Nell、sell、tell 押韻

尼爾，請把這份檔案帶到人事部給戴爾。

2 ✗ The reporter asked me another personnel question, "Are you in love with Sue?"

✓ The reporter asked me another personal question, "Are you in love with Sue?"

記者又問了我一個私人的問題：「你在和蘇談戀愛嗎？」

- personnel director（人事主任）
- personal taste（個人的興趣）
- get personal in an argument（在爭論中進行人身攻擊）

413 pick/pick up 挑選／接（人）；取（東西）

1 ✗ Lulu is at the airport to pick Sue and Andrew.

去某處接人，然後把這人帶到另一個地方，要用 pick up 而不用 pick

✓ Lulu is at the airport to pick up Sue and Andrew.

露露在機場接蘇和安德魯。

意思是「挑選；摘」

- Please pick a good cookbook for Brooke.
（請為布露可挑選一本好的烹飪書。）

414 PIN/PIN number 個人識別碼

1 口語 I'll key in my PIN number and get some money to pay Dr. Mile.

書寫 I'll key in my PIN and get some money to pay Dr. Mile.

= personal identification number 個人識別碼

我要輸入我的個人識別號碼，領出一些錢來付給麥爾醫生。

(1) 既然 PIN 已經包含 number 了，那為什麼許多人要重複 number，說成 PIN number，即 personal identification number number。那不是重複 number 了嗎？

(2) 主要是因為 PIN 的發音與名詞 pin（別針）的發音是一樣的，

比如，safety pin（安全別針），a bobby pin（髮夾）等。如果我們說 PIN number，那麼就很清楚是指個人識別號碼，而不是指那些別針。但在書寫時，就沒有必要重複 number，只需要寫 PIN。

415 play soccer/kick a soccer ball
踢足球

1

❌ Kay likes to kick soccer every day.

這是學生常犯的錯誤。中文說「踢足球」，但英文不能用動詞 kick（踢），而要用動詞 **play**（play soccer）

✅ Kay likes to play soccer every day.

凱喜歡每天踢足球。

如果有名詞 ball，就可以用動詞 kick，比如：kick the ball、kick a soccer ball。

416 pleasant/pleased 令人愉快的／高興的

1

❌ I was pleasant with the chance to practice tennis with Dennis.

意思是「令人愉快的；討人喜歡的；和藹可親的」

✅ I was pleased with the chance to practice tennis with Dennis.

（= happy; satisfied）意思是「高興的；滿意的」，常與 with 連用

我對能有機會與丹尼斯練習網球很滿意。

pleasant 和 pleased 的區別有點類似 interesting 和 interested 的區別。

- a pleasant walk（令人愉快的散步）
- an interesting walk（有趣的散步）
- a pleasant manager（和藹可親的經理）
- an interesting manager（有趣的經理）
- Kirk is a pleasant person, and I am very pleased with his work.（柯克是一個非常和藹可親的人，我對他的工作很滿意。）

417 plural/singular

請參見 all、couple、family、fewer/less、his/her、neither、news、none、number、math/maths、media、one、police、politics 和 youth。

418 police 員警

1 ✗ The police is searching for some terrorists from Greece.

集合名詞 police 形式上是單數，但意義上是複數名詞，所以動詞要用複數動詞

✓ The police are searching for some terrorists from Greece.

員警在搜索從希臘來的一些恐怖分子。

(1) 如果 police 要表示單數意思，就用 a police officer、a policeman 或 a policewoman。

(2) 類似的集合名詞還有：people、cattle。這些字作主詞時，要接複數動詞。

- Matt's cattle are always healthy, and that's why he is wealthy.（麥特的牛總是很健康，這正是他富有的原因。）
- Maria's mom said, "Different people have different ideas."（瑪麗亞的媽媽說：「不同的人有不同的看法。」）

文法加油站

people 還可以指民族、國民

- peoples from central Asia（來自中亞的民族）
- a proud, dignified people (a people = a nation)（一個自豪、有尊嚴的民族）

419 politic/political 精明的／政治的

1

✗ Jenny Nation won't join that politic organization.

精明的；有策略的；謹慎的；考慮周到的

✓ Jenny Nation won't join that political organization.

政治（上）的；與政治有關的

珍妮 ‧ 納欣不願意加入那個政治組織。

- political ideas/views（政治觀點）
- political history（政治史）
- political party（政黨）
- political system（政治制度）
- a politic decision（一個考慮周到的決議）
- a politic reply（一個謹慎的回答）
- Emma is a politic manager and will find an answer to this dilemma.
  （愛瑪是一位精明的經理，會找到解決這個困境的答案。）

420 politics 政治學

1

指「政治；政治學」，形式上看起來是複數，但意義上是單數名詞（不可數名詞），動詞用單數

✗ Are politics mainly about cooperation and are economics mainly about competition?

指「經濟學」，是單數名詞，用單數動詞

✓ Is politics mainly about cooperation and is economics mainly about competition?

政治是否主要與合作有關，而經濟主要與競爭有關？

- Politics is a difficult subject for me, and so is economics.
  （對我來說，政治學是很難的一門學科，經濟學也是。）

文法加油站

複數形式、單數意義的名詞

① **類似以 -ics 結尾的名詞（複數形式，單數意義）**：下列是類似以 -ics 結尾的名詞，雖然形式上是複數，但意義上卻是**單數**，在句中作主詞時動詞要用單數：

- economics（經濟）
- mathematics（數學）
- physics（物理學）
- statistics（統計學）

② **其他類似的字（複數形式，單數意義）**：下列的字形式上是複數，但意義上卻是**單數**，在句中作主詞時動詞要用單數。請參見 math/maths、news。

- news（新聞）
- maths（數學）英式
- the United States（美國）
- headquarters（司令部、總部）

③ **politics 的複數用法**：當 politics 意指「政見；政治立場；政治運動；政策」時，是複數，在句中作主詞時，動詞用複數。

- Rick's politics are more conservative than Dick's.
  政治態度和政治立場（political attitudes and positions）
  （瑞克的政見比迪克的更保守。）

④ **statistics 和 physics 也有類似的用法**：同樣道理，statistics 指「統計學」時，是單數名詞，用單數動詞。而當 statistics 指「統計資料、統計數字」時，是複數名詞，用複數動詞。同理，physics 指學科「物理」時，單數概念；指「物理現象」時，為複數概念。

- Statistics is of little interest to Felix.
  一門學科〔a branch of study〕
  （菲力克斯對統計學一點也不感興趣。）
- Eve told me some statistics that were difficult to believe.
  一組數據〔a group of numbers〕
  （伊芙告訴了我一些讓人難以置信的統計資料。）

⑤ **提示**

- 如果我們把以 -ics 結尾的字當作**泛指**（比如一門學科），那麼這個以 -ics 結尾的字就是**單數**。
- 但如果我們把以 -ics 結尾的字當作**特指**（比如某個人的信念），那麼這個 以 -ics 結尾的字就是**複數**。
- 請參見 acoustics。

421 popular 大眾的、得人心的

1

❌ Professor Sun is very popular to everyone.

意為「得人心的、受歡迎的」，後面接 **with** 或 **among**，不接 to

✅ Professor Sun is very popular with everyone.

孫教授很受大家歡迎。

- Vincent is popular among the voters and could become the President.（文森特很受選民的歡迎，有可能會成為總統。）

422 possessive 兩個人的所有格用法

1

指共同的所有權時，在最後那個人的名字上加「's」或「'」

❌ Jane's and Ted's wedding was delayed for an hour because of the wind and rain.

如果兩個人（Jane and Ted）共同擁有同樣的東西（wedding），應把這兩個人看成是個整體（as the whole），只需在後面的人名加上「's」或「'」

✅ Jane and Ted's wedding was delayed for an hour because of the wind and rain.

珍和泰德的婚禮因風雨而被延誤了一個小時。

2

❌ The Whites and the Knights' houses were brightly lit with Christmas lights.

這句的 the Whites 指的是 the White family；the Knights 指的是 the Knight family。每一家都獨自擁有一棟房子。要表示獨立的、各自的所有權，在每一個家庭後面加一個「'」

✅ The Whites' and the Knights' houses were brightly lit with Christmas lights.

✅ The houses belonging to the Whites and Knights were brightly lit with Christmas lights.

懷特家和奈特家的房子都被聖誕燈照得亮晶晶的。

如果兩個人各自擁有某東西，而不是共同擁有，每一個人的名字後面都得加上「's」或「'」。換言之，指各自的、獨立的所有權時，每一個人的名字後面都要加「's」或「'」。

3 ✗ I spent many hours designing their and our houses.

如果兩個擁有者都是由人稱代名詞所有格來表示（比如 your、my、our、his、her 等），不要把兩個代名詞所有格放在一起

✓ I spent many hours designing their house and ours.

要把名詞（擁有的東西）house 放在兩個擁有者之間，即放在第一個人稱代名詞所有格之後，把第二個改成（獨立）所有格代名詞這樣聽上去更順耳，更符合習慣用法

我花了很多個小時設計他們的房子和我們的房子。

423 possibility 可能性

1 ✗ What is the possibility to sell our home in Rome?

後面接 of，不接不定詞

✓ What is the possibility of selling our home in Rome?

賣掉我們在羅馬的住宅可能性有多大？

possibility of (doing) something：possibility 後面接 of，不接不定詞。

- Is there any possibility of catching a train that is going to Spain?（還有沒有可能趕上一班去西班牙的火車？）

424 post

請參見 mail。

425 practice/practise 練習

1 ✗ Ray told Alice, "To learn English well, you need two hours of listening practise every day."

英式英語的 practise 不能作名詞

✓ Ray told Alice, "To learn English well, you need two hours of listening practice every day."

雷告訴艾麗絲：「要學好英語，你需要每天做兩小時的聽力練習。」

2

❌ Did that pretty alien practice to fly/practise to fly her UFO over New York City?

動詞 practice 美式／practise 英式，後面接 V-ing 形式，不能接不定詞

英式 Did that pretty alien practise flying her UFO over New York City?

美式 Did that pretty alien practice flying her UFO over New York City?

那位美麗的外星人在紐約城上空練習駕駛她的不明飛行物了嗎？

(1) 英式 practice (n.)/practise (v.)

(2) 美式 practice (v./n.)

426 prefer/would prefer 寧願（選擇）

1

❌ I prefer to walk with Rae today.

I prefer 是泛指。如果特指一個決定，要用 **would prefer**

✅ I would prefer to walk with Rae today.

= I would rather walk with Rae today.

我寧願今天跟芮一起散步。

- Dee **prefers** tea to coffee.（蒂喜歡茶勝過咖啡。）

泛指

427 prevent

請參見 forbid。

428 prevent/protect 阻止／保護

1

❌ Dwight wears glasses that prevent his eyes from ultraviolet sunlight.

指「阻止某人做某事／阻止某事發生」。
句型：prevent sb./sth. + from + V-ing

✅ Dwight wears glasses that protect his eyes from ultraviolet sunlight.

表達「維護某人／某物的安全」的含意

杜威特戴的眼鏡可以保護他的眼睛不受紫外線的傷害。

· Dan tried to prevent Ann from going to Japan.
（丹試圖阻止安去日本。）

429 price of/price for 價格／代價

1

❌ Margo says the price for rice is low. — price 表示「**價格**」時後面要用介系詞 **of**

✅ Margo says the price of rice is low.

瑪歌說，米的價格不高。

(1) price of something：price 表示「價格」時後面要用介系詞 of。

(2) pay the price for something：price 表示「代價」時，後面要用介系詞 for。

· Brad Sun paid a heavy price for what he had done.
（布萊德・孫為他所做的事付出了沉痛的代價。）

430 principal/principle 主要的；校長／原則

1

❌ What was the principle reason Lars gave for his decision to live on Mars?

✅ What was the principal reason Lars gave for his decision to live on Mars? — 當形容詞時意為「**主要的**」（main）

拉斯決定在火星上居住的主要原因是什麼？

2

❌ "Encouraging everyone to do extensive reading for fun" is one of the important principals that guide our country's principles.

✅ "Encouraging everyone to do extensive reading for fun" is one of the important principles that guide our country's principals.

principles — 意為「**原則、原理**」（rule）

principals — 當**名詞**時，意為「**主要的人物**」（main person），比如首長、校長

「鼓勵大家做大量的趣味閱讀」是用來指導我國校長們重要的原則之一。

(1) principal：當形容詞時意為「主要的」（main）；main 和 principal 兩個字都包含有字母 a。當名詞時，principal 自然就成

A B C D E F G H I J K L M N O P Q R S T U V W X Y Z

了權威人士，即「主要的人物」（main person），比如首長、校長、社長、主要演員、主角、首席演奏者等。

⑵ 名詞 principle 的意思是「原則、原理」（rule）；rule 和 principle 都包含了字母 -le。希望這一點有助於你記住這個字的正確拼寫。

⑶ 再提供一個小提示：如果你能記得 the principal（校長）是你的 pal（好友），那麼 你就不會把 principal 與 principle 搞混了。

- the principal aim of the project (main aim)
  （這個項目的主要目標）
- the school principal (the main person of a school)（校長）
- live by one's principles (rules)（按照某人的原則生活）

431 pronoun agreement

代名詞要與先行詞一致

1

非正式 Everyone wants to get their pets on the Margo Monroe TV show.

人稱代名詞（he、she、her、his、their 等）必須與先行詞（先行所指的名詞）的數（單數或複數）和性（男或女）一致

單數主詞 + 單數動詞 + 單數人稱代名詞

正式 Everyone wants to get his or her pet on the Margo Monroe TV show.

正式 They all want to get their pets on the Margo Monroe TV show.

人人都想讓自己的寵物上瑪歌．門羅的電視節目。

2

非正式 Each of the girls ate their peaches.

主詞（即先行詞）each 是不定代名詞，永遠是單數，其後面的人稱代名詞也應該用單數

正式 Each of the girls ate her peach.

正式 Each of the girls ate a peach.

每一個女孩都吃了一個桃子。

(1) 有些不定代名詞，雖然可能感覺它們的意思是「複數」，但實際上是單數，要接單數動詞和單數人稱代名詞。基本規則是：用單數動詞和單數人稱代名詞與下面這些**單數不定代名詞**搭配。

- each
- either
- neither
- everyone
- everybody
- no one
- nobody
- anyone
- anybody
- someone

(2) 在口語中，一些人常用複數人稱代名詞 their 來與單數不定代名詞 each、everyone 等搭配。這種現象雖然比較普遍，但不符合文法規則，受到大多數文法學家、編輯、嚴謹的作家反對。所以，在正式文體中（商務信函、學術報告、考試），應該遵循文法規則，避免出錯。

(3) 如何避免代名詞的性別歧視，請參見 sexist language。

3

✗ Sam says some of the water have gone over the top of the dam.

不可數名詞，後面要接**單數動詞**

✓ Sam says some of the water has gone over the top of the dam.

山姆說，一些水已經溢出了水壩。

(1) 有些不定代名詞（比如：none、any、some、all 和 most）根據其含意，後面既可以接單數動詞和單數代名詞，也可以接複數動詞和複數代名詞。

(2) 如果從上下文中看這些不定代名詞的複數含意不是很清楚，那麼就用單數動詞和單數代名詞。

(3) 請參見 none、all 以及 subject-verb agreement（第 I 點）。

some（= a quantity）是單數；這句的 some 從上下文中很難確定含意是單數還是複數，動詞就要用單數

- **Some is** better than none, so let's have a little bit of fun.
  （有總比沒有好，就讓我們娛樂一下吧。）

some（= a number of people）是複數；這句的兩個 some 明顯指 some people，因此應該用複數動詞

- **Some are** wise and **some are** full of lies.
  （一些人明智，而一些人愛撒謊。）

4 美式 口語 "None of you like me," cried Sue.

在美式口語中，如果 none 指代的是複數名詞或複數代名詞，常用複數動詞

正式 "None of you likes me," cried Sue.

在正式用語中，「none of + 複數名詞／複數代名詞」後面接單數動詞

「你們當中沒有一個人喜歡我。」蘇哭著說。

(1) 當 none 清楚地指「not one」（一個也不）時，需要單數動詞。

這句 none 指「not one」，是單數

- Gail has all of Ed's paintings, but **none is** for sale.
  （蓋兒擁有埃德的所有畫作，但沒有一幅畫要銷售。）

(2) 當 none 指代不可數名詞，作主詞時，需要單數動詞。

這句 none 明顯指代不可數名詞 mail，因此只能用單數動詞

- Though all the mail has arrived, **none is** for Gail.
  （儘管所有的郵件都到達了，但沒有一封是給蓋兒的。）

432 pronouns with collective nouns
人稱代名詞和集合名詞

(1) 集合名詞（collective noun）根據其含意，後面可以接單數動詞和單數代名詞，或接複數動詞和複數代名詞。

(2) 美式英語在集合名詞後面常用單數動詞和單數代名詞，或用複數名詞取代集合名詞；而英式英語在集合名詞後面常用複數動詞和複數代名詞。

(3) 不過，如果集合名詞在句中的單複數含意不是很清楚，最好選用單數動詞和單數代名詞，或者重寫句子，使句子清楚表示複數的含意。

(4) 請參見 family 以及 subject-verb agreement（第 C 點）。

(5) 常見的集合名詞有：

- audience（觀眾）
- class（班）
- committee（委員會）
- company（公司）
- crew（全體船員／機員）
- crowd（人群）
- family（家庭）
- group（群；組）
- staff（全體職員）
- team（組；隊；班）

1

美式英語更常用 members、classmates 等複數名詞來取代集合名詞，後接**複數動詞**和**複數人稱代名詞**

美式 英式 My classmates couldn't say their ABCs or spell "please."

英式英語的集合名詞強調個體時（my class = my classmates），常用**複數動詞**和**複數代名詞**

英式 My class couldn't say their ABCs or spell "please."

我班上的同學不會說英文字母，也不會拼寫 please（請）。

2

美式 The team practices at school according to its schedule.

強調**一個整體**（a whole）時，美式用**單數動詞**和**單數代名詞**

英式 The team practises at school according to its schedule.

強調整體時，英式可以用單數動詞和單數代名詞

The team practise at school according to their schedule.

即使是強調整體，英式仍然更常用**複數動詞**和**複數代名詞**

小組根據自己的計畫表在學校進行練習。

練習 動：美式 practice 英式 practise

3

✖ Her staff are learning how to raise its baby giraffe.

動詞用複數 are，而後面的代名詞用單數 its，無論是英式還是美式，這種用法都是錯誤的

美式 Her staff is learning how to raise the baby giraffe.

英式 Her staff are learning how to raise their baby giraffe.

用 members 表示複數

美式 英式 Her staff members are learning how to raise their baby giraffe.

她的職員們在學習如何飼養他們的長頸鹿寶寶。

在同一個句子裡，集合名詞不能同時看作是單數和複數。單數動詞要與單數代名詞搭配，複數動詞要與複數代名詞搭配。

433 pronoun reference 代名詞指代先行詞

1

語意不清 Sue told her mother she would have to move to Honolulu.

代名詞 she 是指代 Sue 還是指代 her mother ？這句可能有兩種含意：
(1) Sue's mother would have to move to Honolulu.
（蘇的媽媽不得不搬去檀香山。）
(2) Sue would have to move to Honolulu.
（蘇不得不搬去檀香山。）

語意清楚 Sue said to her mother, "I will have to move to Honolulu."

改用直接引語就可以糾正第一句含糊的指代

蘇對她媽媽說：「我不得不搬去檀香山。」

(1) 先行詞的定義：為了避免重複，可以用代名詞來代替句子前面出現過的名詞或一組有名詞作用的字，**這類名詞就是先行詞**。先行詞也可以是不定代名詞，比如：everyone、each、anybody、anything 等。

(2) 含糊的先行詞：上面以及下面範例中的「語意不清」的句子或錯誤句子，代名詞與先行詞的關係指代不清楚。

2

✗ Sue Righter has always been interested in writing and finally has decided to become one.

這句沒有一個先行詞可以和代名詞 one 搭配，應該用名詞 a writer，而不能用代名詞 one

✓ Sue Righter has always been interested in writing and finally has decided to become a writer.

蘇・賴特一直都對寫作感興趣，她最終決定要成為一名作家。

3

✗ Kangaroo Hill was a lush green, the flowers were in full bloom, and the sky was a bright blue. It filled Roy with joy.

代名詞 it 的先行詞很含糊，指代 the sky 還是 Kangaroo Hill？究竟是 the sky、the flowers 還是 Kangaroo Hill 使羅伊充滿了歡樂？

✓ Kangaroo Hill was a lush green, the flowers were in full bloom, and the sky was a bright blue. The scene filled Roy with joy.

當代名詞指代的先行詞不清楚時，最好改用名詞，不用代名詞

袋鼠山上一片翠綠，鮮花盛開，天空蔚藍。這片景色使羅伊充滿了喜悅。

4

語意不清 Dad is speaking to Brad, and he looks sad.

指代不清楚，既可以指 Dad，也可以指 Brad

語意清楚 Dad is speaking to Brad, who looks sad.

本句改變了句型，刪除了代名詞 he。形容詞子句 who looks sad 在 Brad 後面，修飾先行詞 Brad，清楚指明是 Brad 在傷心

爸爸在對布萊德說話；布萊德看起來很傷心。

5

語意不清 Jake's paper about energy is too long, too general, and full of spelling and grammar mistakes, which means he has to rewrite it tonight.

語意不清 Jake's paper about energy is too long, too general, and full of spelling and grammar mistakes. This means he has to rewrite it tonight.

句中的 which 和 this 的先行詞是哪一個？代名詞 which 和 this 的指代不清楚，指代一個籠統的概念

語意清楚 Jake's paper about energy is too long, too general, and full of spelling and grammar mistakes. These problems mean he has to rewrite it tonight.

當代名詞指代抽象的觀念，而不是具體的事物，代名詞指代的先行詞通常不是很清楚。這種情況，最好用名詞（these problems）來代替代名詞（which、this）

傑克寫關於能量的論文太長、太籠統，而且還有許多拼寫錯誤以及文法錯誤。這些問題的存在意味著他今晚必須重新寫論文。

關係代名詞 which 清楚地指代先行詞 the Kennedy Space Center

- Today I am at the Kennedy Space Center, **which** has a lot of big rockets on display.
  （今天我來到甘迺迪太空中心，這裡展示了許多大火箭。）

434 pronunciation/pronounce 發音

1

名詞 pronunciation 中間的拼寫是「nun」（尼姑）

❌ "Your pronounciation of "nation" and "space station" was very good," declared Ms. Sun.

✅ "Your pronunciation of "nation" and "space station" was very good," declared Ms. Sun.

孫女士宣布：「你對 nation 和 space station 這兩個字的發音很標準。」

(1) 名詞 **pronunciation** 的第二個音節（-nun-）與單字 nun 或 sun 押韻。記住名詞 pronunciation 中間的拼寫是「**nun**」（尼姑）。

(2) 動詞 **pronounce** 的第二個音節（-noun-）與單字 announce、ounce、bounce 押韻。記住動詞 pronounce 後面的五個字母是 **ounce**（盎司）。也請記住 pronounce 後面的六個字母和 **announce**（宣布）後面的六個字母一樣。

- The Queen wants me to announce the news that her baby daughter has learned how to **pronounce** the words "ounce" and "bounce."
  （女王要我宣布，她的小女娃已經學會了 ounce〔盎司〕和 bounce〔蹦跳〕的發音。）

435 proof 證據、證物

1

❌ Is the water dripping on my bed proof for my need for a new roof?

「證據；物證」的意思，後面接 **of**，不接 for

✅ Is the water dripping on my bed proof of my need for a new roof?

水滴落在我的床上，這是否可以證明我需要一個新屋頂？

436 proof/resistant 防……的／抵抗的

1 ✗ Lex lives in an earthquake-proof apartment complex.

water-proof/waterproof（防水的）
earthquake-resistant（抗震的）

✓ Lex lives in an earthquake-resistant apartment complex.

賴克斯居住的社區公寓大樓是可以抗震的。

文法加油站

-proof 的用法

-proof：與一些名詞連用，構成形容詞，表示「防……的」；或構成動詞，表示「使防……」。

- a bulletproof vest（防彈衣）
- rustproof（不鏽的）
- fireproof（防火的；使具防火性能、為……安裝防火裝置）

waterproof、water-resistant、watertight 的區別

waterproof、water-resistant、watertight 都是指「防水的」，但意思有細微的區別。

① waterproof：指「完全不透水」。
- waterproof clothes（防水衣）
- waterproof tape（防水膠帶）
- a waterproof camera（防水相機）

② water-resistant：指「能暫時防水；不容易被水毀壞或沖掉」。
- a water-resistant suntan lotion（耐水性防曬乳）
- a water-resistant jacket（防水夾克）

③ watertight：指「（容器）不漏水的」或指「（措辭等）嚴密的」。
- watertight compartments（水密艙室）
- a watertight submarine（不透水潛艇）
- a watertight excuse（無懈可擊的藉口）

437 pupil/student 學生

1 美式 Molly is a third grade student on the island of Bali.

現代美語用來指所有年齡的學生（可以是孩子也可以是成人）和所有層次的學生（小學生、中學生、高中生、大學生、研究生、博士生）

英式 Molly is a third grade pupil on the island of Bali.

= Molly is a grade-three pupil on the island of Bali.

茉莉是峇里島上一個三年級的小學生。英式英語指小學生

	student	pupil
美式	指所有年齡的學生（可以是孩子也可以是成人）和所有層次的學生（小學生、中學生、高中生、大學生、研究生、博士生）。	
英式	指年齡大一點的學生，比如大學生、高中生等。	指小學生

- I won the best pupil award at a primary school in London, and my sister Kitty won an art contest for college students in New York City.

英式英語指年齡大一點的學生，比如大學生、高中生等

（我獲得了倫敦一所小學的最佳學生獎，我姐姐姬蒂在紐約城大學生的藝術競賽中獲勝。）

→ **小學：** 英式 primary school

美式 elementary school

文法加油站

graduate student/postgraduate

大多數美國人用 graduate student 指已經獲得學士學位（B.A.、B.S.）而正在攻讀碩士學位的學生。而英國人用 postgraduate 來表達這個意思。

Q

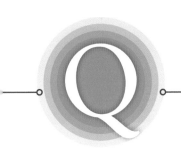

438 quiet/quite 安靜／相當

1

❌ Joe was thinking about his diet on a quite afternoon when he heard the roar of a tornado.

意思是「相當、十分」，與這句的句意不符。quite 與 bite 押韻，兩者都以 -te 結尾。quite 也和 light、night 押韻

✅ Joe was thinking about his diet on a quiet afternoon when he heard the roar of a tornado.

意思是「安靜的」；與 diet 押韻，兩者都以 -et 結尾

在一個寧靜的下午，喬正在考慮飲食問題，突然聽見了龍捲風的轟隆聲。

quite 和 quiet 混淆是一個常見的錯誤，這種錯誤甚至電腦的拼寫及文法檢查工具有時也檢查不出來，所以使用時必須小心，不要把這兩個字弄混淆了。只要發音正確，就不會拼錯這兩個字。

- Joe Todd was quite thankful that he had survived the tornado, and he said a quiet thank-you prayer to God.
  （喬・陶德對從龍捲風中倖存下來感到非常萬幸，他輕聲地禱告，對上帝說了一聲：「謝謝」。）

R

439 raise/raise up 舉起；提高

1

❌ Ed will show us some easy ways to raise up Liz above his head.

raise 已經包含了 up 的意思，兩者不要同時使用

✅ Ed will show us some easy ways to raise Liz above his head.

艾德要向我們示範一些如何把莉茲舉到他頭頂上的簡易方法。

請參見 continue/continue on、doublets/wordiness、repeat/repeat again、reply/reply back 和 return/return back。

440 raise/rise 加薪；提高／上升

1

美式 Lorelei's brother asked Ms. Days for a raise.

名詞，意思是「加薪」

英式 Lorelei's brother asked Ms. Days for a rise.

英式 Lorelei's brother asked Ms. Days for a pay rise.

蘿芮萊的哥哥向戴斯女士要求加薪。

2 ✗ Since 2007, they have risen the level of education in their nation.
rise 的意思是「上升；（自己）升高」；是**不及物動詞**，不能接受詞。動詞變化形：rose, risen, rising

✓ Since 2007, they have raised the level of education in their nation.
及物動詞，後面需要接受詞，意思是「舉起;增大;增多;籌款;提高；提出」。動詞變化形：raised, raised, raising

自 2007 年以來，他們國家的教育水準已經提高了。

- Mary and Gary are raising money to buy books for the library.
（瑪麗和蓋瑞正在為學校的圖書館籌款買書。）
- Rose was worried that she might freeze in this big basket hanging under the huge balloon as it rose high in the sky.
（蘿絲坐在由大氣球垂吊的大籃子裡，高高升上天空時，她擔心會凍僵。）

441 rather/would rather 相當／寧願

1 ✗ I rather work than play all day.
副詞，意思是「**相當**」，比如：rather tired（相當疲倦）。用於此句與句意不符

✓ I would rather work than play all day.
rather 與 would 用在一起，意思是「寧願」。句型為：**would rather do something**

= I'd rather work than play all day.
would rather do something 縮寫形式是：**'d rather do something**

我寧可工作也不願意整天玩耍。

2 ✗ I would rather study at the library than going to the beach with Mary.
此處 than 後面不能接 V-ing 形式，否則結構不平行

✓ I would rather study at the library than go to the beach with Mary.
平行結構：「would rather + 原形動詞 . . . than + 原形動詞」

我寧願在圖書館念書，也不願意跟瑪麗去海灘。

後面省略了相同的動詞 move
- I would rather move to Vancouver than to Sydney.
（我與其搬去雪梨，還不如搬去溫哥華。）

3 ✗ I would not rather see Scot.

✓ I would rather not see Scot.

否定詞 not 要放在 would rather 後面：**would rather not do**（寧可不做某事）

我寧可不要見史考特。

4 ✗ I would rather they come on Saturday or Sunday.

✗ I would rather they will come on Saturday or Sunday.

✓ I would rather they came on Saturday or Sunday.

如果要表達「某人寧願讓另一個人（不要）做某事」，would rather 後面就要接子句，子句中一般用動詞過去式來表示現在或將來要做的事，這是一種假設語氣。句型為：「**would rather + 子句（過去式）**」

我寧願他們星期六或星期天來。

(1) 如果要表達「某人寧願讓另一個人（不要）做某事」，would rather 後面就要接子句，子句中一般用動詞的過去式來表示現在或將來要做的事，這是一種假設語氣。句型為：「would rather + 子句（過去式）」。

- I would rather Ann went to Japan.（我寧願安去日本。）

(2) 注意重音的落點使句意產生的變化（以下句子中的藍色字，表示重音落在的地方。）

- I would rather Ann went to Japan. (not me)
  寧願安去，我不去
- I would rather Ann went to Japan. (not stay)
  寧願安去日本，不要留下來
- I would rather Ann went to Japan. (not to America, China, Britain, etc.)
  寧願安去日本（而不是去美國、中國、英國，或其他國家）

文法加油站

比較：'d rather（= would rather）和 'd better（= had better）

① would rather/'d rather

（= would prefer that; would choose to）（寧可）

· I'd rather you were my boss than Sue.

「我寧願你⋯⋯」（I'd rather you . . .），在子句中用簡單過去式動詞（were, did not）來表示現在或將來要做的事

（我寧可你當我的老闆，而不願蘇當我的老闆。）

· I'd rather you and Coco did not try to gather all the flowers in my meadow.（我寧可你和可可不要摘掉我草地上所有的花朵。）

② had better/'d better（= ought to; would be wise to）（最好）

had better/'d better 後面接原形動詞（stay）

· You'd better stay here until the end of May.
（你最好留在這裡一直到五月底。）

否定式：had better/'d better 後面接「not + 原形動詞」（not hang out）

· Sue's brother Jim is bad news, and you'd better not hang out with him.（蘇的哥哥吉姆是個麻煩人物〔俚語〕，你最好不要跟他混在一起。）

· 請參見 better/had better。

442 real/really 十分、很

1 美式 口語 I'll take a long look at the starry night and try real hard not to think about my English grammar textbook. —— 美語中的 real 可作形容詞，也可作副詞，特別是在口語中 real 常作副詞用。英式英語 real 只能當形容詞

美式 英式 I'll take a long look at the starry night and try really hard not to think about my English grammar textbook. —— 美語中的 really、real 都可作副詞，英式英語只用 really 作副詞

我要久久望著布滿星星的夜空，儘量不要去想我的英語文法課本。

	really	real
美式	副詞	形容詞／副詞（口語常見）
英式	副詞	形容詞

正式用語中 real 作形容詞，修飾名詞 necklace

- He'll give her a kiss and a real diamond necklace.
（他要吻她一下並給她一條真鑽項鏈。）

正式用語中 really 作副詞，修飾形容詞 tired。美式口語中也可以用 real 作副詞來修飾形容詞，比如：real tired

- Lynn's mom has been really tired since she gave birth to the twins.（自從生了雙胞胎後，琳恩的媽媽一直非常疲倦。）

443 reason 理由

1

✗ We need to know the reason of that terrible explosion in the Pacific Ocean.

reason 後面用 **for**，而不用 of

✓ We need to know the reason for that terrible explosion in the Pacific Ocean.

片語 reason for (doing) something 意思是「做某事的原因」

我們需要知道太平洋那起可怕爆炸事故的原因。

2

✗ Lynn wondered whether the reason for the fight was because each boy thought he would win.

reason 等於 because。在句型「the/somebody's reason for . . . is/was . . .」中，is/was 後面用 that，不能用 because

✓ Lynn wondered whether the reason for the fight was that each boy thought he would win.

琳恩在琢磨，這場打架的原因是否是因為這兩個男孩都以為自己會贏。

⑴ because 的意思是 for the reason that。如果說「the reason . . . is because . . .」，就相當於在說「the reason . . . is for the reason that . . .」，這顯然是多餘的。所以儘管中文可以重複說「……原因是因為……」，英語兩者只用其中一個。

⑵ 請參見 although/but 和 doublets/wordiness。

444 redundancies 冗詞

⑴ redundancies 是一些重複字，比如 past history、repeat again 等。

⑵ 請參見 although/but、continue/continue on、doublets/wordiness、ideal、other/similar、raise/raise up、reason、repeat/repeat again、reply/reply back、return/return back。

445 regard/regards 關心／問候

1

✗ Mr. Card's mother asked me to give you her best regard.

✓ Mr. Card's mother asked me to give you her best regards.

卡德先生的媽媽要我代她向你問好。

(= good wishes) 用複數 **regards** 表示「**問候；致意**」

2

✗ Mr. Weeds always expects us to work hard and yet never shows any regards for our needs.

✓ Mr. Weeds always expects us to work hard and yet never shows any regard for our needs.

(= concern; attention; a fixed look; respect; reference) 作**不可數名詞**，意思是「**關心；注視；尊重；關係**」

威茲先生總是期待我們努力工作，然而他對我們的需求卻從來不關心。

446 regret 遺憾；懊悔

1

✗ Skip didn't have time to regret for the loss of his spaceship.

regret 後面直接跟受詞，不需要加 for

✓ Skip didn't have time to regret the loss of his spaceship.

regret something 指「因某事而遺憾」

史基普沒有時間為失去太空船而遺憾。

2

表達「**後悔**」時，regret 後面只能接**動名詞**，不接不定詞

✗ I regret to leave both Lorelei and Vienna.

✓ I regret leaving both Lorelei and Vienna.

regret doing something 表示「為已經做過的事或說過的話而後悔」

我後悔離開了蘿芮萊和維也納。

文法加油站

regret 的其他用法

① regret 接不定詞：regret 後面接不定詞，表示「對將要說出的話感到遺憾或抱歉」（express with regret），通常後面只接 tell、inform、 say、announce 等動詞（regret to tell/inform/say/announce + that 子句），用來告訴某人壞消息。

· I regret to say that I can't marry you.
（很抱歉，我不能嫁給你。）

· I regret to inform you that Sue is going to marry Norm.
（我很抱歉地通知你，蘇要嫁給諾姆。）

② regret 接 that 子句。

· I regret that my disease will stop me from marrying Louise.
（我的病將使我不能娶露易絲，為此我感到遺憾。）

447 relation/relationship 關係

1

✗ Do you have good relations with your sister-in-law Sue?

複數 relations 表示「**國家或團體之間的關係、往來**」，與句意不符

✓ Do you have a good relationship with your sister-in-law Sue?

指「**親戚或朋友之間的關係好或壞**」，要用 relationship

你和你嫂子蘇的關係好嗎？

· develop friendly relations with the neighboring countries
（與鄰近國家發展友好關係）

· Does Bahrain maintain good relations with Spain?
（巴林與西班牙保持了友好關係嗎？）

448 remember 記得

1

✗ Remember emailing Gail your video of that huge whale.

✓ Remember to email Gail your video of that huge whale.

remember to do something：記住（需要做某事）；不要忘記（應該做某事）

= Do not forget to email Gail your video of that huge whale.

記得把你拍的那頭大鯨魚的影片用電子郵件寄給蓋兒。

2 ✗ I remember to meet her last September.

✓ I remember meeting her last September.

記得去年九月我見過她。

remember doing something：記得、想起、回憶起（已經做過某事）

與 forget 的用法是一樣的。請參見 forget。

449 remind somebody of/ remind somebody about 使……回想起／提醒

1 ✗ Does the beautiful view remind you about Honolulu?

如果某事或某人使你回想起了什麼（相似的事或人），要用 remind somebody **of**，不用 about

✓ Does the beautiful view remind you of Honolulu?

這美麗的景色使你想起檀香山了嗎？

(1) 某事或某人使你回想起了什麼，要用 remind somebody of。

(2) 如果要提醒某人不要忘記某事，就用 remind someone about something。在這個意義上，remind 後面常用 about，但也可以用 of。

這句也可以用 remind me of

- Please remind me about that meeting with Louise.
  （請提醒我與露易絲的會面。）

(3) remind 後面也常接不定詞，表示「提醒某人做某事」。

- Please remind me to call Dwight tonight.
  （請提醒我今晚打電話給杜威特。）

450 repeat/repeat again 重複

1 repeat 和 again 通常不要放在一起，因為 repeat 已經包含了 again 的意思。中文可以說「再重複」，但英語不能說 repeat again，至少在書面語中應該避免這類多餘的重複

✗ I'll have to repeat again to Sue what I have just told you.

✓ I'll have to repeat to Sue what I have just told you.

我必須把我剛告訴你的事重複給蘇聽。

文法加油站

不要用意思與動詞一樣的副詞來修飾動詞

① 下面的例子雖然在口語中常見，但在書面語和正式文體中要避免。

✗ Lee saw the huge dragon and began to **advance forward** slowly.
✓ Lee saw the huge dragon and began to **advance** slowly.
（李看見了那頭巨龍，然後開始緩慢地前進。）

- **advance** (not "advance forward")（前進）
- **begin** (not "first begin")（開始）
- **continue** (not "continue on")（繼續）
- **cooperate** (not "cooperate together")（合作）
- **finish** (not "finish up")（完成）
- **follow** (not "follow after")（跟隨）
- **raise** (not "raise up")（舉起；增加；提高）
- **return** (not "return back")（回來、返回）

② 請參見 continue/continue on、doublets/wordiness、raise/raise up、repeat/repeat again、reply/reply back 和 return/return back。

451 replace with

請參見 substitute for。

452 reply/answer 回覆

1

✗ Do you expect a mermaid on a whale to **reply** your email?

✓ Do you expect a mermaid on a whale to **reply to** your email?

reply to (an email, a letter, an invitation) 意為「回信、回邀請等」；reply 作不及物動詞，後面要接 **to**

✓ Do you expect a mermaid on a whale to **answer** your email?

answer 後面直接接受詞，不要 to

你期待騎在一條鯨魚上的美人魚會回你電子郵件嗎？

- Has Eve **answered** the text message from Steve?
（伊芙回史蒂夫的手機簡訊了沒？）

453 reply/reply back 回覆

1 ✗ Jack Ride has written three text messages to her, but she has never replied back.

動詞 reply 已經包含了 back 的意思，所以不能與 back 連用

✓ Jack Ride has written three text messages to her, but she has never replied.

= Jack Ride has written three text messages to her, but she has never written back.

傑克・賴德寫過三封手機簡訊給她，但她從來沒有回覆過。

請參見 continue/continue on、doublets/wordiness、other/similar、raise/raise up、repeat/repeat again 以及 return/return back。

454 reported speech 間接引語

請參見 indirect speech/reported speech。

455 request 請求、要求

1 ✗ The Brooks Library in Nigeria has requested for our old books.

及物動詞，後面直接接受詞，不需要介系詞 for

✓ The Brooks Library in Nigeria has requested our old books.

request something (= ask for something) 表示「請求給予某物」

= The Brooks Library in Nigeria has asked for our old books.

奈及利亞的布魯克斯圖書館請我們把舊書給他們。

A B C D E F G H I J K L M N O P Q R S T U V W X Y Z

2

❌ I took down my sail and requested that I was allowed to ride on the whale.

美式英語：「某人 request 另一個人」做什麼事情，在 request 後的子句中要用**原形動詞**表示假設語氣，比如用 be、do 等，而不用 are、is、was、were、did、does 等

✅ I took down my sail and requested that I be allowed to ride on the whale

我放下帆布，請求讓我騎在鯨魚上面。

(1) 上面的例句主詞是 I，子句雖然主詞仍然是 I，但子句是被動語態，表示「我請求別人讓我……」。意思仍然是：「某人 request 另一個人」做什麼事情。

(2) 英式英語在 request 後面的子句中用 should + 原形動詞。

(3) 請參見 suggest。

文法加油站

that 子句用原形動詞的假設語氣句型

① 下面的動詞用在 that 子句前面，that 子句裡的動詞要用原形來表示重要性。英式英語用 should + 原形動詞。注意，這種句型要求**主句的主詞和子句的主詞不同**，意思是「某人要求（寧願／提議）另一個人做某事」。

- advise（建議）
- insist（堅持要求）
- request（請求）
- ask（請求）
- order（命令）
- require（要求）
- command（命令）
- prefer（寧願）
- suggest（建議）
- demand（要求）
- propose（提議）
- urge（強烈要求）
- desire（要求）
- recommend（建議）

- Ann suggested that I move to Japan.（安建議我搬去日本。）
- I recommend that Trish listen to lots of fun and easy English.（我建議翠西大量聽趣味簡易的英語。）

② 同類的名詞用法一樣。

- demand
- insistence
- order
- preference
- proposal
- recommendation
- request
- requirement
- suggestion

- My recommendation is that he read *Building a Rich Nation*.
  （我的建議是，他讀一讀《打造一個富有的國家》一書。）

③ 請參見 important (essential/vital/necessary/desirable）。

④ 如果這些動詞或名詞表達的意思不是「某人要求（寧願／提議）另一個人做某事」，那麼，這類字後面接的 that 子句裡就不用假設語氣原形動詞。

這句的 suggest 的意思是「暗示；表示」，而不是「建議」，因此這句不用假設語氣原形動詞

- The lime juice on her blouse and blood on her shoes suggest that she was involved with the crime.
  （她襯衫上面的萊姆汁以及鞋上的血跡表示她與犯罪活動有關。）

這句 insists 的意思是「堅持認為」，而不是「堅持要求」。這時主句和子句的主詞是同一個人，而不是兩個人，因此不能用假設語氣原形動詞

- Coco insists that she saw a UFO.
  （可可堅持認為她看到了一架幽浮。）

456 respect 尊敬、尊重

1

✗ Nancy has no respect to my privacy.

✗ Nancy doesn't respect for my privacy.

✓ Nancy has no respect for my privacy.

✓ Nancy doesn't respect my privacy.

南西不尊重我的隱私。

作**名詞**時，後面接介系詞 **for**（have respect for somebody/something），不接 to

作**動詞**時，後面直接接**受詞**（respect somebody/something），不接 for

- have respect for the elderly = respect the elderly（尊敬長者）

片語 with respect to（用 to）的意思是「有關」

- questions and answers with respect to the German Air Force
  （有關德國空軍的問題和回答）

457 responsible 負責的

1

✗ You are responsible to bring this kangaroo back to the zoo.

對（做）某事負責用 **responsible for (doing) something**，不接不定詞

✓ You are responsible for bringing this kangaroo back to the zoo.

由你負責把這隻袋鼠帶回動物園。

(1) responsible for (doing) something（不接不定詞）
對（做）某事負責；對某事承擔責任；是某事發生的原由

是某事發生的原由（the cause of）

- Jack wanted to know who was responsible for the terrorist attack.
（傑克想知道是誰發動了這次的恐怖攻擊事件。）

(2) responsible for someone（= having charge or control over）照顧或掌管某人（通常用 for）

照顧或掌管某人（in charge of）

- Megan is responsible for a class of 22 children.
（梅根負責管理一個有 22 名孩童的班級。）

(3) responsible to somebody 對……要負責任（通常接 to）

如果你 responsible to someone（= able to answer for one's own conduct），那麼這個人就可以要求你證實你的行為或決定是正確的、合理的，相當於 answerable。

- responsible to my immediate superior
（對我的直屬上司負責）
- President Gus Wu is responsible to us.
（總統加斯．吳對我們負有責任。）

458 rest/stay 休息／停留、暫住

1

✗ I am resting at my friend's house in Dubai all week.

✓ I am staying at my friend's house in Dubai all week.

我這一週都要住在朋友位於杜拜的房子裡。

你如果疲倦了，你就 rest。如果暫住在某人家裡，要用 stay。

- Gwen is going to rest for an hour before she starts to work again.（葛雯要休息一個小時，然後再開始工作。）

459 return 返回

1

✗ Fay has returned from Norway for a week.

表示**短暫動作**，而不是延續動作，通常不與表示延續時間的片語（for a month、for a year）連用。要與過去時間 yesterday、a month ago、a year ago 等連用

✓ Fay has been back from Norway for a week.

菲從挪威回來已經一週了。

✓ Fay returned from Norway a week ago.

✓ Fay came back from Norway a week ago.

菲一週前從挪威回來。

(1) 類似短暫動作的字或片語還有 come、die、go、leave、pass away、stop 等。

(2) 請參見 ago/for。

460 return/return back 返回

1

✗ On Wednesday I will return back to Melbourne.

動詞 return 已經包含了 back 的意思，所以不能與副詞 back 連用。要不用 return，要不用 go back 或 come back

✓ On Wednesday I will return to Melbourne.

= On Wednesday I will go back to Melbourne.

我星期三要回墨爾本。

請參見 continue/continue on、doublets/wordiness、raise/raise up、repeat/repeat again、reply/reply back。

461 return ticket/round-trip ticket 來回票

1 美式 I found the round-trip rocket ticket in my jacket pocket.

美式英語用 **round-trip ticket/round trip ticket** 表示「**來回票**」(a ticket to a place and back, usually over the same route)。用 **one-way ticket** 來表示「**單程票**」

英式 I found the return rocket ticket in my jacket pocket.

英式英語用 **return ticket** 來表示「**來回票**」。用 **single ticket** 來表示「**單程票**」

我在我的上衣口袋裡找到了那張來回火箭票。

462 rob/steal 偷竊

A) steal something

rob 的受詞是「人」或「地方」,不是「物」

1 ✗ Why did Neal rob that wheel?

✓ Why did Neal steal that wheel?

尼爾為什麼要偷那個車輪?

steal something 偷東西(錢、珠寶首飾、汽車、財產等)。steal 後面直接接被盜的東西

- My hotel room key was stolen by that monkey! (我飯店的房間鑰匙被那隻猴子偷了!)
- Alice stole Doug's diamond ring so she could buy illegal drugs. (為了買毒品,艾麗絲偷了的道格的鑽石戒指。)

B) rob somebody/rob a place

1 ✗ Ann sobbed, "I've been stolen!"

✓ Ann sobbed, "I've been robbed!"

安哭著說:「我被搶了!」

rob somebody (of something) 或 rob a place (= break into a place) 指「搶劫;盜取」。rob 後面直接跟「人」或「地方」。

- Robbers rob banks. (強盜搶劫銀行。)
- Robbers rob people. (強盜搶劫人們。)
- When Alice tried to rob a bank, she was shot and soon died. (艾麗絲企圖搶劫一家銀行時,遭到槍擊,隨即死亡。)

文法加油站

steal 通常後面接「物」

請注意下句 steal somebody 的含意。

- Lenore Ride would like to steal your boyfriend just to hurt your pride.（蕾諾兒・賴德想要搶你的男朋友，只是為了傷害你的自尊心。）

463 run-on sentences/ run-together sentences 連寫句

1

✗ Michael drove off on his new motorcycle, Eve just watched him leave.

僅僅一個逗號不能連接獨立子句

✓ Michael drove off on his new motorcycle. Eve just watched him leave.

這是兩個獨立句子（即簡單句）。兩個簡單句後面都要用**句號**

✓ Michael drove off on his new motorcycle; Eve just watched him leave.

如果要把兩個獨立子句連接起來，應該使用**分號**或者「**逗號 + 對等連接詞**」（and、but、or 等）

✓ Michael drove off on his new motorcycle, and Eve just watched him leave.

麥克騎著他的新摩托車走了，伊芙只是望著他離去。

2

✗ June must get up soon, she could cause us to miss the bus.

✓ June must get up soon. She could cause us to miss the bus.

分號後面的獨立子句首字母要小寫（除非是專業名詞）

✓ June must get up soon; she could cause us to miss the bus.

✓ June must get up soon, or she could cause us to miss the bus.

茱恩必須馬上起床，否則她可能使我們錯過班車。

(1) 用不恰當的標點符號連接獨立子句是英語中常見的錯誤。這種錯誤的句子叫「**連寫句**」（run-on sentence/run-together sentence），指兩個獨立子句之間遺漏了連接詞或用錯了標點符號。

(2) 一個獨立句子（即，簡單句）應該以**句號**、**問號**或**感嘆號**結尾。

(3) 掌握以下三種給獨立子句加標點符號的方法，就可以避免「連寫句」：

(a) 把兩個獨立子句改成兩個簡單句。兩個簡單句後面都要用句號。
(b) 用分號分開兩個獨立子句。
(c) 用逗號以及以下的其中一個連接詞把兩個獨立子句連接起來。
· and　· but　· or　· nor　· for　· so　· yet

文法加油站

可以接受的連寫句（acceptable run-on sentences）

① 在一些名人名言中，偶爾會有只用一個逗號連接兩個獨立子句的情況，比如下面三種情況：
1) 句子很短並用同一種句型。
2) 語調從容、流暢而且是會話體。
3) 句子的押韻所需要。

· Did Abraham Lincoln sound sad when he said, "We cannot dedicate, we cannot consecrate, we cannot hallow this ground"?
（當亞伯拉罕・林肯說：「我們不能奉獻、我們不能聖化、我們不能神聖這塊土地。」時，他聽起來很傷心嗎？）

② 但英語為第二語言的學生或老師，最好遵守基本文法規則，避免使用連寫句，否則會寫出錯句。

464 RV 休旅車

1

✗ Ivy and Ann live in a RV.
✓ Ivy and Ann live in an RV.
愛葳和安住在一輛休旅車裡。

縮寫詞 RV 前面用不定冠詞 an，因為 R 是母音發音 [ɑr]。（請參見 a/an。）

RV = recreational vehicle 休旅車。當要說 a recreational vehicle 時，要用不定冠詞 a

· Midge lived in a recreational vehicle while she was in college.（米姬讀大學時住在一輛休旅車裡。）

S

465 scenery 風景、景色

1

✗ Oliver rowed his boat and enjoyed the beautiful sceneries along the river.

scenery 是不可數名詞，沒有複數形式

✓ Oliver rowed his boat and enjoyed the beautiful scenery along the river.

奧利弗划著船，欣賞著沿岸一帶的美景。

466 see/look

請參見 hear/listen。

467 see off/send off 送行／寄出

1

✗ Mort came along with Pat to send me off at the airport.

send off 與信件、包裹等相關，意思是「**寄出**」

✓ Mort came along with Pat to see me off at the airport.

莫特和蓓特一起去機場為我送行。

see somebody off 表示去機場、車站等向某人告別

與信件、包裹等相關，意思是「寄出」

- Has Kay sent off her resume?
（凱已經把她的個人簡歷寄出了嗎？）

也可以表示「派遣」（dismiss）

- My math teacher was angry and sent me off to the principal's office.（我的數學老師生氣了，把我送到校長辦公室。）

A B C D E F G H I J K L M N O P Q R S T U V W X Y Z

注意：名詞 send-off 表示「送別、送行」。

- We gave Mort a warm send-off at the airport.
（我們在機場熱烈歡送了莫特。）

468 -self 自身的（反身代名詞）

1

✗ *Amy Can See the Icy Sea* is a play written by Nancy and myself.

反身代名詞 oneself 不能取代普通代名詞 I、me、she、her 等

✓ *Amy Can See the Icy Sea* is a play written by Nancy and me.

《艾咪能看見結滿冰的大海》是南西和我寫的劇本。

反身代名詞（myself, herself, ourselves, themselves 等）用於下面兩種情況（請參見 myself/I/me）：

(a) 為了**強調**，意為「親自；本人」。

(b) 作**反身代名詞**（主詞和受詞是相同的）。

強調

- Midge **herself** found enough courage to walk across the shaky bridge.
（米姬自己鼓起了勇氣走過那座搖晃的橋。）

反身（主詞和受詞指同一個人）

- **Dee**, a pretty elf, loves nobody but **herself**.
（蒂是一隻只愛自己、不愛別人的美麗小精靈。）

469 send/take 送去／帶去

1

✗ Maxie didn't have time to send the kangaroo back to the zoo, so she **sent** him there in a taxi.

如果帶某人去某地（與這個人一起去），要用 **take** somebody to a place

✓ Maxie didn't have time to take the kangaroo back to the zoo, so she sent him there in a taxi.

如果送某人去某地（不與這個人一起去），用 **send** somebody to a place

邁克塞沒有時間把袋鼠帶回動物園，於是她用計程車送牠回去。

公司不與我一起去夏威夷

- Every year my company sends me to Hawaii.
（公司每年都派我去夏威夷。）

我和蘿芮萊一起去峇里島

- Every July I take Lorelei to Bali.
（我每年七月都帶蘿芮萊去峇里島。）

470 senior 年紀較大的

1

✗ Jane is fourteen months senior than her brother Dean.

意思是 older，反義詞是 junior。比某人歲數大，用 **senior** to someone，比某人歲數小，用 **junior** to someone

✓ Jane is fourteen months senior to her brother Dean.

= Jane is fourteen months older than her brother Dean.

珍比她弟弟迪安大一歲零兩個月。

- senior to = older than
- junior to = younger than

471 sexist language 性別歧視語言

1

性別歧視 A new teacher will soon find out that his students are not always kind.

暗示所有的老師都是男性，與現實不符

一名新教師將很快發現他的學生並不總是友好的。

當提及一種包括兩性類型的人（醫生、護士、老師等），用**複數先行詞**（比如：doctors、teachers、nurses），然後再用一個**複數代名詞**（無性別的字 gender-free），這樣就可避免性別歧視語言（sexist language）

無性別詞 New teachers will soon find out that their students are not always kind.

新教師將很快發現（他們的）學生並不總是友好的。

A B C D E F G H I J K L M N O P Q R S T U V W X Y Z

文法加油站

先行詞指男性也指女性時

① 如果單數先行詞既指男性也指女性，那麼應該用哪一個單數第三人稱代名詞呢？是用 he 還是用 she ？在過去，he 是正確的選擇。注意：下面三個例句都是性別歧視用語（sexual bias）。

- If anyone wants a ride home, he can go with Jerome.
- Joe, if anybody calls, just tell him that I'm in Chicago.
- Let the traveler himself decide whether he wants to go through Chicago.

② 現代人試圖用下面幾種方法來避免性別歧視：

(a) 用複數第三人稱代名詞 **they**、**them**、**their** 或 **themselves**。
注意：下面三句不符合文法規則，在正式用語中要避免。

- If **anyone** wants a ride home, **they** can go with Jerome.

  即使先行詞是單數（**anyone**、**anybody**、**the traveler**），許多人也使用複數第三人稱代名詞 **they**、**them**、**their** 或 **themselves**。不過，用複數代名詞去搭配單數先行詞是文法錯誤

- Joe, if anybody calls, just tell them that I'm in Chicago.
- Let the traveler themselves decide whether they want to go through Chicago.

(b) 用 he/she、him/her 或 himself/herself。

- If **anyone** wants a ride home, **he/she** can go with Jerome.
- Joe, if **anybody** calls, just tell **him/her** that I'm in Chicago.
- Let the **traveler himself/herself** decide whether **he/she** wants to go through Chicago.

  使用 he/she、him/her 或 himself/herself，不過這種結構很笨拙

(c) 用 he or she、him or her 或 himself or herself。

- If **anyone** wants a ride home, **he or she** can go with Jerome.

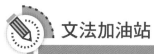

· Joe, if **anybody** calls, just tell **him or her** that I'm in Chicago.

· Let the **traveler himself or herself** decide whether **he or she** wants to go through Chicago.

使用 he or she、him or her、或 himself or herself。he or she 這種結構比 he/she 結構好一些。然而，如果在句子裡不斷重複 he or she，會使句子不流暢

(d)重寫句子。

· Anyone who wants a ride home can go with Jerome.
（任何想搭車回家的人可以跟傑羅姆一起走。）

· Joe, tell anybody who calls that I'm in Chicago.
（喬，告訴任何來電者，我在芝加哥。）

· Let the travelers themselves decide whether they want to go through Chicago.（讓遊客自己決定他們是否想遊經芝加哥。）

→ 最佳方法是改寫句子，使句子文法正確，而且也避免了性別歧視，還避免了笨拙的 he/she 結構以及冗長的 he or she 結構，如上面三個改寫後的句子。

→ 建議：

1. 首先選擇方法 (d)，即改寫句子。
2. 如果無法改寫句子，選擇方法 (c)，即用 he or she 結構。

選擇無性別的辭彙

① 在正式英語或書面英語中，要選擇無性別的辭彙（gender-free terms），避免用性別歧視的語言（sexist language/sexual bias），以免引起對方的不快。

② 請參見 his/her 和 one。

性別歧視的語言	無性別的辭彙	字義
businessman, businesswoman	businessperson, employer, manager, owner, storekeeper	商人；實業家；經理
fireman	firefighter	消防隊員
housewife, househusband	homemaker	管家

mailman	letter carrier, mail carrier	郵差
mankind	people, humanity, humankind, the human race, human beings	人類
manpower	workers, work force, staff, human resources	人力資源
policeman	police officer	員警
salesman, saleswoman	salesperson, salesclerk, sales representative	推銷員
stewardess	flight attendant, steward	空服人員

472 shadow/shade 影子／陰涼

1

✗ Ella likes to read in the shadow of her beach umbrella.

意思是「影子」，通常是由你的身體形成的，在自己的影子裡閱讀似乎有點困難

✓ Ella likes to read in the shade of her beach umbrella.

當天氣熱時，你坐在由大樹或大樓形成的陰涼處（shade）

愛拉喜歡在她的海灘傘下乘涼閱讀。

- Little Margo is sometimes afraid of her own shadow.
（小瑪歌有時候會害怕自己的影子。）

473 shopping 購物

1

✗ On Sundays I like to go for shopping or swimming.

要表示「去打保齡球、去露營、去爬山、去釣魚、去購物、去游泳」等，用「go + V-ing」，不用介系詞 for

✓ On Sundays I like to go shopping or swimming.

星期天我喜歡去購物或游泳。

- go bowling（打保齡球）
- go shopping（去購物）
- go fishing（去釣魚）
- go camping（去露營）
- go climbing（去爬山）
- go swimming（去游泳）

474 similar/same 相似的／同樣的

1 ✗ Lenore's voice is similar as yours.

意思是「相似的」，用介系詞 **to**，不用 as

✓ Lenore's voice is similar to yours.

蕾諾兒的聲音與你的聲音相似。

same 意思是「同樣的」，要與冠詞 the 連用，後面接介系詞 as；the same as 意思是「跟……一樣」。

- My views about the dangers of smoking are the same as Lulu's.（對於吸菸帶來的危險，我的看法與露露一樣。）

475 simple past tense/ present perfect tense (did/have done) 過去簡單式／現在完成式（與時間副詞搭配）

1 ✗ Margo has arrived in Tokyo two hours ago.

只能用於**過去簡單式**

✓ Margo arrived in Tokyo two hours ago.

瑪歌兩小時前抵達了東京。

(1) 句中有表示過去時間的副詞（比如：at eight、this morning、yesterday、last night、last month、five minutes ago、in 2008），常用於過去式。

(2) 有關現在完成式的用法，需要記住的最重要一點是，它絕不會跟描述已經結束了的過去時間副詞連用。

(3) 如果現在完成式需要與一個時間副詞連用，這個時間副詞必須是描述一個還沒有結束的時間（比如：today、this week、this evening、tonight），因為現在完成式表示的是「到現在為止已經完成或尚未完成的事」。現在完成式既與過去有關聯，也與現在有關聯。

(4) 請參見 past perfect tense/simple past tense (had done/did) 及 past perfect tense/present perfect tense (had done/have done)。

- Kay went to the city library twice yesterday.
（凱昨天去過市立圖書館兩次。）
- Fay has been to the city library twice today.
（菲今天已經去過市立圖書館兩次了。）

2

✗ It was a long time since I last talked to Vince.

談論一個從過去開始而持續到現在（持續到說話的時刻）的動作，主要子句要用**現在完成式**（不用過去式），從屬子句用過去簡單式

✓ It's been a long time since I last talked to Vince.
(It's been = It has been)

有時主要子句也可以用現在簡單式

✓ It's a long time since I last talked to Vince.
(It's = It is)

自從我上次跟文斯談話後，已經過了很長的時間了。

現在完成式常與下面的時間副詞或時間副詞片語連用：

- since（自……從）
- already（已經）
- still（依舊）
- yet（還沒）
- ever（至今、從來）
- never（從不）
- so far（到目前為止）
- recently（最近）
- for two weeks（長達兩週）
- in/during/over the past/last decade/5 years/3 months/4 days（在過去的十年／五年／三個月／四天期間）

1) 他們的友誼從過去開始（他們過去是朋友），他們現在仍然是朋友。
2) 現在完成式涉及過去和現在。
3) 主要子句用現在完成式（have been）+ since 從屬子句用過去式（were）。

- Clive and Kay **have been** friends **since** they **were** five.
（克萊夫和凱自從五歲起就一直是朋友。）

476 simple present tense/ present perfect tense 現在簡單式／現在完成式

1

✗ How long are you in Macao? — Since July 3.

談論多長時間，不用現在簡單式，要用**完成式**。請參見 simple past tense/present perfect tense

✓ How long have you been in Macao? — Since July 3.

你在澳門多久了？——自從七月三號起就在澳門了。

現在簡單式用來描述永久的、重複的事件或動作。事實、慣例、習慣常用現在簡單式來表示。

事實

· Kris has a small waist, and she is very tall.
（克莉絲的腰很細，個子很高。）

習慣

· Does your brother Lee often get up early?
（你哥哥李常早起嗎？）

477 simple present tense/ present progressive tense 現在簡單式／現在進行式

1

✗ The city water tank is standing behind the new bank.

通常不用進行式來談論「持續比較長」或「永久」的情形

✓ The city water tank stands behind the new bank.

用**簡單式**來談論「持續較長的情形」

城市的蓄水塔聳立在那家新蓋的銀行後面。

2

✗ I am going to Guam to visit my relatives **every July**.

通常不用現在進行式來談論「與講話當下沒有密切聯繫的反覆行為、動作或事件」

✓ I go to Guam to visit my relatives **every July**.

談論「永久的情形或真理」、「習慣」或「反覆的動作和事件」時，用**現在簡單式**。這句表反覆的事件（every July）

我每年七月都要去關島拜訪親戚。

文法加油站

兩個現在時態

① 現在簡單式	・總是事實的事 ・經常發生	・一直在發生 ・有時發生	・反覆發生 ・從未發生過的事情
② 現在進行式	・此時此刻正在發生的事		・即將發生的事

反覆發生

・Dwight watches the news on the Internet almost every night.
（杜威特幾乎每天晚上上網看新聞。）

此刻正在發生

・Margo is reading a book about a UFO.
（此刻瑪歌正在讀一本關於不明飛行物的書。）

這裡的進行式 is staying 不表示「正在進行」，而是表示將要發生的事

・How long is Ming staying in Taipei?
（敏要在台北待多久？）

3

✗ "I am not understanding what to do," complained Sue.

understand 是表示心理狀態的字，不用於進行式

✓ "I don't understand what to do," complained Sue.

蘇抱怨說：「我不懂該做什麼。」

(1) 一些動詞通常用於簡單式，不用於進行式。

(2) 常見的非進行式動詞：

(a) 表示心理狀態和感情的動詞（mental and emotional states）

・believe（相信）
・dislike（不喜歡）
・doubt（懷疑）
・feel (= have an opinion)（認為、覺得）
・guess（猜測）
・imagine（想像）
・know（知道）
・like（喜歡）
・hate（討厭）
・prefer（更喜歡）
・realize（意識到）
・recognize（認出）
・remember（記得）
・see (= understand)（明白）
・suppose（假設）

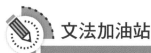

- think (= have an opinion)（認為）
- understand（懂、明白）
- want（想要）
- wish（但願、希望）

(b) 感官動詞（verbs showing perception）

- hear（聽見）
- see（看見）
- smell（聞起來）
- sound（聽起來）
- taste（嚐起來）

(c) 連綴動詞（linking verbs）

- be（是）
- seem（似乎是）
- look (= seem)（看起來）
- appear（好像是）

(d) 其他非進行式的動詞

- agree（同意）
- belong（屬於）
- contain（容納）
- consist of（由……構成）
- fit（合身；適合）
- owe（欠債；歸功於……）
- promise（承諾）
- weigh (= have weight)（有……重量；秤起來）
- disagree（不一致;不同意）
- deserve（應得）
- include（包括）
- own（擁有）
- prove（證明是；結果是）
- need（需要）
- possess（擁有）
- surprise（吃驚）
- satisfy（滿意）

不能用進行式 was hearing

- Lenore heard a strange noise from under the floor.
（蕾諾兒聽見從地板下面傳來一個奇怪的聲音。）

weigh 意思是「有……重量、稱起來」（have weight），非進行式動詞，不能用進行式 am weighing a lot

- Do I weigh a lot just because I eat an apple pie every day?
（我的體重很重，就只是因為我每天都吃一個蘋果派嗎？）

比較：上面列舉的動詞中，有些可兼作一般行為動詞，這時就可以用於進行式，與非進行式動詞的意思不一樣。

秤某物的重量

- Jake is weighing the ingredients for the cake.
（傑克正在秤做蛋糕的原料。）

478 simple present tense/ simple future tense 現在簡單式／未來簡單式

1

✗ After Michael will pass his driving test, he'll buy a new electric motorcycle.

主要子句是**未來式**，但要在子句裡表示「未來」的含意時，**子句**應該用**現在式**，而不是未來式。一般說來，如果你明顯在指將來，子句裡就不要用 will

✓ After Michael passes his driving test, he'll buy a new electric motorcycle.

子句也可以用現在完成式

✓ After Michael has passed his driving test, he'll buy a new electric motorcycle.

通過駕照的考試後，麥克就要去買一輛新的電動摩托車。

(1) 這類的子句是由 when、until、before、after、as soon as、once、if、whether、as long as、on condition that 等引導。

if 子句用現在式 are buried

- **If** they **are buried** deep in the tunnel, Faye and Kay **will** have to dig **until** they **see** the light of day.

主要子句用 will have to dig

until 子句用現在式 see

（如果菲和凱被深深埋在隧道裡，他們就不得不一直挖下去，直到看見光線。）

(2) 請參見 after 和 if。

479 since 自從

since + 過去時間（2003），句子的動詞要用完成式或完成進行式（用完成進行式是為了強調動作的持續性），不用過去簡單式。請參見「simple past tense/present perfect tense」

1

✗ Since 2003, the City Power Company produced a lot of solar electricity.

用來表示某件事從過去某一時間開始，並持續到現在或持續到另外一個過去時間

✓ Since 2003, the City Power Company has produced a lot of solar electricity.

自從 2003 年，城市能源公司已經生產出了很多太陽能電。

✓ Since 2003, the City Power Company has been producing a lot of solar electricity.

自從 2003 年，城市能源公司就一直在大量生產很多太陽能電。

(1) since 後面接過去的某一時間、日期或事件；如果 since 引導的是子句，子句動詞用過去式。

(2) 請參見 ago/since、during/since、in/since/on。

- It has always been windy here, and this huge wind farm **has been making** electricity **since** last year.

  過去的某一個具體時間（last year），句子的動詞用現在完成進行式（has been making）

  （這裡一直都多風，自去年以來，這座巨大的風力發電廠就一直在發電。）

  since 引導一個子句，子句裡的動詞用過去式（were）；主句裡的動作用現在完成式（have known）

- I **have known** Jade **since** we **were** in first grade.
  （自從小學一年級開始，我就認識了潔德。）

480 since/for 自從／多長（時間）

1

✗ We have lived here since one year.

✓ We have lived here for one year.

我們在這裡已經住了一年了。

談論「一段時間」（a period of time）或「有多長時間」（how long），用 **for**

(1) 避免把 for 用在一個具體的時間前面。for 表示時間的持續（duration）。

(2) since 用在一個「具體的日期或具體的時間」（a specific date or time）前面，不能用在一段時間前面。since 回答這個問題：beginning when（從什麼時候開始的）。用 since 來表達某個行為是從何時開始的。

- for + 一段時間（for three years, for a week）
- since + 某一時間點（since 2009, since Sunday）

(3) 現在完成式（have + 過去分詞）常和 for 和 since 連用。

- I **have been** in Norway for one day.（我在挪威已經一天了。）
- **I've been** in Barcelona since July.
  （自從七月起我就在巴賽隆納。）

481 since/from 從……開始

1

✗ Jim Jet was there since 2 p.m., but nobody came to meet him.

現在完成式

✓ Jim Jet has been there since 2 p.m., but nobody has come to meet him yet.

現在完成式

從下午兩點開始，吉姆 ‧ 傑特就在那裡了，但（還）沒有人來見他。

過去式

✓ Jim Jet was there from 2 p.m. to 4 p.m., but nobody came to meet him.

過去式

吉姆 ‧ 傑特從下午兩點一直到四點都在那裡，但沒有一個人來見他。

(1) since 用來說明某件事從過去某個時刻開始，一直持續到現在或持續到過去的某一時刻。since 後面接一個具體的過去時間、日期，或一個過去事件（用過去式），主要子句中動詞要用現在完成式或現在完成進行式（不用一般過去式或未來式）。句型為：

- 完成式 + since + 過去某一具體時間／日期
- 完成式 + since 子句（過去式動詞）

(2) from 指「從某一個具體時間開始並持續下去」，意思與 since 差不多，但在 from 的句子裡可以用過去式、現在式或未來式。

過去式

- Evan taught at a ballet school **from** 2002 **to** 2007.
（從 2002 年到 2007 年，伊文在一所芭蕾舞學校教書。）

現在式

- Gem is usually at home **from** 9 p.m. **to** 7 a.m.
（從晚上 9 點到早上 7 點，潔姆通常都在家。）

未來式

- Gem will interview you tomorrow **from** 2 p.m. **to** 3 p.m.
（潔姆明天從下午 2 點到 3 點要來採訪你。）

482 skip school

請參見 escape from school/skip school。

483 sleep 睡覺

1

✗ Dwight slept late last night.

sleep late（= sleep in）指的是「起床晚；睡懶覺」，與句意不符

✓ Dwight went to bed late last night.

✓ Dwight stayed up late last night.

杜威特昨晚很晚才睡覺。

stay up late 的意思才是「熬夜」

- Bing read until midnight, so he slept late this morning.
  （昨晚賓看書一直看到半夜，所以今天早上他起床晚了。）
- On Sundays Kate likes to sleep late.
  （星期天凱特喜歡睡懶覺。）

2

✗ Every night Ted has to put his baby sister to sleep.

✓ Every night Ted has to put his baby sister to bed.

put somebody to bed 通常指「把孩子放上床睡覺 」，千萬不能錯用 put somebody to sleep 來表示這個意思

每晚泰德都要把他的小妹妹放上床睡覺。

put a person or an animal to sleep 有下面兩個意思：

(1) 給某人或某動物打麻醉藥使之失去知覺；使麻醉。

(2)（委婉語）注射藥物，然後讓人或動物無痛苦地死去；安樂死。

- Dr. Nation is your doctor, and she will put you to sleep before your operation.
  （你的醫生是納欣醫生，在動手術之前，她會給你打麻醉藥讓你睡著。）
- I had to put my old dog Clyde to sleep, and then I cried and cried.
  （我不得不給我的老狗克萊德注射藥物，讓牠無痛苦地死去，然後我傷心地哭啊哭。）

484 so/such 如此

1

✗ Merle is so a strong girl!

so 修飾形容詞或副詞，不修飾名詞

✓ Merle is such a strong girl!

such 修飾名詞

梅兒真是一個堅強的女孩啊！

(1) so + 形容詞；so + 副詞

so 後面接形容詞 smart

· Bart is so smart!（巴特真聰明！）

(2) such（+ 形容詞）+ 不可數名詞／複數名詞

such 後面接複數名詞 people

· "Mary and Harry are such friendly people," said Jerry.
（傑瑞說：「瑪麗和哈利真是非常友善的人。」）

(3) such a/an（+ 形容詞）+ 單數可數名詞

such 後面接單數可數名詞

· Our trip to Alaska was such an exciting trip that we've decided to go there again next year.
（我們去阿拉斯加的旅程如此令人興奮，我們決定明年再去那裡。）

485 society 社會、社團

泛指「社會」（people in general）時，society 前**不要加 the**

1

✗ "Are lies a danger to the society?" asked Mr. Wise.

✓ "Are lies a danger to society?" asked Mr. Wise.

懷斯先生問：「謊言對社會構成威脅嗎？」

(1) 當泛指「社會」（people in general）時，society 前不要加 the。

· the evolution of human society（人類社會的發展）
· Dr. Miller is not respected by society because he's a killer.
（米勒博士因為是一個殺人犯，所以不受到社會的尊重。）

(2) 如果 society 指特定的社團、俱樂部、協會等，則為可數名詞，須與 the 連用。

· Dan joined the film society after he met Ann.
（丹認識安後就加入了電影協會。）

486 sometime/some time/sometimes
某時候／一段時間／有時候

1

✗ Kay will visit me some time in May.

指「一段時間」，與句意不合

✓ Kay will visit me sometime in May.

指未確定的時間，用作副詞，意思是「在（將來或過去）某一時候」

凱在五月的某天會來探望我。

2

✗ Amy some time comes to visit me.

✓ Amy sometimes comes to visit me.

指「有時候、間或」（at times）

艾咪有時會來探望我。

- Rick needs to take some time off, or he'll get sick.
  （瑞克需要休假一段時間，否則他會生病。）

487 sort of 請參見 kind of。

488 specialize/specialized/specialist
專攻／專門的、專業的／專家

1

✗ Vance is specialized in modern dance.

✓ Vance has specialized in modern dance.

✓ Vance specializes in modern dance.

萬斯專攻現代舞蹈。

(1) specialize in something：專攻（某專業）；專門從事。

(2) specialized：為形容詞，用在名詞前，表示「專門的；專科的；專業化的」。

- specialized skills/training/tools, etc.
  （專門技術／訓練／工具等）

(3) specialist：為名詞，意思是「專家；專科醫生」，後面常接 in。

- To build a house on the moon, you'll need some specialized tools and a specialist like June.
  （要在月球上修建一棟房子，需要一些專門的工具和像茱恩那樣的專家。）

文法加油站

major in something：主修

- Trish **majors in** English.（翠西主修英語。）

489 spend 花費（金錢、時間等）

1

✗ Vance spent $50 for a new pair of pants.

在「spend an amount of money on something」（在某事或某物上花錢）的句型中，用 **on** 而不用 for

✓ Vance **spent** $50 **on** a new pair of pants.

萬斯花了五十塊美金買了一條新褲子。

2

✗ Sue Flower usually spends less than five minutes on taking a shower.

在「spend (a period of) time doing something」（花時間做某事）的句型中，要直接用「**V-ing** 」形式，不要用「介系詞 on + V-ing 形式」

✓ Sue Flower usually **spends** less than five minutes **taking** a shower.

蘇 · 弗勞爾沖個澡通常花不到五分鐘的時間。

在「spend (a period of) time on something」（某事上花時間）用 on

- Alice **spends** a lot of time **on** basketball practice.（艾麗絲花很多時間練習打籃球。）

在「spend (a period of) time at/in a place」（花時間在某地）用 at 或 in

- Kim is slim, because she **spends** a lot of time **at** the gym.（金姆很苗條，因為她很多時間都待在體育館。）

在「spend (a period of) time with someone」（花時間與某人在一起）用 with

- Joe is going to **spend** Christmas Eve in Chicago **with** Margo.（喬要在芝加哥與瑪歌一起度過聖誕夜。）

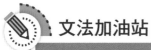

490 staff （全體）職員

1 ✗ The staffs at the Clear Days Hotel are expecting a pay raise.
當指全體成員（職員）的時候，staff 是集合名詞，不要用複數 staffs

美式 The staff at the Clear Days Hotel is expecting a pay raise.
美式用 is

英式 The staff at the Clear Days Hotel are expecting a pay rise.
英式英語常用 are

= The staff members at the Clear Days Hotel are expecting a pay raise.

晴天大飯店的職員們期待著加薪。

⑴ staff 作主詞時，**美式英語**動詞常用**單數**；英式英語動詞可用單數也可用複數，如果把 staff 看成是一個整體（as a whole），動詞就用單數，如果把 staff 看成是個體（individuals），動詞就用複數。不過，英式更常用複數。

⑵ 請參見 family、subject-verb agreement（第 C 點）。

- Sue has hired a staff of 22 for the new zoo.
- = Sue has hired 22 staff members for the new zoo.
  （蘇為新建的動物園招收了 22 名員工。）

⑶ **加薪**： 美式 pay raise　　英式 pay rise

491 statistics

請參見 politics。

492 step 腳步

1 ✗ Russ, watch your steps when getting off the bus.

✓ Russ, watch your step when getting off the bus.
watch one's step 意思是「留意腳下」或「謹言慎行」

魯斯，下公車時留意腳下！

文法加油站

step 的習慣用語

① in step (with)（步調一致；與周圍環境一致）
- in step with the times（與時代一致）
- Kitty and her mother wore pretty pink dresses and danced in step with each other.
（姬蒂和她媽媽穿著漂亮的粉紅洋裝，舞步一致地跳著舞。）

② out of step（步調不一致；與周圍環境不一致）
- out of step with the modern world（與現代世界不協調）
- Wade is out of step with this new decade.
（韋德跟不上這新的十年。）

③ step by step = one step at a time = by degrees（逐步地）
- Sue told Bob, "Let's take our relationship slow and one step at a time, because I need to complete my education and get a job."
"Yes," he agreed and then added, "We'll take our time and go step by step, because that's what we both need."
（蘇對鮑伯說：「讓我們緩慢地發展我們的關係吧，一步一步來，因為我需要完成學業，找份工作。」——「好。」鮑伯贊成，接著他補充道：「我們不急，逐步發展，因為我倆都需要如此。」）

493 stock/stocks 存貨／股票

1

✗ We don't have that kind of lock in stocks.

✓ We don't have that kind of lock in stock.

那種鎖我們沒有現貨了。　in stock：有現貨

(1) in stock 的反義詞是 out of stock（沒有現貨、缺貨）。
- You bought my shop's last Big Ben Clock, and it is still out of stock.（你買了我們商店最後一個大笨鐘，現在那種鐘仍然缺貨。）

(2) 複數 stocks 指「公司股票」。

- Ann sells stocks, and her husband Lars sells cars.
 （安買賣股票，她先生拉斯買賣汽車。）

494 stop 阻擋、停止

1

❌ That hurricane stopped Wayne to go to visit Jane.

✅ That hurricane stopped Wayne from going to visit Jane.

颶風阻止了韋恩去探望珍。（由於颶風，韋恩不能去探望珍。）

- stop somebody/something from doing something
= prevent somebody/something from doing something
（阻止；阻擋）

2

❌ Doctor Ride told me to stop to work so hard, and the next day he died.

stop **to do** something 指「中斷或停下來，以便做某事」，在這裡與句意不符

✅ Doctor Ride told me to stop working so hard, and the next day he died.

stop **doing** something（= not continue）指「停止做某事〔不要繼續做某事〕」

賴德醫生要我不要如此過分辛苦地工作，第二天他卻去世了。

(1) stop doing something（= not continue）。
指「停止做某事〔不要繼續做某事〕」。

- When we heard Mom say, "Bedtime," we all stopped laughing and jumping.（當我們聽見媽媽說：「睡覺時間到了」，我們都停止了歡笑和蹦跳。）

(2) stop to do something 指「中斷或停下來，以便做某事」：
to do something 是表示「目的」的不定詞片語。

- Bart stopped to listen to Sue talk about art.
 （巴特停了下來，以便聽蘇談論藝術。）

495 stress 強調

1

意思是「強調」，是及物動詞，後面**直接接受詞**，不需要接 on

✗ Dr. Fish stressed on reading for fun as the best way to learn English.

✓ Dr. Fish stressed reading for fun as the best way to learn English.

費許博士強調，趣味閱讀是學習英語的最佳方法。

當 stress 用作名詞時，用於片語 lay/place/put stress on，這時就需要 on。

- Larry lays stress on reading for fun as the best way to gain a large vocabulary.
 （賴瑞強調，趣味閱讀是掌握大量辭彙唯一最有效的方法。）

496 subject-verb agreement 主詞和動詞的數要一致

A) 單數第三人稱主詞 + 單數動詞

1

單數第三人稱主詞（third person singular），要接一個以 -s 結尾的單數動詞（loves）

✗ Mary love peach pie, our children love apple pie, and I love blueberry pie

複數名詞，要接動詞的複數形式（一般動詞的複數形是原形動詞，如 love）

✓ Mary loves peach pie, our children love apple pie, and I love blueberry pie.

代名詞 I 要接原形動詞（love）

瑪麗愛吃桃子派，我們的孩子們愛吃蘋果派，而我愛吃藍莓派。

現在簡單式中，單數第三人稱主詞需要單數動詞（Mary walks and talks.），而其他主詞（包括複數主詞）需要複數動詞／原形動詞（I walk and talk./You walk and talk./They walk and talk.）。

動詞 + -s = 單數 lives

- My friend Eli lives in Johannesburg.
 （我的朋友伊萊住在約翰尼斯堡。）

名詞 + -s = 複數 friends

- All my close friends live in Johannesburg.
 （我所有的摯友都住在約翰尼斯堡。）

B) 不可數名詞 + 單數動詞

1 ✗ Dad said, "This milk taste really bad."

當不可數名詞作主詞時，動詞要用**單數動詞**

✓ Dad said, "This milk tastes really bad."

爸爸說：「這牛奶味道很不好。」

(1) 不可數名詞（uncountable noun）是不能數的事物，比如 food、money、water、health、news 等。

(2) 當不可數名詞作主詞時，動詞要用單數動詞。

there 開首的句子（there is/there are/there was/there were），主詞是動詞 be 後面的名詞。而動詞要與 be 後面的名詞一致。這句的主詞是不可數名詞 money，動詞要用單數 is

- There is not enough **money** to buy the honey.
（沒有足夠的錢買這些蜂蜜。）

C) 集合名詞

1 美式 Pakistan's basketball team is playing against Japan's.

美式英語通常把集合名詞看成一個**整體單位**，含有單數意義，要用**單數**動詞

英式 Pakistan's basketball team are playing against Japan's.

英式英語通常把集合名詞當作**複數**，含有複數意義。作主詞時，動詞用**複數**

巴基斯坦籃球隊正在與日本籃球隊打籃球。

(1) 集合名詞（collective noun）雖然指的是一組人或一組東西，但有單數形式（a team）也有複數形式（two teams）。

(2) 美式英語通常把集合名詞（committee、family、jury、group、team 等）看成一個整體單位（a unit），含有單數意義，要用單數動詞。

(3) 英式英語通常把集合名詞當作複數，強調一群體裡單獨的行為（independent actions of the group）或強調一個群體裡的成員（its members as individuals），含有複數意義。作主詞時，動詞用複數。

把 government 看成一個整體單位，
美式要用單數動詞。

美式 · Jane says the government is going to increase the taxes on nicotine.
[ˋnɪkəˏtin] 尼古丁：香菸裡含有的一種有毒、能讓人上癮的水溶性生物鹼

· Jane says the government are going to increase the taxes on nicotine.
把 government 看成是一群執政官員，英式用複數動詞
（珍說，政府要給尼古丁加稅。）

美式 · The crowd was very loud.

英式 · The crowd were very loud.（人群很嘈雜。）

(4) 假若用了複數動詞搭配集合名詞的句子聽起來很彆扭，那就加上表示成員的字（members），如 family members、club members。美式英語尤其如此。

· My family members are gathering for the wedding.
（我家人正聚集起來準備去參加婚禮。）

(5) 請參見 family、staff。

2

美式 Next week the biology club is going on its yearly field trip to Italy.
美式常用**單數**動詞和**單數**代名詞

英式 Next week the biology club are going on their yearly field trip to Italy.
英式常用**複數**動詞和**複數**代名詞

美式 英式 Next week the biology club members are going on their yearly field trip to Italy.

下週生物學俱樂部要去義大利進行一年一次的考察旅行。

D) 複合主詞 + 複數動詞

1

✗ A cup of tea and a glass of milk often helps me to wake up.
由對等連接詞（coordinating conjunction）**and** 連接起來的複合主詞（compound subjects）常接**複數動詞**

✓ A cup of tea and a glass of milk often help me to wake up.

一杯茶再加一杯牛奶常幫助我清醒過來。

· Claire and Omar are over there.（克萊兒和歐馬就在那裡。）

E)（作為一個整體的）複合主詞 + 單數動詞

1 ✗ Bacon and eggs are a great brunch or lunch.

被看成是一個**整體單位**（一頓餐；一份菜），動詞要用**單數**

✓ Bacon and eggs is a great brunch or lunch.

培根蛋是一頓豐富的早午餐或一頓豐富的午餐。

(1) 通常用 and 連接的複合主詞要用複數動詞，比如：Mom and Dad **love** Tom.（媽媽和爸爸愛湯姆。）

(2) 如果由 and 連接的兩個或更多的主詞是指同一個人或東西，或指一個整體單位，就要用單數動詞去搭配主詞（比如：a knife and fork〔一副刀叉〕）。

F) every 或 each 連接的複合主詞 + 單數動詞

1 ✗ Every man and woman in our village want to become as rich as Mitch.

由 each 或 every 修飾的複合主詞要接單數動詞

✓ Every man and woman in our village wants to become as rich as Mitch.

這句重複 every，沒有上面的句子簡潔

✓ Every man and every woman in our village wants to become as rich as Mitch.

我們村裡的男男女女都希望像米奇一樣富有。

· Each CD and DVD that she owns is funny.
（她擁有的每一片 CD 和 DVD 都很滑稽。）

· Every boy and girl that I coach in Hong Kong is quick and strong.
（我在香港訓練的每一個男孩和女孩都敏捷、強壯。）

G) 單數不定代名詞 + 單數動詞

1

✗ Nobody and nothing are going to stop Dan from visiting Ann.

單數不定代名詞被 and 連接起來，並作句子的複合主詞時，也要用單數動詞

✓ Nobody and nothing is going to stop Dan from visiting Ann.

沒有任何人、任何事物會阻止丹去探望安。

(1) 下面的不定代名詞是**單數**，與**單數動詞**在一起使用：

- another
- any one of
- anybody
- anyone
- anything
- each
- each one
- either
- every one of
- everybody
- everyone
- everything
- little
- many a
- much
- neither
- no one
- nobody
- nothing
- one
- somebody
- someone
- something

(2) 即使這類單數不定代名詞被 and 連接起來，並作句子的複合主詞時，也要用**單數動詞**，如上面的例句（Nobody and nothing is going to . . .）。

- Amy declared, "**Nobody listens** to me, but when **something goes** wrong, **everybody blames** me!"（艾咪聲稱：「沒人聽我的話，但一旦發生了不好的事，人人都責備我！」）

H) 複數不定代名詞 + 複數動詞

1

✗ Several of my friends is in love with that movie star.

✓ Several of my friends are in love with that movie star.

總是與**複數動詞**搭配

我的朋友中有好幾個都愛上了那位電影明星。

下面的複數不定代名詞總是與**複數動詞**搭配：

- both（兩者〔都〕）
- few（幾個；一些）
- many（許多）
- others（其餘）
- several（幾個；數個）

I) 不定代名詞 + of + 複數名詞 + 複數動詞
不定代名詞 + of + 單數名詞／不可數名詞 + 單數動詞

1

✗ Dad said, "Some of the beef have gone bad."

不可數名詞，動詞要用**單數**

✓ Dad said, "Some of the beef has gone bad."

爸爸說：「一些牛肉已經壞掉了。」

有一些不定代名詞可以與單數動詞、也可以與複數動詞搭配，依據它們所指的名詞的數而決定。

- all/any/most/more/some of + 複數名詞 + 複數動詞

some of + 複數名詞 + 複數動詞

- Elwood said, "Some of the novels are good."
  （埃爾伍德說：「這些小說中有一些很好。」）

- all/any/most/more/some of + 單數名詞／不可數名詞 + 單數動詞

- Elwood said, "Some of the novel is good."

「some of + 單數可數名詞」不常用

= Elwood said, "Some parts of the novel are good."

此種句型較常見

（埃爾伍德說：「這本小說中的一部分內容很好。」）

J) neither of/either of/none of + 複數名詞 + 單數動詞（正式）

1

非正式 Neither of the boys are over there with Claire.

「neither of/either of/none of + 複數名詞」
在**非正式寫作**中或**口語**中，有人用**複數**動詞

正式 Neither of the boys is over there with Claire

「neither of/either of/none of + 複數名詞」
在**正式用語**中被看成是單數，要用**單數**動詞

那兩個男孩沒有一個在那裡與克萊兒一起。

(1)「neither of/either of + 複數名詞」在正式用語中被看成是單數，要用單數動詞。但在非正式寫作中，有人用複數動詞。注意：考試中要按照文法規則，用單數動詞。

(2) 請參見 either 和 neither。

2 美式口語 Gail knew none of the skirts were on sale.

正式 Gail knew none of the skirts was on sale.

蓋兒知道那些短裙沒有一條在打折。

(1)「none of + 複數名詞」在正式用語中被看成是單數，要用單數動詞。但在美式口語中，常用複數動詞。**注意**：考試中要按照文法規則，用**單數動詞**。

(2) 請參見 none。

K) one of + 複數名詞／複數代名詞 + 單數動詞

1

✗ One of you are going to have to tell Sue the truth about Ruth.

one 在句中作主詞，動詞要用**單數**

✓ One of you is going to have to tell Sue the truth about Ruth.

你們當中有一個人需要把露絲的實情告訴蘇。

請參見 one 條目裡的「文法加油站」。

L) the + 形容詞 + 複數動詞

1

有些形容詞與 the 連用（the + adjective），變成了**含複數意義的名詞**，作主詞時，動詞要用**複數**

✗ "Does the rich get richer and the poor get poorer?" asked Mitch.

✓ "Do the rich get richer and the poor get poorer?" asked Mitch.

米奇問：「富人越來越富有了，而窮人越來越貧苦了嗎？」

請參見 p. 442（第 D 點）。

M) 一些不規則形式的名詞（Irregularities）

1

✖ The news are not interesting to Ms. Andrews.

看起來是複數，但意義上是單數，
作主詞時，要用**單數動詞**

✔ The news is not interesting to Ms. Andrews.

這消息並未引起安德里女士的興趣。

(1) 一些名詞形式上看起來是複數，但意義上是單數，作主詞時，要用單數動詞。比如：the United States（美國）、mathematics（數學）、statistics（統計學）、The New York Times（紐約時報）等。請參見 politics、math/maths、news。

(2) 而有些名詞形式上是單數，但意義是複數，作主詞時，要用複數動詞。比如：people、police、youth。請參見 police 和 youth。

- The police are searching for a terrorist from Greece.
（員警在搜索來自希臘的一個恐怖分子。）

N) 測量（Measurements）

1

以時間、金錢、距離、重量的測量（measurements of time, money, distance, weight）作主詞時，通常接**單數動詞**

✖ Eight hours of sleep are enough for Kate.

✔ Eight hours of sleep is enough for Kate.

八小時的睡眠對凱特來說就足夠了。

- Eight hundred kilometers is not too far to travel by car.
（開汽車旅行，八百公里的距離並不太遠）

- 參見 numerical expressions 和 time 時間或次數表達法。

O) the number + 單數動詞；a number + 複數動詞

1

the number of（……的數量），作主詞時，
是單數片語，要用**單數動詞**

✖ The number of students in my biology class are twenty.

✔ The number of students in my biology class is twenty.

我的生物學班上有二十名學生。

(1) the number of（……的數量），作主詞時，是單數片語，用單數動詞。

(2) a number of（一些），作主詞時，用複數動詞。

- Kate noticed a large number of her classmates were late.（凱特注意到有許多同學遲到了。）

(3) 請參見 number: a number of 和 number: the number of。

P) 倒裝句子：動詞的數與修飾語無關

1

✗ Outside was the three horses I had learned to ride.

動詞要與**複數主詞**一致，與句首的修飾副詞 outside 無關

主詞

✓ Outside were the three horses I had learned to ride.
= The three horses I had learned to ride were outside.

我已經學會騎的那三匹馬就在外面。

主詞在動詞後面：當句子是倒裝句時，即主詞和動詞的順序顛倒，此時動詞要與主詞一致，不與句首的修飾語一致。

因為主詞是由 and 連接起來的複合主詞（Lenore and Kate），動詞要用複數

- Behind that door **wait Lenore and Kate**.
（蕾諾兒和凱特在門後等待著。）

Q) 動詞數與補語無關

1

✗ The cause of Jade's big smile were her good grades.

本句的主詞為單數

動詞的數應該與**主詞**一致，而不與補語一致

複數詞 grades 在句中作補語

✓ The cause of Jade's big smile was her good grades.

潔德滿面笑容的原因，是因為她獲得了好成績。

R) 肯定主詞和否定主詞

1

✗ The physics department **members, not the dean, has decided** to have a party for Alex.

如果句子裡有一個肯定的主詞和一個否定的主詞，其中一個是複數而另一個是單數，動詞的數應該與**肯定主詞**的數一致

用逗號把否定主詞分開，複數動詞（have）與**複數肯定主詞**（The physics department members）一致

✓ The physics department **members, not the dean, have decided** to have a party for Alex.

用 but 連接否定主詞，不用逗號

✓ The physics department **members but** not the dean **have decided** to have a party for Alex.

決定為艾力克斯召開聚會的是物理系的成員，而不是系主任。

如果句子裡有一個肯定的主詞和一個否定的主詞，其中一個是複數而另一個是單數，**動詞的數應該與肯定主詞的數一致**。通常要用逗號把否定主詞分開，但如果否定主詞前面有連接詞 and 或者 but，就不用逗號分開。

肯定主詞　否定主詞

- **The dean**, **not the physics department members**, **has decided** to have a party for Alex.

動詞要與單數肯定主詞 dean 一致，需用單數動詞 has

= **The dean but** not the physics department members **has decided** to have a party for Alex.

（決定為艾力克斯召開聚會的是系主任，而不是物理系成員。）

S) 關係子句中的動詞要與先行詞一致（形容詞子句中的動詞要與先行詞一致）

1

✗ Ming often writes **short stories, which is** her favorite form of writing.

關係代名詞 which 的先行詞，子句中的動詞應該與之一致，須用複數 are

✓ Ming often writes **short stories, which are** her favorite form of writing.

補語，非主詞。記住，補語不是關係代名詞的先行詞

敏常寫短篇故事，因為那是她最喜歡的體裁。

(1) 如果關係代名詞在關係子句中作主詞，那麼子句中的動詞就要與先行詞一致。先行詞即關係子句所修飾的詞。

(2) 請參見 one of those。

T) 成對連接詞／關聯連接詞／相關連接詞（Correlative Conjunctions）

1

如果成對連接詞 not only . . . but also . . . 連接的是主詞，且都是單數，那麼動詞也要用**單數**

✗ "Not only English but also Spanish are widely used in the world," declared Trish.

✓ "Not only English but also Spanish is widely used in the world," declared Trish.

翠西宣稱：「全世界廣泛使用的語言不只有英語，還有西班牙語。」

(1) 如果成對連接詞（either . . . or . . . 、neither . . . nor . . . 、not only . . . but also . . . ）連接的是主詞，且都是單數，那麼動詞也用單數；如果都是複數，那麼動詞也就用複數。如果主詞有單數也有複數，那麼動詞就應該遵循靠近原則。也就是說，動詞的單複數由最靠近動詞的主詞單複數而定。

- Either Brooke or her mom has my cookbook.
  （布露可或她的媽媽有我那本烹飪書。）
- Either Brooke or her parents have my cookbook.
  （布露可或她的父母有我那本烹飪書。）
- Neither Claire nor her son is there.
  （克萊兒不在那裡，她的兒子也不在那裡。）
- Neither Claire nor her daughters are there.
  （克萊兒不在那裡，她的女兒們也不在那裡。）

(2) 請參見 either . . . or . . . 、neither . . . nor . . . 、as well as。

U) 主詞不在介系詞片語裡（Subjects Not in Prepositional Phrases）

1

如果作主詞的名詞有介系詞片語修飾，動詞的數要與該名詞一致

主詞

✗ That book on the problems of global warming are interesting to Brooke.

可用**排除介系詞片語或插入語**的方法來確認主詞單複數。如果刪除了這個介系詞片語，只剩下「The book is interesting to Brooke」，就很清楚主詞是單數 book，要用單數動詞 is

✓ That book on the problems of global warming is interesting to Brooke.

布露可對那本有關全球暖化問題的書很感興趣。

(1) 如果作主詞的名詞有介系詞片語修飾，動詞的數要與該名詞一致。

複數主詞 Christmas stories 與複數動詞 are 一致，而不是與介系詞片語 about Santa Claus 以及 for example 一致

- **Christmas stories about Santa Claus, for example, are** numerous.（比如，有許多關於聖誕老人的聖誕故事。）

there be 句型後面的第一個名詞是 people，看上去好像是主詞，但它不過是介系詞片語的一個部分，把這個介系詞片語刪除後，下一個名詞是 longing，這個名詞才是決定動詞的主詞。主詞是單數 longing，那麼動詞也應該用單數動詞 is

- **There is** now, especially among young **people** like June, a **longing** to visit the moon.
（尤其是在像珍那樣的年輕人當中，現在有一種要去參觀月球的渴望。）

(2) 如果主詞有插入語，動詞的數不受插入語的影響。常見的主詞插入語有 as well as、accompanied by、(together) with、such as 等。主詞插入語常常用逗號與主詞隔開。

(3) 請參見 as well as。

靠近動詞的複數名詞 children 只不過是過去分詞片語的一部分，不是主詞。如果刪除這個附加的分詞片語，就可以清楚看見主詞是單數 President Jane Wu，動詞也要用單數 is

- **President Jane Wu, accompanied by her children, is** on a trip to Spain.
（總統珍・吳由她的孩子們陪伴著去西班牙旅行。）

497 subjunctive mood 假設語氣

請參見 if、rather/would rather（第 4 個範例）、request、suggest、time 時間或次數表達法（第 5 個範例）和 wish。

498 substitute for 取代

1

✗ I cannot substitute with astronaut Scott.

正確的片語是 substitute for

✓ I cannot substitute for astronaut Scott.

我不能取代太空人史考特。

文法加油站

substitute 和 replace

比較 **substitute one thing/person for another** 和 **replace one thing/person with another**

- Margo knew he had **replaced** the original Picasso **with** a fake copy.

= Margo knew he had **substituted** a fake copy **for** the original Picasso.（瑪歌知道他用一幅贗品代替了畢卡索的原畫。）

499 suck 吸

在美式俚語裡，suck 也可以指「很糟糕、令人討厭」。但即使在非正式用語中，還是應該避免這種用法

1

非正式 Trish asked, "How is your English?"—"It sucks!" replied Brooke with an unhappy look.

翠西問：「你的英語好嗎？」——「糟糕透了！」布露可神色不悅地回答。

正式 Trish asked, "How is your English?"— "It's not good," replied Brooke with an unhappy look.

翠西問：「你的英語好嗎？」——「不好！」布露可神色不悅地回答。

(1) suck 的意思是「吸」。

- suck air into the lungs（吸氣入肺部）
- suck on a straw（用吸管吸）

(2) suck 用在骯髒的俚語（Vulgar Slang）裡。許多學生從電影裡聽見這個字，就把它用在日常生活中，而沒有意識到如果用的不恰當，就成了髒話。

500 suggest 建議

1

✗ Pete is a nurse, and he suggests to take Vitamin D right after you eat.

後面接 V-ing 形式，不能接不定詞

✓ Pete is a nurse, and he suggests taking Vitamin D right after you eat.

彼特是一名護士，他建議飯後吃維他命 D。

(1) suggest doing something「建議某人做某事」，suggest 後面接 V-ing 形式，不能接不定詞。

(2) suggest that（子句）+ 假設語氣（原形動詞）。

不能用 Kay gets

- I **suggest that** Kay **get** her tooth fixed right away.（我建議凱立刻把她的牙齒治好。）

(3) 請參見 request 和 important。

文法加油站

「建議或要求某人做某事」的表達

① 下面這些動詞後面如果接 that 子句，就要用**原形動詞**。這是美式英語「建議或要求某人做某事」的一種特殊的**假設語氣**表達法。

· advise	· demand	· propose	· require
· ask	· insist	· recommend	· suggest
· command	· order	· request	· urge

② 在這種情況下，英式英語在子句中不用原形動詞表示假設，而用「should + 原形動詞」

美式 Kay's dad asked that Kay be excused from class for two days.

不能用 Kay was excused

英式 Kay's dad asked that Kay should be excused from class for two days.

（凱的爸爸請求讓凱停課兩天。）

美式 Lulu insisted that I listen to you.

不能用 I listened

英式 Lulu insisted that I should listen to you.

（露露堅持我應該聽你的話。）

501 superior 優越的、較好的、較大的

1

✗ Does Nate's sister act as if she were superior than all of her classmates?

superior 後面接 **to**，不接 than

✓ Does Nate's sister act as if she were superior to all of her classmates?

superior to（= better than）意思是「優於……」

內特的妹妹表現得好像她比同班同學都優秀嗎？

文法加油站

與 superior 相關的字

① 反義詞：inferior to（= not as good as）（比……差；不如）

- Are these little lakes inferior to big Lake Superior?

  （這些小湖泊比不上〔北美的〕蘇必略湖嗎？）

② junior、inferior、prior、senior、superior 等後面都接介系詞 to。

- junior to（年幼的／地位較低的）
- senior to（年長的／地位高的）
- inferior to（不如）
- superior to（優於）
- prior to（優先的、在前的）

502 sure/surely 確信的／當然、的確

1 美式 口語 "It's sure windy," declared Lee.

sure 是形容詞，修飾名詞。在美式口語中，sure 用作副詞

正式 "It's surely windy," declared Lee.

surely 是副詞，修飾形容詞和動詞

李大聲說：「風的確很大。」

- Lily surely is kind and lovely.（莉莉的確又友善又可愛。）

503 surroundings/environment 環境

1 ✗ Bing's grandparents have a nice surrounding.

✓ Bing's grandparents have nice surroundings.

賓的爺爺和奶奶身處的周遭環境很好。

複數形 surroundings 表示「環境；四周狀況」

- The king's daughters spent a lot of time exploring the castle and its surroundings.
（國王的女兒們花了大量的時間探索那座城堡以及周遭的環境。）

2 ✗ Mary likes the quiet environments in the library.

✓ Mary likes the quiet environment in the library.

瑪麗喜歡圖書館裡安靜的環境。

作單數用時，意思等於 surroundings，指「環境；四周狀況」

the environment：自然環境；生態環境（包括土地、水、空氣、植物、動物，尤其是受人類活動影響的自然界）。**注意：**environment 指「自然環境」時要有 the。

- a happy home environment（一個快樂的家庭環境）
- the natural environment（自然環境）
- If our city gets its electricity from the sun and wind, the environment will be clean and green.
（如果我們的城市從太陽和風生產電力，生態環境就會很乾淨，綠油油的。）

· Margo grew up in a small town environment and then attended a university in Chicago.

= Margo grew up in a small town surroundings and then attended a university in Chicago.

（瑪歌在一個小鎮環境裡長大，然後去了芝加哥念大學。）

a happy home environment

the natural environment

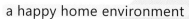

T

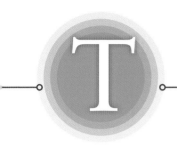

504 taxi stand/taxi rank 計程車招呼站

1 美式 If you want to go somewhere, take a taxi from that **taxi stand** over there.

英式 If you want to go somewhere, take a taxi from that **taxi rank** over there.

如果你想去什麼地方，你可以在那邊的計程車招呼站搭計程車。

505 technique/technology 技巧；技術／科技

1 ✗ Maggie understands modern rocket techniques.

技巧；方法；手段 — techniques

✓ Maggie understands modern rocket technology.

瑪姬懂現代的火箭科技。

科技 — technology

- statistical/analytical/surgical **techniques**（統計技術／分析技術／外科技術）
- a useful **technique** for doing something（做某事有用的方法）
- information/computer/military/software **technology**（資訊科技／電腦科技／軍事科技／軟體科技）
- I had only two weeks to learn about modern management **techniques**.（我只有兩週的時間可以學習現代管理技術。）
- Maggie is able to live on the moon because of modern **technology**.（由於有現代科技，瑪姬能夠在月球上居住。）

506 teens/teenager 十幾歲／青少年

1

非正式 Those four teens are camping out next to Lake Rose.

雖然可以指青少年，但屬於美國俚語，不要用於正式語中

指十幾歲的青少年

正式 Those four teenagers are camping out next to Lake Rose.

那四個十幾歲的年輕人要在玫瑰湖旁露營。

在正式語中，teens 通常指的是從十三歲開始至二十歲之前的這些年齡，因為從 thirteen（十三）到 nineteen（十九）都是以 -teen 結尾的。

- in one's teens（十幾歲〔在某人 13 至 19 歲的時間裡〕）
- in one's early/late/mid teens（某人的青少年前期／後期／中期）
- That singer wearing the pink jeans is excellent, and she is only in her teens.
  （那名身穿粉紅牛仔褲的歌手很優秀，而且她只有十幾歲。）

507 tense choice 時態選擇

1

✗ Stop jumping on your bed, because a bed was a place for sleeping.

指一般性的事實，要用現在簡單式

✓ Stop jumping on your bed, because a bed is a place for sleeping.

停止在床上跳，因為床是用來睡覺的地方。

2

✗ I was going to send a text message to Scot, but I forget.

談論過去發生的事，要用過去式

✓ I was going to send a text message to Scot, but I forgot.

我本來打算發一封手機簡訊給史考特，但我忘記了。

3

✗ Of course Ann expected that I will divorce Dan.

談論過去發生的事，要用過去式（包括過去未來式）

✓ Of course Ann expected that I would divorce Dan.

安原本當然是以為我會和丹離婚。

過去簡單式 expected 與過去未來式 would 搭配

✓ Of course Ann expects that I will divorce Dan.

安當然是預期我將會和丹離婚。

現在簡單式 expects 與未來簡單式 will 搭配

(1) 基本規則：如果談論一件過去發生的事，要用過去式，包括過去簡單式、過去完成式、過去未來式等（**did**、**had done**、**would do**）。否則就要用現在式，包括現在簡單式、現在完成式、簡單未來式等（**do/does**、**has/have done**、**will do**）。

(2) 請參見 past perfect tense/present perfect tense、past perfect tense/simple past tense、simple past tense/present perfect tense、simple present tense/present perfect tense。

現在簡單式

- Dan: What **does** Ivy **look** like?

現在簡單式

Ann: Ivy **is** cute and strong, and she **has** long black hair.
（丹：愛葳長什麼樣子？
安：愛葳漂亮，身強體壯，有一頭黑色長髮。）

過去簡單式

- Amy **was** not with Ray yesterday. She **was** with me.
（艾咪昨天沒有和雷在一起，她和我在一起。）

現在完成式

- Jerome **has never been** to Rome.
（傑羅姆從來沒有去過羅馬。）

過去完成式 had read；過去簡單式 entered。
過去完成式常與過去簡單式連用，表示「過去的過去」

- Martin **had read** lots of American books before he **entered** kindergarten.（馬丁進幼稚園之前就讀過許多美國書籍。）

未來簡單式

- **Will** Joe go climbing tomorrow?（喬明天要去爬山嗎？）

談論過去事件時（in 2005 I arrived in Yellowknife），若是談及過去某時刻的未來要發生的事情，就要用過去未來式（would spend）

- In 2005 I **arrived** in Yellowknife, Canada, where I **would spend** the next three years of my life.
（我在 2005 年時來到加拿大的黃刀城，將在那裡度過我一生中的三年。）

A B C D E F G H I J K L M N O P Q R S T U V W X Y Z

508 temporary/short action 短暫行為

請參見 ago/for、dead/die、return

509 term/terms 術語／條款

1

❌ I accept your term for buying my truckload of worms.

✅ I accept your terms for buying my truckload of worms.

複數形 terms 指契約或合約的「條款；條件」

我接受你們購買我一貨車蟲蟲的條款。

(1) 當指契約或合約的「條款；條件」時，用複數形 terms。

- the terms of a treaty（契約條款）
- under the terms of（按照條款……）

(2) term（= word or phrase）當指「術語」時，是可數名詞，有單數形式，也有複數形式。

- a technical/medical/legal/scientific term
  （一個技術／醫學／法律／科學術語）
- I use the term "alcoholic" to describe Dick.
  （我用「酒鬼」這個名稱來描述迪克。）

510 than 比……還

1

❌ Do any of those banks offer better salaries than does your company?

比較級 than 後面不用問句形式，即使句子本身是個疑問句

✅ Do any of those banks offer better salaries than your company?

than 後面的子句常省略動詞（= than your company **does**）

那些銀行有沒有哪家提供的薪水比你公司提供的薪水還高？

= than Sue is（省略了動詞 is）

- Are you shorter **than Sue**?（你比蘇矮嗎？）

❌ **Are you shorter** than is Sue?

511 thank 感謝

1

✗ Sue: Thank you so much for your help, Lulu.
Lulu: No thanks, Sue.

用於委婉地拒絕別人給你的東西

✓ Sue: Thank you so much for your help Lulu.
Lulu: You are welcome, Sue.

蘇：露露，非常感謝你的幫助。
露露：蘇，不客氣。

(1) 這是學生常犯的習慣性錯誤。中文常說「不客氣、不謝」，但用英文說時，就不應該用 no 或者 not 這樣的否定詞語。回答別人對你的道謝，其中一個正確的回答是：「You are welcome.」。

(2) 當你委婉地拒絕某人給你的東西時，才應該把 thanks 和 no 用在一起，並在中間放一個逗號。

- Margo: Would you like some tea or coffee?
  Dan: No, thanks, Margo.
  （瑪歌：你想要喝茶還是咖啡？
  丹：不用了，謝謝，瑪歌。）

2

✗ "Thanks God it's Friday!" exclaimed Tod.

可以說 thanks for something，但不能說 thanks something

✓ "Thank God it's Friday!" exclaimed Tod.

及物動詞 + 受詞

陶德驚呼道：「謝天謝地，今天是星期五！」

(1) 可以說 thanks for something，但不能說 thanks something，因為 thanks 是複數名詞，不是動詞，後面不能接受詞。

- Lulu, thanks for inviting me to Singapore.
  （露露，謝謝妳邀請我去新加坡。）

(2) 名詞 thanks 後面可以接 a lot 等修飾詞語。

- A thousand thanks!/Thanks a lot!（非常感謝！）

512 that 引導受詞子句

1

❌ I guess that that girl over there is Tess.

連接詞 — 形容詞／限定詞。在這種情況下，不要重複使用 that

✅ I guess that girl over there is Tess.

限定詞，修飾名詞 girl。連接詞 that 被省略了

✅ I guess that the girl over there is Tess.

連接詞，連接主要子句和受詞子句。girl 前面用定冠詞 the 限定

我猜那邊那個女孩就是黛絲。

513 that/which 引導形容詞子句

1

❌ The robot, that Dawn kept in the garage, is gone.

非限定形容詞子句，只能用 which，不能用 that

✅ The robot that Dawn kept in the garage is gone.

限定子句，指「朵安存放在車庫裡的機器人，而不是存放在別處的機器人」

✅ The robot, which Dawn kept in the garage, is gone.

非限定子句，指「朵安只擁有一個機器人，沒有兩個機器人」。which 子句只是對主詞 the robot 提供進一步補充說明

朵安存放在車庫裡的機器人不見了。

(1) 非限定子句：

(a) which 和 that 常用來引導形容詞子句。

(b) 如果刪除子句，主要子句的意思仍然清楚正確，那麼這個子句就是非限定的，應該用逗號和主要子句隔開。

(c) 雖然 which 和 that 都可以引導形容詞子句，用來指代「物」，但如果是非限定形容詞子句，就只能用 which，不能用 that。

(2) 限定子句：

(a) 為了句子的清晰和準確，有時必須要用子句限定或修飾，則這個子句就是限定的，這時不能在主句和子句之間加逗號。

(b) 限定子句通常用 that 引導。that 既可以指代「人」，也可以指代「物」。

(c) that 子句只能引導限定子句，不用逗號。限定性子句指代「物」時，有時也可以用 which 來引導。

文法加油站

A 限定性子句（which/that）

① 如今很多作家既用 which 也用 that 來引導限定子句，但更常用 that。

② 但在下列情況中，人們更常用 which，而不是 that。

(a) 當句中已經用過了 that 時，用 which。

- That is a movie which Alice should not miss.
（那是一部艾麗絲不應該錯過的電影。）

(b) 當先行詞前面有 that/this/these/those 修飾時，用 which，比如：this . . . which 、that . . . which 、these . . . which 或 those . . . which。

- Rose was explaining to Sam those words which she had already taught Pam.
（蘿絲此刻正在對山姆解釋她已經教過潘姆的那些字。）

B which 要放在恰當的位置

把 which 放在恰當的位置對清楚表達句子的含意至關重要，位置放錯了會造成混淆。注意下面語意不清的例子多麼容易產生混淆：

是我的大腳趾還是喬的椅子腳斷了？這句意思沒有表達清楚。腳斷的當然應該是椅子，不是我大腳趾上的

語意不清　Joe Wu's chair fell on my big **toe**, which had a broken leg.

非限定子句：含意是「Joe Wu 只有這一把椅子」。子句只作補充說明

語意清楚　Joe Wu's chair, which had a broken leg, fell on my big toe.

子句靠近所修飾的名詞 chair，清楚指明「椅子有一根腳斷了」

（喬・吳的椅子倒在我的大腳趾上，那把椅子有一根腳斷了。）

限定子句：子句限定「斷了一根腳的那把椅子，而不是其他椅子」。總之，which、that 應緊跟所修飾的名詞之後，才能避免意思上的混淆。請參見 which（作關係代名詞的 which）

語意清楚　Joe Wu's chair that had a broken leg fell on my big toe.（喬．吳斷了一根腳的椅子倒在我的大腳趾上。）

C 關係代名詞 that

一些作家認為，關係代名詞 that 不能用來指代「人」。但如果沒有明確說這個人的名字時，那麼，可以用 that 來指代「人」。

- Dr. West's main idea is "**People** who love to read do great on language tests."

= Dr. West's main idea is "**People** that love to read do great on language tests."
（韋斯特博士的主要觀點是「愛閱讀的人在語言考試中都考得很好」。）

這句只能用 who，主詞是專有名詞 Nell，刪除子句後意思非常清楚 (Nell is doing well.)。非限定子句在這裡只是作補充說明。非限定子句只能用 who 指代「人」，不能用 that

- **Nell**, who joined the army last month, is doing well.
（尼爾上月入伍了，現在過得很不錯。）

514 the（不應該用 the 的情況）

A) 獨一無二的身分（special roles）名稱前，不用 the

1

✗ Why was Jill Nation elected the president of that corporation?

elect 後面如接表示人們「特殊身分」的名詞，通常省略 the

✓ Why was Jill Nation elected president of that corporation?

為什麼吉兒．納欣被選為那家股份公司的董事長？

(1) 在某些動詞（elect、make、appoint 等）後面，表示人們「特殊身分」，即「獨一無二的身分」的名詞，通常省略 the。（比如：董事長，在公司裡只有一個。）

・Penny Roger will be appointed manager of our company.

= Penny Roger will be appointed our company's manager.

（潘妮・羅傑將被任命為我們公司的經理。）

這句話在口語中說「Dennis Beam is the captain of our tennis team.」也是可以接受的。但在正式文體中最好省略 the

・Dennis Beam is captain of our tennis team.

（丹尼斯・比姆是我們網球隊的隊長。）

(2) 下面表示人們特殊身分的字，都可以省略 the。

・boss（老闆）
・captain（隊長）
・center（中鋒）
・chairman（〔男〕主席）
・chairperson（主席）
・chairwoman（女主席）
・director（主任）
・goalkeeper（〔足球〕守門員）
・head（首領）
・king（國王）
・manager（經理）
・president（董事長；總統）
・prime minister（首相）
・queen（女王）

(3) 在這些名詞前面省去 the，必須具備兩個條件：

(a) 這些都是獨一無二的身分（比如在一個足球隊裡，只有一個隊長；在一個國家，只有一個國王）。

(b) 這些字在句中是補語，而不是主詞，即，必須用在動詞 appoint、be、elect 或 make 等後面。 如果這些字是句中的主詞就必須要用冠詞 the，因為我們指的是「個人」，而不是指職務或身分。

句中主詞必須用冠詞 the，因為我們指的是「個人」，而不是指職務或身分

・The captain of the women's volleyball team is Liz Wall.

（這支女排的隊長是莉茲・沃爾。）

B) 不需要 the 的地點名稱

1

❌ How long will it take Michael to cross the Queen Park by bicycle?

一些地名（比如：公園名）不用 the

✅ How long will it take Michael to cross Queen Park by bicycle?

麥克騎自行車穿過女王公園需要多久時間？

許多地點名稱是由兩個字構成，而第一個字往往是人名（如：Kennedy）或地名（如：Canterbury），所以這些名稱前面一般不加 the。

(1) airports 機場名稱（地名／人名 + Airport）

- Ms. Short lives close to **Vancouver International Airport.**（肖特女士住在溫哥華國際機場附近。）

(2) bays/harbors 海灣／港口名稱（地名 + Bay/Harbor）

- Kay lives next to **San Francisco Bay**.
（凱住在舊金山灣附近。）
- **Pearl Harbor** is where I met Earl.
（我就是在珍珠港遇見厄爾。）

> ✅ 例外：如果用 of 連接的海灣名稱，就要用 the。
> - the Bay of Bengal（孟加拉灣）
> - the Bay of Fundy（芬地灣）

(3) cathedrals/abbeys/monasteries/convents
大教堂／大寺院／修道院名稱（地名 + Cathedral/Abbey 等）

- Canterbury Cathedral（坎特伯里大教堂）
- Abby loves to visit **Westminster Abbey**.
（艾比喜歡參觀西敏寺。）

> ✅ 例外：如果用 of 連接的教堂名稱，就要用 the。
> - the Abbey of Cluny（克倫尼修道院）
>
> ✅ 比較：「地名（形容詞）+ Church」前，常用 the。
> - the Roman Catholic Church（羅馬天主教會）

(4) cities/towns 城鎮名稱

- New York（紐約）
- London（倫敦）
- Hong Kong（香港）
- Dubai（杜拜）

(5) continents 大洲名稱

- Africa（非洲）
- Europe（歐洲）
- Antarctica（南極洲）
- North America（北美洲）
- Asia（亞洲）
- Oceania（大洋洲〔即 Australia 澳洲〕）
- South America（南美洲）

> 例外：如果洲名包含 continent 這個字，就需要 the。這時的 the 不是修飾大洲名稱，而是修飾 continent 這個字。其寫法變成「the + 地名（形容詞）+ Continent」。
> - the African Continent（非洲大陸）
> - the Asian Continent（亞洲大陸）
> - the European Continent（歐洲大陸）
> - the Antarctic Continent（南極大陸）
> - the Australian Continent（澳洲大陸）
> - the North American Continent（北美洲大陸）
> - the South American Continent（南美洲大陸）

(6) countries 國家名稱

- America（美國）
- Italy（義大利）
- Great Britain（英國）
- Germany（德國）
- Japan（日本）
- New Zealand（紐西蘭）

> 例外：國家名稱如果是**複數**，或帶有 Republic、Kingdom 等字的國家名，就需要 the。
> - the Philippines（菲律賓）
> - the Netherlands（荷蘭）
> - the United States of America（美利堅合眾國）
> - the United Kingdom（大英聯合國）
> - the Dominican Republic（多明尼加共和國）

(7) lakes 湖泊名稱（Lake + 地名；地名 + Lake）

- Lake Superior（蘇必略湖）
- Deer Lake（鹿湖）

> 例外：如果是複數 **Lakes**，或「**兩個以上的字 + Lake**」，就需要 the。
> - the Great Lakes（北美五大湖）
> - the Great Salt Lake（大鹽湖）

A B C D E F G H I J K L M N O P Q R S T U V W X Y Z

(8) **mounts** 山峰名（Mount + 地名）
- Mont Blanc（白朗峰）
- Mount Fuji（富士山）

(9) **parks** 公園名稱（地名 + Park）
- Disney World（迪斯尼世界）
- Hyde Park（海德公園）
- New York Central Park（紐約中央公園）

(10) **states/provinces** 州名／省分名
- California（加州）
- Quebec Province（魁北克省）

(11) **spacecraft** 太空船名稱
- Challenger（挑戰者號）
- Apollo 13（阿波羅十三號）

> 例外：如果有 **spacecraft** 這個字，就需要 **the**。
> - the Apollo 13 spacecraft（阿波羅十三號太空船）

(12) **streets/roads/squares/avenues** 街名／路名／廣場名（地名／序數詞／人名 + Street/Road/Square/Avenue）
- Tenth Street（第 10 街）
- MacDonnell Road（麥克唐奈道）
- Times Square（時代廣場）
- Fifth Avenue（第五大街）

> 例外：the High Street（高街）

(13) **train stations** 火車站名（地名 + Station）
- Oxford Station（牛津火車站）
- Saigon Railway Station（胡志明市火車站）
- Vancouver Train Station（溫哥華火車站）

> 例外：許多美國人會在火車站名前用冠詞 **the**。
> - the Taipei Train Station（臺北火車站）

(14) **universities/colleges/institutes** 學校／大學／學院名稱（地名 + University/College/Institute）
- Oxford University（牛津大學）
- Niagara College（尼加拉學院）

> 例外：如果用 **of** 連接的大學名稱，就要用 **the**。
> - the University of California at Los Angeles（加州大學洛杉磯分校）
> - the Industrial Institute of Madrid（馬德里工業學院）

文法加油站

要用 the 的地理名稱、地點名稱和專有名詞

① canals 運河名稱
- the Panama Canal（巴拿馬運河）
- the Suez Canal（蘇伊士運河）

② channels/straits 海峽名稱
- the English Channel（英吉利海峽）
- the Formosa Straits/the Taiwan Straits（臺灣海峽）

③ basins（河川的）流域名稱
- the Amazon Basin（亞馬遜河流域）
- the Colorado River Basin（科羅拉多河流域）

④ gulfs 海灣名稱
- the Gulf of Mexico（墨西哥海灣）
- the Persian Gulf（波斯灣）

⑤ oceans 海洋名稱
- the Atlantic Ocean（大西洋）
- the Pacific Ocean（太平洋）

⑥ seas 大海名稱
- the Arabian Sea（阿拉伯海）
- the Mediterranean (Sea)（地中海）
- the Black Sea（黑海）
- the South China Sea（南海）

⑦ rivers 江河名稱／河流名稱
- the Mississippi（密西西比河）
- the Rhine（萊茵河）
- the Nile（尼羅河）
- the Yangtze River（長江〔揚子江〕）

⑧ island groups 群島名稱（複數形式）
- the British Isles（不列顛群島）
- the Hawaiian Islands（夏威夷群島）
- the Florida Keys（佛羅里達群島）
- the West Indies（西印度群島）

> 注意：如果不是群島，就不要 the。
> - Hainan Island（海南島）
> - Hispaniola Island（希斯盤紐拉島〔即海地島 Haiti〕）

⑨ mountain ranges 山脈名稱（複數形式）
- the Alps（阿爾卑斯山脈）
- the Himalayas（喜馬拉雅山脈）
- the Rockies/the Rocky Mountains（落磯山脈）

> 注意：如果是山峰，不是山脈，就不用 the。
> - Mount Everest（聖母峰）
> - Mount Gongga（貢嘎山）

⑩ ranges of hills 丘陵名稱
- the Black Hills（黑崗）

⑪ deserts 沙漠名稱
- the Kalahari Desert（喀拉哈里沙漠）
- the Sahara（撒哈拉沙漠）

⑫ cinemas/theaters 電影院名／劇院名
- the Kennedy Center for the Performing Arts（甘迺迪表演藝術中心）
- the Playhouse（普利豪斯劇院）

> 比較：
> - the Whitehall（懷特豪爾劇院〔劇院名要用 the〕）
> - Whitehall（倫敦官府大道〔街名不用 the〕）

⑬ hotels 飯店名
- the Hilton（希爾頓大飯店）
- the Holiday Inn（假日酒店）

⑭ museums/galleries 博物館名稱／美術館名稱
- the British Museum（大英博物館）
- the National Gallery（國家藝術館）

⑮ ships 船名
- the Queen Mary（瑪麗皇后號）
- the Titanic（鐵達尼號）

⑯ trains 火車名
- the Golden Arrow（黃金之箭）
- the Orient Express（東方特快車）

⑰ bridges 大橋名
- the Golden Gate Bridge（金門大橋）

⑱ towers 塔樓
- the Eiffel Tower（埃菲爾鐵塔）
- the Tower of London（倫敦塔）

C) 節日名稱（festival names）前不要 the

在節日名稱前面不要加 the

1

✗ "Is the New Year's Day celebrated on January 1 all over the world?" asked little Fay.

✓ "Is New Year's Day celebrated on January 1 all over the world?" asked little Fay.

小菲問：「全世界都是在一月一號慶祝新年嗎？」

(1) 在節日名稱前面不要用 the：

- Christmas（耶誕節）
- Easter（復活節）
- Thanksgiving（感恩節）
- Mother's Day（母親節）
- Father's Day（父親節）
- Valentine's Day（情人節）

(2) 但是 the Fourth of July（美國獨立紀念日）需要用 the。

(3) 中國傳統節日通常要加定冠詞 the，如：

- the Spring Festival （春節）
- the Dragon Boat Festival （端午節）

D) 三餐（meals）前不要 the

1

✗ Kay, why don't we get together for the lunch today?

在三餐前面不要加 the

✓ Kay, why don't we get together for lunch today?

凱，我們今天聚在一起吃午餐，好不好？

(1) 三餐名稱（breakfast, lunch, dinner) 前，通常不要 the。

(2) 如果特指提供的具體一餐時，通常要用 the。

(3) 如果三餐前面有一個形容詞，可以用不定冠詞 a。

- a free lunch（一頓免費午餐）
- a wonderful dinner（一頓美好的晚餐）
- Dee, dinner is ready.（蒂，晚餐準備好了。）
  泛指　特指
- Thank you, Kate. The dinner was great.
  （凱特，謝謝你。這頓晚餐很好吃。）

E) 交通方式前不要 the

1

✗ Does Russ go to work on the foot or by the bus?

談論以某種交通方式旅行，不用 the

✓ Does Russ go to work on foot or by bus?

注意：步行 on foot，不能用 by foot

魯斯步行去上班還是搭公車去上班？

談論以某種交通方式旅行，不用 the。下面的字與 by 連用，無需用 the。

- by bike（騎自行車）
- by boat（乘小船）
- by bus（搭公車）
- by ferry（搭渡輪）
- by sea（海運）
- by ship（乘船）
- by tram（搭電車）
- by train（搭火車）
- by taxi/by cab（搭計程車）

F) 抽象名詞前不要 the

1

✗ You should mention that we all need the love and the attention.

在 love 和 attention 這類抽象名詞前不要加 the

✓ You should mention that we all need love and attention.

你應該提及我們都需要愛和關懷

(1) 在抽象名詞（比如：anger、attention、hatred、liberty、love 等）前不要用 the。

(2) 抽象名詞後若有修飾語（比如：介系詞片語、形容詞子句），就需要用 the。此時，抽象名詞因為使用了 the 而變成具體名詞，具有特定的性質。

(3) 抽象名詞前如果有形容詞，可以用不定冠詞 a/an，比如：a passionate love（一種強烈的愛）。

抽象名詞 anger 前不要冠詞

- Brad, do you understand that anger isn't all bad?
  （布萊德，你明白憤怒並非完全不好嗎？）

that 子句修飾抽象名詞 anger。這時的 anger 已經具有特定性質了，特指「造成我離開朗的那股憤怒」

- The anger that had separated me from Ron was finally gone.
  （那股造成我離開朗的憤怒，最終平息了。）

介系詞 of 片語修飾抽象名詞 anger。這時的 anger 已經具有特定性質了，特指「暴民的憤怒」

- The anger of the mob made her sob.
  （暴民的憤怒使她哭泣。）

G) 所有格形式的人名／所有格形式的專有名詞不要 the

1

❌ Brent quietly parked his electric bike near the Eva's tent.

所有格形式的人名前面，不要 the

✅ Brent quietly parked his electric bike near Eva's tent.

布蘭特輕輕地把他的電動自行車停在伊娃的帳篷附近。

2

❌ Are any of the Russia's factories producing this type of electric car?

所有格形式的專有名詞前面，不要 the

✅ Are any of Russia's factories producing this type of electric car?

歐馬問：「有沒有任何一家俄國工廠在生產這類的電動汽車？」

所有格形式的人名或所有格形式的專有名詞不要 the 或 a/an，因為所有格形式本來就屬於限定詞，再用冠詞作限定就重複了。

❌ the/an Ann's coat　✅ Ann's coat（安的大衣）

❌ a Shakespeare's play　✅ a Shakespearean play

❌ the Shakespeare's play　✅ a play by Shakespeare

（莎士比亞寫的一部戲劇）

H) 表示行星的名詞前是否要 the ？

1

❌ Lars wants to explore the Mars. — Mars（火星）不用冠詞

✅ Lars wants to explore Mars. — Mars（火星）要大寫

拉斯想探索火星。

(1) 通常我們在 earth、moon、sun 等前面要用 the：the earth、the moon、the stars、the sun、the sky 等。但也有例外，請參見 the（必須加 the 的情況）。

- I dreamed about the birth of the sun and the earth.（我夢見太陽和地球的誕生。）
- The stars and the moon are shining brightly in the sky tonight.（今晚的天空群星閃爍、月光燦爛。）

⑵ 其他行星和星座前面不用 the。

(a) 行星（planets）

- Mercury（水星）
- Venus（金星）
- Mars（火星）
- Jupiter（木星）
- Saturn（土星）
- Uranus（天王星）
- Neptune（海王星）

(b) 星座（constellations）

- Ursa Minor（小熊座）
- Ursa Major（大熊座）
- Scorpion（天蠍宮座）
- Dragon（天龍星座）

I) 太空（space）不需要 the

1

✗ Grace knew that humans had just taken another step in exploring the space. —— space 如果指「太空」，不用冠詞

✓ Grace knew that humans had just taken another step in exploring space.

葛蕾絲知道人類朝太空探索又邁進了一步。

space 如果指「太空」，不用冠詞。

- humanity's grand adventure into space（人類偉大的太空冒險）
- live in space（住在太空中）

J) society 泛指「社會」，不要 the

1

✗ Does Kitty want to be respected by the polite society?

society 泛指「我們生活在其中的這個社會」，一般不用冠詞 the

✓ Does Kitty want to be respected by polite society?

姬蒂希望受到上流社會的尊重嗎？

請參見 society。

- the evolution of human society（人類社會的發展）

K) industry 泛指不要 the，特指要 the

1

❌ Overall, the industry has not done well during the last eight months, but **the entertainment industry** has done great.

泛指 industry 時，不用 the

✅ Overall, industry has not done well during the last eight months, but the entertainment industry has done great.

特指某個行業時，就需要用 the

大體上這八個月以來，工業進展不太好，但娛樂業的發展卻非常好。

- the automobile industry（汽車業）
- the movie industry（電影業）
- the tourist industry（旅遊業）
- the chemical industry（化學工業）
- the service industry（服務業）
- the wind power industry（風能發電工業）
- the solar power industry（太陽能發電工業）

L) 泛指（或半泛指）的事物或人物不要 the

1

❌ "I like the nineteenth-century literature," said Eli.

這裡雖不是泛指一切文學，不過談的仍然是「一般概念」，是「**半泛指的**」，而不是特指。在這類「半泛指的」的名詞前面，通常不用冠詞 the

✅ "I like nineteenth-century literature," said Eli.

伊萊說：「我喜愛十九世紀的文學。」

(1) 泛指事物或人物時（比如：adults、children、literature），通常不用 the。

泛指

- Maggie says **children** are always full of energy.
  （瑪姬說，兒童總是充滿活力。）

(2) 但如果名詞後面有 of 連接，我們通常用 the。

- the literature of the eighteenth century（十八世紀文學）

2 ✗ Tonight I am going to watch the program on TV about the rats and cats.

the rats and cats 是指一些特定的老鼠和貓。電視節目談論的 rats and cats 是泛指，不用冠詞 the

✓ Tonight I am going to watch the program on TV about rats and cats.

今晚我要觀看關於「老鼠和貓」的電視節目。

M) 表示民族的名詞用來泛指，不要 the

1 ✗ Kim says the Americans love to swim.

意思是「所有美國人都喜歡游泳」，不符合現實

✓ Kim says Americans love to swim.

表示民族的複數名詞不是類指（整體），也不是特指，而是泛指時，不加 the

金姆說美國人喜歡游泳。

⑴ 跟其他複數名詞一樣，當表示民族的複數名詞不是類指（整體），也不是特指，而是泛指時，不加 the，比如 Americans（美國人），Russians（俄國人）等。換言之，如果把表示民族的複數名詞（美國人）看成是個體（as individuals），而不是整體，那麼就不用 the。

- I like Nigerians.（我喜歡奈及利亞人。）

泛指個體

⑵ 不過，如果是在特殊的場合下，比如，在一個海灘，你挑出一群美國人來，並把他們與別的人（民族）進行比較，表示「特指」，你可以說 the Americans。

特指。挑出一群美國人來，與別的人做比較

- Kim said, "The Americans love to swim."

不過，在這種情況下，習慣上更常用 those，而不用 the

= Kim said, "Those Americans love to swim."
（金姆說：「那些美國人喜歡游泳。」）

文法加油站

① 表示民族的名詞如果是類指（一個整體），那麼我們就要加 the。

- the Americans = the American people（指全體美國人）
- the Canadians = the Canadian people（指全體加拿大人）
- the Chinese = the Chinese people（指全體中國人）

② 當表示民族的名詞用來特指時，我們要加 the。

這裡的 the Canadians 和 the Americans 相當於 those Canadians 和 those Americans。不過，在這種情況下，我們更常用 those，而不用 the

- I agreed with **the Canadians** and **the Americans**.
  （我同意那些加拿大人和美國人的意見。）

N) 一些固定片語省略 the

1

✗ We were walking the arm in the arm around the farm.

arm in arm 是固定片語，不加 the

✗ We were walking an arm in an arm around the farm.

arm in arm 是固定片語，不加 an

✓ We were walking arm in arm around the farm.

我們臂挽著臂地繞著農場散步。

下面片語常常省略冠詞 the 或 a/an：

- cheek to cheek（臉貼著臉的）
- day after day（日復一日）
- face to face（面對面）
- from head to toe（從頭到腳）
- from top to bottom（從上到下）
- hand in hand（手牽手）
- on land and sea（在陸地和海上）
- side by side（肩並肩）

O) 學科名稱前不要 the

1 ✗ Maggie is majoring in the psychology and minoring in the biology.

學科名稱是不可數名詞，不需要 the

✓ Maggie is majoring in psychology and minoring in biology.

瑪姬主修心理學，兼修生物學。

(1) 學科名稱是不可數名詞，不需要 the。比如：biology、chemistry、education、English、history、math、philosophy 等。

泛指，不加 the

- I don't like philosophy, biology, and psychology.
（我不喜歡哲學、生物學和心理學。）

(2) 但有些不可數名詞後面有 of 片語修飾，就變成具體名詞，要用 the。

不可數名詞後面有 of 片語修飾，變成具體名詞，要加 the

- the philosophy of mathematics（數學原理）

philosophy 後面有 of 片語限定，需要 the；這時 philosophy 變成具體名詞， 具有特定的性質，特指「柏拉圖的哲學」

- Is Margo interested in the philosophy of Plato?
（瑪歌對柏拉圖的哲學感興趣嗎？）

515 the（需要加定冠詞 the 的情況）

A) 獨一無二的人或物要加 the

1 ✗ Joan knew she would not feel alone in world if she bought a cellphone.

「世界」（the world）是獨一無二的事物，通常要加 the

✓ Joan knew she would not feel alone in the world if she bought a cellphone.

裘恩知道，如果她買了一支手機， 就不會覺得在這個世界上只有她獨自一個人了。

2 ❌ Our nation will send her to International Space Station. ——「國際太空站」，獨一無二的事物，要加 the

✅ Our nation will send her to the International Space Station. —— 這類獨一無二的「建築物」類似專有名詞，需要大寫

我們國家要派遣她去國際太空站。

(1) 世界上獨一無二的人或物，如「國王」（the king）、「世界」（the world）、「建築物」（如：the International Space Station、the Great Wall）等，通常要用 the。

- Ella thought the sun was too hot, so she sat under her beach umbrella.
  （愛拉覺得太陽太熾熱，於是她撐著海灘傘坐了下來。）
- Why should I try to count all the stars in the sky?
  （為什麼我應該數天空中所有的星星呢？）
- Is the U.S. President going to visit India in July?
  （美國總統 7 月要訪問印度嗎？）

(2) 這類獨一無二的名詞類似專有名詞，目前其中有一些有大寫的傾向，特別是 the Devil、the Earth、the North Pole、the Pope、the South Pole 等。

- the Devil（撒旦）
- the earth/the Earth（人間／地球）
- the moon（月亮）
- the king（國王）
- the North Pole（北極）
- the planets（行星）
- the Pope（羅馬教皇）
- the president（總統；董事長）
- the sky（天空）
- the solar system（太陽系）
- the South Pole（南極）
- the stars（恆星）
- the sun（太陽）
- the Taj Mahal（泰姬瑪哈陵）
- the United Nations（聯合國）
- the universe（宇宙）
- the weather（天氣）
- the world（世界）

文法加油站

① Earth（地球）也有不加冠詞的用法，特別是片語 on earth/Earth。

片語 on earth/Earth 不加冠詞

- Lars lives on Earth, but his wife and son live on Mars.
（拉斯住在地球上，但他的妻子和兒子住在火星上。）

② 上面提及的一些獨一無二的事物有時可以用 a/an，成為可數名詞。

如果太陽前有一個形容詞，就可以加 a/an

- Is it hard to have fun under a hot sun?
（在艷陽高照下要玩得開心很難嗎？）

B) 人體部位的名詞要加 the

1

✗ She took me by arm, and we walked slowly back to the farm.

人體部位名詞出現在表示「接觸」的字後，需要加 the

✓ She took me by the arm, and we walked slowly back to the farm.

她挽著我的手臂，我們慢慢地走回農場。

代表人體部位的名詞出現在表示「接觸、打擊、疼痛或傷患（beat、take、bite、pat、pain、wound）」的字後時，常加 the，而且這類人體部位的名詞要用單數。

- pat somebody on the shoulder
（拍某人的肩）
- a sharp pain in the chest
（胸部劇烈疼痛）
- With a stick, Ted beat the wolf on the head.
（泰德一棍子打在狼的頭上。）
- Did Meg bite Peg on the leg?
（梅格咬了佩格的腿嗎？）
- When I talk to your dad, I try hard to look him in the eye.
（當我跟你爸爸說話時，我盡量直視他。）

文法加油站

當談及某人的身體部位時，我們通常用所有格形式，而不用 the。

不說 turned the head

- Tim was ready to dive, and Kim **turned her head** to look at him.
（迪姆準備好了要跳水，金姆轉過頭去看他。）

不說 twist the ankle

- Did Nicole **twist her ankle** in that hole?
（妮可是在那個洞裡扭傷了腳踝嗎？）

不說 cut the finger

- My wife accidentally **cut her finger** with this knife.
（我妻子就是用這把刀不小心割傷了她的手指。）

不說 break the leg

- How did Meg **break her leg**?（梅格是怎麼折斷腿的？）

C) 用 the 的單數可數名詞（類指）

1

✗ Soon rocket will be able to send people to Neptune.

✓ Soon the rocket will be able to send people to Neptune.

類指所有的火箭

✓ Soon rockets will be able to send people to Neptune.

很快地火箭就能夠把人送到海王星。

如果用一個單數可數名詞概括某一類人或事物或動物，需要加 the。換言之，定冠詞 the 常與單數可數名詞連用，表示類指（generic）。這種情況在討論科技問題、發明創造的時候很常見。

表示類指，在討論科技問題、發明創造的時候很常見

- Joan loves living in the age of **the computer** and **the cellphone**.（裘恩喜歡生活在這個電腦和手機的時代裡。）

A B C D E F G H I J K L M N O P Q R S T U V W X Y Z

D) 一些形容詞和 the 連用

1

✗ Mitch helps both rich and poor.

✓ Mitch helps both the poor and the rich.

米奇既幫助窮人，也幫助富人。

the 和某些形容詞（不加名詞）的結合，具有**複數名詞**的意義，用來指**所有具有那種特性的人**

(1) **the** 和某些**形容詞**（不加名詞）的結合，具有**複數名詞**的意義，用來指所有具有那種特性的人、事或某個國家的民族。

- the rich
  = the rich people（富人）
- the foolish
  = the foolish people（蠢人）
- the aged（老人）
- the blind（盲人）
- the brave（勇敢者）
- the dead（死者）
- the deaf（聾人）
- the disabled（殘疾的人）
- the educated（受過教育的人）
- the elderly（上了年紀的人）
- the free（自由人）
- the handicapped（殘疾的人）
- the homeless（無家可歸的人）
- the hungry（飢餓的人）
- the poor
  = the poor people（窮人）
- the wise
  = the wise people（智者）
- the oppressed（受迫害的人）
- the powerful（掌權者）
- the sick（病人）
- the starving（飢餓者）
- the strong（強者）
- the supernatural
  （超自然現象）
- the uneducated
  （未受過教育的人）
- the unemployed（失業者）
- the unexpected
  （出乎意料的事）
- the unknown（無名小卒）
- the impossible（不可能的事）
- the unthinkable
  （難以想像的事）
- the weak（弱者）
- the wealthy（有錢人）
- the wounded（傷員）
- the young（年輕人）
- the injured（傷者）
- the living（活著的人）
- the needy（窮人）
- the old（老人）

(2) 這類形容詞與 **the** 的結合，相當於複數名詞，在句中作主詞時，要用**複數動詞**。

- The rich never miss a meal, but all the good food in the world won't help them to live forever.
  （富人從來沒有少吃過一頓飯，但世上所有的美食都無法幫助他們永生。）
- The foolish tell lies to the wise.（蠢人對智者撒謊。）

E) 特定的日期和一段時間要用 the

1

❌ Eli will fly to Athens on 4th of July.

✅ Eli will fly to Athens on the 4th of July.

表特定日期要加 the

伊萊在 7 月 4 日美國獨立紀念日時飛往雅典。

- the 1990s（二十世紀九〇年代）
- the Iron Age（鐵器時代）
- the Tang dynasty（唐朝）
- the eighties（八〇年代）
- the nineteenth century（十九世紀）

F) 相對的地理名詞要用 the

1

❌ I'm going to country this weekend to see Nancy Wu.

在用 country（鄉村）這類相對的地理名詞時，一般要加 the

✅ I'm going to the country this weekend to see Nancy Wu.

= the countryside

這週末我要去鄉間探望南西・吳。

(1) 在用 country（鄉村）、sea、seaside、town 和 mountains 這類相對的地理名詞時，即使不特指哪一個海、哪一座山，一般也要加 the。

- We take most of our vacations on the coast.
  （我們的假期大都是在沿海地區度過。）
- She prefers the mountains to the sea.
  （她喜歡山勝過喜歡海。）

(2) 但在一些固定片語裡，sea 前不用 the/a。

- at sea (= in a boat or ship on the sea)（在海上）
- go to sea (= become a sailor)（當水手；當海員）
- lost at sea (= died at sea or died in the sea)（死於大海）

G) 特指某一事物或人物要 the

1

✗ Margo locked door and closed window.

這是特指的一扇門和一扇窗，說話人和聽話者都知道指的是哪一扇門和窗。因此要加 the

✓ Margo locked the door and closed the window.

瑪歌鎖了門、關了窗戶。

在一個特指的物或人前要用 the，這個物或人是已經在前面提及過或是已知的

比較下面兩個句子：

聽者和說話者都知道指的是哪一個機場

- I have to pick up Mort at the airport.
  （我得去機場接莫特。）

「地點名稱 + Airport」 是專有名詞，不用 the。
請參見 the（不應該用 the 的情況）之「地點名稱」

- I have to pick up Mort at Tampa International Airport.
  （我得去坦帕國際機場接莫特。）

H) 特指的行業名稱要 the

1

✗ She works in service industry.

特別指稱某行業時要加 the

✓ She works in the service industry.

她在服務業工作。

the service industry 告訴我們具體是哪一個 industry

請參見第 435 頁第 K 點（industry 泛指不要 the ，特指要 the）。

I) 姓氏的複數形式要 the

1

✗ Kay's sister has been hiking and camping with Browns for ten days.

表示某一家人，要在專有名詞（姓）前加 the（the + 複數姓）

✗ Kay's sister has been hiking and camping with the Brown for ten days.

表示某一家人，要在專有名詞（姓）後加一個 s

✓ Kay's sister has been hiking and camping with the Browns for ten days.

凱的妹妹跟布朗一家徒步旅行和露營已經十天了。

the Browns 指 Brown 一家（the Brown family）。在專有名詞（姓）後加一個 s，在專有名詞（姓）前加 the（the + 複數姓），表示某一家人

2 ✗ Dwight had a great time at Johnsons' last night.

✓ Dwight had a great time at the Johnsons' last night.

昨晚杜威特在詹森家過得很愉快。

這裡的「the + 複數姓所有格形式」（the Johnsons'）表示省略了 home、house 或 apartment 等

注意：複數姓前必須要 the，無論這個複數姓是所有格形式還是一般形式，都不能刪除 the。

- the Wangs = the Wang family（王家）
- at the Wilsons' = at the Wilsons' home (house, apartment, etc.)（在威爾森家）

文法加油站

用名字（first name）時，就不要 the

- at Mary's（在瑪麗家）
- at Mike's（在麥克家）
- Louise had a great afternoon at Annie's.（露易絲在安妮家過了一個非常愉快的下午。）

J) 表示樂器的名詞通常要 the

1 ✗ Lynn has started playing violin.

談到某人演奏某種樂器或某人演奏某種樂器的能力時，通常要加 the

✓ Lynn has started playing the violin.

琳恩開始學小提琴了。

美國人常在口語中省略 the，說 play piano 或 play the piano。但在正式語中，最好保留樂器前的 the。

- play the drum（打鼓）
- play the guitar（彈吉他）
- play the flute（吹笛子）

K) 政治機構名稱、著名的組織名稱、銀行名稱要 the

1 ⊗ BBC reported on the huge wind farm in the North Sea.
在著名的組織名稱前，通常要加 the。這類名稱縮寫時，仍要有 the

✓ The BBC reported on the huge wind farm in the North Sea.

英國廣播公司對北海巨大的風力發電廠做了報導。

2 ⊗ State Department will send Dan to Japan.
在政府部門、政治機構等的名稱前，通常要加 the

✓ The State Department will send Dan to Japan.

美國國務院要派遣丹去日本。

在銀行、著名的組織、政府部門、政治機構等的名稱前，通常要用 the。這類名稱縮寫時，仍要有 the（比如：the VOA、the BBC）。

(1) **Banks**：銀行的名稱前通常要 the

- the Development Bank of Singapore（新加坡發展銀行）
- the Toronto-Dominion Bank（多倫多道明銀行）

> ✓ 例外：
> - Bank of America（美國銀行）
> - Barclays Bank（柏克萊銀行）
> - Bank of China（中國銀行）

(2) **Famous organizations**：
著名組織名稱前要 the（包括縮寫名稱）

- the BBC (the British Broadcasting Corporation)（英國廣播公司）
- the Red Cross（紅十字會）
- the United Nations (the UN)（聯合國）
- the VOA (the Voice of America)（美國之音）
- the World Trade Organization (the WTO)（世貿組織）

(3) **Government departments/Political institutions**：
政府部門或政府機構的名稱前通常要 the（包括縮寫名稱）

- the New York City Police Department (the NYCPD)
（紐約市政府警察局）
- the CIA (the Central Intelligence Agency)（〔美國〕中央情報局）
- the U. S. Department of State（美國國務院）
- the U. S. Justice Department（美國司法部）
- the French Embassy（法國大使館）
- the House of Representatives（眾議院）
- the Library of Congress（國會圖書館）
- the Senate（參議院）
- the White House（白宮）
- the House of Commons 英式（下議院）
- the Labor Party 英式（工黨）
- the Ministry of Education（教育部）
- the Supreme Court（最高法院）

文法加油站

但如果縮寫的組織名稱可以讀成一個字時，就不用 the

- NATO [ˋneto] (the North Atlantic Treaty Organization)
（北大西洋公約組織）
- OPEC [ˋopɛk] (the Organization of Petroleum Exporting Countries)
（石油輸出國組織）
- UNICEF [ˋjunɪsɛf]（聯合國兒童基金會）
→ UNICEF 是 the United Nations International Children's Emergency Fund 的縮寫，而現在的全名是 the United Nations Children's Fund。

L) 公司名稱是否要 the ?

1

✗ Maggie says General Electric Company is good at developing new technology.

公司名稱裡含有 company 這個字，要加 the

✓ Maggie says the General Electric Company is good at developing new technology.

瑪姬說，美國通用電氣公司對發展科技很在行。

⑴ 如果公司名稱裡含有 company 這個字，就要用 the。

· the General Electric Company（美國通用電氣公司）

⑵ 如果公司名稱裡沒有 company 這個字，就不用 the。

· General Electric（通用電氣公司）
· General Motors（通用汽車）

⑶ 公司名稱是縮寫形式，不用 the。

· ABC（美國廣播公司）
· CBS（哥倫比亞廣播公司）
· CNN（美國有線電視新聞網）
· NBC（美國全國廣播公司）
· GE（美國通用電氣公司）
· IBM（國際商務機器公司）
· ICI（英國帝國化學工業公司）
· KLM（荷蘭皇家航空公司）

· ABC showed a movie about living under the sea.
（美國廣播公司播放了一部關於在海底生活的影片。）
· Was *Snow White* the first movie on HBO last night?
（《白雪公主》是昨晚美國 HBO 有線電視臺播放的第一部影片嗎？）

⑷ 注意公司名稱的縮寫形式與政府部門／政治機構的縮寫詞有區別。

(a) 政府部門／政治機構的縮寫詞如果不讀成一個字，就要用 the（the CIA）；讀成一個字，就不加 the（NATO）。

· I will go on a long vacation, and after that I'll go to work for the Federal Bureau of Investigation.
= I will go on a long vacation, and after that I'll go to work for the FBI. ——政府部門的縮寫詞，如不讀成一個字，要加 the
（我要度一個長假，然後就去美國聯邦調查局工作。）

(b) 而公司名稱的縮寫形式都不用 the。

· Penny and Rick stood under a huge wind turbine made by General Electric. ——公司名稱沒有 company 這個字，不用 the
= Penny and Rick stood under a huge wind turbine made by the General Electric Company. ——公司名稱含有 company 這個字，要用 the
= Penny and Rick stood under a huge wind turbine made by GE. ——公司名稱的縮寫形式，不用 the
（潘妮和瑞克站在一個由美國通用電氣公司製造的巨大風力發電機下面。）

M) at this time of the day

1

✗ It may take Kay an hour to get here at this time of a day. — at this time of the day 是固定片語，應該用定冠詞 the，不用不定冠詞 a

✓ It may take Kay an hour to get here at this time of the day.

✓ It may take Kay an hour to get here at this time of day. — 也可以在 day 的前面什麼冠詞也不加，而說 at this time of day

在這種時候，凱去那裡可能要花一小時的時間。

516 their/there/they're 他們的／那裡／他們是

1

✗ Both Claire and Sue dyed they're hair blue.

they are 的縮寫形式，與句意不符

✓ Both Claire and Sue dyed their hair blue.

克萊兒和蘇都把頭髮染成藍色。

they 的所有格，意思是「他（她、它）們的」

2

✗ Their both silly friends of Millie.

✓ They're both silly friends of Millie.

他們都是米莉傻乎乎的朋友。

(1) their 是 they 的所有格，意思是「他（她、它）們的」。

(2) they're 是 they are 的縮寫形式。

(3) there 與「地點」有關，意思是「在那裡」；也用於片語 there is/are/was/were 等中，表示「有……」。

- Claire and Sue wondered what their boss at the Great Ice Cream and Pizza Shop would say about their blue hair.
  （克萊兒和蘇納悶，不知道她們在「美味霜淇淋和披薩店」的老闆，會對她們的藍色頭髮說些什麼。）
- There was a lovely cheese pizza sitting there on the table when they arrived at work a little early.
  （她們提早到達上班地點，桌上有一個誘人的起司披薩。）
- Their boss gave them the pizza and didn't even look at their blue hair.
  （她們的老闆給了她們披薩，對她們藍色的頭髮看都沒有看一眼。）

517 though/although 雖然；不過／雖然

1 ✗ Snow is not predicted; we expect some rain, although.

though 作副詞（通常放在句尾），意思是「不過；可是」時，不能用 although 替換。此時 though 的意思是 however，而不是 although

✓ Snow is not predicted; we expect some rain, though.

沒有預報會下雪；不過，我們預料會下雨。

⑴ **though** 當**連接詞**時，意思是「雖然」，可以與 although 互換。

⑵ **though** 作**副詞**（通常放在句尾），意思是「不過；可是」的時候，就不能用 although 來替換。在這種情況下，though 的意思是 however，而不是 although。

連接詞

- Though/Although our city is old, it is very pretty.
（雖然我們的城市很古老，但卻很美麗。）

- Ann: I'll see that show in Chicago. 副詞
Dan: Aren't Chicago musicals expensive, though?
（安：我要在芝加哥看那場演出。
丹：不過，芝加哥的音樂劇不是很昂貴嗎？）

518 thousand

請參見 hundred。

519 through/to 從……到

1 美式 From June 27 through July 2, I'll be with Lee in Italy.

在美式英語裡意思是「從……直到」，用來確認「最後提及的日期、頁碼等」包括在內，像本例句就包括 7 月 2 號

英式 From June 27 to July 2, I'll be with Lee in Italy.

英式英語用 to 來表示「從……直到」，以及「最後提及的日期、頁碼等」包括在內

從六月二十七號到七月二號，我和李會在義大利。

英式

· Olive will be in New York City from the third to the ninth inclusive.（從三號到九號，奧莉芙將在紐約市。）

英式英語有時為了強調「最後提及的日期、頁碼等」也包括在內，會用 inclusive 補充

520 till 直到……為止

1

❌ I'd like to walk till the riverside.

till/until 作介系詞時，只能與時間連用，不與地點連用

✅ I'd like to walk to the riverside.

✅ I'd like to walk as far as the riverside.

✅ I'd like to walk until/till I reach the riverside.

我想要一直走到河邊。

這句的 until 或 till 是連接詞，後面接子句

(1) till/until 作介系詞時，只能與時間連用，而不與地點連用。

(2) till 沒有 until 正式，在書面語中也沒有 until 常見。

介 till/until+ 時間

· Kay is going to stay with my family till/until the end of May.
（凱要和我家人住在一起，一直到五月底。）

521 time 時間或次數表達法

1

❌ Three years are a long time to wait for Amy to get out of the army.

three years 雖然是複數名詞，但在這裡被看成是一個整體單位（a total amount），動詞應該用單數

✅ Three years is a long time to wait for Amy to get out of the army.

等待艾咪退伍要三年，等待的時間太長了。

2

❌ Three years has passed since the last time I talked to Dee.

這句的 three years 與上面的不同，不是指一個整體單位，而是指一組個體單位（a number of individual units），指「分開的三個年份：一年、兩年、三年過去了」，所以動詞要用複數

✅ Three years have passed since the last time I talked to Dee.

自從我上次和蒂說過話後，已經過了三年了。

文法加油站

① 表達 periods of time（一段時間）、amounts of money（一定數量的錢）或 quantities（數量）的主詞代表 a total amount（**一個整體數字**），要用單數動詞。 當這些主詞代表 a number of individual units（**一組個體單位**）時，就用複數動詞。

② 請參見 numerical expressions 、and/plus 和 subject-verb agreement 的第 N 點（測量）。

一個整體單位

- That $2,000 was spent by Mat.（那兩千美金是麥特花掉的。）

一組個體單位

- Sam knows that two hundred million dollars have already been spent on this dam.
（山姆知道，修建這個水壩已經花了兩百萬美金了。）

3

✖ Janet knows it is a matter of time before that huge comet hits our planet.

片語 a matter/question of time 通常要與 **just/only** 連用。其意思是，某事肯定要發生，只不過不知道何時發生而已，「只是取決於……時間」

✔ Janet knows it is just a matter of time before that huge comet hits our planet.

珍妮特知道，那顆巨大的彗星遲早要撞擊我們的行星。

4

✖ Louise had tried to quit smoking for four times before she died of lung disease.

當表達「做某事四次、五次、二十次等」時，不與 for 連用

✔ Louise had tried to quit smoking four times before she died of lung disease.

露易絲死於肺病之前戒過四次菸。

It is (high/about) time + (that) 子句，子句裡要用**過去式**；這是一種**假設語氣**，其含意是**現在或將來**，而不是過去；表達的意思是「某事應該現在發生」

5 ✗ It is time our nation do more to defend this world civilization.

✓ It is time our nation did more to defend this world civilization.

= It is time for our nation to do more to defend this world civilization.

我們國家採取更多行動來保衛世界文明的時候到了。

6 ✗ Is this the third time Monique falls down this week?

It's the first/second/third/last, etc. , time + (that) 子句，子句通常要用**現在完成式**

✓ Is this the third time Monique has fallen down this week?

這是莫妮可這週第三次摔倒嗎？

文法加油站

其他類似 the first time + 子句（完成式）的句型

✗ This is one of the loveliest and greenest valleys I ever see.

✓ This is one of the loveliest and greenest valleys I've ever seen.
（這是我見過最美麗、最綠油油的山谷之一。）

當先行詞前有**形容詞最高級**修飾，或有**序數詞**修飾，或有 **last**、**only** 等字修飾時，形容詞子句中的動詞要用**完成式**形式。在下列表達方式後面要用完成式：

- This/That/It is the best/worst/most . . .
- This/That/It is the last/first/second/third . . .
- This/That/It is the only . . .
- "Night of the White Knight" is the second story Dwight has placed on his website.
（《白衣騎士的夜晚》是杜威特放在他自己網站上的第二篇故事。）

522 timetable/schedule/itinerary
時刻表／日程安排表／旅行計畫

1 ❌ As the Dime Store Manager, I always have a busy <u>timetable</u> during Christmastime.

> 無論是美式英語還是英式英語，timetable 都不用來指人們的行程安排

✅ As the Dime Store Manager, I always have a busy <u>schedule</u> during Christmastime.

> 計畫表、行程安排表：美式和英式都用 schedule

身為「廉價商店」的經理，耶誕節期間我的日程安排總是滿滿的。

課程表	飛機、火車、公車等的時刻表	計畫表、行程安排
美式 schedule	常用 schedule，也可以用 timetable	都用 schedule
英式 timetable	timetable	

- a class schedule（課程表）美式
- a work schedule（工作預定表）美式 英式
- behind schedule（行程落後）美式 英式
- Mabel found out her train's departure time in this timetable. 美式 英式

 （美博在這張時刻表上找到了她的火車出發時間。）

- You'll find out the ship's schedule after she gets a full load of fuel. 美式

 （當船裝滿了燃料後，你就會查到船的時刻表。）

- If everything follows the schedule, we'll leave for the moon this afternoon. 美式 英式

 （如果一切都按照計畫表進行，我們今天下午就能去月球。）

2

✗ Mary gave Joe his schedule for his sales trip around Mexico.

當我們談論旅行計畫（travel plan），尤其是被推薦的路程，要用 itinerary

✓ Mary gave Joe his itinerary for his sales trip around Mexico.

瑪麗把喬在墨西哥巡迴銷售的旅程計畫給了他。

- depart from one's **itinerary**（改變自己的旅行計畫）

523 tired/tiring 請參見 excited/exciting。

524 to 請參見 between . . . and/between . . . to、through/to。

525 toast 吐司

1

✗ Meg wants two pieces of burnt bread and a hard-boiled egg.

用 burnt bread 來表示「烤麵包」是典型的中式英語

✗ Meg wants two toasts and a hard-boiled egg.

烤麵包（吐司）的英文是 toast，是**不可數名詞**，沒有複數形式，也不能用不定冠詞 a 修飾

✓ Meg wants two pieces of toast and a hard-boiled egg.

梅格想要兩片吐司和一個煮熟的雞蛋。

不可數名詞，沒有複數形式，也不能用不定冠詞 a 修飾

- My cat ate most of the buttered **toast**.
（那片塗奶油的吐司被我的貓吃了一大半。）

526 toilet 請參見 bathroom/toilet/restroom。

527 too/also 請參見 also/too 和 also/too/either。

528 too/very 太過於……／很……

1

✗ My friend Lily is too lovely.

✓ My friend Lily is very lovely.

「too + adj.」帶否定意義，意味「有毛病；有問題」。稱讚朋友可愛要用 very lovely

我的朋友莉莉很可愛。

(1) 當你真心稱讚你的朋友可愛，用 very lovely ，而不要用 too lovely。

(2) too + adjective 意味著「有毛病；有問題」。

含否定意義

- Mort thinks this mini-skirt is too short.
（莫特覺得這條迷你裙太短了。）

含肯定意義

- "That dress is very cute," thought Tess.
（黛絲心想：「那件洋裝很漂亮。」）

529 too much/much too 太過於……

1

✗ Amos is always too much generous on Christmas.

too much 不能用在形容詞前，要放在名詞前或動詞後面

✓ Amos is always too generous on Christmas.

too + 形容詞

✓ Amos is always much too generous on Christmas.

much too 用來強調，用在形容詞或副詞前面

阿摩司總是在耶誕節時非常地慷慨。

- much too young〔形 前面〕（太年輕了）
- much too soon〔副 前面〕（太快了）
- too much work〔名 前面〕（太多的工作）
- cry too much〔動 後面〕（哭得太多）

too much 放在名詞 noise 前

- I can't sleep because there is **too much noise** from the boys.
（我睡不著覺，因為那群男孩的吵鬧聲太大了。）

too much 修飾 talks，放在該動詞後面

- Jane **talks too much** about her jewels and jet airplane.
（珍大談她的首飾和她的噴射機。）

530 torch/flashlight 手電筒

1 美式 I got the flashlight that was on the porch and gave it to Scot.

英式 I got the torch that was on the porch and gave it to Scot.

我從門廊上拿到手電筒，然後把它交給了史考特。

531 total 總數

請參見 couple。

532 toward/towards 朝（某方向）

1 美式 I didn't want to swim anymore, so I swam toward the shore. 美式常用

英式 I didn't want to swim anymore, so I swam towards the shore.

我不想再游了，於是朝著岸邊游去。

(1) 美語更常用 toward，而英式英語用 towards。

(2) 類似的還有 forward、backward、onward、downward 等，在美語中都不加 s。

- June asked, "Will humans soon move outward toward Neptune?"（茱恩問：「人類很快就要向外朝著海王星發展嗎？」）
- She looked backward at the surface of the sea.（她回頭看著海面。）

533 traffic 交通

1 ✗ Rush hour traffics are heavy in both London and Rome. traffic 是不可數名詞，沒有複數 s，也沒有冠詞 a

✓ Rush hour traffic is heavy in both London and Rome.

在上下班尖鋒時間，倫敦和羅馬的交通都很擁擠。

「交通擁擠」可用 heavy 來修飾。「不擁擠」可用 light 來修飾。

· heavy traffic（交通擁擠）　　· light traffic（交通不擁擠）

· rush hour traffic（〔上下班時〕交通擁擠時間；尖峰時間）

不可數名詞，沒有複數 s，也沒有冠詞 a

· Stick Avenue was closed to **traffic**.（「枝條大街」禁止通行了。）

534 trash

請參見 rubbish/trash。

535 travel 旅行

1

非正式 Do you and Bing love travel?

正式 Do you and Bing love traveling?

正式 Do you and Bing love to travel?

你和賓喜歡旅行嗎？

如果泛指喜歡旅行，要用「love traveling」或「love to travel」，而不用名詞 travel

536 travel/trip 旅行

1

❌ In July I am going on a business travel to Cairo.

不可數名詞，不能與冠詞 a 連用；但可以用作複數（travels）

✅ In July I am going on a business trip to Cairo.

我七月要去開羅出差。

可數名詞，可加冠詞 a

· go on a trip/take a trip（去旅行）

· ten days of travel by train/ten days of travelling by train/ten days' travel by train（搭火車旅行十天）

· on her travels abroad = on her trips abroad（在她出國旅行時）

· In July I am going to have six days of travel by train from Moscow to Shanghai.
（七月我要搭火車旅行六天，從莫斯科到上海。）

537 trouble 麻煩、煩惱

1

✗ I thought all my **troubles** were over, and then Sue Hubble caused me new troubles.

指「煩惱、煩心的事」，用複數 troubles

✓ I thought all my troubles were over, and then Sue Hubble caused me new trouble.

指「麻煩」，用於固定片語「cause trouble」，是不可數名詞，不可加 s

我以為我所有的煩惱就此消失了，結果蘇・哈伯給我製造了新麻煩。

(1) 指「煩惱、憂慮」（worries、difficulties）；社會動亂、衝突（civil disorder, disturbance, or conflict），常用複數 troubles，比如：labor troubles（勞工紛爭）。

(2) trouble 指「不便；折磨；困難；麻煩；打擾；苦痛」時，是不可數名詞。

(3) 不可數名詞 trouble 常用於下列片語：

- ask for trouble/look for trouble（找麻煩）
- be in (big/deep/serious) trouble（深深陷入麻煩之中）
- get somebody into trouble（使某人陷入麻煩）
- be in trouble with somebody（與某人有麻煩）
- keep/stay out of trouble（迴避麻煩）
- little/much trouble doing something（做某事不費力／很費力）
- cause/make trouble for somebody/something（給某人／某事製造麻煩）
- run into trouble（遭遇麻煩）

這裡的 trouble 是不可數名詞，用於片語「little trouble doing something 做某事不費力」，a 與 trouble 沒有關係，而是與 little 構成片語 a little

- Brent had a little trouble getting his dog to sleep outside the tent.（要讓狗睡在帳篷外面，讓布蘭特傷了點腦筋。）

指 health problems（苦痛；疾病）

- "Do you have any of back, heart, or stomach trouble?" asked Sue.（蘇問：「你有任何背部、心臟或腸胃的毛病嗎？」）

指 worries（煩惱）

- Ann thought, "I could tell my troubles to Dan."（安想：「我可以把我的煩惱告訴丹。」）

538 trousers/pants 褲子

1 美式 Amos and his aunts wore red pants last Christmas.
英式 Amos and his aunts wore red trousers last Christmas.
去年耶誕節，阿摩司和他的姨媽們都穿著紅褲子。

	pants	trousers
美式	長褲	在「正式場合」穿的長褲
英式	underpants 的縮寫，意思是「內褲」	長褲

2 ✗ Is your pants made in France?
英語裡，pants 用作複數，在句中作主詞時，動詞要用複數
✓ Were your pants made in France?
你的褲子是法國製嗎？

(1) 在一些語言中，「trousers、pants」是單數，但在英語裡，「trousers、pants」用作複數，在句中作主詞時，動詞要用複數。

(2) 如果想要表達單數意思，就用 a pair of trousers/pants（一條褲子）。

(3) 類似的字還有：

- underpants（內褲）
- shorts（短褲）
- blue jeans（藍色牛仔褲）
- glasses（眼鏡）
- panties（女用內褲）

539 truck/lorry 卡車；貨車

1 美式 Lori told Bud that her truck was stuck in the mud.
美國人駕駛 truck
英式 Lori told Bud that her lorry was stuck in the mud.
英國人駕駛 lorry
蘿麗告訴巴德，她的卡車陷在泥漿裡。

540 trunk/boot （汽車車尾的）行李箱

1 美式 I'm going to shoot some water at the skunk on my trunk. —— 美國人用 trunk 表示「車尾行李箱」

英式 I'm going to shoot some water at the skunk on my boot. —— 英國人用 boot 表示「車尾行李箱」

我要對著車尾行李箱上的那隻臭鼬射一些水。

541 try not to/try to not 試著不……

1 ✖ When it is cold, Ted tries to not lose any heat from his head.

儘量不要把不定詞拆開。動詞不定詞的否定式是在 to 前面加 not 構成「not + to」

✔ When it is cold, Ted tries not to lose any heat from his head.

天冷時，泰德努力不讓頭部失溫。

(1) 嚴格來説，應該盡量不要把不定詞拆開。動詞不定詞的否定式是在 to 前面加 not 構成「**not + to**」。

(2) 在非正式的場合下，**try to not lose** 也許可以被人們接受。實際上，這類錯誤變得如此常見，聽起來似乎就順耳了。不過，在正式文體中，還是儘量不要違反文法規則（try **not to break** the grammar rule）。

(3) 請參見 infinitive。

542 try to do/try doing 努力／試試

try to do something 意思是「努力或試圖做某事」，與句意不符

1 ✖ Larry tried to send Mary a poem every day, but she still wanted to marry Harry.

try doing something 意思是「嘗試、試驗做某事，看看會有什麼結果」，這個意思不能用 try to do

✔ Larry tried sending Mary a poem every day, but she still wanted to marry Harry.

賴瑞試著每天寄一首詩歌給瑪麗，但她仍然想嫁給哈利。

(1) try to do something：意思是「努力或試圖做某事」。有時也可以用 try doing something 來表達這個意思，但更常用不定詞 try to do。

(2) try doing something：意思是「嘗試、試驗做某事，看看會有什麼結果」。這個意思只用 try doing something，不能用 try to do。

努力、試圖保持

- Sue, just be honest and **try to stay** calm during your interview.（蘇，當妳在面試時，只需要誠實，並且儘量保持鎮靜。）

543 try and/try to 試圖

1

非正式 I'll try and smile at Kyle for a while.

正式 I'll try to smile at Kyle for a while.

我會努力對著凱爾微笑一會。

書面語中要用 try to do something，不用 try and do something

544 turn someone on 使人興奮

1

✗ "Andrew, will you give me your painting of the kangaroo?"—"Sure, Lily, if that's what turns you on."

指「激起某人對某物感興趣」、「使某人興奮起來」。此對話是關於「想要一幅袋鼠畫」，用 turn somebody on 不恰當

「安德魯，把你的那幅袋鼠畫給我行嗎？」
——「當然可以，莉莉，只要能使妳興奮起來。」

✓ "Andrew, will you give me your painting of the kangaroo?"—"Sure, Lily, if that will make you happy."

「安德魯，把你的那幅袋鼠畫給我行嗎？」
——「當然可以，莉莉，只要能使妳高興起來。」

(1) turn someone on 可以指「激起某人對某物感興趣」、「使某人激動起來」。

(2) turn someone on 在美式英語中，常指「引起某人性興奮、性激動」。這是五十年代開始的美國俚語，而現在已經變成常見口語。

(3) 反義詞是 turn somebody off，也是有兩種含意：
a) 使某人對某事失去了興趣；b) 使某人失去性興奮。

545 type of 請參見 kind of。

U

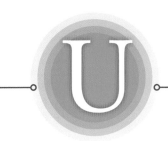

546 uncle 叔叔（伯父、姑夫、姨夫、舅父）

1

❌ Uncle Smith is coming for dinner tonight.

Smith 是姓。用英語稱呼叔叔、姑姑、姨媽時，應該「Uncle/Aunt + 名」（first name）

✅ Uncle Dwight is coming for dinner tonight.

杜威特叔叔今晚要來吃晚餐。

用英語稱呼叔叔、姑姑、姨媽時，應該「**Uncle/Aunt + 名**」（first name）。因為你家裡也許有好幾個叔叔或姑姑（而他們都同姓），用「Uncle/Aunt + 名」才清楚你提及的是哪一個叔叔或姑姑。

- Aunt Ann（安姑姑）
- Uncle Jerry（傑瑞叔叔）

文法加油站

稱謂

① 中西方的區別

(a) 我們稱呼和自己父母同輩的人為「叔叔、阿姨」（非親戚），並在前面加上那人的姓。比如：李阿姨、王叔叔、張伯伯。

(b) 在西方，人們只稱呼自己的親戚為「uncle, aunt 」，並在後面加上名。

- Aunt Lynn is Mom's identical twin. She is married to Dad's elder brother, Uncle Reed.
  （琳恩姨媽是我媽媽的雙胞胎妹妹。她嫁給了我爸爸的哥哥，里德伯伯。）

② 應該大寫「Uncle/Aunt/Cousin + 名」嗎？

(a) 當 uncle、aunt 或 cousin 這幾個字與人名用在一起組成一個整體單位時，要大寫。

(b) 前面有所有格代名詞（比如：his Uncle Dwight、my Aunt Dawn、her Cousin Mary 等），uncle、aunt、cousin 通常也要大寫，因為 Uncle Dwight、Aunt Dawn、Cousin Mary 被看成是一個整體。

(c) 如果只是在描述家庭關係，前面有所有格代名詞時，就不必大寫 uncle、aunt、cousin。

在這裡，Cousin Ann 被看成是「一個整體」

· My Cousin Ann is in Japan.（我的安堂妹在日本。）

在這裡，cousin 這個字只表明家庭關係。可以把她看作是 Kay

· My cousin Kay may go to Norway at the end of May.
（我的堂妹，凱，五月底可能會去挪威。）

· I visited Uncle Dan in Japan.（我去日本探望了丹叔叔。）

必須大寫 Uncle

前面即使有 my 修飾，也可以大寫 Uncle，把 Uncle Dan 看作是一個整體

= I visited my Uncle Dan in Japan.（我去日本探望了我的丹叔叔。）

= I visited my uncle Dan in Japan.（我去日本看望了我的叔叔，丹。）

前面有 my，可以小寫 uncle。uncle 在句中只表明家庭關係

547 underwear 內衣褲；衛生褲

1

✗ Claire felt very cold, because she didn't wear her long winter underwears. —不可數名詞，沒有複數形式，也不和 an 連用

✓ Claire felt very cold, because she didn't wear her long winter underwear.

克萊兒感覺很冷，因為她沒有穿長衛生褲。

(1) underwear 是不可數名詞，沒有複數形式，也不和 an 連用。

(2) 其他類似的不可數名詞：

· menswear（男裝）
· footwear（鞋類）
· sportswear（運動服裝）

548 unique 獨一無二的

1 ✗ Monique says the American July 4th holiday is very unique.

unique 意思是「獨一無二的；獨特的；無可匹敵的」，表示絕對性。不能說什麼東西「more unique」、「less unique」或「very unique」

✓ Monique says the American July 4th holiday is unique.

莫妮可說，七月四日是美國特有的一個節日。

請參見 doublets/wordiness。

549 until

請參見 till。

550 use 用途

there is no use 後面應該接**動名詞** (in) doing something; it is of no use 才是接**不定詞** to do something

1 ✗ There is no use to look for that silly goose.

✓ There is no use looking for that silly goose.

✓ It's of no use to look for that silly goose.

尋找那隻蠢鵝沒有什麼用的。

(1) there's no use (in) doing something

= it's of no use to do something 做……沒有用

· There is no use complaining about all the snow covering Chicago.

= It is of no use to complain about all the snow covering Chicago.

（抱怨白雪覆蓋了芝加哥是沒有意義的。）

(2) 有人用 it is of no use + V-ing，但這不是常見的用法。

551 use/utilize/usage 使用／慣用法

1

✗ Mary makes good usage of her time when she is in the library.

意思是「（詞的）使用」，與句意不符

✓ Mary makes good use of her time when she is in the library.

意思是「使用」。「make use of」是固定片語，不要用 usage 來取代 use

在圖書館時，瑪麗充分利用她的時間。

⑴ utilize 和 use 都可以指「使用」。有些人傾向於用動詞 utilize 來取代 use，用名詞 utilization 來取代 use。但最好使用 use 這個簡單的字，沒必要用多音節詞 utilize 或 utilization。

⑵ usage 的意思是「習慣；慣用法；（詞的）使用」。

- Midge wrote a book about modern American English usage.（米姬寫了一本關於現代美語慣用法的書。）

552 used to/get (be) used to 曾經／習慣

A) used to do 過去常做某事

「used to + 原形動詞」這個片語沒有現在式（use to do），只有過去式（used to do）

1

✗ When I was a young woman, I use to climb Slim Mountain and swim across Lake Kim.

指「某事過去常發生；過去一向、過去曾（而現在不再）做某事」

✓ When I was a young woman, I used to climb Slim Mountain and swim across Lake Kim.

我還是年輕女子時，我時常攀登苗條山，游泳橫跨金姆湖。

used to+ 原形動詞：指「某事過去常發生；過去一向、過去曾（而現在不再）做某事」。

- My name is Roy, and when I was a little boy in France, I used to sing and dance with my Cousin Joy.
（我名叫羅伊，當我住在法國，還是一個小男孩時，我時常跟我的喬伊堂妹一起唱歌跳舞。）

文法加油站

used to 在美式英語與英式英語中用法不同

	疑問句	否定句
美式	did + 主詞 + use to	didn't use to
· Did Kay use to play basketball with Paul? （凱過去常和保羅一起打籃球嗎？） · Kim didn't use to smile at Jim.（金姆過去不常對吉姆微笑。）		
英式	used+ 主詞 + to	usedn't to
· Used Kay to play basketball with Paul? （凱過去常和保羅一起打籃球嗎？） · Kim usedn't to smile at Jim.（金姆過去不常對吉姆微笑。）		

used to 主要用在肯定句中，很少用在否定或疑問句中。上面的美語和英式英語的形式都顯得很笨拙，尤其是英式英語的形式。所以最好不要用疑問句和否定句的形式。

B) get/be used to (doing) something 習慣

1

✗ Kirk is use to hard work.

應該用形容詞 used

✓ Kirk is used to hard work.

意思是「習慣的、適應的」

柯克習慣辛勤地工作。

2

✗ Lily is not used to get up so early.

形容詞　介系詞，後面接**名詞**或 **V-ing** 形式，不能接不定詞

✓ Lily is not used to getting up so early.

莉莉不習慣那麼早起床。

get/be used to (doing) something：意思「習慣的、適應的」。在這個片語中的 used 是形容詞，to 是介系詞，後面接名詞或 V-ing 形式，不能接不定詞。

· It took Lulu more than a month to get used to living with Sue.（一個多月後，露露才適應了跟蘇在一起生活。）

文法加油站

be used to do 意為「被用來……」

· That amount of money **was used to pay** for the truckload of honey.

└─動詞 use 的過去分詞，在這裡用在被動語態裡

（那筆錢用來買了一貨車蜂蜜。）

553 usual/common 慣常的／常見的

1

✗ Erica is a very usual name in America.

└─指「通常的、慣常的」，與句意不符

✓ Erica is a very common name in America.

└─指「常見的」

在美國，艾芮卡是一個常見的名字。

common 指「常見的」，usual 指「通常的、慣常的」，比如：

· Tomorrow we will meet Grace at the usual time and place.

（明天我們要在老時間、老地方與葛蕾絲見面。）

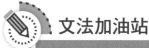

V

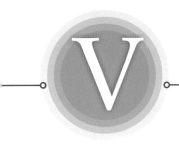

554 vacation/vocation 假期／職業

1

✗ Lily Nation is going to Russia for her summer <u>vocation</u>. —— 意思是「職業；行業」，與句意不符

✓ Lily Nation is going to Russia for her summer <u>vacation</u>. —— 意思是「假期；休假」

莉莉・納欣暑假時要去俄國。

請參見 holiday/vacation。

- Leading vacation tours is my vocation, and today Egypt is our destination.
  （我的職業是帶領假期旅遊團，今天埃及是我們的目的地。）

555 verb + 動名詞 (V-ing 形式)／verb + 不定詞

A) verb + 不定詞

1

✗ Dwight <u>promised</u> coming home before midnight. —— 後面要接不定詞作直接受詞，不接動名詞

✓ Dwight promised to come home before midnight.

杜威特答應要在半夜之前回家。

(1) 有些動詞後面要接不定詞作直接受詞（也可以稱這類不定詞為「不定詞補語」），不接 V-ing 形式（即不接動名詞）。

- Kind Tom deserves to live a good life.
  （善良的湯姆應該要有好的生活。）

· Mary had agreed to marry Henry, and then she found out he was already married to Sherry.
（瑪麗已經答應嫁給亨利，但後來她發現亨利已經跟雪瑞結了婚。）

⑵ 下面的動詞後面接不定詞為直接受詞。（動詞 + 不定詞）

- afford（負擔得起）
- agree（同意）
- appear（似乎）
- arrange（安排）
- ask（請求）
- attempt（試圖）
- beg（請求）
- begin（開始）
- can't bear（無法忍受）
- care（想要）
- choose（選擇）
- claim（聲稱）
- consent（同意）
- continue（繼續）
- dare（竟敢）
- decide（決定）
- demand（要求）
- deserve（應得）
- desire（渴望）
- expect（期待）
- fail（不能）
- forget（忘記）
- get（有機會；有可能）
- go on（繼續）
- happen（碰巧）
- hate（討厭）
- help（幫助）
- hesitate（猶豫）
- hope（希望）
- intend（想要）
- know how（知道如何）
- learn（學習）
- like（喜歡）
- love（熱愛）
- manage（設法做到）
- mean（意圖；打算）
- need（需要）
- neglect（忽視）
- offer（提議）
- plan（計畫）
- prefer（寧願）
- prepare（準備）
- pretend（假裝）
- promise（承諾）
- propose（提議）
- refuse（拒絕）
- regret（後悔）
- remember（記得）
- seem（好像）
- start（開始）
- swear（發誓要）
- tend（傾向）
- threaten（威脅）
- trouble（費心）
- try（努力）
- undertake（著手做；從事）
- volunteer（自願）
- vow（發誓）
- wait（等待）
- want（想要）
- wish（希望；想要）
- would like（想要）

注意：上面列的動詞若畫線者，也可以接 V-ing 形式。

· prefer to live in the countryside
= prefer living in the countryside（寧願在鄉村居住）

· I can't bear to see her suffer like that.（我不忍心見她如此受罪。）

· I can't bear being bossed around by a useless playboy.
（我受不了一個無能的花花公子對我發號施令。）

· This bill needs to be paid. 美式

This bill needs paying. 英式（這張帳單該繳費了。）

(3) 請參見 avoid、begin/start、consider、enjoy doing、forget、like to do/like doing、like to do/like doing/would like to do、practice、regret、remember、stop、suggest、try。

B) verb+ 動名詞

1

✗ Ming believes there are many things that parents can do to encourage to read.

✓ Ming believes there are many things that parents can do to encourage reading. —— encourage + 動名詞

敏相信，父母可以做許多事來鼓勵閱讀。

✓ Ming believes there are many things that parents can do to encourage their children to read. —— encourage + 受詞 + 不定詞

敏相信，父母可以做許多事來鼓勵他們的孩子閱讀。

(1) 有些動詞要接 V-ing 作直接受詞，不接不定詞。

· Mort finished writing his report.
（莫特寫完了報告。）

· Lance practices dancing whenever he has the chance.
（蘭斯只要有機會就要練習跳舞。）

(2) 下列單字是接 V-ing 形式（即動名詞）為直接受詞的常見動詞。

· admit（承認）
· anticipate（期望）
· appreciate（欣賞；感謝）
· avoid（迴避）
· begin（開始）
· burst out（突然……起來）
· can't help（忍不住）
· can't see（無法想像）
· can't stand（不能忍受）
· cease（停止）
· complete（完成）
· consider（考慮）
· contemplate（仔細考慮）
· continue（繼續）
· delay（延緩）
· deny（否認）
· detest（厭惡）
· *discuss（討論）
· dislike（討厭）
· don't mind（不介意；不反對）
· *encourage（鼓勵）
· endure（忍耐）

· enjoy（欣賞；喜歡）
· escape（逃避）
· excuse（原諒）
· face（正視）
· fancy（想像）
· feel like（想要）
· finish（完成）
· forget（忘記）
· forgive（原諒）
· get through（辦完）
· give up（放棄）
· go (fishing/swimming)（去釣魚／去游泳）
· hate（討厭）
· imagine（想像）
· involve（意味著）
· keep (on)（繼續）
· leave off（停止）
· like（喜歡）
· love（熱愛）
· mention（提到）
· mind（介意；反對）
· miss（錯過）
· postpone（延遲）
· practice（練習）
· prefer（寧願）
· put off（推遲）
· quit（放棄）
· recall（回想起）
· *recommend（推薦；勸告）
· *regret（懊悔；遺憾）
· remember（記得）
· *report（報告）
· resent（怨恨）
· resist（抵抗；忍耐）
· risk（冒……的風險）
· start（開始）
· *stop（停止）
· suggest（建議）
· tolerate（容忍）
· try（嘗試）

注意：上面列的動詞若畫線者，也可以接不定詞。表格裡帶有星號 * 的單字，請看下面解說。

(a) 動詞 **discuss** 後面可以接 how/why/whether 等 + 不定詞。

· discuss **how to avoid** mistakes（討論如何避免犯錯）
· discuss **doing** something（討論做某事）

(b) 動詞 **encourage** 和 **recommend** 也可以接「受詞 + 不定詞」結構（encourage/recommend **somebody to do** something）。

(c) 動詞 **regret** 也可以接「to say, to report」等，常用在宣布一個壞消息時。（請參見 regret）。

· I **regret to say** . . .（很遺憾，我得說……）宣布一個壞消息
· I **regret saying** . . .（我後悔說過……）為過去做過的某件事後悔

(d) 動詞 **report** 也可以接不定詞。不過，不定詞結構通常用在被動語態裡（somebody **is reported to do** something）。

(e) 動詞 **stop** 也可以接不定詞，表示目的。（請參見 stop。）

· stop **to do** something 表示「結束一個行為以便開始做另一事」
· stop **doing** something 表示「停止做某事」

(3) 請參見 avoid、begin/start、consider、enjoy doing、forget、like to do/like doing、like to do/like doing/would like to do、mind、practice、regret、remember、shopping、stop、suggest、try。

556 very/very much 非常、很

1

✗ I very liked those apes, but they stole my grapes.

very 用來修飾副詞或形容詞（very fast、very good、very happy、very sad），不用來修飾動詞（not "very liked"）

✓ I liked those apes very much, but they stole my grapes.

very much 用來表示「非常；很」，修飾動詞

我很喜歡那些黑猩猩，不過牠們偷了我的葡萄。

2

用來表示「非常；很」，修飾動詞，不可修飾形容詞 sad

✗ Those apes were very much sad, because I stopped them from taking your grapes.

用來修飾形容詞 sad

✓ Those apes were very sad, because I stopped them from taking your grapes.

那些大猩猩很傷心，因為我阻止了牠們拿走你的葡萄。

557 vital

請參見 important (essential/vital/necessary/desirable)。

558 voice 表達、說出

1

✗ My wife voiced out her anger about all the changes in her life.

及物動詞，意思是「用言語表達；說出」，後面不需要加 out

✓ My wife voiced her anger about all the changes in her life.

我妻子對她生活中的所有變化表示憤慨。

W

559 wage/salary 薪水

1

❌ Margo loves her job, but her monthly wage is a little bit low.

指因工人的勞動或提供的服務而付給工人的報酬，尤其指按小時、按日、按週計算的薪水，或是計件薪水

✅ Margo loves her job, but her monthly salary is a little bit low.

指年薪、季薪或月薪；通常專業人員（professionals）每月領取 salary

瑪歌喜歡她的工作，但她的月薪有點偏低。

- daily wage（日薪）
- hourly wage（時薪）
- weekly wage（週薪）
- minimum wage = living wage（夠維持生活的薪水）
- Mr. Page's workers get excellent wages.
（佩吉先生的員工獲得很不錯的薪水。）

560 wake me up

請參見 knock me up。

561 walk

請參見 a/an（需要冠詞 a/an）。

562 wash up/do one's dishes
洗（臉、手）／洗碗

1 美式 Mr. Cup will go for a walk after he finishes doing the dishes.

英式 Mr. Cup will go for a walk after he finishes washing up.

卡普先生洗完碗後就會去散步。

	洗臉和手	洗碗
美式	wash up	do one's dishes/do the dishes/ wash one's dishes
英式		wash up

美式英語，指「洗臉；洗手」

- Do we have to wash up and look neat before we can sit down to eat?
（我們必須先洗手洗臉，看起來乾淨後才能坐下來吃飯嗎？）

美式英語，指「洗碗」

- Pete will wash the dishes after we eat.
（我們吃完飯後，彼特會洗碗。）

英式英語，指「洗碗」

- Pete will wash up after we eat.（我們吃完飯後，彼特會洗碗。）

563 weather 天氣

1 ✗ Heather Plum hoped for a good weather.

weather 表示「天氣」，是不可數名詞。
不能用不定冠詞 a 來修飾，也不能用複數

✓ Heather Plum hoped for good weather.

✓ Heather Plum hoped for some good weather.

海瑟・普盧姆希望有（一些）好天氣。

564 weather/whether 天氣／是否

1

✗ Heather doesn't know weather she can go to Chicago.

名詞，意思是「天氣」

✓ Heather doesn't know whether she can go to Chicago.

連接詞，相當於 if，指「是否」，後面接子句

海瑟不清楚她是否能去芝加哥。

漁夫出海，特別要看天氣，「天氣」與「大海」有關聯，而 **weather** 和 **sea** 都包含有「**-ea**」，記住這一點，就可以區分 weather 和 whether 這兩個單字的拼寫。

- **Whether** Heather will go camping or not depends on the **weather.**（海瑟是否去露營，要看天氣狀況。）

565 weekend 週末

1

美式 Do you want to see the movie *Pretend* on the weekend?

英式 Do you want to see the film *Pretend* at the weekend?

週末你想去看電影《假裝》嗎？

(1) 美國人說 **on** the weekend，而英國人常說 **at** the weekend。

(2) 注意：美國人觀看 **movie**，而英國人卻觀看 **film**。

566 welcome 受歡迎的；歡迎

1

✗ You're welcomed to our Plum Store.

be **welcome** to a place 意思是「受歡迎的」，片語中的 welcome 是形容詞，不可用 welcomed

✓ You're welcome to our Plum Store.

歡迎光臨我們的梅子商店。

(1) be welcome to do something 或 be welcome to a place 意思是「受歡迎的」，片語中的 welcome 是形容詞。

(2) be welcomed by somebody 意思是「受到某人歡迎」，片語中的 welcomed 是動詞 welcome 的過去分詞，用於被動語態。

- a welcome guest（一位受歡迎的客人）
- Millie was warmly welcomed by Lily and Lee.（米莉受到了莉莉和李的熱情歡迎。）

567 what（用作關係代名詞）

1

關係代名詞 what 是主詞子句的動詞 said 和 did 的受詞

✗ What Miss Bliss said and did are none of your business.

句子的補語，是單數，因此句子的動詞應該用單數 is，與句子的補語一致

what 引導的子句在句中作主詞

✓ What Miss Bliss said and did is none of your business.

布利斯小姐說了什麼以及做了什麼，都不關你的事。

2

關係代名詞 what 是主詞子句的動詞 says 和 does 的受詞

✗ "What Sue says and does is two different things," said Omar.

句子的補語，是複數，因此句子的動詞應該用複數 are，與句子的補語一致

what 引導的子句在句中作主詞

✓ "What Sue says and does are two different things," said Omar.

歐馬說：「蘇言行不一致。」

文法加油站

以 what 引導的子句必須根據語義來決定其單複數

① 當 what 引導主詞子句，而 what 是子句動詞的受詞時：句子的動詞用單數還是複數主要取決於補語是單數還是複數。句子的補語是單數，句子的動詞總是用單數；句子的補語是複數，句子的動詞常用複數。

A B C D E F G H I J K L M N O P Q R S T U V W X Y Z

what 引導的主詞子句指的是單數名詞 a piece of apple pie，因此句子的動詞應該用單數 is

· What I want is a piece of apple pie.（我想要的是一片蘋果派。）

what 引導的主詞子句指複數名詞 pictures，因此句子的動詞用複數動詞 are

· What I want are some pictures of June exploring the moon.
（我想要的是一些茱恩探索月球的照片。）

② 比較：主詞不是 what 引導的主詞子句時，動詞要與主詞的單複數一致。

複數主詞 trucks 和複數動詞 are 搭配，不與單數補語 product 搭配

· Electric trucks are the only product we make.
（電動貨車是我們生產的唯一產品。）

568 what/which 什麼／哪一個；哪一些

A) 疑問限定詞／疑問形容詞

在具體的兩者之間（two cellphones）進行選擇，要用 which

1

✖ What cellphone is more useful—the one bought by Rich or the one bought by Mitch?

✔ Which cellphone is more useful—the one bought by Rich or the one bought by Mitch?

哪一支手機更有用——瑞奇買的那支，還是米奇買的那支？

(1) which 和 what 用作疑問限定詞（也稱「疑問形容詞」）時，可以修飾「人」，也可以修飾「物」。

(2) 通常 which 涉及的東西或人物比 what 更具體，因此在具體的兩者之間（two cellphones）進行選擇，要用 which。

(3) 如果要從未知的數目／數量中進行選擇，就用 what。

what 是疑問限定詞／疑問形容詞，提問時並沒有限定顏色讓對方選擇，選擇的顏色數目未知，對方需要從泛指的各種顏色中選出一種顏色（比如：米色、猩紅色、橄欖色、棕褐色、紅色、藍色）

· What color are Lulu's new shoes?
（露露的新鞋是什麼顏色？）

which 是疑問限定詞／疑問形容詞，提問時有限定的顏色讓你選擇，要求你從特指的三種顏色中做出選擇

· Which color do you prefer—red, green, or blue?
（你比較喜歡哪種顏色：紅色、綠色，還是藍色？）

B) 疑問代名詞

1
✗ What of you stole the candy from Mitch?
疑問代名詞 what 用來指「物」，不能指「人」。後面也不接 of

✓ Which of you stole the candy from Mitch?
疑問代名詞 which 通常指「物」，但如果後面有 of，也可以指「人」

你們當中哪一個偷了米奇的糖？

疑問代名詞 which	疑問代名詞 what
意思是「哪一個」，指「物」，如果後面接有 of，也可以指「人」（which of us、which of them）	意思是「什麼」，用來指「物」，不能指「人」
後面可以接介系詞 of	後面不接 of，不能說 what of you、what of these dolls

which 是疑問代名詞，指「物」（dolls）

- Which of these dolls did you get from Rich?
（這些玩偶中，哪一個是你從瑞奇那裡得到的？）

what 是疑問代名詞，指「事物」

- What did Kay say?（凱說了什麼？）

569 whatever 不管什麼

1
✗ Whatever Fay said and did were OK with Kay.
意思是 anything 或 everything。anything 和 everything 只能接**單數動詞** was
不要誤以為菲所說的和所做的是兩件事，就用複數動詞 were。把「說什麼以及做什麼」看作是一個整體

✓ Whatever Fay said and did was OK with Kay.
無論菲說什麼以及做什麼，凱都覺得可以。

由 whatever、whomever、whether、that 引導的子句作句子的主詞時，動詞要用單數

- Whatever Lulu enjoyed in school was also enjoyed by Sue.
（露露在學校喜歡什麼，蘇也同樣喜歡。）

570 when and where 何時與何地

1

✗ When and where Joe learned to fly that UFO are a secret that he has only shared with Margo.

這裡把 when 和 where（何時何地）看成是一個整體，而不是兩件事，應該用單數動詞

✓ When and where Joe learned to fly that UFO is a secret that he has only shared with Margo.

喬何時何地學會駕駛那個幽浮，是一個祕密，而這個祕密他只告訴過瑪歌。

571 which（作關係代名詞的 which）

1

語意不清 My package arrived on Friday, which Kay had mailed from Norway.

which 引導的形容詞子句與其修飾的字 package 分開了。子句靠近名詞 Friday，讓人不清楚子句究竟是修飾 package 還是 Friday ？從句型上看，好像 Kay 從挪威寄來的是 Friday

語意清楚 My package, which Kay had mailed from Norway, arrived on Friday.

which 引導的形容詞子句靠近所修飾的字 package，意思表達清楚。**關係代名詞引導的形容詞子句一定要靠近所修飾的先行詞**

凱從挪威寄給我的包裹星期五到達了。

- 請參見 that/which 的「文法加油站」的第 B 點（which 要放在恰當的位置）。

2

非正式語中的 which 是泛指 her apartment looks dirty 這一個事實

非正式 Her apartment looks dirty, which is why June will do a thorough cleaning today at noon.

正式 Her apartment looks dirty, and this is why June will do a thorough cleaning today at noon.

她的公寓看起來很髒，這就是為什麼茱恩要在今天中午做一次徹底的大掃除。

(1) 非正式語中常用 **which** 來泛指前面主要子句的整個意思，而不是修飾某一個先行詞。這裡的 which 是指 her apartment looks dirty 這一個事實。

(2) 正式語中 which 用來修飾特定的先行詞。比如上面第一個範例的 which 特指 package。又比如下面的例句：

- Ms. Bell is very fond of Chinese, which she speaks very well.

= Ms. Bell is very fond of Chinese, and she speaks it very well.

（貝兒女士很喜歡中文，她的中文講得很好。）

572 which/whose

（關係代名詞 which 和關係形容詞 whose）

1

不自然 The toy dinosaur the legs of which are broken is behind Roy.

指「物」時，用關係形容詞 whose 比用 of which 自然得多

自然 The toy dinosaur whose legs are broken is behind Roy.

斷了雙腿的那個玩具恐龍就在羅伊的身後。

whose 用作關係形容詞，修飾前面的先行詞，表示「……的」，可以指「人」，也可以指「物」。指「物」時，用關係形容詞 whose 比用 of which 自然得多。

whose 指「人」
（the princess Jade's）

- Jade is a bold princess, whose shoes are made of gold.

（潔德是一位大膽的公主，她的鞋是金子做的。）

573 who/whom 誰

1

口語 Who will Harry Bloom marry?

正式 Whom will Harry Bloom marry?

哈利・布盧姆要娶誰？

	主詞	受詞
正式用語	who	whom、whomever
口語／大眾用語	who	who 常可以取代 whom 作受詞
正式／非正式	whom 和 whomever 都不能作主詞	

2

❌ Lulu knows whom tried to kill you.

✅ Lulu knows who tried to kill you.

who 在受詞子句中作動詞 tried 的主詞，不是受詞，所以不能用 whom

露露知道是誰試圖殺害你。

無論在子句還是簡單句中，都要用 who 或 whoever 作主詞。

who 是子句的主詞

- Is that the woman who interviewed you?
（那位就是面試過你的女士嗎？）

whom 是子句動詞 introduced 的受詞

- Is that the woman whom you **introduced** to Harry Bloom?
（那位就是你介紹給哈利 · 布盧姆的女子嗎？）

whom 是介系詞 with 的受詞。介系詞可以直接放在 whom 前面，也可以與 whom 分開，放在後面

- That is the woman with whom Joe ate breakfast in the dining room.

= That is the woman whom Joe ate breakfast with in the dining room.
（那位就是與喬一起在餐廳吃早餐的女子。）

3

❌ To who did you give the key to the room?

在簡單句中，無論是口語或書面語，無論是正式或非正式，在介系詞後面都要用受格形式 whom（to whom、with whom 等）

✅ To whom did you give the key to the room?

這間房子的鑰匙你給了誰？

(1) 在**簡單句**中，無論是口語或書面語，無論是正式或非正式，在介系詞後面都要用受格形式 whom（to whom、with whom 等）。

(2) 在**從屬子句**中，要用 who 或 whoever 作主詞，即使它們出現在主要子句的介系詞後面。

名詞子句

- A free trip into space is given to whoever wins the annual Miami Rocket Plane Race.

整個名詞子句是介系詞 to 的受詞。whoever 是子句裡動詞 wins 的主詞，即使在介系詞後面，仍然要用 whoever 當主詞。正如你不可能說 to anyone whom wins the annual Miami Rocket Plane Race 一樣

形容詞子句，修飾先行詞 anyone

= A free trip into space is given to anyone who wins the annual Miami Rocket Plane Race.

（無論誰贏了邁阿密的年度火箭飛機大賽，都會獲得一次免費去太空旅行的機會。）

(3) 請參見下面 who ever/whoever/whomever。

574 who ever/whoever/whomever

究竟是誰／無論誰

1

✗ Will the president of our company be whomever marries Jill?

在子句中，動詞 marries 的主詞要用主格形式 whoever，而不能用受格形式 whomever

✗ Will the president of our company be who ever marries Jill?

who ever 意思是「究竟是誰」。在 who ever 中，ever 是副詞，用來強調；who ever 不用來引導名詞子句

✓ Will the president of our company be whoever marries Jill?

（引導名詞性子句）無論誰；任何人

無論誰娶了吉兒，他就將擔任我們公司的總裁嗎？

who ever 意思是「究竟是誰」。在 who ever 中，ever 是副詞，用來強調。

- "Who ever said I had all the answers?" Lulu asked Sue.
  （「究竟是誰說我知道所有的答案？」露露問蘇。）
- "Who ever can it be?" asked Sue.（蘇問：「那究竟會是誰呢？」）

介系詞 to 的受詞易誤用為受格 whomever。實際上，介系詞 to 的受詞是整個名詞子句：whoever asks for one。而子句的主詞應該用主格形式 whoever。主詞永遠都要用 who 或 whoever

2

✗ Give a picture of the sun to whomever asks for one.

✓ Give a picture of the sun to whoever asks for one.

= Give a picture of the sun to anyone who asks for one.

無論誰想要一張太陽的照片，就給他／她一張。

who 引導形容詞子句，修飾先行詞 anyone；who 是形容詞子句的主詞

· The Green Environment King is usually selected **by whomever** we elect as the Green Environment Queen.

整個子句是介系詞 by 的受詞。
whomever 是子句裡動詞 elect 的受詞

= The Green Environment King is usually selected **by** the **woman whom** we elect as the Green Environment Queen.

引導一個形容詞子句，修飾先行詞 woman；
whom 是子句中 elect 的受詞

（綠色環境國王通常是由我們選為綠色環境皇后的女子來選定。）

575 who's/whose ……是誰／誰的

1

✗ Claire, whose that young man over there?

代名詞所有格形式，指「誰的」，與句意不符

✓ Claire, who's that young man over there?

who is 的縮寫詞，符合句意

克萊兒，那邊那位年輕男子是誰？

2

✗ Who's shoes are prettier than Sue's?

who is 的縮寫詞。本句句意指「誰的」，應該用代名詞所有格形式 whose

✓ Whose shoes are prettier than Sue's?

誰的鞋比蘇的鞋還漂亮？

(1) who's 是 who is 或 who has 的縮寫詞。

(2) whose 是代名詞所有格形式。

· Who's going to tell me whose robot threw away my shoes?
（誰要告訴我，是誰的機器人把我的鞋扔掉了？）

· Who's going to tell me whose statues have beautiful tattoos?
（誰要告訴我，誰的雕像刻有美麗的花紋？）

576 will 將會（縮寫形式 'll 的用法）

1
非正式 When'll you see Ben?
正式 When will you see Ben?
你何時會去看班？

(1) 'll 是 will 的縮寫形式，通常用於以下人稱代名詞：
- I'll = I will
- we'll = we will
- he'll = he will
- you'll = you will
- she'll = she will
- they'll = they will
- it'll = it will
- who'll = who will

(2) 在正式文體中，'ll 通常不和名詞和其他代名詞連用（比如 that'll、this'll、when'll、there'll）。

(3) 縮寫形式 're、've、'd 的用法和 'll 的用法一樣。下面例句中的縮寫體在非正式用語中是可以的，但在正式用語中需要迴避。

2
非正式 Where're you going with Claire?
正式 Where are you going with Claire?
你跟克萊兒要去哪裡？

3
非正式 Where've you and Gwen been?
正式 Where have you and Gwen been?
你和葛雯去過哪裡？

4
非正式 That'd be good.
正式 That would be good.
那很好啊。

577 will/shall 將（用於單純的未來式）

1
美式 I will be home by noon.
英式 I shall be home by noon.
我中午以前會回家。

從前無論在英國還是在美國，學校都教學生當表示單純的未來式時，第一人稱必須用 I shall 和 we shall。然而語言在不斷進化，隨著時代的演變，shall 也就逐漸被 will 所代替。特別是在美國，表示未來式的 shall 幾乎完全被 will 所代替，甚至當今的英國人也越來越少用 shall 了。

文法加油站

shall 的現代用法

shall 在一些問句中依然和 I/we 用在一起，尤其是當「提議」或「提出建議」的時候。

- Shall I make a pizza for Jake?（我做一個披薩給傑克好嗎？）
- Shall we dance and enjoy this evening in France?
（我們來跳舞，盡情享受在法國的這一晚上好嗎？）

578 will/would 將、會

句型「believe + (that) + 從屬子句」中，如果動詞是現在式，「that + 子句」裡要用 will，不用 would

1

✗ Scot believes that global warming is a big problem and that the sea level would rise a lot.

✓ Scot believes that global warming is a big problem and that the sea level will rise a lot.

史考特認為，全球暖化是一個大問題，海平面將大幅度地升高。

- 請參見 tense choice。

2

✗ I hope Vance would enjoy France.

句型「hope + (that) + 從屬子句」中，如果動詞是現在式，「that + 子句」裡要用 will，不用 would

✓ I hope Vance will enjoy France.

我希望萬斯會喜歡法國。

句型「I/we, etc. , **would be grateful** if you could/would . . .」的意思是「如果你能／願意……，我／我們會非常感激的」。這個句型要用 **would**，不用 will

3 ✗ I will be grateful if you would explain why Jane is going to leave Spain.

✓ I would be grateful if you would explain why Jane is going to leave Spain.

如果你向我解釋茱恩為什麼打算離開西班牙，我會很感激的。

579 wish 希望、但願

1 非正式 英式 I wish I was in Spain with Jane.

wish 表達一種願望，當這種願望與現在或未來事實不一樣時，子句裡要用**過去式動詞**，be 動詞要用 were，英式非正式可以用 was

正式 I wish I were in Spain with Jane.

但願我和珍一起在西班牙。

當 wish 所表達的願望與未來事實不一樣時，子句裡要用**過去式動詞** could

2 ✗ I wish I can get Louise to quit smoking before she gets a deadly disease.

✓ I wish I could get Louise to quit smoking before she gets a deadly disease.

但願我能使露易絲戒菸，以免她罹患致命的疾病。

wish 表達的願望與過去事實不一樣時，子句裡要用**過去完成式**（had + 過去分詞）

3 ✗ I wish I did not say that to Trish.

✓ I wish I had not said that to Trish.

當我們為過去所做過的事情或者過去還沒有做過的事情感到懊悔或失望時，我們就要用「wish + 子句（had done something）」

但願我沒有對翠西說過那些話。

文法加油站

由 I wish、she wishes 等開始的句子，後面的從屬子句用假設語氣的動詞

① 如果子句表示現在（present time），動詞要用過去式。

現在事實：Omar does not know that movie star.

- Omar wishes he knew that movie star.
（歐馬希望他認識那位電影明星。）

② 如果子句表示過去（past time），動詞要用過去完成式。

過去事實：I told that lie.

- I wish I had never told that lie.（但願我從來沒有撒過那個謊。）

③ 如果子句表示未來（future time），動詞要用 could/would + 原形動詞，不要用 can/will。

未來事實：I will not be able to visit Mars and the planets of a thousand stars.

- I wish I could visit Mars and the planets of a thousand stars.
（但願我能參觀火星，還能參觀成千個行星。）

④ 當我們用表達願望的假設語氣時，be 動詞用 were，但英式非正式也可以用 was

現在事實：Joe is not on that UFO.

- Joe wishes he were on that UFO.
（喬但願他就在那架幽浮上面。）

580 word order 語序

1

✗ Why you don't like Sue?

✓ Why don't you like Sue?

你為什麼不喜歡蘇？

在直接疑問句中，要把（情態）助動詞或連綴動詞（比如 do、have、be、can、will）放在主詞前面

2

在間接疑問句中，主詞 my birthday 應該要出現在動詞 is 前面，與直述句的語序一樣，也不要用問號

✗ Liz wants to know when is my birthday?

✓ Liz wants to know when my birthday is.

莉茲想知道我的生日是哪一天。

在間接疑問句中，助動詞 will 不要放在主詞前，也不要用問號

3 ❌ Lynn wants to know how long will it take to go by bus from Vienna to Berlin?

✅ Lynn wants to know how long it will take to go by bus from Vienna to Berlin.

間接疑問句中的主詞出現在助動詞或主要動詞前面。實際上這是帶疑問詞的直述句，而不是真正意義上的疑問句

琳恩想知道，從維也納搭公車到柏林要多久時間。

4 ❌ Under no circumstances you should go inside that UFO.

如果句子是以一個否定詞或含有否定意義的字開始，主詞和（助）動詞必須交換位置（should you），即用倒裝結構

✅ Under no circumstances should you go inside that UFO.

無論在什麼情況下，你都絕對不能進入那架幽浮。

請參見 not only . . . but also . . . 的「文法加油站」（倒裝結構）。

581 work 工作

片語 go to work（上班），不要插入 my、your、his 等

1 ❌ Ray goes to his work on foot every day.

✅ Ray goes to work on foot every day.

雷每天步行去上班。

582 work/job 工作

1 ❌ Bob has a good work.

work 的意思不是職業，而是「勞動；作業」（labor），是不可數名詞，不與 a 連用

✅ Bob has a good job.

每天做同樣的工作是 job「職業」

鮑伯有份好工作。

work 的意思不是職業，而是「勞動；作業」（labor）。你可以今天完成了一個 work 後，明天開始做另一個 work。work 指「勞動；作業」時，是不可數名詞，不與 a 連用。

- June will finish her work by noon.
  （茱恩要在中午前完成她的工作。）

583 work for/work in 在……工作

1 非正式 Penny works in a solar power company.

正式 Penny works for a solar power company.

當告訴別人關於你的雇主時，用 **for**

潘妮在一家太陽能發電公司工作。

當表達「具體在公司某部門工作」時，用 **in**

- Kitty **works in the English department** at Yale University.
  （姬蒂在耶魯大學英語系工作。）

584 would （表示過去的習慣）總是

不要用 would 來談論一件現在反覆發生的事，除非談論的是過去反覆發生的事

1 ✗ Margo Row is a lazy woman, and she would often throw cigarette butt out of her car window.

✓ Margo Row is a lazy woman, and she often throws a cigarette butt out of her car window.

瑪歌 • 羅是一個懶惰的女人，她常把菸頭從汽車窗戶往外扔。

不要用 would 來談論一件現在反覆發生的事，除非談論的是過去反覆發生的事。比如下面例句：

- Many years ago, Margo Row lived above my apartment, and she **would** often **throw** a cigarette butt out of her kitchen window.

  過去重複發生的一件事

  （許多年前瑪歌・羅住在我樓上的公寓裡，她常把菸頭從廚房窗戶往外扔。）

585 would like to do

請參見 like to do/like doing/would like to do。

586 wrong 錯誤的、出毛病的

1 ✗ Is there anything wrong about the cellphone you bought in Hong Kong?

要用 wrong **with**，不用 wrong about

✓ Is there anything wrong with the cellphone you bought in Hong Kong?

wrong with somebody/something 表示「某人／某物有問題」

你在香港買的那支手機有什麼問題嗎？

- What's wrong with Kay today?（凱今天怎麼了？）

Y

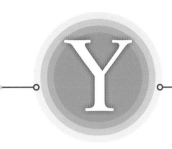

587 year 歲數、年

1

❌ Reed is a child of three years old who likes to read.

談到某人或某物的「年齡」，介系詞後面不要用 years old

a child of + 數字

✅ Reed is a child of three who likes to read.

里德是一個愛看書的三歲小孩。

片語 three years old 用在連綴動詞 is 後面

✅ Reed is only three years old, and he likes to read.

里德只有三歲，卻愛看書。

years old 用在連綴動詞 be 後面

當談到某人或某物的「年齡」時，介系詞 of 後面不要用「years + old」（請參見 . . . old）。以下是正確的用語：

· a girl who is five years old（一個五歲大的女孩）
= a girl of five
= a five-year-old girl

· a boy three years of age（一個三歲大的男孩）
= a boy of three
= a three-year-old boy

2

❌ Penny just signed a two-years contract with that movie company.

two-year 是複合名詞，修飾 contract，year 後面不要加 s

✅ Penny just signed a two-year contract with that movie company.

潘妮剛與那家電影公司簽訂了一份兩年的合約。

當修飾語用的複合名詞（即出現在另一個名詞前面的名詞），通常用單數形式。

- a **three-month** training course
= a training course that lasts **three months**
（一個三個月的訓練課程）

- a **two-hour** exam
= an exam that lasts **two hours** （一次兩小時的考試）

- a **twenty-thousand-mile** trip
= a trip of **twenty-thousand miles**（一次兩萬英里的旅程）

588 your/you're 你（你們）的／你（你們）是

1 ❌ <u>You're</u> Japanese is much better than my Chinese.
└── you are 的縮寫形式，在這裡與句意不符

✅ <u>Your</u> Japanese is much better than my Chinese.
└── you 的所有格形式，意思是「你／你們的」

你的日文比我的中文好得多。

┌── = you 的所有格，
│　　表「你／你們的」　　　　　　　　┌── = you are 的縮寫
- Lulu, <u>your</u> Japanese is excellent, and <u>you're</u> also the best singer in Honolulu.
（露露，妳的日語很棒，而且妳還是檀香山最優秀的歌手。）

589 youth 年輕人

1 ❌ Mexico needs to educate its <u>youths</u> in order to prosper and grow.
當 youth 泛指年輕人（young people considered as a group）時，沒有複數形式

✅ Mexico needs to educate its **youth** in order to prosper and grow.

為了繁榮和發展，墨西哥需要教育其年輕人。

當 **youth** 泛指年輕人（young people considered as a group）時，沒有複數形式。作主詞時，動詞通常用複數，也可以用單數。

· **Are the youth of America** inspired and motivated?

當 youth 泛指年輕人作主詞時，動詞通常用複數，也可以用單數

= **Is the youth of America** inspired and motivated?

（美國的年輕人有激情、有積極性嗎？）

這句只能用複數 are，不要單數 is，因為後面子句的主詞是複數代名詞 they

· **The youth** in our village **are** not reading enough, so they will have trouble getting into college.

（我們村裡的年輕人閱讀量不夠，所以他們要進大學有點難。）

文法加油站

youth 的用法

當 youth 作可數名詞時，意思是「青少年；小夥子」（a young person, especially a young man or boy）。

· Can each of the five youths play both the banjo and the piano?

（這五個青少年都會彈奏五弦琴和鋼琴嗎？）

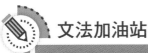

Z

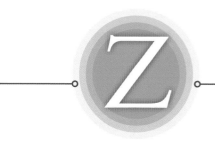

590 zero/nil 零（指「得分」）

1 美式 Jill beat Margo by twenty-one to zero.

美式英語，如果要表示球賽（橄欖球、曲棍球）中的「零分」，要用 zero

英式 Jill beat Margo by twenty-one to nil.

英式英語用 nil 來表示球賽（橄欖球、曲棍球）中的「零分」

吉兒以 21 比 0 擊敗瑪歌。

591 zero/naught/nought 零（指「數字」）

1 美式 Vincent says our yearly rate of economic growth is six point zero percent.

美式英語，如果「零」是號碼中的一部分，尤其是一個小數，要用 zero

英式 Vincent says our yearly rate of economic growth is six point naught/nought percent.

英式英語用 naught 或 nought 來表示這個意思。naught 和 nought 的發音一樣，都與 caught 押韻

文森特說，我們每年的經濟成長率是 6% 。

(1) 在美式英語中，如果「零」是號碼中的一部分，尤其是一個小數，要用 zero。

(2) 英式英語用 naught 或 nought 來表示這個意思。naught 和 nought 的發音一樣，都與 caught 押韻。

(3) 美式無論是指**數字**「零」還是指**比賽得分**「零分」，都是用 zero。這又是一個證據，美式英語在用詞方面比英式簡單。

· "Is a million written with one followed by six zeros/noughts/naughts?" asked Liz.

（莉茲問：「一百萬是不是要在數字 1 後面加 6 個零？」）

592 zero article 零冠詞

請參看 a/an 和 the。

593 zip/zipper 拉鏈

1 美式 Is your jacket's zipper undone so you can get some sun?

英式 Is your jacket's zip undone so you can get some sun?

你上衣的拉鏈沒有拉，是為了想曬曬太陽嗎？

594 zip code/postcode 郵遞區號

1 美式 Norm put his zip code on the form.

英式 Norm put his postcode on the form.

諾姆把他的郵遞區號寫進表格裡。

· Kate says that a zip code is usually placed after the name of a province or a state.

（凱特說，郵遞區號通常是放在省名或州名後面。）

國家圖書館出版品預行編目資料
Don't Say It! 600 個你一定會錯的英文
= Easy Ways to Avoid Errors in English / Dennis Le Boeuf /
景黎明 -- 初版 . --【 臺北市 】: 寂天文化,
2017 .7 面； 公分 . --
ISBN 978-986-318-603-8（ 20K 平裝）
1 . 英語 2 . 詞彙
805.16 98015296

Don't Say It!
600 個你一定會錯的英文

作者 Dennis Le Boeuf ／景黎明
編輯 丁宥暄
校對 陳慧莉
內頁排版設計 鄭秀芳／林書玉
封面設計 林書玉
製程管理 洪巧玲
出版者 寂天文化事業股份有限公司
電話 02-2365-9739
傳真 02-2365-9835
網址 www.icosmos.com.tw
讀者服務 onlineservice@icosmos.com.tw

出版日期 2017 年 7 月 初版一刷 200101

郵撥帳號 1998620 -0 寂天文化事業股份有限公司
劃撥金額 600（含）元以上者，郵資免費。訂購金額 600 元以下者，請外加 65 元。
【若有破損，請寄回更換，謝謝。】